William Harrison

Bibliotheca Monensis

A Bibliographical Account of Works Relating to the Isle of Man

William Harrison

Bibliotheca Monensis
A Bibliographical Account of Works Relating to the Isle of Man

ISBN/EAN: 9783337407049

Printed in Europe, USA, Canada, Australia, Japan

Cover: Foto ©Andreas Hilbeck / pixelio.de

More available books at **www.hansebooks.com**

BIBLIOTHECA MONENSIS

BIBLIOTHECA MONENSIS

The Manx Society

ESTABLISHED IN THE YEAR

MDCCCLVIII

VOL. XXIV.

DOUGLAS, ISLE OF MAN
PRINTED FOR THE MANX SOCIETY
MDCCCLXXVI

N. B.—Members at a distance are requested to acknowledge their copies to the Honorary Secretary, Mr. JOHN GOLDSMITH, 7 Peel Road, Douglas, to whom also their Subscriptions may be remitted.

President.

His Excellency the Lieutenant-Governor.

Vice-Presidents.

The Hon. and Right Rev. Horace, Lord Bishop of Sodor and Man.
The Honourable Charles Hope.
James Gell, H.M.'s Attorney-General of the Isle of Man.
Ridgway Harrison, Receiver-General, Water-Bailiff, and Seneschal.
The Venerable Joseph C. Moore, Archdeacon.
J. S. Goldie Taubman, Speaker of the House of Keys.

Council.

Henry Cadman, Howstrake.
T. C. Callow, Douglas.
John F. Crellin, Orrysdale.
Geo. W. Dumbell, H.K., Belmont.
Edward Curphey Farrant, H.K., Ballakillinghan.
P. L. Garrett, Douglas.
William Gell, Douglas.
Henry Goldsmith, Ramsey.
Samuel Harris, High Bailiff of Douglas.
William Harrison, Rock Mount.
Rev. Wm. M. Hutton, Vicar of Lezayre.
John M. Jeffcott, H.K., High Bailiff of Castletown.
Rev. Joshua Jones, D.C.L., Principal of King William's College.
Rev. Wm. Kermode, Vicar of Maughold.
Robert J. Moore, H.K., High Bailiff of Peel.
William Fine Moore, Cronkbourne.
H. B. Noble, Villa Marina, Douglas.
Richard Sherwood, H.K., Douglas.
Rev. Theophilus Talbot, Douglas.

Treasurer.

P. L. Garrett, Douglas.

Hon. Secretary.

John Goldsmith, 7 Peel Road, Douglas.

BIBLIOTHECA MONENSIS

A

BIBLIOGRAPHICAL ACCOUNT OF WORKS

RELATING TO THE

ISLE OF MAN

NEW EDITION
REVISED, CORRECTED, AND ENLARGED

By WILLIAM HARRISON

DOUGLAS, ISLE OF MAN
PRINTED FOR THE MANX SOCIETY
MDCCCLXXVI

Printed by R. & R. CLARK, *Edinburgh*.

PREFACE.

THE first edition of this work was issued in 1861, at which time the Compiler had not the opportunity of consulting sufficient authorities which a work of this nature required, but had mainly to rely upon such as he possessed in his own library. Since that time he has been enabled to add considerably to the information contained therein by the addition of numerous particulars to the works there enumerated, and has also recorded some 300 more works connected with the Isle of Man or that particularly allude to it.

The Council of the Manx Society, considering the great importance that a work of this nature is to the student of Manx history as a guide to the sources from whence information is to be derived, have decided that this enlarged edition shall form one of their series.

The study of Bibliography, or a knowledge of particular books, was, until of late years, singularly neglected; however, there has now sprung up a desire to become acquainted with whatever has been published that will in any way elucidate the history of a country or a place. It was with this view the Compiler was induced to continue his labours, in the hope that the result might be useful not only to the Manx student, but to others as well. Those only who have been engaged in similar pursuits can have an adequate idea of the vast amount of labour required in wading through a multiplicity of books in order to find out a single fact that may be of use; this requiring no great amount of literary knowledge, but assuredly a vast amount of patience, and as such the Editor trusts it has not been spent in vain. The list has not been extended beyond the year 1870, and such works as have escaped research (for the list does not profess to be exhaustive) will only be an amusement to the reader to fill up.

From John Frissel Crellin, Esq., of Orrysdale, I have received constant contributions for this list of works; and have to express my thanks for his kindness in affording me access to his valuable collection of books and coins relating to the Isle of Man.

An extensive Index has been added for the more easy mode of reference.

WILLIAM HARRISON.

Rock Mount, *May* 1876.

INTRODUCTION TO THE FIRST EDITION,
1861.

FOR many years previous to the establishment of the Manx
Society, the Editor had been collecting from time to time
such Works as related in any way to the Isle of Man, and
making a list of the same. On the formation of the Society
it was suggested that it would be very desirable if such could
be brought before the members at some future day. The im-
pression that such a work might be useful to those engaged
in similar pursuits has led to the compilation of the present
volume. An obscure tract or scarce work no doubt may have
here and there escaped the notice of the Editor, or not have
been sufficiently described for want of the work to refer to,
but it is presumed none of any great importance ; and
such omission will be the sooner pardoned when it is considered by those who can form an estimate of the labour and
research required in the compilation of works of this description, and that the more readily when it is known there is no
Public Library in the Island containing stores of this kind to
which he could resort for reference, but had mainly to rely on
the collections contained in his own library.

Some of the articles may appear too trivial to have been
noticed, but everything to the Historian is of value, and
everything requires his perusal ; a date may be fixed or a fact
established from a sermon, a report, or a lampoon. It is to
be hoped that the new materials which the Manx Society has
been the means of bringing before the public will make the
task of the future Historian of the Island less difficult by the

very valuable documents which have for the first time been brought to light in their volumes.

The full title is described in most instances, thereby enabling the reader to learn what subjects are treated upon by the writer, with the date and place of publication. A few remarks and biographical notices are added where any peculiarity or important information was thought requisite to be noticed. To have extended these would only have retarded the publication of the volume, and might not have increased its usefulness.

Some few notices of works in MS. are appended, but no doubt this might be considerably extended, as also notices of works where incidental remarks are made relative to the history, government, or customs of the Island; but these having been so fully given in Dr. Oliver's *Monumenta*, where he reprints the most important passages, it was considered only necessary to enumerate them. In the various pages of the *Gentleman's* and other Magazines may be found occasional remarks relative to the Island, some of which are noticed, also the publications of the Chetham Society, as well as other sources, all which may be added by any one wishful to extend the present list.

An Alphabetical Index is annexed, which it is hoped will be found sufficiently copious to answer all the purposes of reference, the value of which will be acknowledged by all who have experienced the want of one.

I have to express my thanks to Robt. J. Moore, Esq., High-Bailiff of Peel, for his readiness in answering inquiries, and constant access to the valuable and extensive collection of documents relating to the Island in his possession.

WILLIAM HARRISON.

Rock Mount, *November* 1861.

A BIBLIOGRAPHICAL ACCOUNT OF WORKS

RELATING TO

THE ISLE OF MAN.

RANULPH HIGDEN.—1482.

THE Polycronycon, conteynyng the Berynges and Dedes of
many Tymes, in eyght Books, etc.   Imprinted by William
Caxton. *Folio.*   1482.

This very curious historical miscellany was written in
Latin, circa 1350, by Ranulph Higden, a Benedictine monk
of the Order of St. Werburg, Chester, who died about the
year 1360.   It was translated into English by John de
Trevisa in 1357, at the request of Thomas, Lord Berkeley,
from which Caxton made this version, and added an eighth
book, being a continuation from 1357 to 1460.

Polycronycon.   West-mestre by Wynkyn de Worde.   *Folio.*
1495.

Polycronycon.   Imprented in Southwerke by my Peter
Treveris, at ye expences of John Reynes, Bookseller, at
the sygne of Saynt George in Poule's Churchyarde, the
Yeare of our Lorde God 1527, the xvi. daye of Maye.
Folio.

A paginary reprint of Wynkyn de Worde's edition, with
the introduction of a few woodcuts.

B

Isle of Man. Lib. 1, cap. xv. An early mention of the Island.

This very rare work is fully described by Mr. Haslewood in the "British Bibliographer," vol. iii. p. 348-54. London. 1812.

WM. CAMDEN.—1586.

Britannia, sive florentissimorum regnorum Angliæ, Scotiæ, Hiberniæ, et insularum adjacentium, ex intima anti-quitate chorographica descriptio. Londini : 1586. *Octavo.*

This is the first edition, dedicated to Sir W. Cecil, Lord Burghley. This work passed through eight editions between 1586 and 1590. The editions of 1587 and 1590 are in octavo ; 1594 and 1600 in quarto ; that of 1607 in folio, the last edition corrected by the author. The monks of Rushen Abbey wrote the three first sheets of the account of the Chronicle of Man and the Isles up to the year 1270, the time of the Scottish conquest ; the latter portion continues the history down to 1316, in another hand, probably by the monks of Furness Abbey. Bishop Merrick is said to have drawn up the account of the sketch of the Isle of Man. He was bishop from 1577 to 1599.

William Camden was born in the Old Bailey, London, May 2, 1551. His father, Sampson, was a painter, and his mother was one of the ancient family of Curwens of Cumberland. His great work has been said to be "the common sun, whereat our modern writers have all lighted their little torches."

RALPH HOLINSHED.—1586-7.

Chronicles of England, Scotland, and Ireland. London. 2 vols. *Folio.* 1586-7.

The first edition appeared in 1577. It was first collected

and published by Ralph Holinshed, William Harrison, and others.

The Isle of Man. Vol. i. p. 37, and book ii. chap. ii. p. 146.

An edition was published in quarto, 6 vols. London. 1807-8.

THOMAS DURHAM.—1595.

The Isle of Man exactly described and into several Parishes divided, with every Towne, Village, Baye, Creke, and River therein conteyned. The bordringe Coasts where-with it is circulated in their situations sett and by the Compasse accordingly shewed, with their true distance from every place unto this Island, by a severall scale observed. Described by Tho. Durham. Ano. 1595. *Large Folio.*

The oldest map of the Island. Shows the existence of lakes in the northern district. Mirescogh was the most important ; and Thomas, Earl of Derby, in 1505, made a grant of one-half of the fishery in it to Huan Hesketh, Bishop of Man. On an island in this lake was a state prison.

—— HOOPER.—1608.

Survey of the Revenue, Farm Rents, etc., of the Isle of Man. By Mr. Hooper, commissioner appointed by the Lords Salisbury and Northampton in 1608. Rents were first established here in 1505.

A MS. copy is in possession of M. H. Quayle, Esq., Clerk of the Rolls.

JOHN MONIPENNIE.—1612.

The Abridgement or Summarie of the Scots Chronicles, etc. etc. With a true Description of the whole realme of

Scotland and of the Isles in general, etc. By John Moni-pennie. Printed at Brittaines Bursse. By John Budge. 1612.

A short description of the Isle of Man, in which he states "there was a towne in it named Sodora, the Bishop of the Isles seat."

This work is reprinted in "Miscellanea Scotica," vol. i. Glasgow. John Wylie and Co.   1818.

JOHN SELDEN.—1614.

Titles of Honor, by John Selden. Lucilius, Persium, non curo legere; Lelium decimum volo. London : By William Stansby for John Helme, and are to be sold at his Shop in St. Dunstan's Churchyard. 1614. *Quarto*, pp. 391.

"Of the Title of Kings, as it is subordinate in subject Princes, with some particulars of the kingdom of the Isle of Man."

A second edition, with additions, in folio, was published in 1631, and a third in 1672. The latter is considered the best edition.

That portion relating to the Isle of Man is printed in Oliver's "Monumenta," vol. i. pp. 107-110, Manx Society, vol. iv. 1860. Also in Gell's "Abstract of the Laws of the Isle of Man," vol. i. pp. 156-8, Manx Society, vol. xii. 1867.

JOHN SPEED.—1627.

The Theatre of the Empire of Great Britaine. As also A Prospect of the most Famous Parts of the World. By John Speed. A briefe description of the Ciuill Warres, etc. The Invasions of England and Ireland, etc. The Theatre of Great Britain, etc. Are to be sold in Pops-head Alley by G. Humble. London. *Royal Folio.* 1627.

This appears to be the third edition, the first in 1611, and the second edition in 1614.

This work contains numerous engraved plates of various dates. Man Island is in book i. chap. xlvi. pp. 91-92, giving a description of it. "A table of the Townes, Villages, Castles, Riuers, and Hauens." Also "A Chronicle of the Kings of Man." On the back of pages 91 and 92 is a map, "Described by Tho. Durham. Ano. 1595. Performed by John Speed. Anno 1610."

This map was copied from Durham's map of 1595, and recopied by Daniel King, 1656, on a reduced scale, for "Chaloner's Short Treatise," with the omission of the ships and the figures of marine animals bearing the standards of the British Isles, with the addition on the margin of eight small views in the Isle of Man, the arms of the Island, and the arms of Lord Fairfax. The map accompanying the Manx Society's edition of "Chaloner's Treatise," vol. x. 1863, is on a still further reduced scale.

The portion relating to the Isle of Man is reprinted in the Manx Society's series, vol. xviii. 1871, "Old Historians," pp. 36-44, with Durham's map, reduced.

1635.

Mercator's Atlas. Printed in London. *Small Folio.* 1635.

At p. 96 is a description of the Isle of Man, taken from Camden, with a map.

PETER HEYLIN, D.D.—1636.

Microcosmus, or a little Description of the great World. London. 1636. *Quarto.*

The Isle of Man, pp. 512-513.

Editions of this work have appeared in 1622, small

quarto; 1624-1627, Oxford; and London, 1652-1664; and enlarged in 1674, 1677, 1682, folio. Also in 1703, folio.

PETER HEYLYN, D.D.—1641.

A Help to English History, containing a succession of all the Kings of England, the English, Saxons, and the Britains; the Kings and Princes of Wales, the Kings and Lords of Man and the Isle of Wight; as also of all the Dukes, Marquesses, Earls, and Bishops thereof; with the descriptions of the places from whence they had their Titles; together with the Names and Ranks of the Viscounts, Barons, and Baronets of England. By Robert Hall, Gent. Printed at London. *Quarto*, pp. 379. 1641.

This was compiled by Dr. Heylyn, under the assumed name of Robert Hall. The second edition was published in 1652. Other editions appeared after Dr. Heylyn's death, continued by various hands, in 1671, 1680, 1709, and 1773. The latter contains many additions, and is the best edition of this useful work.

EARL OF DERBY.—1649.

A Message sent from the Earl of Derby, Governor of the Isle of Man, to his dread Sovereign Charles II., King of Scotland, etc. And his Lordship's Declaration to his Majesty concerning the Treaty, and Major-General Ireton, etc. Printed at York, and reprinted for W. R. *Quarto.*

Concerning the Parliament's attempted treaty with the Earl, respecting a surrender of the Island to them, in consideration of taking off the sequestration of his estates, and his celebrated indignant reply to Commissary-General Ireton, dated July 12, which has been often printed.

EARL OF DERBY.—1649.

A Declaration of the Right Honourable James, Earl of Derby,
Lord Stanley, Strange of Knockin and of the Isle of Man,
concerning his resolution to keep the Isle of Man, for his
Majesties Service, against all force whatsoever. Together
with his Lordship's letter in answer to Commissary-
General Ireton. London. *Quarto*, pp. 8. 1649.

This Declaration bears date July 18th as the composition
of Lord Derby. Sir Marmaduke Langdale and Sir Lewis
Dives were commissioned by King Charles II. (June 5th) to
repair to the Isle of Man and assist the Earl in keeping the
same, both "by counsell and personal service." They arrived
two days after the letter had been written to Ireton, and
advised the Earl to publish his declaration of July 18, and
which was considered by them to be a "meer fiction," and
"no whit the sence of Derby." On this account they published their declaration, highly complimentary to the Earl.

LANGDALE AND DIVES.—1649.

A Declaration of the Noble Knights Sir Marmaduke Langdale and Sir Lewis Dives, in vindication of the Right
Honourable James, Earl of Derby, and remonstrating
their resolutions to keep the Isle of Man against all oppo-
sition in his Majesty's service, August the 5th, 1649.
London. *Quarto*. Printed in the year 1649.

For a notice of these three scarce tracts, see "The Civil
War Tracts," edited by George Ormerod, Esq., in the 2d
volume of the Chetham Society's publications, 1844, pp. 280-
285.

1649.

Mercurius Pragmaticus. In this newspaper, published for
Charles II., are articles relating to the surrender of the

Isle of Man by the Earl of Derby, and other matters. *Small Quarto.*

1651.

Mercurius Politicus. In this newspaper is " An exact relation of the manner of our enterprise upon the Isle of Man, with the successe it pleased God to give there unto our forces." By a Gentleman that was ane eye witnesse.

It includes also articles touching the surrendering of Castle Rushen and Peel Castle, account of the arms and ammunition and provision in Andrew Fort, the Proposals of the Countess of Derby, etc. *Small Qvarto.* The first number was published June 13th, 1650.

1651.

A perfect Diurnal of some passages of the Armies in England and Ireland.

The first number was published December 27th, 1649. It was licensed by the Secretary of the Army, which gave its papers authenticity connected therewith. That from Monday, November 10th, to Monday, November 17th, 1651, contains a similar account of transactions in the Isle of Man as are to be found in " Mercurius Politicus " of the same year.

JAMES CHALONER.—1656.

The Vale Royall of England, or the County Palatine of Chester, Illustrated. Wherein is contained a Geographical and Historical Description of that famous County, with all its Hundreds and Seats of the Nobility, Gentry, and Freeholders : its Rivers, Towns, Castles, Buildings, ancient and modern, adorned with Maps and Prospects, and the Coats of Arms belonging to every individual Family of the whole County. Performed by Wm. Smith and Wm. Webb, Gentlemen. Published by Mr. Daniel King. To which is annexed an exact Chronology of all its Rulers and Governors both in Church and State, from the time of the Foundation of the stately City of Chester to this very day : Fixed by Eclipses, and other Chronological Characters. Also an excellent Discourse of the Island of Man ; treating of the Island ; of the Inhabitants ; of the state Ecclesiastical ; of the Civil Government ; of the Trade ; and of the Strength of the Island. London. Printed by John Streater, in Little S. Bartholomews, and are to be sold at the Black Spread Eagle, at the West End of Paul's. *Small Folio.* 1656.

The portion relating to the Isle of Man has a separate title, as follows :—

A Short Treatise of the Isle of Man. Digested into six Chapters. Containing, I. A Description of the Island. II. Of the Inhabitants. III. Of the state Ecclesiasticall. IV. Of the Civill Government. V. Of the Trade. VI. Of the Strength of the Island. Illustrated with severall Prospects of the Island. By Daniel King. London. Printed by John Streater. 1656.

This Treatise is written by James Chaloner, and dedicated " For His Excellencie, Thomas Lord Fairfax, Lord of Man and of the Isles," and dated " Middle Park, December 1, 1653." 3 pp. The Island described, pp. 1 to 33. There is a Map of the Island, with eight small Views on the sides, Arms of the Island and Lord Fairfax ; two Plates with each three Views, and a Plate with three Coats of Arms.

Lord Fairfax made Commissioners for the governing of the Isle in 1652 (Aug. 17th), James Chaloner and Robt. Dynely, Esqrs., and Mr. Joshua Witton, Minister of the Gospel.

James Chaloner was also Governor from 1658 to 1660,

and was one of the Judges of Charles I. He was the fourth son of Sir Thomas Chaloner, of Gisborough, in the county of York, born in London in 1603, and married Ursula Fairfax, by whom he had one son, Edmund Chaloner, born in 1635, and three daughters. He died in 1660.

In Gough's " History of the People called Quakers," Dublin, 1789, is the following note :—" This James Chaloner had been a member of the Long Parliament, and after the King's return had been sent for to London, in order, as was thought, to be tried among the regicides. The day he was to go he took something under pretext of physick, which killed him in a short time." " He had been a violent persecutor, and was heard to say, a little before his death, that *he would quickly rid the Island of Quakers.*"

This Treatise has been reprinted in the 10th volume of the Manx Society's series, 1863, edited by the Rev. J. G. Cumming, M.A.

SIR W. DUGDALE AND R. DODSWORTH.—1655-61-73.

Monasticon Anglicanum, a History of the Abbeys, and other Monasteries, Friers, Cathedral and Collegiate Churches in England and Wales. Plates by Hollar and King. *Folio.* 3 vols.

Bishop Simon, in 1229, published the Statutes of the Constitution of the Diocese of Sodor, in the Isle of Man, which are printed in vol. i. pp. 711-12. A second edition, 1673-83.

An edition in 1718-23, with additions. A greatly enlarged edition, edited by Caley, Ellis, and Bandinel, in 8 folio volumes. London. 1817-46.

Sir William Dugdale was born at Shustoke, in Warwickshire, on the 12th September 1605, and died 10th February 1685-86. His ancestors were of Clitheroe, County Lancaster.

Roger Dodsworth was born on the 24th July 1585, and died in August 1654. The portion relating to the Isle of Man is reprinted in the Manx Society's series, vol. xviii. 1871, "Old Historians," pp. 46-77.

1658.

Map of the Isle of Man. Published at Amsterdam. Forming part of Bleau's "Atlas." This is Thomas Durham's.

Bleau's "Le Grand Atlas" was published at Amsterdam in 12 volumes, imperial folio, with upwards of a thousand large maps. Vol. v., England, contains maps of all the English counties, etc., by Speed and others, surrounded by portraits of old English kings, and numerous coats of arms, etc.

1659.

The Crown Garland of Golden Roses. London. 1659.

"The Lamentable fall of the Great Duchess of Gloucester, the wife of Duke Humphrey; how she did penance in London streets, barefooted, with a wax candle in her hand ; and how at last she was banished the land, where, in exile, in the Isle of Man, she ended her days in woe."

This ballad was reprinted by the Percy Society in 1845. Reprinted in the Manx Society's series, vol. xvi. 1869, "Mona Miscellany," pp. 48-53.

Georgè Fox, John Stubbs, and Benj. Furley.—1660.

A Battledoor for Teachers and Professors to learn Singular and Plural ; You to Many, and Thou to one. (In many Languages.) *Small Folio.* 1660.

Amongst the "many languages," besides the Oriental, are the Saxon, Welsh, *Manx*, Irish, Cornish, Bohemian, Slavonian,

Polonian, Lithuanian, etc.   There is an Appendix of curious colloquial and free phrases in English, which are stigmatised as improper.   This work contains an early printed record of the Manx language.

WM. CHRISTIAN.—1663.

Judgment of the King in Council in William Christian's Case.   Ordered to be printed in folio, as Acts of Parliament are, 14th August.

William Christian was executed at Hango Hill, 2d January 1663.

A Memoir of his Life, with full particulars of his Trial, from the documents in the Rolls Office, would form a very acceptable volume, and it is to be hoped the Manx Society will be able to accomplish this.   He has been by various writers represented as a martyr and a traitor : the latter, I fear, is too true.   By the Manx he is called " Illiam Dhône," —Fair-haired William.   He was buried in the Chancel of Kirk Malew.

WILLIAM PRYNNE.—1669.

Brief Animadversions and additional explanatory Amendments of Records to the Fourth part of the Institutes of the Lawes of England concerning the Jurisdiction of Courts.   Compiled by the late Sir Edward Coke, Knt. By William Prynne, Esqre.   London.   *Small Folio.*   1669.

Of the Isle of Man, pp. 201-205, cap. 69 ; also cap. 69, pp. 384-386, additional records ; and, last page after the table, an omitted record.   Various records relating to this Island are printed in this volume.

In Oliver's " Monumenta," Manx Society, vol. i. p. 111, 1860, is a record of the Earl of Warwick's imprisonment in the Isle of Man, 22 Richard II., 1397, extracted from Prynne

Lord Edward Coke.—1671.

The Fourth part of the Institutes of the Laws of England, concerning the Jurisdiction of Courts. 1671. Fifth edition. *Folio.* Cap. 69.

Has passed through many editions, 1644, 1648, 1660, 1669, 1671, 1680. The 16th, with notes by Hargrave and Butler, in 3 vols. royal octavo, in 1809. Printed in "Abstract of the Laws," etc., by James Gell, Esq., vol. i. p. 153. Manx Society, vol. xii. 1867.

Peter Heylyn, D.D.—1671.

A Help to English History, containing a succession of all the Kings of England, the English-Saxons, and the Britains : the Kings and Princes of Wales, the Kings and Lords of Man, the Isle of Wight. As also of all the Dukes, Marquesses, Earls, and Bishops thereof. With the description of the places from whence they had their titles ; together with the Names and Ranks of the Viscounts, Barons, and Baronets of England. By P. Heylyn, D.D. And since his death, continued to this present year, 1671, with the Coats of Arms of the Nobility, blazoned. London. Printed by E. Leach for T. Basset, at the George, in Fleet Street, and Chr. Wilkinson, at the Black Boy, over against St. Dunstan's Church. 1671. 12*mo*, pp. 557. Preface, pp. 6. "Kings and Lords of Man," pp. 43 to 46. "Bishops of Man," pp. 182 to 184.

The list of Kings, etc., commences with Godred, the son of Syrric, in 1065, and ends with "Charles Stanley, Earl of Derby and Lord of Man, now living, 1670."

The Bishops of Man—Amphibalus, first Bishop of Man, A.D. 360, and ends with Bishop Barrow.

Rev. Samuel Clark.—1671.

A Mirrour or Looking Glass both for Saints and Sinners, held forth in some thousands of Examples ; wherein is presented God's wonderful mercies to the one, so his severe judgments against the other. Collected out of the most Classique Authors, both ancient and modern, with some late examples observed by myself and others. Whereunto are added a geographical description of all countries in the known world ; as also the wonders of God in nature ; and the rare stupendious and costly works made by the Art and Industry of Man, the most famous Cities, Temples, Structures, Cabinets of Rarities, etc., which have been, or are now in the world. By Sa. Clark, late Pastour in Bennet Fink, London. London. Printed by Thos. Milbourn. 1671. The fourth edition in 2 vols. *Folio.* The first edition in 1646, 12*mo.*

The Isle of Man described.

R. Blome.—1673.

Britannia, or a Geographical Description of England, Scotland, and Ireland, and the Isles and Territories thereto belonging. London. *Folio.* 1673. With Maps and Arms of Subscribers, and Plan of London, by W. Hollar.

The Isle of Man, pp. 320-322.

Taken from Camden and Speed.

1678.

England's Remarques ; giving an exact account of the several Shires, Counties, and Islands in England and Wales, etc. etc. London. Printed for Langley Curtis, in Goat Court upon Ludgate Hill. *Small* 12*mo,* pp. 276. 1678. Also an Account of all Monasteries, etc., Table of Kings, Bishops, etc., and Map of England.

The Isle of Man described at pp. 268-270.

CHRISTOPHER IRVINE.—1682.

Historiæ Scoticæ Nomenclatura, Latino vernacula.   Edinbro'.
1682.   *Octavo.*

An edition in 1819, foolscap octavo.

It states the Isle of Man to have been of much larger
dimensions than at present.

1683.

The London Gazette.   Containing the humble Address of the
Governor and Principal Inhabitants of the Isle of Man to
King Charles the Second.   *Folio.*   1683.

G. GUL. LIEBNITZ.—1693.

Codex juris Gentium Diplomaticus.   Hanoveræ.   *Folio.*

The Act of Surrender made by Reginald to the See of
Rome, 10th of October 1219, p. 5.

This is printed in Seacome's "History of the House of
Stanley," p. 515, and Train's "History," vol. i. p. 135, 1845.
Also in Oliver's "Monumenta," Manx Society, vol. ii. pp.
53-57, 1861.

BISHOP WILSON.—1699.

The Principles and Duties of Christianity ; for the Use of the
Diocese of Man, with short and plain directions and
prayers.   In English and Manks. London. *Octavo.*   1699.

With preliminary Instructions to the Clergy of the Isle
of Man, rules for marrying couples, and Devotions to put into
their hands after marriage, "all which are here translated
into Manks, and, I hope as well as can be expected, considering that this is *the first Book published in this language.*"—P. 4,
Introduction.

The second edition appeared in 1707.   *Octavo.*

This book was afterwards corrected and improved, and published under the title of "The Knowledge and Practice of Christianity made easy to the meanest capacities ; or an Essay towards an Instruction for the Indians," under which title it was first published in 1740.

Chaloner states the Book of Common Prayer was translated into Manx by Bishop Philips in 1605, but it appears doubtful if this was ever printed.   In the report of the Society for Promoting Christian Knowledge, for 1764, May 4th, p. 115, they state it "never appeared."

WILLIAM SACHEVERELL.—1702.

An Account of the Isle of Man, its Inhabitants, Language, Soil, Remarkable Curiosities, the Succession of its Kings and Bishops down to the present time, by way of Essay, with a Voyage to I-Columb-kill.   By William Sacheverell, Esq., late Governor of Man ; to which is added a Dissertation about the Mona of Cæsar and Tacitus ; and an account of the Ancient Druids, etc.   By Mr. Thomas Brown, addressed in a letter to his learned friend Mr. A. Sellars.   London : printed for J. Hartley, next the King's Head Tavern ; R. Gibson, in the Middle Row ; and Thos. Hodgson, over against Gray's Inn Gate, in Holborn, 1702.   *Small Octavo*, pp. 175, dedicated "To Robert Sacheverell, Esq. of Barton, in Nottinghamshire," 4 pp. ; Preface, 2 pp. ; the Introduction, 7 pp. ; Isle of Man, p. 1 to 122 ; Voyage to I-Columb-kill, p. 123 to 144 ; Dissertation on Mona, p. 145 to 175.

William Sacheverell was Governor of the Isle of Man in 1692, and from the following letter, published in the " Norris Papers," by the Chetham Society, 1846, appears to have been dismissed from the Governorship of the Isle :—

" Mr. Richard Norrys, Liverpool.

" Dear Mr. Norrys—I am extremely obliged to you for your great care and trouble in assisting my wife in her passage hither, which, as it was a great comfort to me, so I doubt will be very short, for I hear I am out of my imployment after all my care and diligence. All I can say is, I have served an unthankfull man, and I doubt it will turn very much to my prejudis ; but God's will be done. I cannot yet leave the Island myself, but would have her goe for England, but she resolves to stay a winter with me. I desire my service to your brother when you see him. Pray remember me to Mr. Cooke and Mr. Holt, and believe me, etc.

" WM. SACHEVERELL.

" Castle Rushen, 15th August 1694."

A reprint of this edition forms the first volume of the Manx Society's publications, and has been most ably edited by the Rev. J. G. Cumming, M.A., with numerous valuable notes, 1859.

M. MARTIN.—1703.

A Description of the Western Islands of Scotland ; a particular Account of the Second Sight, etc. By M. Martin, Gent. London : printed for Andrew Bell, at the Cross Keys and Bible, in Cornhill, near Stock's Market. 1703. *Octavo,* pp. 392.

The only distinct references to the Isle of Man are in the description of Iona, p. 257, and in the account of the instances of Second Sight, p. 313.

Many of the old customs and strange superstitions described in this curious book as prevailing in the Western Isles of Scotland, are similar to those formerly existing in the Isle of Man. An edition, the second and best, *octavo.* London. 1716.

The perusal of this book is said to have infused in Dr. Johnson the desire to visit the Hebrides.

T. RYMER.—1704-35.

Fœdera, Conventiones, Litteræ et cujuscunque generis Acta Publica, inter Reges Angliæ, et alios quos vis Imperatores, Reges, etc., ab anno 1101, ad nostra usque tempora habita aut tractata. London. 20 vols. *Folio.* Vol. i. p. 137. A.D. 1205. Time of King John. Vol. i. p. 342.

Under date 1246 is a safe conduct from Hen. III. for Harald, King of Man. Also for Reginald, in 1249. Vol. i. p. 451 and p. 489. Vol. i. p. 586, respecting the Murder of Reginald, second son of Olave II.

Vol. ii. p. 492. The Men of the Isle of Man place themselves under the protection of King Edward I., 1290, by which the Manx people cancelled all previous engagements betwixt themselves and their Norwegian rulers, under a penalty of two thousand pounds of silver.

This interesting document is reprinted in the Manx Society's first volume, in note, pp. 152-3. "Sacheverell's History."

Vol. ii. p. 1058. Ed. I., Anno 1307. A *Scire Facias*, to Anthony Beck, Bishop of Durham, to show cause why he should not render the Isle of Man. This is also printed, with a translation, in the Manx Society's first volume, pp. 157-8.

Vol. iii. pp. 223-238. In 1310 Gilbert De M'Gaskill is mentioned as having custody of the Isle of Man under Anthony De Beck.

Vol. iv. p. 562. Grant of Isle of Man to Sir Wm. Montacute, first Earl of Salisbury, by Edward III. Anno 1333. In the Manx Society's first volume, p. 170.

Vol. iv. p. 574. Anno 7 Ed. III., 1333. Grant of Isle of Man to the same, with all rights and claims.

Vol. v. p. 558.

Vol. viii. p. 95.   Anno 1399.   Hen. IV., p. 410.   Concerning the grant of the Isle of Man.

In addition to the foregoing, the following are reprinted from the "Fœdera" in Oliver's "Monumenta," vol. iii., Manx Society, 1862 :—

P.   1. A.D. 1414. Treaty between England and France.

„   24. A.D. 1476. The claims of Lords Scroop and Stanley to the Arms of Man.

„   38. A.D. 1546. 37 Henry VIII. Respecting the gift of the Bishopric to Henry Man.

„   42. A.D. 1546. Significavit for the Bishop of the Isle of Man.

„   46. A.D. 1546. Concessions for Henry, Bishop of the Isle of Man.

„   53. A.D. 1570. 12th Eliz. Significavit for the Bishop of the Isle of Man.

„   58. A.D. 1575. 17th Eliz. Royal Assent for the Bishop.

„   62. A.D. 1576. 18th Eliz. Of the Royal Assent, upon the presentation to the Bishopric of the Island.

„   133. A.D. 1626. 2d Charles I. Gift for Life to Queen Henrietta Maria.

„   135. A.D. 1633. 9th Charles I. Certificate of Presentation to the Bishopric of Man.

„   137. A.D. 1633. Royal Assent for the Bishop of Man.

„   142. A.D. 1635. 11th Charles I. Royal Assent for Richard Parre, Bishop of Man.

The second edition, edited by G. Holmes, London, 1727-35, *folio*, 20 vols. Third edition, 1745, 10 vols. *folio*. Also a new edition, edited by John Caley and Fred. Holbrooke, London, 1816-30, 3 vols. *folio*, extending from the year 1066 to 1377.

Mr. Rymer was born in the north of England, and educated at the Grammar School at Northallerton, Yorkshire, from whence he went to Sidney College, Cambridge. His warrant to search the public offices for this undertaking is dated August 26th, 1693. He died 14th December 1713. The "Fœdera" is an invaluable work, equally interesting to the antiquary and historian, the documents having been copied from the originals.

Thomas Brown.—1707.

A Short Dissertation about the Mona of Cæsar and Tacitus, the several names of Man, whether it was the principal Seat of the Ancient Druids, etc.; together with a short Account of the Institution, Discipline, and Opinions of the Druids. By Mr. Thomas Brown. London. 1707. *Small Octavo.*

This appeared at the end of Sacheverell's *Account of the Isle of Man* in 1702.

Mr. Brown considers that Cæsar alluded to the Isle of Man in his Account, though he never visited it, and Tacitus the Isle of Anglesea, and that the Isle of Man was not likely to be the head-quarters of the Druids, as they were more calculated for a stirring active life.

Bishop Wilson.—1707.

The Church Catechism. Translated into Manks, and also printed in English. 1707.

Edward Lhuyd.—1707.

Archaeologia Britannica, an Account of the Languages, Histories, and Customs of the original Inhabitants of Great Britain. Oxford. 1707. *Folio.*

This valuable work comprises a comparative Etymology, an Armoric Grammar and Vocabulary, Cornish Grammar, British Etymologicon, Irish-English Dictionary, Catalogue of Irish MSS., Account of the Manx language, etc. etc.

No more was ever published. It contains : I. Comparative Etymology—II. Comparative Vocabulary of the Original Languages of Britain and Ireland—III. and IV. An Armoric Grammar and Vocabulary by Julian Manoir, Englished by M. Williams—V. Welsh words omitted in Dr. Davies' Dictionary—VI. Cornish Grammar—VII. Antiqua Britanniæ Lingua Scriptorum, quæ non impressa sunt Catalogus—VIII. A British Etymologicon, or the Welsh collated with the Greek and Latin, and some other European languages, by D. Parry—IX. A brief Introduction to the Irish or ancient Scottish language—X. Focloir ; an Irish-English Dictionary—XI. Catalogue of Irish MSS.

A. D. CHANCEL, M.A.—1714.

A New Journey over Europe from France thro' Savoy, etc., by a late Traveller, A. D. Chancel, M.A. London. 1714. *Small Octavo.*

Isle of Man at pp. 233-234. Speaks of only twelve men as Keys.

—— MISSON.—1714-19.

Misson's Travels over England, Scotland, and Ireland. 5 vols. *Octavo.*

A short notice (about 16 lines) relating to the Isle of Man.

JOHN LE NEVE.—1716.

Fasti Ecclesiæ Anglicanæ : or an Essay towards deducing a regular succession of all the principal dignitories in each

Cathedral, Collegiate Church or Chapel (now in being) in those parts of Great Britain called England and Wales, from the first erection thereof, to this present year, 1715. Containing the Names, Dates of Consecration, Admission, Preferment, Removal, or Death of the Archbishops, Bishops, Deans, Præcentors, Treasurers, Chancellors, and Archdeacons in their several Stations and Degrees, etc. etc. Attempted by John Le Neve, Gent., late Fellow Commoner of Trinity College, in Cambridge. In the Savoy : printed by J. Nutt, etc., MDCCXVI. *Folio*, pp. 535.

Sodor or the Isle of Man, pp. 356 to 359, commences with A.D. 360 Amphibalus ; 447 Germanus ; and ends with 1697 Thomas Wilson.

Browne Willis says Bishop Kennet was the real author.

Rev. Thomas Cox.—1720-31.

Magna Britannia et Hibernia, antiqua et nova ; or a new Survey of Great Britain. Collected and composed by an impartial Hand. London, 1720-31. 6 vols. *Quarto.* Maps.

The Isle of Man, pp. 417-22. Ends with " Dr. Thomas Wilson, the present Bishop."

The portion relating to the Isle of Man has been reprinted in the Manx Society's series, vol. xviii. 1871, " Old Historians."

Bishop Wilson.—1721.

A farther Instruction for such as have learned the Church Catechism, and plain short Directions and Prayers. By Thomas, Lord Bishop of Man. London. 1721. 24*mo.*

Herman Moll.—1724.

Map of the Isle of Man. To the Right Honble. William, Earl of Derby, Lord of ye Isle of Man, etc., humbly dedicated by Captn. G. Collins. *Folio.* Engraved by H. Moll. A View of Peel Castle, with the Round Tower and Spire top.

William, ninth Earl of Derby, was Lord of Man 1672 to November 1702.

Moll's maps were attached to various works.

BISHOP WILSON.—1724.

On the Education of Rich and Poor Children, for ye Masters and Mistresses of Charity Schools. London. 1724. *Small Quarto.*

Especially published for the use of the Inhabitants of the Isle of Man. A Sermon, etc., pp. 60. The Sermon, pp. 35.

JOHN MACKY.—1724.

A Journey through England in familiar Letters from a Gentleman here to his Friend abroad. 2d Edition, with large additions. 2 vols. London : printed for J. Pemberton, etc. 1724. *Octavo.* No name on the Title, but the Dedication signed Jo. Macky.

The Isle of Man in 2d vol., Letter xvii., 1721-22, pp. 228-257. The 5th Edition appeared in 1732. *Octavo.* 2 vols.

BROWNE WILLIS.—1727-30.

A Survey of the Cathedrals of York, Durham, Carlisle, Chester, Man, Lichfield, Hereford, Worcester, Gloucester, Bristol, Lincoln, Ely, Oxford, and Peterborough. By Browne Willis. London. 1727-30. 3 vols. *Quarto.*

Vol. i. p. 5, Preface. The S.E. Prospect of the Cathedral was supplied by Bishop Wilson, at p. 369. Diocese of Man, Vol. i. pp. 369-380. Vol. ii. pp. 817-821.

An edition published in 1742, in 4 vols. *quarto.* The

Survey of the Isle of Man is reprinted in the Manx Society's series, vol. xviii. 1871, " Old Historians," pp. 126-151.

1731.

A Book of Rates, of the Customs of all Goods and Commodities that are imported into and transported from the Isle of Man. Dublin. 1731. 12*mo*. 8 leaves.

GEORGE WALDRON.—1731.

The compleat Works in Verse and Prose of George Waldron, Gent., late of Queen's College. Oxon : printed for the Widow and Orphans, MDCCXXXI. Price 2 gs. *Folio*.

The portion relating to the Isle of Man commences—

" A Description of the Isle of Man, with some useful and entertaining reflections on the Laws, Customs, and Manners of its Inhabitants." Pp. 91 to 191.

" The great many leisure hours he had in the Isle of Man, where for some years he resided, in a post under his late and present Majesty, gave him an opportunity of writing a description of that place, with the customs and manners of the inhabitants, in a much more particular manner than any author before him has done. Most of those who treat on that subject have contented themselves with barely mentioning the situation, soil, produce, chief towns, and markets, whereas the chief curiosities consist in tradition, and a superstitious observance of old customs."—*Preface.*

Only 110 copies of this work were printed. Mr. Waldron resided on the Island in the capacity of a commissioner from the British Government. He was a gentleman of an ancient family in Essex, and received his education at Queen's College, in Oxford, and died in England just after he had obtained a new deputation from the Government.

The volume is dedicated " To the Right Honourable William O'Brian, Earl of Inchiquin," and signed "Theodosia Waldron."

The "History of the Isle of Man" is said to have been printed in 1726, 12*mo*, but I have not met with a copy. It was, however, written in that year.

An edition of the "History of the Isle of Man" appeared in 1744. Reprinted in volume xi. of the Manx Society's series, 1865, with numerous Notes, by the present Compiler.

1732.

The Independent Whig; or a Defence of Primitive Christianity, and of our Ecclesiastical Establishment against the Exorbitant Claims and Encroachments of Fantastical and Disaffected Clergymen. The 5th edition, with additions and amendments. In 2 volumes. London : printed for J. Peele, at Luke's Head, in Amen Corner, Paternoster Row, and sold by J. Osborn, at Dock Head, near Rotherhith, MDCCXXXII. *Small Octavo.*

In vol. i. pp. xxxvii. to lxxxi., is a letter to the publisher, signed W. A., Dec. 14th, 1731, detailing the whole of the particulars of Bishop Wilson's mandate against the introduction of this work in the Isle of Man.

The 6th edition was published in the same year, in one volume. The work commenced in 1720.

Many other editions were published, but the only interest the work possesses relative to the Island is Bishop Wilson's order for its seizure wherever found. It was ordered to be burnt.

FRANCIS PECK.—1732-5.—JAMES, SEVENTH EARL OF DERBY.

Desiderata Curiosa ; or a Collection of divers scarce and curious Pieces (relating chiefly to matters of English History), in six books, containing upwards of one hundred and sixty choice Tracts, Memoirs, Letters, Wills, Epitaphs, etc., transcribed, many of them from the originals themselves, the rest from divers ancient MS. copies, or the MS. collections of sundry famous Antiquaries and other eminent Persons, both of the last and present age : the whole, as near as possible, digested into an order of time, and illustrated with ample Notes, Contents, additional Discourses, and a complete Index.   By Francis Peck, M.A., Rector of Godeby, near Melton, in Leicestershire.

> ——" Referam toto notissima Regno
> Facta."   *Metam. Lib.* XIV.

Adorned with Cuts. London : printed MDCCXXXII. 2 vols. *Folio.*

In the 2d. vol., printed in 1735, No. xii., Lib. xi., is " The History and Antiquities of the Isle of Man.   By James (Stanley), Earl of Derby, and Lord of Man : beheaded at Bolton, 15th Oct. 1651, with an Account of his many troubles and losses in the Civil War ; and of his own proceedings in the Isle of Man during his residence there in 1643, interspersed with large and excellent advices to his son Charles, Lord Strange, upon many curious points.   From the original (all of his Lordship's own handwriting) in the hands of the Honourable Roger Gale, Esq., the whole divided into Chapters, and illustrated with Contents and Notes ; as also an Introduction and Appendix, collected by the Editor."

Pp. 18-50. Contains Introduction, 18 Chapters, and an Appendix.

An edition was published in 1779, in 2 vols. *quarto.*

This has been reprinted by the Manx Society in their 3d volume, 1860, edited by the Rev. William Mackenzie.

1733-38.

An Abstract of the Sufferings of the People called Quakers,

for the Testimony of a good Conscience, from the time of their being first distinguished by that name, taken from original Records and other authentick Accounts, from the year 1650 to the year 1660. London : printed and sold by the Assigns of J. Cowle, at the Bible, in George Yard, Lombard Street. 1733. 3 vols. *Octavo.*

The 2d volume, published in 1738, contains the Records from the year 1660 to 1666. The Isle of Man, pp. 217 to 223.

BISHOP WILSON.—1734.

A short and plain Instruction for the better understanding the Lord's Supper. By Bishop Wilson.

This is the first edition, and has been repeatedly printed. It is universally esteemed for the elegant simplicity of its language, and its unaffected piety.

1736.

The Case of James, Duke of Athol, Lord of Mann and the Isles, etc., claiming the Barony of Strange, created by Writ of Summons, 3 Car. 1., directed to his Great-Grandfather (whose Heir he is) James, the Son of William, Earl of Derby, by the name of James Strange, Chevalier, in virtue of which the said Lord Strange sat and voted in several Parliaments. *Folio.* Pp. 4, with a Pedigree at the end. Privately printed, 1736.

An important Case, giving the List of Proofs.

JOHN SEACOME.—No date (1736).

Memoirs of the House of Stanley, with a full description of the Isle of Man. By John Seacome. A. Sadler, printer, Liverpool. *Quarto.*

This is the first edition. It was one of the earliest productions of the Liverpool press.

BISHOP WILSON.—1740.

The Knowledge and Practice of Christianity made easy to the meanest Capacities ; or, An Essay towards an Instruction for the Indians, 1740.   12*mo*.

In Manx and English.   A corrected and improved version of "The Principles and Duties of Christianity," which was first published in 1699.

Several editions in Manx and English have appeared.

JOHN SEACOME.—1741.

Memoirs of the House of Stanley, with a full Description of the Isle of Man.   By John Seacome.   Printed by A. Sadler, Liverpool.   1741.   *Quarto*, pp. 203.

This is the second edition.   Dedicated to the Duke of Atholl.   Adorned with woodcuts.

GEORGE WALDRON.—1744.

The History and Description of the Isle of Man : viz.—Its Antiquity, History, Laws, Customs, Religion, and Manners of its Inhabitants, its Animals, Minerals, curious and authentic Relations of Apparitions of Giants that have lived under the Castle time immemorial.   Likewise, many comical and entertaining Stories of the Pranks played by Fairies, etc., the whole carefully collected from original papers and personal knowledge, during near twenty years' residence there.   London : printed for W. Bickerton, in the Temple Exchange Passage, Fleet Street, 1744.   (Price one shilling and sixpence.)   12*mo*, pp. 154.

This is exactly the same "description" as in Waldron's folio edition, published in 1731, with an enlarged Title. Some copies have the date 1745.   The plate of Medals, etc., as given on page 145 of the 1731 edition, is here omitted. Reprinted in the Manx Society's series, vol. xi.

WALTER HARRIS.—1747.

Life of St. Patrick, the Apostle and Patron of Ireland, with
an Historical Account of the City and Diocese of Dublin,
the Isle of Man, etc. By Walter Harris. Dublin. 1747.
Octavo.

1748.

Commission issued upon the Petition of John Stevenson of
Balladoole, in the Isle of Man, to certain Estates belonging
to his brother, who died in April 1742 ; the questions and
proceedings as regards the legality of his claims, with the
evidence and cross-examination of witnesses (Eliza Sher-
lock and Anne Trydell, etc.) ; with the order of His
Majesty in Council ; and office copies. G. Quayle,
Comptroller-General ; D. Mylrea, C. Stanley, J. Taubman,
and J. Borles. *Folio.* 1748.

JOHN BALDWIN.—1748.

A new Act of an Inferior Parliament, or probably an Act of
Arbitrary Power lately made in the Isle of Man, to
imprison all Women under Covert Baron, Natives of that
Isle only excepted, for Debts contracted singly by their
Husbands, exemplified in the case of an English Gentle-
woman, already fifteen months a prisoner, etc. By John
Baldwin. London. 1748. *Octavo.*

This is the first of three pamphlets published relating to
Mrs. Hingston being imprisoned in the Island for the Debt
of her husband.

1748.

Yn Sushtal Scruit liorish yn Noo Mian. Prentyt ayns Lun-
nyng. Liorish Ean Oliver, ayns Bartholomew's Close.
MDCCXLVIII. *Octavo,* in 4s., pp. 106.
St. Matthew's Gospel in Manx.

1748-49.

Earl of Derby v. Duke of Athol, Feby. 8, 1748-9. Vesey's Reports, Vol. i. p. 202.

The decision of Lord Chancellor Hardwicke as to the effect of clauses against alienation, and the general title of the Isle of Man.

Printed in Gell's "Abstract," etc., vol. i. pp. 65-67. Manx Society, 1867.

JOHN BALDWIN.—1750-1.

Liberty Invaded ; or, the Remarkable Case of an English Lady, presumptuously held in a Slavish Imprisonment within these his Majesty's Dominions, without Crime against, or any Demand upon, her. Addressed to the Honourable House of Commons.

> Is Albion's once fam'd Spirit wholly flown ?
> Shall Britons under worst of Slaveries groan,
> In Mankish Jails immured !—
> What ! shall the Fair, whose Right is to be free,
> Crimeless in Dungeons mourn lost Liberty ?
> And England not resent the base Indignity !

London : printed for and sold by W. Owen, near Temple-Bar ; and G. Woodfall, near Charing-Cross, 1750-1. (Price one shilling.) *Octavo*, pp. 86.

Addressed "To the Honourable Representatives of the People in Parliament assembled," and signed John Baldwin, pp. i. to v.

"Advertisement to the Reader," pp. vi. to viii.

Case of Mrs. Mary Hingston, with the pleadings in 1747.

JOHN SEACOME.—1750.

Memoirs, containing a Genealogical and Historical Account of the Ancient and Honourable House of Stanley, from 1066 to 1735. Also a full description of the Isle of Man, of which they are the Lords. Liverpool : printed by A. Sadler. 1750. *Quarto*, pp. 250. Numerous Coats of Arms.

Gentleman's Magazine.—1751.

Reasons for Annexing the Isle of Man to the Crown of Great Britain. *Gentleman's Magazine*, May 1751, pp. 201-2.

London Magazine.—1754.

A Description of the Isle of Man, with a Map. *London Magazine*, p. 7.

Gentleman's Magazine.—1754.

On Annexing the Isle of Man to Great Britain. *Gentleman's Magazine*, p. 485.

JOHN BALDWIN.—1755.

British Liberty in Chains, and England's Ruin on the Anvil, in the Isle of Man, now commonly called Little France, addressed to all Free Britons, zealous for the glory of the King, the Liberties of the People, and safety of the Realm; especially to the laudable Association of Antigallicans. By John Baldwin, Esq.

> " Truth is bolder than a Lion,
> Will ever stand upright and unshaken,
> For God himself is truth.
> Who, then, are they that durst oppose it ? "

" With her there is no receiving of Persons nor Difference ; but she doth the things which are just, and abstaineth from unjust and wicked things, and all good men favour her works : neither is there any unjust thing in her judgment ; and she is the Strength, and the Kingdom, and the Power and Majesty of all ages. Blessed be the God of Truth."—1 *Esd.* 4.

London : printed for G. Woodfall, at Charing Cross ; R. Griffiths, in Paternoster Row ; and W. Owen, at 7 Temple Bar. MDCCLV. *Octavo.* Pp. 93.

A Pamphlet, on Mrs. Mary Hingston of Bristol's Imprisonment in the Isle of Man, for the Debt of her Husband. The author represents the Manx as enemies to the Interests of Great Britain, and inveighs against them for their treatment of Mrs. Hingston.

REV. JOHN F. DURAND.—1760.   CAPTAIN THUROT.

Genuine and Curious Memoirs of the Famous Captain Thurot. Written by the Rev. John Francis Durand, with some of Monsieur Thurot's Original Letters to that gentleman, now in England ; to which is added a much more faithful and particular Account than has hitherto been published, of his proceedings since his sailing from the Coast of France.   Oct. 18, 1759.

> " He was a man, take him for all in all,
>   I shall not look upon his like again."
>   *Shakespeare.*

London : printed for J. Burd, at the Temple Exchange Coffee House, and J. Williams, under St. Dunstan's Church, Fleet Street. 1760. Price one shilling. 12*mo.*

This Memoir was reprinted by the Percy Society in 1845. This pamphlet is referred to in the " Gentleman's Magazine " for March, 1760, p. 110 ; with an Account of the Action with Captain Elliot, who brought his prize into Ramsey Bay, and gave a Ball on board his frigate " The Æolus," to the principal inhabitants and strangers. This action between Elliot and Thurot became the subject of two pictures, painted by Wright of Liverpool, and have been engraved. Some relics of Thurot still exist, I believe, at Bishop's Court.

The various songs written on Captain Thurot are printed

in the 21st volume of the Manx Society's series, " Mona Miscellany," second series, pp. 73-87, with a short Memoir.

The Scots Magazine.—1760.

An entertaining Account of Thurot's Naval Engagement with Captain Elliot in Ramsey Bay.

This Magazine commenced in 1739, and records many events connected with Manx History.

Bishop Wilson.—1761.

The Principles and Duties of Christianity, for the Use of the Diocese of Man, with short and plain directions and Prayers. In English and Manx. Liverpool: printed by John Sadler, Harrington Street. 1761. *Octavo.*

The first edition appeared in 1699.

1762.

Plain Instructions for Young Persons in the Principles of the Christian Religion, in three Conferences between a Minister and his Disciples, designed for the use of the Isle and Diocese of Mann. By a Resident Clergyman. London: printed by J. and W. Oliver, Printers to the Society for promoting Christian Knowledge, in Bartholomew Close, near West Smithfield. 1762. *Octavo*, pp. 118.

1763.

The Four Gospels and Acts, in Manx. London. 1763. *Octavo.*

This was the first edition, and only a few copies were supplied to the Clergy, with a request "that they would insert freely their remarks on the blank pages, as the best method that can be proposed for furnishing from the whole one correct edition." I have only met with a very few of these earlier editions of the Scriptures translated into the Manx language, but prior to this the Manx were probably the only Christian Church in the world which were absolutely destitute of a printed Copy of the Holy Scriptures in the vulgar tongue. This was afterwards amply supplied under the auspices of the Society for promoting Christian Knowledge. For a full account of the progress of these Translations, *vide* Appendix to the Memoirs of Bishop Hildesley, by the Rev. W. Butler, 1799, pp. 211-260, for " Narrative of the origin, progress, and completion of the Manx Version of Holy Scripture, and other religious Books, for the use of the native Inhabitants of the Isle of Mann."

An edition of the Gospels and Acts was published in 1765.

1763.

The Christian Monitor, in Manx and English. London. 1763. *Octavo*.

This is the first edition of this work, " and was very eagerly received by the grateful natives."—Hildesley's *Memoirs*.

The Rev. Paul Crebbin, Vicar of Kirk Santon, was the translator.

1764.

English Commissioners' Report of 4th January, respecting Smuggling from the Isle of Man. *Folio*.

The Scots Magazine.—1764.

P. 107.—Succession of Lady Charlotte Murray, Daughter of James, Duke of Athol, to the Lordship of Man and the Isles, and the proceedings consequent thereon. P. 167.—Notice of the Death of John Bourke, in the Island, at the age of 112. Pp. 456-7.—Smuggling from the Isle of Man to be totally Suppressed. Clauses of Acts of Parliament relating to the Island. P. 682.—On the Contraband Trade. Edinburgh. 1764. *Octavo.* Vol. xxvi.

The Scots Magazine.—1765.

Pp. 77-82.—Case of John, Duke of Athol, and Charlotte, his Wife, respecting the Isle of Man. Pp. 138-9.—A short Account of the Island. P. 139.—Letter from the Earl of Derby to Cromwell, respecting the Island. P. 165.—Proceedings in Parliament respecting Sale of the Island by the Duke of Athol. Pp. 337 to 344.—Abstract of Act 5 Geo. III., cap. 26, for Purchase of Isle of Man. Pp. 385-6.—Proclamation for Continuing Officers in the Island after purchase. P. 386.—Proceedings in the Island on issuing Proclamation, etc. P. 391.—Appointment of Governor Wood. P. 392.—Appointment of Collector and Comptrollers. P. 398.—Speech of Governor Wood on taking possession of the Island for the King. Pp. 467-8.—Proceedings in Parliament. Edinburgh. 1765. Vol. xxvii.

1765.

The Book of Common Prayer, and Administration of the Sacraments, and other Rites and Ceremonies of the Church, according to the use of the Church of England; together with the Psalter or Psalms of David. Pointed as they are to be sung or said in Churches. Translated into Manx, for the use of the Diocese of Mann. London: printed by J. and W. Oliver, Printers to the Society for Promoting Christian Knowledge, in Bartholomew Close, near West Smithfield. MDCCLXV. *Octavo.* Not paged from A to CCC.

The Society for promoting Christian Knowledge made

grants in aid of the printing of this. Fifty copies were printed in 4to, for the use of the Churches, and for presents.

An edition in 12mo, in Manx, was published at Ramsey in 1768.

This Manx Prayer Book contains no prayer for the High Court of Parliament of Great Britain and Ireland, but instead of it is a prayer for the Members of the House of Keys, together with a prayer for the Lord and Lady of the Isle, as clauses in the Litany, and in the prayer for the Royal Family, viz.—" And with them the Lord and Lady, and Rulers of this Isle."

1765.

State of the Proceedings in the House of Commons, on the Petition of the Duke and Duchess of Athol, against the Bill for the more effectual preventing the Mischief arising to the Revenue and Commerce of Great Britain and Ireland, from the illicit and clandestine trade to and from the Isle of Mann. No place or date. *Octavo.* Pp. 32.

An excellent statement of the Title of the Duke to the Isle of Man, by his Counsel Mr. Maddox and Mr. Cooper.

1765.

The Duke of Athol's Letter of 25th January to the Lords of the Treasury, with Abstract of Revenue, and offer to part with the same for £70,000.

1765.

By the King, a Proclamation for Continuing Officers in the Isle of Man.

Given at our Court at St. James's, the 21st day of June 1765, in the fifth year of our reign.—*London Gazette.*

John Wood, Esq., appointed Governor.

The Scots Magazine.—1766.

Pp. 302-309.—Proceedings in Parliament respecting the
Illicit Trade of the Isle of Man, and Case of the Duke of
Athol.   P. 361.—Case of the Duke of Athol.   Edinburgh.
1766.   *Octavo.*   Vol. xxviii.

JOHN SEACOME.—1767.

Memoirs, containing a Genealogical and Historical Account
of the Ancient and Honourable House of Stanley from the
Conquest to the Death of James, late Earl of Derby, in
the year 1735 ; as also a full Description of the Isle of
Man, etc.   Manchester : printed by Joseph Harrop,
opposite the Exchange.   1767.   *Quarto,* pp. 238.

Isle of Man—A Complete History of the Isle of Man, pp.
189-238.   Another edition was printed by Harrop in
1783.

This is Seacome's History, without name, dedication, or
preface, and otherwise curtailed. The first edition was published without date in 1736, but the work was completed in
1741.   He has borrowed largely from Sacheverell in his
Description of the Isle of Man, but furnishes other valuable
information.   He had the use of Bishop Rutter's papers,
" the historian of the family," and most probably these papers
are now in the archives at Knowsley, and would be well
worth examination by the Manx Society. There is a Portrait
of Bishop Rutter, at Knowsley, as Archdeacon of Man,
painted by Dobson, and engraved in the "Stanley Papers,"
part 3, Chetham Society, vol. lxx. 1867.

1767.

A short View of the present state of the Isle of Man, humbly
submitted to the consideration of the Lords of the

Treasury. By an Impartial hand. London. 1767. Printed for Johnson. (Price 6d.)

1767.

The Epistles and Revelations, in Manx. Printed by Sheppard, of Whitehaven. Ramsey. 1767. *Octavo.*

1000 copies printed, similar to the Gospels and Acts printed in London in 1765.

John Macpherson, D.D.—1768.

A Critical Dissertation on the History of the Norwegian Principality, commonly called The Kingdom of Man. Edinburgh. 1768. *Quarto*, pp. xxvi. and 382.

1768.

The Christian Monitor, in Manx.

1200 Copies distributed by the Society for promoting Christian Knowledge.

1768.

Lewis's Catechism and Prayer for the Fishery, in Manx. Ramsey. 1768. *Octavo.*

2000 Copies distributed by the Society for promoting Christian Knowledge.

1768.

The Book of Common Prayer, in Manx. Ramsey. 12*mo.*

1000 Copies distributed by the Society for promoting Christian Knowledge.

Thomas Snelling.—1769.

View of the Coinage of Great Britain, Ireland, etc. Seven parts in one volume. *Royal Quarto.* London. 1762-69.

Part 5.—Miscellaneous Views of the Coins struck by English Princes in France, Counterfeit Sterlings, Coins struck by the East India Company, those in the West India Colonies, and in the Isle of Man : Also of pattern pieces for Gold and Silver Coins, and Gold Nobles struck abroad in imitation of English. London. 1769. Pp. 64. Title and preface 2 leaves. 7 plates.

NATHANIEL SPENCER.—1771-3.

The Complete English Traveller ; or a New Survey and Description of England and Wales, containing a full account of whatever is curious and entertaining in the several counties of England and Wales, the Isle of Man, Jersey, Guernsey, and other Islands adjoining to and dependent on the Crown of Great Britain, etc. By Nathaniel Spencer, Esq. London : printed for J. Cooke, at Shakespear's Head, in Paternoster Row. 1771-73. *Folio.*

Pp. 669 to 671, respecting the Isle of Man. Written by Robert Sanders, and published in numbers.

1772.

Calendars of Ancient Charters, with Rolls and Schedules of Fealties done in the Isle of Man. London. 1772.

—— WOOD.—1772.

Institute of the Laws of England, etc.

P. 1 states that the Isle of Man is no part of England, and is out of the power of the English Chancery Court.

1772.

Yn Vible Casherick—The Holy Bible, in Manx. J. Ware

and Son, Whitehaven. 1772. 2 vols. *Octavo.* A few copies in 4to, in 1 vol., for the use of the Clergy.

It was first printed in this year under the auspices of Bishop Hildesley, who received the last portion of it on Saturday, November 28, 1772, and died on the 7th December following. The printing of this Manx version of the Holy Scriptures had been a work of great labour, and the latter portion was attended with an accident which had almost proved fatal to the good work. The Rev. Dr. Kelly, author of "The Manx Grammar" (already published by the Manx Society, 1859), was, on the 19th March 1771, on his way from the Island to Whitehaven, with a portion of the MS., from Deuteronomy to Job, shipwrecked in a storm, when, " with no small difficulty and danger the MS. was preserved by holding it above the water for the space of five hours, and this was almost the only article saved." The Rev. Dr. Kelly transcribed the whole of the Old Testament, besides the corrected edition of the New Testament and Prayer Book. The names of the various Translators will be found in Butler's *Life of Bishop Hildesley,* p. 252.

An edition in 8vo. Whitehaven. 1775. Also distributed by the Society for promoting Christian Knowledge.

WM. CAMDEN.—1772.

Britannia : or a Chorographical Description of Great Britain and Ireland ; together with the adjacent Islands, written in Latin by Wm. Camden, Clarencieux King-at-Arms ; and translated into English, with additions and improvements, by Edmund Gibson, D.D., late Lord Bishop of London. London : printed for W. Boyer, W. Whiston, etc. etc. MDCCLXXII. *Folio.* 2 vols. Portraits and Maps.

This fourth edition is printed from a copy of 1722, left corrected by the Bishop for the Press. The former editions by Bishop Gibson are—1695, folio, 1 vol.; 1722, folio, 2 vols.; 1753, folio.

In vol. ii. pp. 391-398, a new Survey and Description of the Isle of Man. Drawn up by Dr. Thomas Wilson, late Bishop of the Island, and communicated by him to be inserted in this work. The first part, pp. 390-391. By John Meryk, Bishop.

Four Runic Inscriptions, pp. 399-400 :—1. Upon a stone cross laid for a lintel over a window in Kirk Michael Church. 2. Upon a stone cross at Kirk Michael. 3. Upon a stone cross at Kirk Braddan. 4. Upon a stone cross in Kirk Andreas Churchyard.

Pp. 479 to 484, " A Chronicle of the Kings of Man" seems to have been written by the Monks of Russin. "A continuation of the foregoing History collected out of other Authors," p. 485.

A reprint is in the Manx Society's series, vol. xviii. 1871, pp. 4-33, "Old Historians."

RICHARD ROLT.—1773.

The History of the Island of Man; from the earliest Accounts to the present time. Compiled from the Public Archives of the Island, and other authentic Materials. By the late Mr. Rolt. London : printed for W. Nicole, No. 51 in Paul's Churchyard. MDCCLXXIII. *Octavo*, pp. 152. Index and Appendix (not numbered) pp. 24.

An edition is said to have been printed in 1782, but I have not met with it.

Mr. Rolt was the author of " The Lives of the principal Reformers, with a general History of the Reformation from 1360 to 1600 :" London, *Folio*, 1759. " Memoirs of the Life of the Rt. Hon. John Lindesay, Earl of Crawford :" London, 1753, *Quarto;* and other works.

Francis Grose.—1773-77.

The Antiquities of England and Wales. By Francis Grose, Esq., F.A.S., with Supplement. London. 1773-77. Six vols. *Royal Quarto.* The first edition.

In the sixth vol. is a description of the following antiquities, accompanied with views of the Abbey Bridge at Ballasalla :—The Cathedral Church of St. German's, in Peel Castle —a plan of the same ; St. Patrick's Church and Armoury in Peel Castle ; a general View of Peel Castle ; Rushen Abbey ; Castle Rushen—two plates ; The Tinwald—two plates ; St. Trinion's Church ; Map of the Island.

Vol. vi. pp. 197-214 ; vol. viii. pp. 161-162. The views were taken in 1774.

Editions of the work were also published in 1783-1797.

Reprinted in the 18th volume of the Manx Society's series, 1871, pp. 153-170, " Old Historians."

John Campbell.—1774.

A Political Survey of Britain : being a series of Reflections on the Situation, Lands, Inhabitants, Revenues, Colonies, and Commerce of this Island. Intended to show that we have not as yet approached near the summit of Improvement, but that it will afford employment to many generations before they push to their utmost extent the natural advantage of Great Britain. By John Campbell, LL.D. London : printed for the Author, and sold by Richardson and Urquart, at the Royal Exchange, etc. 1774. Two vols. *Quarto.*

Vol. i. sec. iii. pp. 524 to 552, the Island and Kingdom of Man.

Also at pp. 493, 558, 560, 563-4, 591, 604.

The portion relating to the Isle of Man is in Oliver's

"Monumenta," vol. i. pp. 233-236.   Manx Society, vol. iv.
1860.

Sir Joseph Ayloffe, Bart.—1774.

Calendars of the Ancient Charters, and of the Welch and
Scotish Rolls, now remaining in the Tower of London :
Also Calendars of all the Treaties of Peace entered into
by the Kings of England with those of Scotland ; and of
sundry letters and public Instruments relating to that
Kingdom, now in the Charter House at Westminster.
Together with Catalogues of the Records brought to
Berwick from the Royal Treasury at Edinburgh ; of such
as were transmitted to the Exchequer at Westminster ;
and of those which were removed to different parts of
Scotland by order of King Edward I.   The Proceedings
relating to the carrying back the Records of Scotland into
that Kingdom ; and the Transactions of the Parliament
there from the 15th May 1639 to the 8th March 1650.
To which are added Memoranda concerning the affairs of
Ireland, extracted from the Tower Records.   With four
Copper plates, exhibiting all the various hands in which
the several Charters have been written, from the Reign of
King William the Conqueror to that of Queen Elizabeth.
To the whole is prefixed an Introduction, giving some
account of the State of the Public Records from the Con-
quest to the present time.   By Sir Joseph Ayloffe, Bart.,
V.P.A.S. and F.R.S.   London :   printed for Benjamin
White, at Horace's Head, in Fleet Street.   MDCCLXXIV.
Quarto.

Introduction, pp. lxx. ; Calendars, etc., pp. 462 ; with a
General Index.

The following List of Rolls and Charters mentioned in this
volume relate to the Isle of Man :—

Anno 19 to 24 Edward I.

P. 105.—Alanus de Wigeton habet literas de presentione ad ecclesiam Sancti Carber in Man.   Anno 19.

P. 109.—De seisina Insulæ de Man liberata Johanni Regi Scotiæ.   Ano. 21.

P. 110.—De summonitioue Regis Scotiæ ex parte Austriciæ, consanguineæ et hæredis magni quondam Regis Manniæ, pro terra de Man.   Ano. 21.

P. 112.—De venire faciendo ad legem usque Berewicum Marcum episcopum Soderin.   Ano. 24.

P. 121.—De navibus mittendis usque Insulam de Man. Ano. 4 Edwardi II.

P. 121.—De arrestando quosdam malefactores in Insula de Man.   4 Ed. II.

P. 122.—Pro Rege, de Navigio Roberti de Brus movendo ab Insula de Man.   Ano. 4 Ed. II.

P. 132.—De navibus providendis et muniendis pro salvatione terræ Man.   Ano. 10 Ed. II.

P. 192.—Pro hominibus Insulæ de Man, de treugis cum Scotis ineundis.   Ano. 16 Edwardi III.

P. 265.—De frumento versus partes Insulæ de Man et alibi ducendo.   Ano. 1 Henrici IV.

P. 283.—De salvo conductu pro Alexandro principe Scotorum, duce Albaniæ, comite de la Marche et domino de Annanderdale, et de Man.   Ed. IV.

P. 327.—Litera majorum Mann, missa Alexandro Regi Scotiæ.

P. 328.—Litera regis Mann quod tenebit terram Mann di Rege Scotiæ.

P. 328.—Finalis concordia inter Reges Norwagiæ et Scotiæ facta apud Mann, et aliis insulis.

P. 329.—Scriptum Regis Scotiæ Alexandri per quod concessit episcopo Sodorensi quod non iret super Mann usque ad tempus.

P. 329.—Protectio Henrici Regis Angliæ, facta domino magno Regi Mann, in partibus Walliæ. A.D. 1100.

P. 334.—In sexto sacculo. Various writings, etc. Et de pluribus negotiis tangentibus terram Man. *Vide* Train, vol. i. p. 143. 1845.

P. 343.—Confirmatio et donatio Regis Norwagiæ, monasterio de Russy in Mannia.

P. 343.—Charta Regis Norwagiæ, super insula de Bot. et quibusdam aliis concessis Regi Manniæ.

P. 344.—Donationes factæ Abbati et conventui de Russy per magnum dictum Regem Manniæ. *Vide* Train, vol. i. p. 132. 1845.

P. 345.—Charta Regis Manniæ super receptione Manniæ ad firmam. Charta de Glenkelk, quæ fuit Regis Manniæ.

P. 431.—Pro Rege Manniæ de custodienda costera Hyberniæ. Rot. Par. 19 Hen. III.

1775.

Conaant Noa nyn Jiarn as Saualtagh Yeesey Creest ; veih my chied ghlaraghyn ; Dy Kiaralagh chyndait ayns Gailck ; Ta shen dy ghra. Chengy ny Mayrey Ellan Vannin. Pointit dy ve lhaiht ayns Kialteenyn. Whitehaven : Prentit liorish Juan Ware as e Vac., 1775. 12*mo.*

JOHN CAMPBELL.—1775.

A Political Survey of Great Britain. Dublin. 1775.

The Island and Kingdom of Man, vol. ii. pp. 546-564.

1776.

Speech of William Christian. Executed 2d January 1663.

A broadside.

BISHOP WILSON.—1777.

A short and plain Instruction for the better understanding of
the Lord's Supper, with the necessary preparation for the
benefit of Young Communicants, in English and Manx,
translated for the use of the Diocese of Mann. By Bishop
Wilson. Whitehaven. 1777. *Octavo.*

This translation was revised by the Rev. Mr. Moore,
assisted by the Rev. Mr. Kelly.

1777.

The Book of Common Prayer, and Administration of the
Sacraments, and other rites and ceremonies of the Church,
according to the use of the Church of England : Together
with the Psalter or Psalms of David. Pointed as they are
to be sung or said in Churches. Translated into Manks,
for the use of the Diocese of Mann. Whitehaven : printed
by J. Ware and Son. MDCCLXXVII. *Quarto.*

Printed in three columns. Arms of the Bishop at the
head of the Table of Contents. At the end are a number of
Psalms in Manx, translated by the Revs. Robert Radcliff and
Matthias Curghey, with the order of Bishop Hildesley, dated
Bishop's Court, Novr. 9, 1761, that they be sung "in the
several Country Churches of this Isle." This was printed for
the Society for promoting Christian Knowledge. 2000 in
duodecimo, and 50 in small quarto, the latter chiefly for the
use of the Clergy.

1777.

The Holy Bible, in 2 vols. Whitehaven : printed by J. Ware
and Son. *Octavo.*

DANIEL COWLEY.—1778.

Aght Ghiare dy heet gys tushtey jeh'n chredjue Chreestee : ny as toiggal jeh catechism ny Killagh Kiarit son ymmyd sleih aegey Ellan Vannin. 24*mo.*

A short summary of the Christian religion, or an explanation of the Church Catechism. Translated into Manx by Daniel Cowley, of Kirk Michael, who was educated by Bishop Hildesley, and by him apprenticed to a printer.

Mr. Cowley also translated Mr. Wesley's Hymns into Manx, for the use of the Methodists.

DANIEL DEFOE AND SAMUEL RICHARDSON.—1778.

A Tour through the Island of Great Britain, divided into Circuits or Journies, etc. Originally begun by the celebrated Daniel de Foe, continued by the late Mr. Richardson, author of " Clarissa," etc., and brought down to the present time by Gentlemen of eminence in the Literary World. The eighth edition, with great additional improvements, in 4 volumes. London : printed for W. Strahan, etc. 1778. 12*mo.* Maps.

Vol. 4. Isle of Man, pp. 246-252.

The additions only are by Richardson. The sixth edition in 4 vols. 12*mo.* London. 1769. The original work was written by Defoe. London. 1724. 2 vols. *Octavo.*

REV. JAMES JOHNSTONE.—1780.

Anecdotes of Olave the Black, King of Man, and the Hebridian Princes of the Somerled Family, to which are added XVIII. Eulogies on Haco, King of Norway, by Snorro Sturlson, poet to that Monarch, now first published in the Original Islandic from the Flateyan and other Manuscripts ; with a literal Version and notes. By the Rev.

James Johnstone, A.M., Chaplain to his Britannic Majesty's
Envoy Extraordinary at the Court of Denmark.   Printed
for the Author, 1780.   *Small Octavo*, pp. 48.

To the Reader, p. 4.—" The work from which this frag-
ment is taken was composed by Thordr, an Islandic writer of
the 13th century, and is extant in the celebrated manuscript
of Flatey, now in his Danish Majesty's library, where the
poems of Snorro are likewise preserved."

Printed in Oliver's "Monumenta," vol. i. pp. 43-46.
Maux Society, vol. iv. 1860.

GEORGE WALDRON.—1780.

The History of the Isle of Man, etc., with a succinct detail of
Enchantments that have been exhibited there by Sorcerers
and other infernal beings, etc.   1780.

This is most likely to be Waldron's " History," taken from
the edition of 1744.   *Vide* Campbell's " Tales of the West
Highlands," vol. iii. pp. 411.   Edinburgh.   1862.

BISHOP WILSON.—1781.

The Works of the Right Reverend Father in God Thomas
Wilson, D.D., Lord Bishop of Sodor and Man.   In 2 vols.
With his Life, compiled from Authentic Papers.   By C.
Cruttwell.

"Though he be dead he yet speaketh."

Bath : printed for C. and R. Cruttwell, and sold in London
by C. Dilly, Poultry ; J. F. and C. Rivington, and J. Johnson, St. Paul's Churchyard ; J. Philips, George Yard,
Lombard Street ; and James Fox, Dartmouth Street,
Westminster.   MDCCLXXXI.   Two vols.   *Quarto.*

The History of the Isle of Man in vol. i. pp. 477 to 492.
A Portrait of Bishop Wilson.   By G. Vertue.

The History reprinted in the 18th volume of the Manx Society's series, 1871, pp. 90-124.

1781.

An Address to the People of the Isle of Man, introductory to the Report of the Attorney and Solicitor-General of England upon the late Bill of the Most Noble John, Duke of Athol, respecting the said Isle. By order of the House of Keys.

> "Nescio quâ natale solum dulcedine cunctos ducit."—*Ovid.*
> " By secret charms our native land attracts."

Whitehaven : printed by J. Ware and Son. MDCCLXXXI. *Quarto.*

The Address, pp. 1 to 12 ; Report, pp. 15 to 28. Address dated Douglas, Isle of Man, Dec. 30, 1780. The Report dated June 7, 1780.

1781.

Copy of the Report of the Deemster, Clerk of the Rolls, and Attorney-General of the Isle of Man, on a Bill proposed to be brought into Parliament, entitled " A Bill to explain and amend an Act made in the Fifth Year of the Reign of his present Majesty, intituled ' An Act for carrying into Execution a contract made pursuant to the Act of Parliament of the Twelfth of his late Majesty King George the First, between the Commissioners of his Majesty's Treasury and the Duke and Duchess of Atholl, the Proprietors of the Isle of Man and their Trustees, for the purchase of the said Island and its Dependencies, under certain exceptions therein particularly named,' and to ascertain and establish the Jurisdiction of the Manorial Courts of the Most Noble John, Duke of Atholl, in the said Island, and to enable the said Duke and his

Heirs to exercise and enjoy certain Powers and Remedies therein mentioned." With Remarks thereon. *Quarto,* pp. 94.

The Report is addressed "To the Honourable Richard Dawson, Esq., His Majesty's Lieutenant-Governor of the Isle of Man," and signed by "John Quayle, Thos. Moore, Wadsworth Busk, 27th April 1780," to which are added further remarks, dated "February 12th, 1781." This is a report on a Bill to amend an Act commonly called the "Vesting Act," and contains many curious particulars respecting the manners, customs, and laws of the Island. £350,000 per annum was at "the Vesting" conceived to be acquired to the public by the Resumption that was made. A tolerably good bargain forced by the Crown from the Duke of Atholl.

John Quayle, Clerk of the Rolls; Thomas Moore, Deemster. Wadsworth Busk, Attorney-General, was knighted in 1781.

1782.

Observations on some Acts of Tynwald enacted in the Isle of Man since the re-vesting thereof in the Crown.

In the "Cumberland Pacquet," February 26.

JOSEPH BRISCOE.—1783.

Acts of Tynwald passed in the years 1776 and 1777. Douglas, Isle of Mann : printed by Joseph Briscoe. MDCCLXXXIII. *Small Quarto,* pp. 68.

This appears to be the first attempt at printing Acts of Tynwald, and is prefaced by a curious Introduction, with Rules to find the meaning of the Acts. There are 18 Acts.

J. BRISCOE.—17—.

Literary Lovers; an original Manks Novel. By J. Briscoe. 12*mo.*

JOHN SEACOME.—1783.

Memoirs of the House of Stanley, from the Conquest to the death of James, late Earl of Derby, in 1735 ; also a full description of the Isle of Man, etc.   Manchester : printed by Joseph Harrop, 1783.   *Quarto*, pp. 238.

BISHOP WILSON.—1783.

Sharmaneyn liorish Thomase Wilson, D.D., Chiarn aspick Sodor as Vannin ; dy kiaralagh chyndait veih Bayrl gys Gailck.   Lioar 1.   Ca dy vel eh marroo, foast t'eh loayrt. Bath : prentit liorish R. Cruttwell, 1783.   *Octavo*, pp. 490.

One volume of Bishop Wilson's Sermons, translated by the Rev. Mr. Corlett, and printed at the expense of the Rev. Dr. Wilson. Twenty-two Sermons. The second volume, I believe, did not appear.

1783.

Cursory Remarks on a Bill, signed by part of the Legislature of the Isle of Mann, in 1781, and intended by them to pass into an Act of Tynwald, if His Majesty shall think fit, entitled " A Bill to establish and regulate the proceedings of the *Manor Courts* of the Most Noble John, Duke of Atholl, within the Isle of Mann, and to enable the said Duke and his Heirs to use, exercise, and enjoy certain Rights, Powers, and Remedies therein mentioned ; and also to obviate the difficulties and inconveniences which have been occasioned by the separation of the Manorial Courts from the Courts of Common Law in the said Isle." (Long Latin and Manx quotations.)   London : printed in the year 1783.   *Octavo*, pp. 29.   No printer's name.

1784.

Chronicon Manniæ, or a Chronicle of the Kings of Man. Supposed to be written by the Monks of the Abbey of Russin, with the Norwegian Account of Olave the Black, King of Man, and of Haco's Expedition against Scotland. Together with the Civil and Ecclesiastical History of the Island, from the earliest accounts to the present time. Perth : printed for John Gillies, MDCCLXXXIV. *Small* 12*mo*, pp. 123. Address "To the Public," pp. iii. and iv.

The Chronicle is from Camden, and Olave and Haco's Account from Johnstone, 1780. This Chronicle is published in Oliver's "Monumenta," vol. i. pp. 125-215, from a MS. in the British Museum, numbered Julius A., VII., of the Cottonian Collection. Manx Society series, vol. iv. 1860. Also in Munch's edition, 1860.

1785.

The Universal Magazine of Knowledge and Pleasure. London. *Octavo.* 1785. Vol. lxxvi. pp. 22-25.

An Account of a Tour through the Isle of Man, made in May 1st to 7th, 1784. Signed "Albert." Notices the cheap living there, and the installation of the Bishop in Peel Cathedral, on Wednesday, May 5th, when the Bishop, etc., dined at the Liverpool Coffee-House in Peel. This was Bishop Cregan.

FRANCIS GROSE.—1785.

The Antiquities of England and Wales. By Francis Grose, Esq. 8 vols. *Octavo* and *Quarto.* London : Hooper, 1785. Vol. vi. p. 205.

Gentleman's Magazine.—1785.

Remarks on Bog Timber in the Isle of Man. *Gentleman's Magazine*, pp. 502.

ROBERT CALLISTER.—1785.

The Poems of Robert Callister. Liverpool. 1785. *Small Octavo*, pp. 104.

Chiefly relating to the Isle of Man. Inscribed to John Frissell and John Lace, Esqs. Liverpool, June 4, 1785.

HENRY BOSWELL, F.A.R.S.—[No date.]—1786.

Historical Descriptions of New and Elegant Picturesque Views of the Antiquities of England and Wales, etc. By Henry Boswell, Esq., F.A.R.S. London : printed for Alexander Hogg. No date. 2 vols. *Folio*.

Views of Castle Rushen, St. Patrick's Church and Armory, Peel Castle, St. German's Cathedral, and Ground-plan of the same.

These are accompanied with short letterpress descriptions, which are copied from Grose.

REV. JAMES JOHNSTONE, A.M.—1786.

Antiquitates Celto-Normannicæ, containing the Chronicle of Man and the Isles, abridged by Camden, and now first published, complete, from the original MS. in the British Musæum ; with an English translation, and notes. To which are added Extracts from the Annals of Ulster, and Sir J. Ware's Antiquities of Ireland ; British Topography by Ptolemy, Richard of Cirencester, the Geographer of Ravenna, and Andrew, Bishop of Cathness : together with accurate Catalogues of the Pictish and Scottish Kings. By the Rev. James Johnstone, A.M., Rector of Maghera Cross ; and Member of the Royal Societies of Edinburgh and Copenhagen. Printed by Aug. Frid. Stein, at Copenhagen. MDCCLXXXVI. *Quarto*, pp. 152.

Dedicated "To the Right Reverend John Hotham, D.D., Lord Bishop of Clogher."

Mr. Johnstone has given the portion omitted by Camden : this gives a list of the Bishops down to 1375. This chronicle has been printed by the Manx Society, in their 4th volume, 1860, from the copy in the British Museum in the Cottonian collection, under the careful editorship of Dr. Oliver, one of the Honorary Secretaries. "Monumenta," vol. i. pp. 125-215. Printed also in Professor Munch's edition, 1860.

Bishop Thomas Tanner.—1787.

Notitia Monastica ; or an Account of all the Abbies, Priories, and Houses of Friers, formerly in England and Wales. And also of all the Colleges and Hospitals founded before A.D. 1540, with many additions, by James Nasmith, M.A. Cambridge : 1787. *Folio.*

Article, "Bishop of Man." The best edition. The greater part was destroyed by the fire at Mr. Nichol's printing-office, 8th March 1808. The first edition, *folio.* London : 1744.

1788.

The Duke of Athol's Claim, under a Parliamentary entail, of the Isle of Man. *Quarto.*

Some few copies were printed and circulated by order of the Duke of Atholl.

Robert Beatson.—1788.

A Political Index to the Histories of Great Britain and Ireland, or a Complete Register of the Hereditary Honours, Public Offices, and Persons in Office, from the earliest periods to the present time. By Robert Beatson, Esq. The second edition, corrected and much enlarged. In two volumes.

London : printed by G. G. and J. Robinson, Pater Noster Row. 1788. *Octavo.*

Vol. i. pp. 181-183. The Bishops of the Isle of Man, giving a list of 58, commencing A.D. 447 with Germanus, and ending in 1782 with Claudius Crigan.

Vol. ii. at pp. 47-49, entitled, " The See of the Isles," the list of Bishops begins with Amphibalus, A.D. 360, then Germanus, 447, and the 36th A.D. 1388, " John 3rd. The Isle of Man was now separated from this See, which contained all Buteshire, and most of the Western Islands."

A third edition was published in three volumes. *Octavo.* London : 1806.

WM. CAMDEN.—1789.

Britannia ; A new translation by Richard Gough, Esq., in 3 vols. folio, from the Edition published by the Author in MDCVII.

This was reprinted, in 4 vols. folio, in 1806 ; a highly valuable work. The Chronicle of the Kings of Man, etc., begins A.D. 1065 and ends A.D. 1266, but has been continued in a later hand to 1316. Vol. iii. p. 705.

Mr. Gough, in his edition of Camden, prefers this copy of the Chronicles of the Kings of Man to that published in 1787 by Mr. Johnstone, from a fine old MS. in vellum in the Cottonian Library, marked Julius A., VII. 3, because in the former the dates are all right in the original, whereas in the latter they are made so by the Editor in his margin. Mr. Camden's MS. begins with the death of the Confessor, rightly putting it A.D. 1065. Mr. Johnstone's begins 47 years sooner, or, as he has corrected it in his margin, 51 years. Mr. Camden's begins at A.D. 1065, and ends A.D. 1266 ; but has been continued in a later hand to 1316. Mr. Johnstone's copy begins at A.D. 1000 or 1015, and ends 1376, and contains some additional matter foreign to the History of the Island. *Vide* Feltham's "Tour," 1798, p. 71.

Peter Fannin.—1789.

A correct Plan of the Isle of Man, by Peter Fannin, Master
   in His Majesty's Royal Navy.

Published January 1, 1789, by the Author, and by H. Ashley, Engraver, King Street, Cheapside, London.

Inscribed to "The most noble Prince John, Duke and Marquis of Atholl," etc.

A large sheet, 20 inches by 28 inches. Was generally esteemed for its nautical correctness. On it is a Plan of Douglas Harbour; and a View of the south side of Douglas Harbour, from his Grace the Duke of Atholl's house.

John Gough.—1789.

A History of the People called Quakers. From their Rise to
   the present time, compiled from Authentic Records and
   from Writings of that People. By John Gough. Dublin :
   printed for Robert Jackson, Meath Street. MDCCLXXXIX.
   Octavo.   4 vols.

The 4th vol. was published in 1790. John Gough was a Bookseller and Quaker.

Vol. ii. chap. xxi. Isle of Man. Pp. 274 to 292. On the persecutions of this sect in the Isle of Man in 1662 to 1666, Wm. Callow and Evan Christian suffered severe imprisonment in Peel Castle, "the former for refusing to pay 16d. and the latter 2d., demanded by a priest for bread and wine for the sacrament."

Vol. i. pp. 298 to 301. In 1656 to 1659 similar acts are recorded. James Chaloner, the Governor, was heard to say, "he would quickly rid the Island of Quakers." P. 300.

John Stowell.—1790.

A Sallad for the Young Ladies and Gentlemen of Douglas. Raised by Tom the Gardener. (Price four pence a bunch.) Liverpool : printed in the year 1790. *Quarto.* Pp. 20.

A Satire : Some copies have the following title :—" Sallad for the young Ladies and Gentlemen of Douglas, in the Isle of Mann. Raised by Tom the Gardener. Price sixpence a bunch. By John Sharp junior. Printed for the Author. 1790."

John Stowell.—[No date.]—1790.

A Switch for Tom the Gardener ; or, the Sallad dressed, and the Lamb roasted. Price three pence, British. No place or printer. *Small Quarto.* Pp. 8.

Inscribed " To the young Ladies of Douglas, the following pages are respectfully inscribed by their most humble, most obedient, and devoted servant, Candidus."

John Stowell.—1790.

The Retrospect ; or, a Review of the Memorable Events of Mona in the year 1790. By Philanthus.

> " Eye Nature's walks, shoot folly as it flies,
> And catch the manners living as they rise."—*Pope.*

Price one shilling.

No name, place, or printer. 8vo, pp. 55. A Poetical Satire : At page 19 is a woodcut of the House of Keys, and a representation of the twenty-four addressed by " Squire Saugrogh " (Major T——), in the act of killing a louse, which he had just taken from his head, and on a label from his mouth is inscribed—

> —— " Thus ev'ry tyrant should be serv'd,
> Who dares to trample on a Manxman's head."

Mr. John Stowell was a native of Peel, and master of the School there; also a Notary Public, to which he was appointed 22d January 1799. He died 21st July 1799.

CHARLES SMALL.—1790.

To the Anonymous Author of a Publication distributed amongst the people of Douglas, and the Inhabitants of the Isle of Man at large, on Saturday, the 12th current; and who signed himself " A Manxman and Friend to his country."

Dated " Douglas, June 25th, 1790." Signed Charles Small. No place or printer. *Quarto*, pp. 16. In favour of the Duke of Atholl. It was also translated into Manx.

CHARLES SMALL.—1790.

Ansoor gys y Screenyn currit magh mastey. Sleih Ghoolish, as Cummaltee Vannin, fón ennym, Mannanagh, as Carrey da ey Heer.

Doolish: prentit Liorish Christopher Briscoe. *Sm. quarto*, pp. 20, dated at end 1790, and signed Charles Small. This translation was made by the Rev. John Cannel, father of the late chaplain of St. Matthews, Douglas.

1790.

Account of the Petition of the Duke of Athol on the Clandestine Trade to the Isle of Man. 1790. *Octavo*.

Right Hon. WILLIAM PITT.—1790.

Mr. Pitt's Speech, on Tuesday, the 4th of May, 1790. On the additional Compensation to the Duke of Atholl.

Mr. P. moved " That the further consideration of this Bill be deferred to this day three months." Christopher Briscoe, Douglas. A broadside.

RICHARD TOWNLEY.—1791.

A Journal kept in the Isle of Man, giving an Account of the
Wind, Weather, Daily Occurrences for upwards of eleven
months : with observations on the soil, clime, and natural
productions of that Island ; also, Antiquities of various
kinds, now extant there : a trait of the Manners and
Customs, both general and peculiar, of the inhabitants :
an Account of their Harbours, great usefulness of Douglas
Harbour ; neglect, and want of repairs. Description of
their noble herring fishery, etc. Together with a large
Appendix : containing an Account of the ancient forms
of Government, and mild administration of justice, under
the noble House of Stanley ; with Transcripts and Extracts from the Ancient Statute Books of the Isle : together with explanatory notes and observations. In two
volumes. By Richard Townley, Esq. Whitehaven :
printed by J. Ware and Son. Sold by T. Cadell, W.
Richardson, and R. Baldwin, London ; D. Prince, Oxford ;
J. and J. Merrill, Cambridge ; and the Booksellers in
Manchester, Liverpool, Leeds, Kendal, Lancaster, etc. etc.
etc. 1791. Two vols. *Octavo.*

Vol. i. pp. 320 ; vol. ii. pp. 322, dedicated " To the Right
Hon. Edward, Earl of Derby," dated " Douglas (Isle of Man),
April 18, 1790." The preface, dated " Isle of Man, April 19,
1790," and " An Apology to the candid Reader," that his
journal appears on so coarse a paper, dated Ambleside, January 1st, 1791. The journal commences on the 30th April
1789, and ends 21st April 1790. Appendix, containing the
Ancient History, etc.,—a gossiping and amusing work, in
which many trifles are recorded and extracts from curious
unpublished MSS. It was severely satirised by John Stowell
of Peel, in his " Literary Quixote." The author was Colonel

Richard Townley, of Belfield Hall, near Rochdale, Lancashire. He was the patron of John Collier, *alias* " Tim Bobbin," the author of " Lancashire Dialect." Colonel Townley died in 1802.

JOHN STOWELL.—1791.

The Literary Quixote ; or, the Beauties of Townley versified. Printed at the Printing Office, in Douglas ; and sold by the Booksellers in Liverpool, Manchester, Whitehaven, Oxford, Cambridge, etc. etc. No date. *Small Quarto,* pp. 16.

A Portrait of Richard Townley, Esq., faces the title, in the act of writing his journal, and underneath,

> " This day might pass for yesterday's own brother :
> Two peas were never seen more like each other."

An amusing Satire on " Townley's Journal," without the author's name, but written by John Stowell, the author of " The Retrospect," etc. Only one number appeared.

Mr. Stowell published several Elegies and occasional Poems, chiefly anonymously, now become exceedingly rare. Also " An Epistle to the Earl of Lonsdale," signed Petrus Pendarus Secundus, Gent. Douglas. Isle of Man. 1794. Pp. 33.

THOMAS STOWELL.—1792.

The Statutes and Ordinances of the Isle of Man, now in force, alphabetically arranged. By T. Stowell, Advocate. Most humbly inscribed to the Honourable Alexander Shaw, Esq., Lieutenant-Governor and Chancellor of the Isle of Man. Douglas : printed by C. Briscoe. 1792. *Octavo,* pp. 166 ; preface 2 pp., appendix 4 pp., and 1 p. of errata.

" It may be deemed a matter of no small surprise that the Statute Laws, or Acts of Tynwald of the Isle of Man (except a few lately passed) have never heretofore been printed and published."—*Preface.* Some Acts of Tynwald were printed by Joseph Briscoe in 1783.

1792.

Manks Mercury and Briscoe's Douglas Advertiser. The first Manx Newspaper, No. 1, published 27th Nov., 1792. Price Two Pence, British. Published by C. Briscoe. Continued fifteen years.

John Stowell.—1792.

On the death of the much-esteemed Mrs. Callow, late wife of Mr. William Callow, of Douglas, merchant. Dated "Douglas, July 26, 1792." No printer. A Broadside.

On the death of Miss M. Bacon, February 11th, 1792. No place or printer. A Broadside.

1792.

Poems, chiefly by Gentlemen of Devonshire and Cornwall. In two volumes. Bath : printed by R. Cruttwell, etc. MDCCXCII. *Octavo.*

In vol. ii. pp. 6 to 11, is an "Ode on the Isle of Mann, to the Memory of Bishop Wilson, written at the request of the late Dr. Wilson, of Bath. 1781." And pp. 21, 22, "Mona, an Ode," both by the Rev. R. Polwhele.

John Seacome.—1793.

The History of the House of Stanley, from the Conquest to the Death of the Right Honourable Edward, late Earl of Derby, in 1776, containing a Genealogical and Historical Account of that illustrious House ; to which is added a Description of the Isle of Man. Preston : printed by E. Sergent, in the Market Place. MDCCXCIII. *Octavo,* pp. 616.

The Title to the latter portion is " A complete History of the Isle of Man, containing the Situation and Geographical

Description thereof; also the Ecclesiastical and Civil Histories, with the whole order of Government, from the earliest accounts: the Lord's Prerogative and Regalities; the several Officers necessarily employed under him: Nature of the Soil: Names of the Chief Towns and Harbours: Number of Parishes: Value of the Livings; with the Produce of the Country and Neighbouring Sea, and a Description of their usual Trade. To which is added an account of its purchase from the Duke of Atholl by Government, under the reign of his present Majesty King George the Third. Preston: printed by E. Sergent, in the Market Place. MDCCXCIII. Pp. 485-616. A portrait of James, Earl of Derby.

Rev. James Douglas.—1793.

Nenia Britannica; or a Sepulchral History of Great Britain from the earliest period to its general conversion to Christianity, including a complete series of the British, Roman, and Saxon Sepulchral Rites and Ceremonies, with the contents of several hundred Burial places opened under a careful inspection of the author. By the Rev. James Douglas, F.A.S. London: 1793. *Folio.*

Pp. 172-5, Description of the Mound, with Plate of Tynwald Hill, and a Plan of the Chapel and Ground at St. John's, Isle of Man. Supplied by Captain Grose. It was published in numbers. 1786-93.

John Stowell.—1793.

An Elegiac Invocation of the Muses, occasioned by the Death of the amiable Miss Nessy Heywood. October 8, 1793. A Broadside. Signed JUVENIS.

Basil Quayle.—1794.

General View of the Agriculture of the Isle of Man, with observations on the means of its Improvement. By Mr.

Basil Quayle, Farmer, at the Creggans, near Castletown, in the Isle of Man. Drawn up for the consideration of the Board of Agriculture and Internal Improvements. London : printed by C. Macrae. MDCCXCIV. *Quarto*, pp. 40.

With a Map of the Isle, not printed for sale, but circulated for the purpose of procuring farther information respecting the Husbandry of this District, and any observations to be written on the margin and returned to the Board of Agriculture, London. The letterpress is in an octavo size for this purpose ; the work is necessarily rare to meet with. Computes the total population at about 20,000.

DAVID ROBERTSON.—1794.

A Tour through the Isle of Man : To which is subjoined A Review of the Manx History. By David Robertson, Esq. The second edition. London : printed for the Author by E. Hodson, Bell Yard, Temple Bar, and sold by Mr. Payne, Mews Gate ; Mr. Egerton, Whitehall ; Whites, Fleet Street ; and Deighton, Holborn. 1794. *Royal Octavo*, pp. 233,

Dedicated to J. C. Curwen, Esq., M.P. The Preface, 3 pp., is dated " London, Oct. 14th, 1793." Contents, 4 pp. Map of the Island, and 8 Plates. A few copies are printed on large paper. The Tour was made during the summer of 1791. The first edition appeared the same year as the second, but had a violent democratical passage at the end of two pages, for which the author was prosecuted. It was suppressed in this edition.

REV. THOMAS CHRISTIAN.—1796.

Paradise Lost. A Poem. By John Milton. Translated into the Manks Language, by the Rev. Thomas Christian of Ballakilley, Kirk Marown. Douglas : printed by and for C. Briscoe. 12*mo*, pp. 120.

Only selections from Paradise Lost. Mr. Christian was Vicar of Marown. This has been reprinted in the Manx Society's series, vol. xx., Manx Miscellanies, vol. i.

JOHN STOWELL.—1796.

Most humbly addressed to Her Grace the Duchess of Athol. Peel, 27th April 1796. A Broadside.

CHRISTOPHER BRISCOE.—1797.

The Statute Laws of the Isle of Mann. Printed in the year MDCCXCVII. *Octavo*, in 4s. pp. 140.

Dated " Douglas, August 24th, 1797," and signed C. Briscoe. *Vide* Lex Scripta. Preface, pp. xiii. Last Act, 8th July 1796, " An Act for the better regulation of the Court of Common Law."

REV. C. CRUTTWELL (Bp. Wilson).—1797.

The Life of the Right Reverend Thomas Wilson, D.D., Lord Bishop of Sodor and Man. Compiled by the Rev. C. Cruttwell. To which is added, his History of the Isle of Man. The fourth edition. Bath : printed by and for R. Cruttwell ; and sold by C. Dilly, Poultry, London. MDCCXCVII. *Octavo*, 4 volumes.

The Bishop's History of the Isle of Man is in vol. i. pp. 297 to 342. In an Appendix is a continuation from Mr. Rolt's History, pp. 343 to 378.

Vols. ii., iii., iv., containing the works, are dated 1796.

The History of the Isle is reprinted in the Manx Society's series, vol. xviii., 1871, " Old Historians," pp. 90-125.

MRS. LEE.—1797.

Clara Lennox ; or the Distressed Widow. A novel, founded
on facts. Interspersed with an Historical description of
the Isle of Man. By Mrs. Lee. Two vols. 12*mo.* Parsons, 1797.

Dedicated to the Duchess of York.

FRANCIS HARGRAVE.—1797.

Juridical Arguments and Collections. 2 vols. *Quarto.*

The sixth article relates to the Duke of Atholl's claim
under a Parliamentary Entail of the Isle of Man.—See 1788,
p. 54.

LORD EDWARD COKE.—1797.

The fourth part of the Institutes of the Laws of England.
Concerning the Jurisdiction of Courts. Authore Edwardo
Coke, Milite, J. C. London : printed for E. and R. Brooke,
Bell Yard, near Temple Bar, MDCCXCVII. *Octavo*, pp. 282-
284, cap. lxix. Of the Isle of Man, *Insula Euboniæ Modo
Manna*, and of the Law and Jurisdiction of the same.

Printed in Gells' "Abstract of the Laws," etc., vol. i. p.
153. Manx Society, vol. xii. 1867.

JOHN FELTHAM.—1798.

A Tour through the Island of Mann in 1797 and 1798 ; comprising Sketches of its Ancient and Modern History, Constitution, Laws, Commerce, Agriculture, Fishery, etc.
Including whatever is remarkable in each parish, its
population, inscriptions, registers, etc. By John Feltham.
Embellished with a Map of the Island and other Plates.
Bath : printed by R. Cruttwell, and sold by C. Dilly,

Poultry, London ; Jones, Liverpool ; Brown, Bristol ; Ware, Whitehaven ; Woolmer, Exeter, etc. 1798. (Price seven shillings.) *Octavo*, pp. 294.

Dedicated to " The Duke of Athol."

The author took considerable pains in procuring information in the various parishes, and left some further Manuscripts relating thereto, which the Manx Society have published in " Memorials of God's Acre." Manx Society series, vol. xiv. 1868.

The " Tour " is also reprinted by the Manx Society, vol. vi. 1861.

MARGARET CRELLIN.—1798.

The Herring Fishery. A Poem. Extracted from Mr. Feltham's " Tour through the Isle of Man." 1798. Bath : printed by R. Cruttwell. *Octavo*, pp. 8.

The authoress' father was vicar of Kirk Michael, the Rev. John Crellin, and sister to Deemster Crellin.

Gentleman's Magazine.—1798.

Sketch of the Runic Monument at Kirk Michael.—*Gentleman's Magazine.* 1798. Part 2, vol. lxviii. p. 749.

It is said to have been removed from a field near Bishop's Court.

DAVID ROBERTSON.—1798.

The British Tourist ; or, Traveller's Pocket Companion, through England, Wales, Scotland, and Ireland. By William Mavor, LL.D. London : 1798. *Small Octavo.*

In vol. v. is " Tour through the Isle of Man. By David Robertson, Esq. Performed in 1791," pp. 87-136. This is condensed from the edition of 1794. An edition also in 1807.

1799.

Methodist Hymn Book. Translated into Manx. Douglas : printed by Thomas Whittam, 1799.

There were two Manx Hymn Books prior to this edition, but were badly printed, and abounded in errors. This edition is beautifully translated.

REV. WEEDEN BUTLER.—1799.

Memoirs of Mark Hildesley, D.D., Lord Bishop of Sodor and Mann, and Master of Sherburn Hospital; under whose auspices the Holy Scriptures were translated into the Manx language. By the Rev. Weeden Butler, morning preacher of Charlotte Street Chapel. London : printed by J. Nichols; and sold by Messrs. Robson, Dilly, Rivingtons, Payne, Cadell and Davies, Egerton and White. 1799. *Octavo*, pp. 691.

Advertisement and Contents, pp. 12. Arms of the See and Bishop II. on the Title. A valuable Memoir, giving also a full account of the Translating and Printing the Holy Scriptures into the Manx language.

T. GARNETT, M.D.—1800.

Observations on a Tour through the Highlands and part of the Western Isles of Scotland, etc. By T. Garnett, M.D. London : 1800. Two vols, *Quarto*, with Fifty-two Aquatint Plates, from drawings by W. H. Watts.

Vol. i. pp. 258-9. Regarding the See of Man.

JOHN SEACOME.—1801.

The History of the House of Stanley, from the Conquest, to the Death of the Right Hon. Edward, late Earl of Derby, containing a Genealogical and Historical Account of that illustrious House. To which is added, a Description of the Isle of Man ; and a brief account of the Travels of the celebrated Sir Wm. Stanley. Liverpool : printed by J. Nuttall, No. 38 Denison Street. No date. *Octavo*.

The Description of the Isle of Man has the same title as the edition of 1793, with " Liverpool : printed by J. Nuttall, Denison Street. 1801." Pp. 485-614.

1801.

Isle of Man. In the Privy Council. Case of the Most Noble John, Duke of Atholl. To be heard, with Petition for his Grace, before the Right Honourable the Lords Committee of His Majesty's Most Honourable Privy Council, at the Cockpit, Whitehall, on Saturday the 27th day of June 1801. Fraser, Lincoln's Inn. *Folio*, pp. 18.

Isle of Man. In the Privy Council. Appendix to Case for the Duke of Atholl. Fraser, Lincoln's Inn. Printed by A. Strahan, Law Printer to His Majesty, Printers' Street, London. *Folio*, pp. 13.

This case gives the early History of the Island, and states " That the Isle of Man was an ancient kingdom of itself, and no part of the Kingdom of England." P. 2.

REV. C. CRUTTWELL.—1801.

A Tour through the whole Island of Great Britain ; divided into Journeys. Interspersed with useful observations ; particularly calculated for the use of those who are desirous of travelling over England and Scotland. By the Rev. C. Cruttwell, author of the "Universal Gazetteer." In 6 volumes. London : printed for G. and J. Robinson, Paternoster Row, etc. 1801. *Octavo*, maps, vol. v.

Isle of Man, pp. 290-309.

1801.

The Manx Advertiser. Commenced August 8th. Published by G. Jefferson. Douglas. 1801. Continued 44 years.

1802.

The Manks Almanack, for the year of our Lord 1802, being sixth after Leap Year, and the 42d year of the reign of King George III. till 25th October, containing the Sun's rising and setting, Moon's age and changes, with her rising, setting, and southing; Weather; Time of High Water; Custom-house Holidays, List of Fairs, Common Law Court Days, etc. etc. Douglas: printed by and for T. Whittam. Price sixpence, British. 32*mo.* Not paged. 31 pp.

In the List of the Keys is the date of their Elections and place of Residence. The Hon. John Taubman, of the Nunnery, 17th February, 1785 ; elected Speaker, 28th November, 1799. The oldest members : J. Stevenson, Larghey Dhoo, 12th July, 1774 ; and P. Moore, Pole Roish, same date.

BRITTON AND BRAYLEY.—1802.

The Beauties of England and Wales ; or, Delineations, Topographical, Historical, and Descriptive. London : published by Vernor and Hood, Poultry. 1802. *Octavo.* Vol. iii.

Isle of Man. Pp. 248-290. Compiled by J. Britton and E. W. Brayley. A View of Douglas, from a drawing, by W. H. Watts.

REV. SAMUEL BURDY.—1802.

Ardglass, or the Ruined Castles ; also the Transformation, with some other Poems. By the Rev. Samuel Burdy, Author of Skelton's Life, Vindication, etc. Dublin :

printed for the Author, by Graisberry and Campbell, 10 Back Lane. 1802. *Octavo.* Pp. 128.

" Ardglass " consists of 37 pp., 1-37, and the notes from pp. 39 to 61. Both chiefly relate to the Isle of Man, to which the author appears to have made a short visit in July 1794, and describes places and persons pretty freely. He says :—

> " Herring's the food of Mona's greedy sons,
> Who eat them up as fast as butter'd buns."

W. H. WATTS.—1802.

Sketch of the State of Manners and present Condition of the Isle of Man. *Monthly Magazine*, September. With a Notice of the late Rev. Joseph Stowell of Peel.

Mr. Watts was an artist and portrait painter, who lived in the Island some years. His name is to the View of Douglas, in the third volume of " The Beauties of England and Wales." See also " Memoir of the Rev. Joseph Stowell," 1821, and in " Garnett's Tour," 1800.

REV. JOHN KELLY.—1804.

A Practical Grammar of the Antient Gaelic ; or Language of the Isle of Mann, usually called Manks.

> —— Si quid novisti rectius istis
> Candidus imperti ; si non, his utere mecum.

By the Rev. John Kelly, LL.D., Vicar of Ardleigh and Rector of Copford, in the county of Essex. London : printed by John Nichols and Son, Red Lion Passage, Fleet Street, and sold by R. Bickerstaff, the Corner of Essex Street, Strand. 1804. *Quarto.* Pp. 75.

Dedicated to the Most Noble George, Marquis of Huntly, etc.

Dated " Ardleigh, 22nd Nov. 1803." This edition is rare. The Society for Promoting Christian Knowledge gave to

Mr. Kelly 10 guineas for composing the Manx Grammar and
Vocabulary, but declined to print it.

Reprinted by the Manx Society in their second volume,
1859. Edited by the Rev. Wm. Gill, Vicar of Malew.

1804.

Report from the Committee on the Isle of Man Port Petition.
Ordered to be printed 5th May 1804. *Folio.* Pp. 7.
Evidence respecting Ramsey Harbour.

No date.—[1804].

The Twenty-four Keys of the Isle of Man ; their mode of
Election : character given of them by the Inhabitants :
with the opinion of the Commissioners of Inquiry : and a
Description of the present Twenty-four Keys. Printed
by B. M'Millan, Bow Street, Covent Garden. No date.
Folio. Pp. 3.

1804.

Return to an Order of Account of Application of Surplus
Revenues of the Isle of Man. 1798. *Folio.*

1805.

Observations on the Atholl Revenue in the Isle of Man.
Octavo.

1805.

Cobbett's Parliamentary Debates. *Octavo*, vol. v.
Duke of Atholl's Claim for Compensation.

1805.

Case on behalf of the Keys of Man. Dated 25th March.

1805.

Report of the Lords of the Committee of his Majesty's Most

Honourable Privy Council; dated the 21st July 1804; upon the Petition of the Duke of Atholl to his Majesty. Ordered to be printed 29th March 1805. *Folio*, pp. 5.

The Duke and Duchess of Atholl offered by letter, 27th February 1765, to accept £70,000 for their Rights in the Isle of Man, and stated he had only recently succeeded to the possession of the Island. John Duke of Atholl was then an infant. See the remark on the "Mischief Act," 1765.

1805.

Observations on the Case now depending in Parliament, respecting the Isle of Man, in reference to the Statement and Appendix circulated in support of the Duke of Atholl's Petition. London : printed by B. M'Millan, Bow Street, Covent Garden, printer to his Royal Highness the Prince of Wales. 1805. *Quarto*, pp. 16.

A Statement of the Duke's case as entitling him to further Compensation.

1805.

To the Gentlemen of the Keys, the Landholders, the Merchants, and Inhabitants of the Isle of Man. (Signed) Atholl. Portman Square, April 10th, 1805. London : printed by B. M'Millan, Bow Street, Covent Garden. A Broadside.

The Address of the Duke of Atholl on his appointment as Governor of the Isle of Man.

1805.

Address of his Grace the Duke of Atholl to the Gentlemen of the Keys the Landholders, the Merchants, and Inhabitants in general of the Isle of Man. London : printed by B.

M'Millan, Bow Street, Covent Garden, Printer to his
Royal Highness the Prince of Wales. 1805. *Quarto*,
pp. 10.

Dated "Portman Square, April 10th, 1805," and signed
"Atholl." This passed through two editions.

This Address gives an account of the sale of the Revenues
of Customs to the Crown, and the Duke's Petition for further
Compensation, and says, p. 8, "Should the Report be that
further Compensation ought to be given or granted, the spirit
of the clauses which I shall have to offer will be for a definite
proportion of the Revenue, leaving a considerable surplus
after payment of the Civil and Revenue establishment and
Herring bounties, and for enabling his Majesty *to apply either
the whole or a part of the remaining surplus*, in such a manner,
and *to such public purposes of the Island*, as may be deemed
needful or expedient."

No date.—[1805.]

Memorial of the Landholders, Merchants, and Inhabitants of
the Isle of Man, to the Honourable the Speaker and Members of the House of Keys of the Island of Man. G.
Jefferson, Printer. A Broadside.

Praying that their "agents be instructed not to oppose
any *fair compensation* his Grace may seek." This accompanied the Duke's Address of 10th April.

1805.

Papers presented to the House of Commons respecting the
Isle of Man. Ordered to be printed 10th April 1805.
Folio, pp. 113.

Contains Copies of Proceedings before the Privy Council,
on a Petition of his Grace, John Duke of Atholl, for a further

Compensation for the Sale of the Feudal Rights of the Isle of Man in 1765.

Sixteen Papers.—Important documents connected with the Stanley and Atholl families in the Isle of Man.

1805.

Further Observations on the Measure of Creating, by Authority of Parliament, an Hereditary Rent Charge, payable out of the Revenue of the Isle of Man, in favour of the Duke of Atholl. On behalf of the House of Keys of the Isle of Man. Printed by R. Willis, 89 Chancery Lane. *Octavo*, pp. 16.

Signed by " John Christian, Thomas Quayle, Agents for the House of Keys of the Isle of Man. 10th May 1805."

A reply to the Duke of Atholl's Address of 10th April, and Statement of his Case.

1805.

Isle of Man.—Analysis of the Petition of the 24 Keys of the 16th April 1805. London : printed by B. M'Millan, Bow Street, Covent Garden, Printer to His Royal Highness the Prince of Wales. 1805. *Quarto*, pp. 21. Dated May.

1805.

Isle of Man.—Letter to their Colleagues, from Messrs. Bridson and Stowell, members of the Committee appointed by the Merchants and other respectable Inhabitants of the Isle of Man, to attend to their Interests before Parliament. London : printed by B. M'Millan, etc. 1805. *Octavo*, pp. 20.

Dated " London, 21st May 1805." Addressed to Messrs. Edward Moore, Edward Forbes, and Wm. Oates, Douglas. This is against the proceedings of the Keys. Signed, Paul Bridson, Will. Stowell.

1805.

Report from the Committee on the Petition of the Duke of Atholl; and other Matters relating to the Isle of Man. Ordered to be printed 23d May 1805. *Folio*, pp. 9.

Recommended that Parliament should grant a further Compensation to the Duke of Atholl and the other Heirs general of the 7th Earl of Derby, and that such Compensation should be charged on the Revenue of the Island.

1805.

Minutes of the Evidence relating to the House of Keys; taken before the Committee to whom the Petition of the Duke of Atholl is referred. Ordered to be printed 27th May 1805. *Folio*, pp. 60.

Contains Extracts from the printed report of the Commissioners of Inquiry for the Isle of Man, 1792, and from the Appendix to the said report.

1805.

Isle of Man.—Amount of Revenues and Payments of the Isle of Man, received and paid by George Watts, Esq., Receiver-General : betweeen the years 1786 and 1799, etc. Ordered to be printed 7th June 1805. *Folio*, pp. 2.

1805.

Amount of the Revenues and Payments of the Isle of Man, received and paid by William Scott, Esq., Receiver-General, between the years 1799 and 1804, etc. Ordered to be printed 7th June 1805. *Folio*, pp. 2.

J. C. CURWEN, M.P.—1805.

Substance of the Speech of J. C. Curwen, Esq., in the House

of Commons, on the 7th June 1805, on the consideration of the Report of the Committee to whom was referred the Petition of John, Duke of Atholl, praying farther Compensation, chargeable on the Revenue of the Isle of Man, for the Interests in that Island ceded by his Family to the Crown in 1765. To which is prefixed a short statement of the proceedings in the House of Commons and the Petition of the Inhabitants and Proprietors of Estates in the Island. London: printed for J. Bell, 148 Oxford Street, by R. Wilks, Chancery Lane. 1805. *Octavo*, pp. 73.

1805.

Papers presented to the House of Lords respecting the Isle of Man. Ordered to be printed 6th July 1805.

Same to the House of Commons.

1805.

Statement of the Case of the Duke of Atholl, claiming a Compensation out of the Surplus Revenues of the Isle of Man. London: printed by R. M'Millan, Bow Street, Covent Garden, Printer to His Royal Highness the Prince of Wales. 1805. *Quarto*, pp. 21 ; Appendix, pp. 33.

No date.—[1805.]

Isle of Man.—Views of the Revenues of Duties and Customs on Imports, as they stood in 1765, showing the Inadequacy of the Compensation. Printed by B. M'Millan, Bow Street, Covent Garden. A Broadside.

There are six Views of the Revenue. Put forth on account of the Duke of Atholl.

1805.

Bishop of Man *v.* Com. Derby ; and Com. Derby *v.* Duke of

Atholl. In Case, 1751, July. House of Commons Paper, No. 79, Session 1805, p. 42. Also in Vesey's Reports, vol. ii. p. 337.

On the Alienation of the Isle.—The Lord Chancellor's Judgment. Printed in Gell's "Abstract," vol. i. pp. 67-74. Manx Society series, vol. xii. 1867.

See on the same Case, 1748.

No date.—[1805.]

Isle of Man.—Statement of the Amount of Customs on Imports into the Isle of Man, for different periods; compared with the estimated Amount of Duties which would have been payable on the same commodities to the Lord Proprietor, according to the Ancient Book of Rates; and calculation of the total produce of the Revenue, and total amount of the Expenditure, from 6th July 1765 to 5th January 1805. R. Wilks, Printer, 89 Chancery Lane. *Folio*, pp. 2.

This was put forth on account of the Keys. Average of Duties on Imported Goods for seven years, from January 1798 to January 1805, £8971 : 19s : 6½.

John Woodhouse.—1805.

Copy of a Letter from John Woodhouse, in answer to one published in the "Manks Advertiser," by Paul Bridson and William Stowell, Esqs. Dated 31st August 1805. W. Jones, Printer, 56 Castle Street, Liverpool. *Octavo*, pp. 8.

Dated "Liverpool, September 6th, 1805."

1805.

Isle of Man.—Memorandum. No. 1. *Quarto*, pp. 2. Printed by B. M'Millan, Bow Street, Covent Garden.

It is stated, "In the year 1711, the British Commissioners of Customs sent some Revenue Officers to the Isle of Man, and the Government of the Island sent Agents to England, in order to concert arrangements that would be mutually advantageous and fair."

This accounts for George Waldron's appointment. *Vide* Insular Act of 1711. Suspended, 25th September 1713.

1805.

Isle of Man.—Memorandum. No. 2. *Quarto*, pp. 2. Printed by B. M'Millan, Bow Street, Covent Garden.

Relates, as Memorandum No. 1, to the intended purchase of the Customs Revenue, etc., of the Isle of Man.

1805.

The Report of the Commissioners of Inquiry for the Isle of Man. 1792. Ordered to be printed 8th July 1805. *Folio.* The Report, pp. 3 to 137. List of Papers, pp. 139 to 150. Appendix, pp. 151-802, A to 5 M.

There are seven Maps, Nos. 1 to 7. Some few were struck off before the Nos. were attached, as Map of Cornah Harbour.

This is one of the most important Documents connected with the History of the Isle of Man, giving an account of the Constitution, Government, Customs, and Statistics of the country. Only a very few copies were printed by order of the British Government, to ascertain the Regal and Manorial Rights of the Duke of Atholl, etc. In the Appendix will be found the various Allegations; Examinations of numerous persons connected with the Government; Resolutions of the House of Keys and other bodies; Petitions and Appeals of the Duke of Atholl; Statutes; Statements of Revenue; on the Constitution and Suggestions for the benefit of the Island, containing altogether a mass of most useful and important information for the Historian.

The Commissioners, appointed 8th September 1791, were, John Spranger, Master in Chancery ; W. Grant, an English Lawyer and Member of Parliament ; William Osgoode, an English Lawyer and Chief-Justice of Quebeck ; William Roe, Commissioner of the Customs at London ; and David Reid, Commissioner of the Customs at Edinburgh, Esquires—all of whom signed the Report, 21st April 1792. Mr. Reid also made a separate Report, with his own opinion upon each head of the Inquiry, dated 16th March 1792. These observations are printed from pages 95 to 133.

The Appendix, containing the information upon which the Commissioners founded their Report, embraces every subject connected with the Island. A list of the papers contained in it is here given, as the work is seldom met with, and bears a high price.

APPENDIX A.—PART I.

ALLEGATIONS.

1. Resolution of the House of Keys, dated 23d September 1791.
2. A Paper of the House of Keys, dated 26th September 1791.
3. Book of Rates, 1692.
4. The Examination of John Quayle, Esq., Clerk of the Rolls, taken at Douglas September 26th and 27th, 1791.
5. The Examination of Mr. Coultry Connell, taken at Douglas September 26th, 1791.
6. The Examination of Mr. William Crebbin, Merchant, taken at Douglas the 26th and 27th September 1791.
7. The Examination of Robert Heywood, Esq., one of the Keys, taken at Douglas the 26th September 1791.
8. The Examination of Thomas Moore, Esq., Deemster of the Isle of Man, taken at Douglas the 26th September 1791.
9. A Letter from Sir Wadsworth Busk, Attorney-General of the Isle of Man, dated Newtown, 29th October 1791, contain-

ing information relating to the Revenue of the Customs in the Isle of Man prior to 1765.

10. The Examination of Thomas Moore, Esq., Deemster of the Isle of Man, taken at Douglas the 27th September 1791.

11. The Examination of Mr. Hugh Cosnahan, taken at Douglas September 27th, 1791.

12. Copy of the Order of the Governor and Council, respecting the application of the Speaker of the House of Keys, 28th January 1765.

13. Copy of a Letter from the Keys to the Speaker, requesting him to apply to the Governor to convene the Keys, dated 8th March 1765.

14. Copy of a Letter from the Speaker of the House of Keys to the Governor, requesting him to convene the Keys, dated 12th March 1765.

15. Copy of a Letter from the Governor to the Speaker of the House of Keys, dated 14th March 1765.

16. Resolution of the Keys, appointing Commissioners, dated 21st March 1765.

17. Instructions to the Commissioners, dated 21st March 1765.

18. Address of the Keys to the Duke and Duchess of Atholl, dated 21st March 1765.

19. Copy of the Petition of the House of Keys to the Commons of Great Britain, in 1765.

20. The Duke of Atholl's reasons for giving in to the Commissioners the Petition of the House of Keys to Parliament in 1765.

21. Rights which the Duke of Atholl conceives were necessary to be vested in the Crown, for the purpose of preventing illicit proceedings.

22. Statutes of the Isle of Man, previous to the revestment.

23.   Do.   do.   since   do.

24. Act of Tynwald, 23d June 1610, for regulating the Herring Fishery.

25. Extract of an Act of Tynwald of 1610, relative to the Herring Fishery.

26. Act of Tynwald, 24th June 1613, for regulating the Castle Maze of Herrings.

27. The Examination of John Quayle, Esq., Clerk of the Rolls, taken at Douglas 28th September 1791.

28. Clear amount of Herring Custom paid to the Lord from 1740 to 1765.

29. The Examination of Senhouse Wilson, Esq., Deputy Receiver-General of the Isle of Man, taken at Douglas the 25th September 1791.

30. The Examination of Mr. Michael Cullen, Searcher at Douglas, taken the 28th September 1791.

31. The Examination of Mr. George Savage, Water Bailiff, taken at Douglas the 28th September 1791.

32. The Examination of John Quayle, Esq., taken at Douglas the 28th September 1791.

33. The Examination of Senhouse Wilson, Esq., Deputy Receiver-General of the Isle of Man, taken at Douglas the 28th September 1791.

34. Copy of Lease of Salmon Fishery.

35. Examination of John Quayle, Esq., taken at Douglas 28th September 1791.

36. Examination of Robert Farrant, Esq., High Bailiff of the town and district of Peel, taken at Douglas the 18th October 1791.

37. The Examination of Alexander Shaw, Esq., Lieutenant-Governor of the Isle of Man, taken at Douglas the 28th September 1791.

38. The Examination of Mr. George Savage, taken at Douglas the 28th September 1791.

39. The Examination of John Quayle, Esq., taken at Douglas the 28th September 1791.

40. The Examination of Mr. George Savage, taken at Douglas the 28th September 1791.

41. An Order of the Court of Exchequer, 7th September 1786.

42. Reasons why the Attorney-General declines entering into the question, Whether certain rights of the Crown are or are not necessary for the prevention of illicit traffic?

43. A Letter from Sir Wadsworth Busk, Attorney-General of the Isle of Man, dated Newtown, 22d November 1791.

44. A Letter from the Duke of Atholl, dated London, January 14th, 1791.

45. A Paper entitled Wrecks of the Sea.   Signed Atholl.
46. Rights meant to be retained, and which have by the operation
       of the Act of 1765 been rendered nugatory, or left in
       a mutilated or unprotected condition.   Signed Atholl.
47. An Account of Wrecks at Sea, anno 1740.
48.   Do.   do.   1744.
49.   Do.   do.   1747.
50.   Do.   do.   1753.
51.   Do.   do.   1754.
52.   Do.   do.   1760.
53.   Do.   do.   1761.
54. An Extract of the Wrecks clear for 1766.
55. Water Bailiff's Account of Wrecks, Flotsam, Jetsam, and
       Ligan, 1765 to 1785.
56. The Examination of John Quayle, Esq., taken at Douglas 28th
       September 1791.
57. The Examination of Senhouse Wilson, Esq., taken at Douglas
       the 28th September 1791.
58. Determination of the Court of Chancery on a Cause respect-
       ing Wrecks, 1783.
59. Petition of the Duke of Atholl on the above Determination,
       and dismission thereof, 12th March 1783.
60. The Duke of Atholl's Appeal, 9th April 1783.
61. Copy of the Act of Settlement, and other Acts relating thereto.
62. The Examination of John Quayle, Esq., taken at Douglas the
       29th September 1791.
63. The Examination of Thomas Moore, Esq., taken at Douglas
       the 7th October 1791.
64. The Examination of Mr. James Banks, taken at Douglas the
       29th September 1791.
65. The Examination of John Kaighin, taken at Douglas the 7th
       October 1791.
66. The Examination of Patrick Shimin, taken at Douglas the
       7th October 1791.
67. The Examination of Mr. William Quine, taken at Douglas the
       7th October 1791.
68. Clear Amount of Money received in lieu of Boon Services out
       of the Lord's Lands, and the disbursements thereout, anno
       1766.

69. A List of the Number of Quarterlands of Lord's Lands in the several and respective Parishes of the Isle of Man.

70. Copy of the Report of the Attorney and Solicitor General, dated 6th March 1780.

71. Report of the Crown Officers in the Isle of Man, dated 27th April 1780.

72. The Attorney and Solicitor General's Report on the Isle of Man Bill, dated 7th June 1780.

73. The Attorney and Solicitor General's Report on the Isle of Man Bill, dated 30th April 1781.

74. Note of Reference to written Evidence in respect of Game.

75. The Examination of Mr. James Banks, taken at Douglas the 5th October 1791.

76. The Examination of Thomas Moore, Esq., taken at Douglas the 5th October 1791.

77. Depositions of Witnesses, taken at an Exchequer Court holden the 4th February 1757, concerning the killing the Lord's Game.

78. The Appeal of Mr. James Banks on the determination of the above Court.

79. The Examination of Thomas Moore, Esq., taken at Douglas the 5th October 1791.

80. The Examination of Robert Heywood, Esq., one of the Keys, taken at Douglas the 5th October 1791.

81. A Paper from the Duke of Atholl, stating that since the revestment of the Isle of Man in the Crown, he has had no legal knowledge of any Acts of Tynwald that have passed.

82. Resolution of the House of Keys, dated 4th October 1791.

APPENDIX B.—PART II.

REVENUE.

1. An Account of His Majesty's Revenue received in the Isle of Man from the 5th January 1790 to the 5th January 1791, with the charges thereon.

2. An Account of all Payments made to Officers on the Civil Establishment of the Isle of Man for the year 1790.

3. An Account of all Incidental Payments (exclusive of Pay-

ments to Officers) made in the Isle of Man on Account of His Majesty's Customs for the year 1790.

4. An Account of the Number of Barrels of Herrings on which the bounty of one shilling per barrel on Herrings cured White has been received in the Isle of Man, from the granting such bounty to the present time, distinguishing the year, the number of barrels, and the amount of the bounty.

5. An Account of the Number of Barrels of Herrings cured Red exported from the Isle of Man for the bounty of one shilling and ninepence per barrel, from the granting such bounty to the present time, distinguishing the year, the number of barrels, to what place exported, and the amount of the bounty ; as also the number of barrels exported to Great Britain within the same period, distinguishing each year.

6. An Account of the Number of Barrels of Herrings cured White exported from the Isle of Man for the bounty of two shillings and eightpence per barrel, from the granting such bounty to the present time, distinguishing the year, the number of barrels, to what place exported, and the amount of the bounty ; as also the number of barrels exported to Great Britain within the same period, distinguishing each year.

7. An Account of the several Officers by whom the Harbour Dues in the Isle of Man are collected, specifying the Officers, the Allowance to the Officers, the Appointment, and the respective Harbour Dues.

8. An Account of the Number of Boats belonging to the Isle of Man for which the Herring Custom has been paid, for ten years ending the 5th January 1791, distinguishing the year, and to what port or creek belonging, and if licensed ; as also the British and Irish boats respectively for which the Herring Custom has been paid within the same period, distinguishing the number and year.

9. An Account of the Revenue Customs, as also of the Harbour Duties, Herring Custom, and Bay Fisheries of the Isle of Man, from the year 1765 to the 5th January 1791, distinguishing the total in each year.

10. An Account of the Revenue of the Harbour Fund, Herring and Salmon Fisheries of the Isle of Man, from the year 1765 to the present period, with the disposal thereof, distinguishing each year.

11. An Account of His Majesty's Revenues received in the Isle of Man from the year 1765 to the 5th January 1791 ; showing the receipt upon each article, at each port, in each year ; the payments made out of the said Revenues ; and how the balance has been accounted for or remitted, to whom, and when.

12. A List of the several Ports and Creeks in the Isle of Man, distinguishing the Ports to which the Creeks respectively belong, and the date of the Commission in virtue of which they were appointed.

13. A Copy of the Return to the Commission for appointing the Extent, Bounds, and Limits of the Ports of the Isle of Man.

14. An Account of the Salaries, Fees, Gratuities, and Allowances received by the Officers of the Customs in the Isle of Man, distinguishing the Port, the name of the Officer, the Employment, by what authority appointed, where paid, the gross produce of the Employment, the several deductions therefrom, and the net produce for the year 1790.

15. An Account of the several Fees taken by the Officers of the Customs in the Isle of Man, distinguishing the Port, the Fee, for what business or document, for whose use, and by what authority.

16. An Account of the Duties which have been laid upon Articles imported into the Isle of Man, the Variations which have taken place in those Duties, and the Duties now payable on each article.

17. An Account of all Articles imported into the Isle of Man by License, and into what Port, from the respective periods at which such Licenses were required by Law ; distinguishing the year, the article, the quantity annually allowed, the quantity imported, and from what ports of Great Britain exported.

18. An Account of Coals imported into the Isle of Man for ten years ending the 5th January 1791, distinguishing the year and quantity.

19. An Account of Salt imported into the Isle of Man from Great Britain or foreign parts for ten years ending 5th January 1791, distinguishing the year, the country, the species of salt, the quantity, whether duty free ; if liable to duty, the amount thereof.

20. An Account of all Wines imported into the Isle of Man from the year 1765 to the present period, distinguishing the year, in what vessel imported, from what port brought, at what part of the Island imported, the species of wine, the quantity, and the amount of the duties.

21. An Account of the different species of Corn and Grain, Meal and Flour, imported into and exported from the Isle of Man for ten years ending the 5th January 1791, distinguishing the quantity of each species in each year.

22. An Account of Linens exported from the Isle of Man to Great Britain for the Bounty, for ten years ending the 5th January 1791, distinguishing the year and quantity : As also those exported elsewhere within the same period, distinguishing the year and quantity.

23. An Account of Bestials exported from the Isle of Man for ten years ending the 5th January 1791, distinguishing the year, species, and number, and to what country.

24. An Account of the total quantities of all articles, the growth, produce, and manufacture of the Isle of Man, exclusive of Grain, Linen, Bestials, and Herrings, which have been exported from thence for ten years ending the 5th January 1791, distinguishing the year, the article, and to what country.

25. An Account of all Goods which have been imported into the Isle of Man from the 5th January 1781 to the 5th January 1782, distinguishing the quantities imported of each article, and the ports from whence brought, and at which imported into the Isle of Man.

26. An Account of all Goods which have been exported from the Isle of Man from the 5th January 1781 to the 5th January 1782, distinguishing the quantities exported of each article, and the ports to which exported.

27. An Account of all Goods which have been imported into the Isle of Man from the 5th January 1790 to the 5th January

1791, distinguishing the quantities imported of each article, and the port from whence brought, and at which imported into the Isle of Man.

28. An Account of all Goods which have been exported from the Isle of Man from the 5th January 1790 to the 5th January 1791, distinguishing the quantities of each article, and the ports to which exported, and the port where shipped.

29. An Account of all Articles brought coastwise from the Port of Douglas for ten years ending 5th January 1791, distinguishing the year, the port of shipping, the vessel, her tonnage, the article, and the quantity.

30. An Account of all Articles carried coastwise from the Port of Douglas from the 5th January 1781 to the 5th January 1791, distinguishing the year, the port of delivery, the vessel, her tonnage, the article, and the quantity.

31. An Account of all Articles brought coastwise to the Port of Derby Haven for ten years ending the 5th January 1791, distinguishing the year, the port of shipping, the vessel, her tonnage, the article, and the quantity.

32. An Account of all Articles carried coastwise from the Port of Derby Haven for ten years ending 5th January 1791, distinguishing the year, the port of delivery, the vessel, her tonnage, the article, and the quantity.

33. An Account of all Articles carried coastwise to the Port of Peel for ten years ending the 5th January 1791, distinguishing the year, the port of shipping, the vessel, her tonnage, the article, and the quantity.

34. An Account of all Articles carried coastwise from the Port of Peel for ten years ending the 5th January 1791, distinguishing the year, the port of delivery, the vessel, her tonnage, the article, and the quantity.

35. An Account of all Articles carried coastwise to the Port of Ramsay for ten years ending 5th January 1791, distinguishing the year, the port from whence, the vessel, her tonnage, the article, and the quantity.

36. An Account of all Articles carried coastwise from the Port of Ramsay for ten years ending 5th January 1791, distinguishing the year, the port of delivery, the vessel, her tonnage, the article, and the quantity.

37. An Account of the number of Ships and Vessels belonging
to the Port of Douglas, Isle of Man, with the Names and
Tonnage, which have been registered in pursuance of an
Act of Parliament passed in the 26th year of his present
Majesty, entitled, "An Act for the further Increase and
Encouragement of Shipping and Navigation," distinguishing such as are British built, such as are foreign built, and
such as are prizes made free ; also distinguishing which of
the said ships have been lost, broken up, or otherwise
destroyed, or condemned as unfit for further service ; the
Trade in which those remaining have been employed, the
number of men and boys by whom they are usually navi-
gated, and such of them as have neither entered inwards
nor cleared outwards at the said port, either for a foreign
or coasting voyage, between the 30th September 1786
and 30th September 1791.

38. An Account of do. belonging to Darby Haven.

39. An Account of do. belonging to Peel.

40. An Account of do. belonging to Ramsay.

41. An Account of the number of Vessels which have cleared inwards and outwards from the different Ports in the Isle of
Man for ten years ending the 5th January 1791, distinguishing the year, the port, whether British or foreign,
with their respective tonnage.

42. An Account of all Seizures which have been made by the
Officers of the Customs in the Isle of Man since the year
1765, distinguishing the year, the article, where seized,
by what officer, before what court prosecuted, whether
condemned, the gross produce, the charges of condemna-
tion and sale, the king's share, and the disposal of the king's
share.

43. An Account of the King's Cruisers or Revenue Cutters which
have been stationed at the Isle of Man for the purpose of
cruising, for ten years ending 5th July 1791, distinguishing the year, their names, and force.

44. An Abstract of the several Laws respecting the Revenue and
Trade of the Isle of Man, distinguishing the Acts.

45. An Account of all Bounties payable on the Fisheries of the
Isle of Man, or on articles exported, distinguishing whether

payable in the Island or in Great Britain, and by what authority paid.

46. An Account of the Articles which may be imported into Great Britain from the Isle of Man, duty free.

47. An Account of the Articles duty free on Importation into the Isle of Man, and from what countries.

48. An Account of the Articles prohibited to be imported into the Isle of Man.

49. An Account of Articles prohibited to be exported from the Isle of Man.

50. Copy of the Warrant appointing Charles Lutwidge, Esq., Receiver-General of the Isle of Man, dated 22d June 1765.

51. Copy of the Warrant appointing George Watts, Esq., Receiver-General of the Isle of Man, dated 9th May 1785.

52. Copy of the Appointment of Mr. Thomas Barber, by Mr. Senhouse Wilson, to be Searcher and Comptroller of the Port of Ramsay, dated 16th March 1790.

53. Examination of Senhouse Wilson, Esq., Deputy Receiver-General and Collector of the Revenues in the Isle of Man, taken at Douglas October 3d, 6th, 7th, 8th, and 20th, 1791.

54. Do. taken at Douglas October 21st, 1791.

55. The Examination of Charles Small, Esq., Collector of the Customs at Douglas, taken the 4th and 19th October 1791.

56. The Examination of Mr. Wm. Scott, Comptroller of the Customs at Douglas, taken October 4th and 20th, 1791.

57. The Examination of Mr. Michael Cullen, Searcher at Douglas, taken October 8th, 10th, and 12th, 1791.

58. The Examination of Mr. Peter Moore, Port Gauger at Douglas, taken October 11th, 1791.

59. The Examination of Mr. Robert Jelly, Riding Officer at Douglas, taken October 10th, 1791.

60. The Examination of Mr. Henry Routledge, extra Waiter and Searcher, and acting Chief Boatman at Douglas, taken October 10th, 1791.

61. The Examination of Mr. Robert Affleck, Tidesman and Boatman at Douglas, taken October 11th, 1791.

62. The Examination of Mr. William Clague, Acting Collector and Riding Officer at Darby Haven, taken at Douglas October 14th and 19th, 1791.

63. The Examination of Mr. John Moore, Comptroller at Derby
    Haven, taken at Douglas October 14th and 19th, 1791.
64. The Examination of Mr. James Webb, Searcher at Derby
    Haven, taken at Douglas October 14th and 19th, 1791.
65. The Examination of Mr. James Webb, Collector of the Harbour
    Duties at Derby Haven, taken at Castletown, October 15th,
    and at Douglas, October 19th, 1791.
66. The Examination of Mr. Joseph Lawson, Chief Boatman at
    Derby Haven, taken at Douglas the 14th and 19th Octo-
    ber 1791.
67. The Examination of Mr. George Savage, Acting Collector,
    Established Tidesman and Boatman, and Extra Riding
    Officer at Peel, taken at Douglas October 11th and 12th,
    1791.
68. The Examination of Mr. Henry Gell, Chief Boatman and
    Acting Searcher at Peel, taken at Douglas October 13th,
    1791.
69. The Examination of Mr. John Gammel, Collector at Ramsay,
    taken at Douglas October 18th and 19th, 1791.
70. The Examination of Mr. Thomas Barber, Acting Comptroller
    and Deputy Searcher at Ramsay, taken at Douglas October
    11th and 12th, 1791.
71. The Examination of Mr. Daniel Gill, Riding Officer at Ram-
    say, taken at Douglas October 12th, 1791.
72. The Examination of Mr. Thomas Hodgson, Chief Boatman at
    Ramsay, taken at Douglas October 20th, 1791.
73. The Examination of Mr. Thomas Brayden, Collector of the
    Harbour Duties at Ramsay, taken at Douglas the 19th
    October 1791.
74. An Account of the several Sums of Money received by George
    Watts, Esq., as Receiver-General of the Isle of Man, since
    his appointment to that office, to the 5th January 1792,
    with the payments made thereout.
75. An Account of Remittances made to the Receiver-General of
    the Isle of Man, by Senhouse Wilson, Esq., Deputy Re-
    ceiver-General, on account of the Revenue of the said
    Island, between the 9th May 1785 (the date of his appoint-
    ment) and the 5th day of January 1792. specifying the
    sums and dates of receipt, with the payments made there-

from, and the dates (exclusive of salaries, etc., paid in the Island), and the balance remaining in his hands on the 5th of January in each year respectively.

76. A Letter from the Deputy Receiver-General of the Isle of Man, dated Douglas, 12th October 1791, containing his Observations on the Present System of Duties in the Isle of Man, etc.

77. Observations on the Trade and Revenues of the Isle of Man, by the Collector and Controller of Douglas, dated 10th October 1791.

78. A Letter from the Collector of Ramsay, dated 26th November 1791, containing his Observations on the Illicit Trade of the Isle of Man, etc.

79. Queries put to the Deputy Receiver-General of the Isle of Man, respecting certain points contained in his letter on the present system of Revenues in the said Island, dated 12th October 1791, with his answers.

80. Queries put to the Collector and Controller of Douglas respecting certain points contained in their Observations on the Trade and Revenues of the Isle of Man, dated October 10th, 1791, with their answers.

81. Opinion of the Deputy Receiver-General of the Isle of Man, and the Collector and Controller of Douglas, as to a new Revenue Establishment in the Isle of Man.

82. Observations on the Revenue of the Isle of Man, by Mr. Robert Jelly, Riding Officer at Douglas, dated 10th October 1791.

83. A Letter from Alexander Shaw, Esq., Lieutenant-Governor of the Isle of Man, dated Castle Rushen, 19th October 1791, containing—

84. Observations and Remarks of the House of Keys repecting the Public Buildings, Harbours, etc., of the Isle of Man. Signed John Taubman, Speaker, dated 19th October 1791.

85. Propositions, etc., of the Merchants of Douglas, in the Isle of Man, dated 20th October 1791.

86. Memorial of the Merchants and Shopkeepers of Castletown, dated 1st November 1791.

87. The Memorial of the principal Inhabitants of the Town of Peel, dated 15th November 1791.

88. Propositions and Information of the Inhabitants of Ramsay, dated 20th October 1791.

89. Transcript of a Paper in the handwriting of the late Bishop Wilson, containing an account of the number of souls in the Isle of Man in 1726.

90. An Account of the number of souls in the Isle of Man, as returned by the several Clergy in answer to the Lord Bishop's twelfth article of visitation, anno 1757.

91. An Account of the number of Inhabitants in the Isle of Man, as returned by the several Clergy thereof, in pursuance of Requisitions from Governor Smith, dated 29th January 1784.

92. Petition of Abraham de la Poyme, dated 21st October 1791.

93. An Abstract of the gross Revenue of the Post-Office in the Isle of Man from the 6th of July 1782 to the 10th October 1791.

APPENDIX C.—PART III.

CONSTITUTION.

1. The Constitution of the Isle of Man, by Thomas Moore, Esq., the Deemster, dated 8th October 1791.

2. A Letter from Sir Wadsworth Busk, Attorney-General of the Isle of Man, dated Newtown, 13th October 1791.

3. A Letter from do., dated Newtown, 6th December 1791.

4. A Letter from John Quayle, Esq., Clerk of the Rolls, dated Rolls Office, Castletown, 17th October 1791.

5. The Examination of Thomas Moore, Esq., Deemster of the Isle of Man, taken at Castletown October 19th, 1791.

6. The Examination of John Quayle, Esq., Clerk of the Rolls, taken at Castletown October 15th, 1791.

7. The Examination of do., taken October 21st, 1791.

8. The Examination of John Taubman, Esq., Speaker of the House of Keys, taken at Castletown October 15th, 1791.

9. Copy of the most ancient Record in the Isle of Man, A.D. 1417.

10. The Memorial of the Right Rev. Claudius, Lord Bishop, and

Evan Christian, Vicar-General, in behalf of themselves and the other Ecclesiastics constitutionally Members of His Majesty's Council in the Isle of Man.

11. The Oath administered to the twenty-four Keys of the Isle of Man, before and since the Revestment.

12. The Oath administered to the Bishop of the Isle of Man before the Revestment.

13. The Oath administered to the Bishop since the Revestment.

14.   Do.   Archdeacon before do.

15.   Do.   do. since do.

16.   Do.   Archdeacon's Official before Revestment.

17.   Do.   do.   since Revestment.

18.   Do.   Vicars-General before Revestment.

19.   Do.   do. since Revestment.

20.   Do.   Attorney-General before and since Revestment.

21.   Do.   Comptroller and Clerk of the Rolls before Revestment.

22.   Do.   Clerk of the Rolls since Revestment.

23.   Do.   Receiver-General before the Revestment.

24.   Do.   do. and Collector since the Revestment.

25.   Do.   Deemster before the Revestment.

26.   Do.   do. since do.

27.   Do.   Water Bailiff before the Revestment.

28.   Do.   do. since the Revestment.

29.   Do.   Judge of the Court of Admiralty since the Revestment.

30. The Governor's Commission, 1764.

31. The Deemster's do.

32.   Do.   do.

33. The Attorney-General's Commission, 1764.
34. The Receiver-General's do.
35. Comptroller and Clerk of the Rolls Commission, 1764.
36. Water Bailiff and Collector's   do.
37. Major-General's   do.
38. The Legislature of the Isle of Man.
39. Minutes of the Attorney-General's Protest respecting Members of the Council.
40. Certificate of the Clerk of the Rolls, that there are no Precepts from the Governor, Lieutenant-Governor, or any other authority, recorded in the Rolls Office, for the convening of the Council of the Isle of Man relative to the Laws made and enacted for the time therein specified.
41. Certificate of the Clerk of the Rolls, that there are no Precepts from the Governor, Lieutenant-Governor, etc., from the year 1742 to 1777.
42. Extracts from the Exchequer Books of the Isle of Man of the proceedings of the Governor and Council, 1720-1721.
43.   Do.   do.
44.   Do.   do.   1722.
45.   Do.   do.   1722.
46.   Do.   do.   1722.
47. List of Proceedings or Acts of the Governor and Council, abstracted from the Records in the Rolls Office.
48. Copies of proceedings of the Governor and Council, taken from the Records in the Rolls Office.
49. Copy of the Patent for the Office of Clerk of the Rolls.
50. Copy of the Commission for the Chaplain at Castletown.
51.   Do.   Constable of the Garrison of Castle Rushen.
52.   Do.   Steward of the Houses, Demesnes, and Garrisons.
53.   Do.   do.   Abbey Lands.
54. Copy of the Oath administered to the Assistants of the Deputy Searcher.
55.   Do.   Governor prior to the Revestment.
56.   Do.   do.   since the Revestment.

57. Copy of the Oath administered to the Lieutenant-Governor since the Revestment.

58.   Do.   Steward of the Garrison before the Revestment.

59.   Do.   Steward of the Abbey Lands since the Revestment.

60. The Examination of Mr. George Savage, Water Bailiff of the Isle of Man, taken at Douglas the 4th and 11th October 1791.

61. The Examination of Mr. Thomas Whittam, Chief Constable of the Town and District of Douglas, taken the 3d of October 1791.

62. The Examination of Mr. Daniel Quark, a Coroner of Garff Sheading, taken the 4th October 1791.

APPENDIX D.—PART IV.

SUGGESTIONS FOR THE BENEFIT OF THE ISLAND THAT HAVE NOT BEEN DISCUSSED UNDER THE FOREGOING HEADS.

1. A Letter from Lieutenant-Governor Shaw, dated Castle Rushen, 17th November 1791.   (A.)

2. Memorial of the principal Proprietors of Land in the Isle of Man, dated 26th and 31st October 1791.

3. Petition of the Inhabitants of the Northern District of the Isle of Man, 1791.

4. The Examination of John Cosnahan, Esq , High Bailiff of the District of Douglas, taken the 6th October 1791.

5. The Constitution of Mr. George Savage, Water Bailiff.

6. A Letter from Lieutenant-Governor Shaw, dated 17th November 1791.   (B.)

7. A Judgment of the Water Bailiff.

8. A Letter from Lieutenant-Governor Shaw, dated 22d October 1791.

9.   Do.   do.   9th November 1791.

10. The Memorial of Norris Moore, Esq., Acting Secretary, Isle of Man.

11. The Examination of the Rev. Mr. Corlett, taken at Douglas October 22d, 1791.

12. The Examination of Thomas Moore, Esq., taken at Douglas the 22d October 1791.

13. The Petition of Mr. John Cotteen, Gaoler of Castle Rushen.

14. The Memorial of the Inhabitants of Kirk Lonan, dated 22d October 1791.

15. Plan of Laxey Harbour in the Isle of Man.

16. Information of the Inhabitants of Kirk Maughold, with a plan of the natural harbour of Cornah.

17. The Examination of Mr. Nicholas Christian, Harbour Master of the Port of Douglas, taken the 3d, 10th, and 11th of October 1791.

18. Plan of the Harbour of Douglas.

19. Plan of Peel Castle and Harbour.

20. Plan of Ramsay Harbour, with the intended new Quay.

21. Plan of Port Earn and Bay.

22. A Letter from Mr. Alexander Cook, dated Douglas, 10th October 1791.

23. Petition of John Taubman and John Stevenson.

24.   Do.   to the Lords Commissioners of Her Majesty's Treasury.

25.   Do.   John Stevenson   to   do.

26. A Paper marked Revenue, No. 1.

27.   Do.   No. 2.

28.   Do.   No. 3.

29. Remarks on the present Establishment of Revenue Officers in the Isle of Man.

30. A Letter from the Duke of Atholl, dated Douglas, Isle of Man, 20th October 1791, inclosing—

31. A Paper marked Harbours.

32. A Letter from the Duke of Atholl, dated London, February 6, 1792, inclosing—

33. Population of the Isle of Man, 1792.

34. A Letter from the Duke of Atholl, dated London, 13th January 1792.

1807.

A Compilation of the different Statements of a late Duel, in the Isle of Man, between Sir John Piers, Bart., and John Meredith, Esq. Douglas : printed by George Jefferson. *Octavo.* Pp. 20. Dated Douglas, 24th March 1807.

The Duel originated in a difference of opinion between Sir J. Piers and Mr. Meredith, relative to a bet at a Dinner, on the 24th of December 1806. Mr. Meredith was afterwards killed in a duel by Mr. Boys, in a field near Mount Murray, and the body left in the field : Boys fled.

1807-9.

The Antiquarian Repertory, a Miscellaneous Assemblage of Topography, History, etc.

Vol. iv. p. 460.—Lid of a Stone Coffin found in the Calf of Man.

This is now in the possession of the Clerk of the Rolls, H. M. Quayle, Esq., Castletown.

London : 1807-9. 4 vols. *quarto.*

S. TURNER.—1807.

To the Public—Statement respecting the Duel between Sir John Piers and Mr. Meredith. Signed " S. Turner. Douglas, January 9th, 1807." G. Jefferson, Printer.

A broadside.

Published and edited by Jeffery the bookseller.

SAMUEL WILLIAM RYLEY.—1808.

The Itinerant, or Memoirs of an Actor. By S. W. Ryley. London : printed for Taylor and Hessey, 93 Fleet Street. 1808. 3 vols. 12*mo.* In the third volume will be found

an account of this eccentric individual's residence in the
Town of Peel, in the Isle of Man, in 1795, with his
remarks on the Country, Inhabitants, and their Customs,
etc.   Pp. 217 to 289.

A very entertaining work, printed in three series, 9 vols.
A second edition of the first series appeared in 1817, and the
three in 1816-27, 9 vols. London. 12mo. There is also
a ludicrous account of Lord Henry Murray and Mr. Back-
house's "spree" to the Isle of Man.

1808.

The Book of Common Prayer, in Manx.   Whitehaven :
   printed by John Ware. 1808.

JUDGE BLACKSTONE.—1809.

Commentaries on the Laws of England. 15th edition. Vol. i.
   p. 105.   *Vide* "Abstract of Laws," etc.   J. Gell, Esq.
   Vol. i. p. 163. Manx Society, vol. xii., 1867.

1809.

Case of Major-General William Stapleton on the Investigation ordered by his Majesty's Principal Secretary of State
   for the Home Department, into the Charges preferred by
   General Stapleton, against his Honor John Lace, Esq.,
   his Majesty's First Deemster in the Isle of Man.   No
   place or date on Title. *Octavo.* Pp. 30. Dated "21st
   October 1809."

Case arose in consequence of an affray at the Theatre, in
Douglas, caused by Major-General Stapleton having in a
mere frolic pushed a Mr. Johnson forward on the stage,
when the General and Sir John Piers and Captain Edwards
were summoned to appear in the Deemster's Court in Castle

Rushen, when Deemster Lace reflected on the character of General Stapleton. Memorial and correspondence of the transaction.

NATHANIEL JEFFERYS.—No date.—[1809.]   (Mr. Bell.)

A Descriptive and Historical Account of the Isle of Man ; with a view of its Society, Manners, and Customs ; partly compiled from various authorities, and from observations made in a Tour through the Island in the summer of 1808. Dedicated to his Majesty, by Nathaniel Jefferys, formerly representative in Parliament for the City of Coventry. To which is added a Map of the Isle of Man, with the roads described, and every information necessary to the convenience of the Pleasurable and Commercial Traveller. Also, a short account of the Towns of White-haven and Workington, with the fashionable Bathing Places of Allonby and Skinburness, on the coast of Cumberland, and the entrance to Scotland across the Solway Frith. Newcastle-upon-Tyne : printed for the Author, by Preston and Heaton ; and sold by R. Miller, Bookseller, Mosley Street, and all other Booksellers in the United Kingdom. (Price 8s.) *Small octavo.* Pp. 200. Dedication, "To the King," pp. iii. to viii. Preface, pp. ix. to xxxviii.

George Woods observes in the preface to his Account of the Isle of Man (1811), that he considers it as stated, to be " a sort of literary license for picking and stealing," and " The authorities of the Jeweller to the Prince of Wales appear to have been Robertson and Feltham. Had the treatise been valuable, it would have checked my own presumption. The period of ten or fourteen years makes considerable alteration in the appearance of an improving country ; and the author has not been careful to separate what continues to be true from that which is so no longer."

Mr. Jefferys was Jeweller to the Prince of Wales (George IV.), against whom he had a claim for nearly £100,000 for Jewels, about 1806. Nineteen pages of the Preface relate to these transactions with the Prince and to his publications connected therewith. He was once M.P. for Coventry.

Mr. Bell, of Gateshead, wrote the Account of the Isle of Man in Jefferys' parlour, and the latter put the Preface to it.

N. JEFFERYS.—1809.   (Mr. Bell.)

The same Title, but without the Author's name, and the date inserted.

In the Preface, at pp. 21 to 38, is the Manx Magna Charta, instead of the Matters relating to the Prince of Wales. The History, pp. 39 to 200.

JAMES NEILD.—1810.

James Neild on Castle Rushen Gaol.   A Letter addressed to Dr. Lettsom.   London : *Gentleman's Magazine*, Dec. 1810. Pp. 514-517.

He states the number of Prisoners, Nov. 10, 1810 :— Debtors, 9 ; Felons, etc., 0 ; and mentions that in one of the rooms is confined, " besides an infant boy, son of *a man and his wife*, who (so strangely is the law here constructed) are both of them confined in this gaol *for the same debt !*"

REV. HUGH STOWELL.—1810.

A Sermon preached at St. George's Chapel, Douglas, Isle of Man, on Sunday, the 26th day of August, 1810, being the anniversary or yearly meeting of the children educated in the Lancasterian School, in the town of Douglas.

By the Rev. Hugh Stowell. Published at the particular request of the Committee of the Lancasterian School, and for the benefit of the Institution. George Jefferson, Printer, Douglas. *Octavo.* Pp. 22.

THOMAS EVANS.—1810.

Old Ballads, Historical and Narrative. By Thomas Evans. London: 1810. *Octavo.* 4 vols.

In vol. ii. pp. 308 to 310, is the "Winning of the Isle of Man by the noble Earl of Salisbury." Reprinted from the "Garland of Delight."

This ballad is reprinted in the sixteenth volume of the Manx Society's Series, 1869. "Mona Miscellany," pp. 45-47.

1810.

Conaant Noa nyn jiarn as saualtagn Yeesey Creest. The New Testament, in the Manks Language. 12*mo.*

1810.

Encyclopædia Britannica. Edinburgh. *Quarto.* 20 vols.

Vol. xii.—Article on the Isle of Man.

GEORGE WOODS.—1811.

An Account of the past and present state of the Isle of Man ; including a Topographical description ; a sketch of its Mineralogy ; an outline of its Laws, with the privileges enjoyed by Strangers ; and a history of the Island. By George Woods.

—— "Quis nescit, primam esse historiæ legem, nequid falsi dicere audeat ? Deinde, neque verè non audeat ?"—*Cicero de Oratore, Lib. II.*

London : printed for Robert Baldwin, 47 Paternoster Row, and William Blackwood, Edinburgh. 1811. *Octavo.*

Pp. 365. Dedicated to Thomas Stewart Traill, of Liverpool, M.D. Preface, pp. v. to vii. A small Map of the Island.

"The best as well as the latest traveller who has laid before the public any account of this Island." — Quayle's *Survey*, Preface, p. 9. 1812. It contains the earliest geological notice of the Island.

1811.

Articles of Agreement between the Duke of Atholl, Earl of Derby, Lord Bishop of Sodor and Man, Lord Stanley, and the Clergy of the Isle of Man, respecting the Ecclesiastical Rights and Properties on the Island. 1811. Privately printed. *Folio.*

J. JOHNSON.—1811.

A View of the Jurisprudence of the Isle of Man : with the History of its Ancient Constitution, Legislative Government, and Extraordinary Privileges ; together with the practice of the Courts, etc. etc. etc. By J. Johnson, Esq. Edinburgh : printed by George Ramsay and Compy. ; sold by Thomas Bryce and Co., No. 13 Infirmary Street ; Longman, Hurst, Rees, Orme, and Brown, London ; and J. Cuming, Dublin. 1811. *Octavo.* Pp. 234.

Index, pp. 6, and List of Subscribers, pp. 15.

FRANCIS HARGRAVE.—1811.

Hargrave's Jurisconsult Exercitations. London : *Quarto.*

Vol. i. pp. 141-70, "On the Case of the Duke of Athol in respect of the Isle of Man."

Vol. iii., 1813, pp. 255-312, "Further opinion in the Duke of Athol's Isle of Man Case."

For this further opinion, *vide* "Abstract of Laws," etc.,

J. Gell, Esq. Vol. i. pp. 158-163. Manx Society, vol.
xii. 1867.

KERMOTTE STOWELL.—1812.

A brief Report of the Transactions of the Committee of the
Douglas Library, for the last twelve months, including
some of the Resolutions passed at the last Annual Meeting. By K. Stowell. Printed by J. Beatson and Co.,
Douglas. Delivered gratis to the Proprietors. 1812.
12mo. Pp. 17.

Mr. Stowell was Secretary, and resigned 30th May 1812.
An exposé of the *management* of the Committee.

About 1810, Samuel Ward, Esq., LL.D., then residing in
Dublin, presented to the Library a great number of valuable
works, for which his name was placed on the list as an
Honorary Member. Some time after, visiting Douglas for
a few months, he availed himself of this privilege, when the
proprietors resolved that no honorary member (there were
only two) could have access to the rooms without paying the
Annual Subscription! Mr. Ward's name was erased, and he
was obliged to leave the rooms. A list of the works Mr. W.
presented is given at p. 13.

THOMAS QUAYLE.—1812.

General View of the Agriculture of the Isle of Man, with
observations on the means of its Improvement. Drawn
up for the consideration of the Board of Agriculture and
internal Improvement. By Thomas Quayle, Esq. London:
Printed by W. Bulmer and Co., Cleveland Row, St.
James's : sold by G. and W. Nicol, Booksellers to his
Majesty, Pall Mall ; and Sherwood, Neely, and Jones,
Paternoster Row. 1812. (Price 7s. 6d., Boards.) *Octavo.*
Pp. 193.

A Map of the Island, same as in Wood's Account, 1811.

KERMOTTE STOWELL.—1813.

A Letter to the Inhabitants of the Isle of Man, or, an Exposition of the circumstances which led to the ruin of the Methodists' Friendly Society of Douglas ; with Notes, containing Interesting Anecdotes of many eminent Persons. By Kermotte Stowell. Price One shilling and sixpence. For the benefit of the Poor belonging to the above Society. 1813. *Octavo.* Pp. 24. Dated "Douglas, Isle of Man, 5th May, 1813." Printed by J. Adlard, Duke Street, Smithfield.

1813.

The third Report on the Day and Sunday Schools. Douglas : 1813.

REV. HUGH STOWELL.—1813.

A Sermon preached at St. John's Chapel, July 5th, 1813, before the Legislature of the Isle of Mann, assembled in Tynwald, by the Rev. Hugh Stowell, Vicar of Kirk Lonan. Published by the expressed command of the Most Noble John Duke of Atholl, Governor in Chief of the Isle of Mann, etc. etc. Douglas : printed and sold by J. Beatson, Custom House Quay. 1813. Price 1s. 6d. *Quarto.* Pp. 15.

REV. HUGH STOWELL.—1813.

A Sermon preached at St. George's Chapel, Douglas, Isle of Man, on Sunday, the 25th July 1813, being the Anniversary or Yearly Meeting of the Children educated in the Daily and Sunday School, in the town of Douglas. By the Rev. Hugh Stowell. Published at the request of the Committee of the School. Douglas : printed by G. Jefferson. 1813. *Post octavo.* Pp. 16.

FRANCIS HARGRAVE.—1813.

Hargrave's Jurisconsult Exercitations. Vol. iii. 255. "Further Opinion on the Duke of Athol's Isle of Man Case."

This is printed in Gell's "Abstract," vol. i. pp. 158-163. Manx Society, 1867.

1813.

The four new Acts of Tynwald, promulgated at a Tynwald Court holden at St. John's, on the 5th day of July 1813. Now published by Authority. Douglas : printed and sold by J. Beatson. (Price only Sixpence British.) (No date.) 12mo. Pp. 29.

MARK ANTHONY MILLS.—1813.

An Impartial Inquiry respecting the Duke of Atholl's right to Licence Intacks, and the tenant's Indefinite Claim as to Turbuary and Depasture on the Mountains of the Isle of Man.

"Quam multa injusta ac prava fiunt moribus."—*Ter. Heaut.*

By Mark Anthony Mills, Esq. Douglas : printed and sold by Beatson and Copeland, Custom House Quay. 1813. (Price One shilling and sixpence British.) *Octavo.* Pp. 27.

1813.

The Isle of Man Weekly Gazette, and General Advertiser. The first number published by Beatson and Copeland. Price 4d. Continued three years.

John Beatson was brother-in-law to Mr. James Harrop, proprietor and printer of *The Manchester Mercury and British Volunteer.*

Nicholas Carlisle.—1813.

A Topographical Dictionary of Scotland and the Islands in
the British Seas, etc. Being a continuation of the Topography of the United Kingdom of Great Britain and Ireland. By Nicholas Carlisle, F.S.A. London: printed for G.
and W. Nicol, Booksellers to his Majesty, Pall Mall; and
Bell and Bradfute, Booksellers, Edinburgh, by W. Bulmer
and Co., Cleveland Row, St. James's. 1813. 2 vols. *Quarto.*

In the Preface he states "The Isle of Man has also been
included upon the grounds of its having constituted part of
the Territories belonging to Scotland in 1266, although it
was taken under the protection of Edward the First in 1290;
and in 1307 assumed as his own."

Each parish, town, etc., in the Island is noticed in alphabetical order.

1814.

Acts of Tynwald promulgated on the Tynwald Hill on the
24th March 1814. Second edition, carefully revised and
corrected. Douglas: printed by G. Jefferson. 1814.
12*mo.* Pp. 24.

Act for the more easy Recovery of Debts contracted out
of the limits of the Isle of Man. Act for the Relief of Insolvent Debtors in the Isle of Man.

Dr. Berger.—1814.

Memoir of a Geological Survey of the Isle of Man. This was
published in the second volume of the first series of the
Transactions of the Geological Society of this year.
London.

A Supplementary Account, by Professor Henslow, was
also published in the fifth volume of the same series. Dr.
Berger resided a considerable time in the Island, and these

accounts furnish the greatest amount of geological information up to this time respecting the Isle of Man.

In the first volume of the Transactions, Dr. Berger gave the heights of the mountains, etc., in the Island, which were obtained by the barometer.—*Vide* vol. ii. pp. 29-65, and vol. v. pp. 482-505.

KERMOTTE STOWELL.—1814.

A Letter to his Grace the Duke of Atholl, embracing various subjects, with notes; containing much valuable information and deserving the particular attention of the Inhabitants of the Isle of Man. By Kermotte Stowell. Price One shilling. 1814. *Octavo*, pp. 12.

Dated "Douglas, Isle of Man, May 10th, 1814." Printed by J. Adlard, Duke Street, Smithfield.

REV. THOMAS HOWARD.—1814.

A Sermon, preached at Kirk Lonan Church, January 16th, 1814, on occasion of the death of Mrs. Amelia Stowell, wife of the Reverend Hugh Stowell, Vicar of Kirk Lonan. By the Rev. Thomas Howard.

"The righteous shall be had in everlasting remembrance."—Ps. cxii. 6.

Douglas: printed by Beatson and Copeland. 1814. *Octavo*, pp. 21.

Scots Magazine.—1814.

View of the State of the Isle of Man in 1814. *Scots Magazine*, p. 508.

1815.

The Isle of Man Weekly Gazette. New series. Published by M. A. Mills. Continued six years.

THOMAS CALLISTER.—1815.

An accurate, interesting, and peculiarly entertaining Description of that lucrative branch of business the Herring Fishery of the Isle of Man, which affords Employment for more than three months every year to above Five thousand poor people, to a number of Coopers all the year round, and to a variety of other crafts periodically. Of the Superior Quality of the Red Herrings manufactured in Douglas, as well as that of the Pickled Herrings, in a comparative point of view with all such as are caught and cured elsewhere. Of the various curious modes of preparing these Monarchs of the Finny Tribe, throughout the Island in their fresh state, for immediate consumption, and also the several amusing ways of making use of Pickled Herrings. A particular and very pleasing account of the flourishing Town of Douglas, which has been long considered as the Emporium of the Island with regard to Commerce ; comprising its present state, its commodious Quay and Harbour, its new Streets, the many genteel Houses built in the Modern Taste in many of the old Streets, the several places of Public Worship, the grand new Public Library, the famous new Charity School, the large new Poor House, etc. Likewise a List of the several Packets and constant Traders, and a correct abstract of the British Act of Parliament passed in July 1814, repealing the old Harbour Dues of the Island and substituting new ones in Lieu thereof, on the Fishing Boats and on all British and Foreign Vessels not only entering its Harbours but even anchoring in its Bays ; also the Duties payable on every kind of Merchandize imported into the Island. To all which is added a very curious, descriptive, entertaining and picturesque view of the much admired Seats and Estates of the Nobility and

Gentry in the Vicinity of the Town. Humbly inscribed to His Excellency the most noble John Duke of Atholl, Governor-in-Chief and Captain General of the Island. By Thomas Callister. Price only One shilling and sixpence British. 1815. *Octavo*, pp. 30. No place or printer.

CHARLOTTE NOOTH.—1815.

Original Poems and a Play. By Charlotte Nooth. London : printed for Longman, Hurst, Rees, Orme, and Brown, Paternoster Row. 1815. *Octavo*.

At p. 21-23 is a Manks Elegy, and at p. 49 lines written at Sea off the Isle of Man.

MRS. ST. GEORGE.—(About 1815.)

Edwardine. A Novel. By Mrs. St. George. In 3 volumes. 12*mo*.

The Scene in the Isle of Man. Mrs. St. George was formerly Mrs. Maddocks, a resident in Douglas.

1815.

Crossman's Cathechism in Manx. Douglas. 1815.

KERMOTTE STOWELL.—1815.

A Letter addressed to the Hon. John Moore (one of the Hon. Commissioners of Harbours) embracing various subjects. By Kermotte Stowell. Presented to ———. By the Society for upholding the Rights of the People. Dublin : printed by Wm. Espy, 14 Cork Hill. 1815. 8*vo*, pp. 34.

KERMOTTE STOWELL.—1816.

An Address to the Inhabitants of the Isle of Man, embracing

various subjects. By Kermotte Stowell. Presented to ——. By the Society for upholding the Rights of the People. Dublin : printed by J. J. Nolan, 3 Suffolk Street. 1816. *8vo.*

On "Paper Currency." "Letter to a Member of the House of Keys on the system of Custom House Fees." In a note, p. 14, "Two Clergymen informed me that to the few Public Institutions which are in this Country, they did not know of his Grace (the Duke of Atholl) contributing *one farthing.*" "Memorials of Kermotte Stowell to the Right Hon. Lord Viscount Sidmouth, on not having the Lamps properly lighted up on the Quays of Douglas, and neglect of the Harbour Lights." Dated "9th March 1816," and 21st April 1816. A Petition of K. S. to the Same, respecting the Duke of Atholl enclosing part of the Sea Beach extending towards Pollock Rocks, and his Grace conveying the same to Mr. Wm. Scott, the Collector of Douglas Port, and nephew (by marriage) to his Grace, and that the said Wm. Scott took the Stones from the Old Fort to enclose the same. Praying that these enclosures may be demolished. Dated "Douglas, 18th May 1816."

In Mr. Feltham's "Tour," 1798, on the title page is given a view of this Old Fort, attributed by Waldron to the Romans, but more probably erected by the Picts. At one time it was commanded by a Constable and Lieutenant, and defended by four pieces of ordnance, and four of the townsmen were bound to keep watch and ward upon the ramparts.

II. A. BULLOCK.—1816.

History of the Isle of Man, with a comparative view of the past and present State of Society and Manners ; containing also Biographical Anecdotes of Eminent Persons connected with that Island. By H. A. Bullock. London : printed for Longman, Hurst, Rees, Orme, and Brown,

Paternoster Row. 1816. 8*vo*, pp. 436. Introduction, Table of Contents, and List of Subscribers, pp. v. to xl. Map and View of Peel Castle at the time of the Revestment.

This History was written by a Lady. Mr. Wm. Cubbon of Denny, N.B., in a letter to Paul Bridson, Esq., January 24th, 1862, says, "She was a lady of no ordinary cleverness. I saw her only once, and I thought at the time that nature had made a mistake at her formation, and made her of the materials designed for a drum-major! She appeared to me to be quite qualified to hold the scissors of destiny, or stir the cauldron with Macbeth's witches! And with her pen she knew not to show mercy to the living or the dead. Stanley Bullock, Esq., her husband, was a man of a much more meek and quiet spirit."

REV. ROBERT BROWN.—1816.

A Sermon preached at St. George's Chapel, Douglas, Isle of Man, on Sunday the 1st September 1816 ; being the Anniversary or Yearly Meeting of the Children educated in the Daily and Sunday School, in the Town of Douglas. By the Rev. Robert Brown. Published at the request of the Committee of the School. Douglas : printed by G. Jefferson. 1816. *Octavo*, pp. 29.

REV. HUGH STOWELL.—1817.

Memoirs of Mrs. Stowell. By the Rev. Hugh Stowell, Rector of Ballaugh, Isle of Man. Wellington, Salop : printed by and for F. Houlston and Son, and sold by G. and S. Robinson, Paternoster Row, London. 1817. 12*mo*. Pp. 143. Introduction pp. iii. to vii.

Dated Ballaugh, Isle of Man, October 7, 1816. Mrs. Amelia Stowell was the wife of the Rev. Hugh Stowell. She died January 9th, 1814.

1817.

The New Criminal Code, or an Act for Altering and Amending the Criminal Law of the Isle of Man. Promulgated at the Tynwald Hill on the 31st July 1817. Published by Authority. Douglas: printed by G. Jefferson. 1817. *Octavo.* Pp. 23.

JAMES CLARKE.—1817.

A View of the Principal Courts in the Isle of Man, founded upon Authentic Documents, accompanied with Practical Remarks. By a Member of the Council. Liverpool: printed by Harris and Co., Water Street; and sold by Jefferson, Douglas, and the Booksellers in the Isle of Man; London, Liverpool, Whitehaven, etc., 1817. *Octavo.* Pp. 60. Dedicated to the Duke of Athol.

The Author was Attorney-General of the Island.

CATHERINE ST. GEORGE.—1817.

Maria, a Domestic Tale. Dedicated by permission to Her Royal Highness the Princess Charlotte of Saxe-Coburg. By Catherine St. George. London: published by J. Porter, Bookseller to Her Royal Highness Princess Charlotte, 81 Pall Mall. 1817. 12*mo*, 3 volumes.

Mrs. St. George kept a Lady's School in Douglas, and was the widow of a Mr. Maddocks. A portion of the Tale is laid in Douglas.

1817.

The Isle of Man Diary and New Almanack. Published for M. A. Mills and Co.

The loss of the Herring Fleet is mentioned as having taken place on the 21st September 1787 at Douglas, and many persons perished.

KERMOTTE STOWELL.—1818.

The Seneschal's Creed. No place or printer. 12*mo.* Pp. 12. Written by Kermotte Stowell, and dated at the end "March 1st, 1818." "N.B.—The Litany and the Old Woman in breeches in a few days."

The latter was never published, the Creed having given so much offence.

REV. ROBERT BROWN.—1818.

Sermons on Various Subjects. By the Rev. Robert Brown, Minister of St. Matthew's Chapel, Douglas, Isle of Man. Wellington, Salop : printed and sold by F. Houlston and Son. Sold also by Scatchard and Letterman, Ave Maria Lane, London. 1818. *Octavo.* Pp. 400. 22 Sermons.

The Rev. Mr. Brown was afterwards Vicar of Braddan.

M. A. MILLS.—1818.

Observations applicable to the existing system of Tithes in the Isle of Man. Douglas : printed at the Phœnix Press, Parade, for M. A. Mills. 1818. *Small Octavo.* Pp. 16.

An extract from a late publication on Tithes, with notes applicable to the Island, and a calculation of the value of the Tithes.

DONALD MONRO.—1818.

Description of the Western Isles of Scotland, called Hybrides. By Mr. Donald Monro, High Dean of the Isles, who travelled through the most of them in the year 1594. Glasgow : printed for John Wylie and Co. by R. Chapman. 1818.

This forms a portion of "Miscellanea Scotica," vol. ii.

Glasgow, 1818. The Isle of Man is the first island described. There are several tracts in the first edition which appeared in 1774. Edinburgh. 12*mo*. Only 50 copies were printed.

REV. H. STOWELL.—1818.

Yn Chied Lioar gailckagh ; ny cooney dy ynsaghey, chengey ny mayrey Ellan Vannin, Liorish y Cheshaght son Cummal seose, as cur er nyn doshiaght, Schoillyn Dhoonee Trooid magh reeriaght hostyn. Lunnin : prentit liorish Harry Teape, Chrork Toor. 1818. 12*mo*. Pp. 24.

A Manx Spelling and Lesson Book, compiled by the Rev. H. Stowell, Rector of Ballaugh.

A Manx Spelling Book was also compiled by —— Corlett, with an explanation at the end, but I have not been able to meet with a copy.

REV. HUGH STOWELL.—1819.

The Life of the Right Reverend Father in God Thomas Wilson, D.D., Lord Bishop of Sodor and Man. By the Rev. Hugh Stowell, Rector of Ballaugh, Isle of Man.

> ——" A friend to human race ;
> Fast by the road, his ever open door
> Obliged the wealthy, and reliev'd the poor."
> *Pope's Homer's Iliad*, vi. 18-20.

London : printed for F. C. and J. Rivington, No. 62 St. Paul's Church Yard, and No. 3 Waterloo Place, Pall Mall. 1819. *Octavo*. Pp. 419. Preface, pp. ix.

Dated "Ballaugh, Isle of Man, April 1819."—A Portrait of Bishop Wilson.

1819.

Bible, in Manks.

Yn Vible Casherick, ny yn Chenn Chonaant, as yn Conaant

Noa ; veih ny chied Ghlaraghyn ; dy Kiaralagh Chyndait ayns Gailck : ta shen dyghra Chengey ny mayrey Ellan Vannin. Pointit dy ve l'haiht ayns Kialteenyn. London : printed by Eyre and Strahan, for the British and Foreign Bible Society. 1819. *Octavo.*

A beautiful and accurate edition of the Manx Bible.

1819.

The Lex Scripta of the Isle of Man ; comprehending the Ancient Ordinances and Statute Laws. From the earliest to the present date. A new Edition published by Authority. Douglas : printed at the Manks Advertiser Office, for G. Jefferson, Bookseller and Stationer, Duke Street. Sold by Baldwin, Cradock, and Joy, Paternoster Row, London, and other Booksellers. 1819. *Octavo.* Pp. 543.

The last Act in the collection was promulgated on the 26th Feb. 1819. A copious Index added.

Dr. John Macculloch.—1819.

A Description of the Western Islands of Scotland, including the Isle of Man, comprising an Account of their Geological Structure, with Remarks on their Agriculture, Scenery, and Antiquities. By John Macculloch, M.D. London : printed for Archibald Constable and Co., Edinbro', and Hurst, Robinson, and Co., Cheapside, London. 1819 Two vols. *octavo.* One vol. *quarto;* plates.

Isle of Man—Vol. ii. p. 516-579.

1819.

The Isle of Man Diary and New Almanack, for the year of our Lord 1819, etc. etc. Douglas : printed at the Phœnix Press, Parade, for M. A. Mills. *Small octavo.*

Gives a list of the Legislature, Manks Bar, Packets, Inns, Principal Estates, Tables of Manks and English Money, etc. etc.

J. BARROW.—1820.

The Mona Melodies. A collection of Ancient and Original Airs of the Isle of Man. Arranged for the Voice, with a Piano Forte accompaniment by an amateur. The words by Mr. J. Barrow. Dedicated by permission to Her Royal Highness the Duchess of Kent. Price 8s. London: published at Mitchell's Musical Library and Instrument Warehouses, 159 New Bond Street, opposite Clifford Street, and 13 Southampton Row, Russell Square. *Folio.* Pp. 26.

Advertisement. Dated "London, 30 May 1820." Contains the following Airs :—

Brown William, or Illiam Dhoan.

Molly Charane.

False Isabel—Isbel Falsey.

The Storm is up—Callin Veg Dhoan—My little Brown Girl.

The Praise of Wine—Skilley Brishm—Kirkbride.

Berry Dowin—The Brown Oxen.

My Hen Whoomey Vien—My dear old Man.

A Sheign Doin.

Ny Kirree fo Sniaghtey—The Sheep under the Snow.

Ma graigh nagh nare doin farraghten?—Had we not better wait, my dear?

Manks Air—Hunt the Wren.

Manks Dances:

Tapsagyn Jeargey—Red Cockade.

Wandescope—The Wanderer.

COUNT BOROWLASKI.—1820.

Memoirs of Count Borowlaski, containing a sketch of his
Travels, with an account of his reception at the different
Courts of Europe, etc. etc. Written by himself. Durham : printed by Francis Humble and Co. 1820. *Octavo.*
Portrait. Pp. 393.

Isle of Man, pp. 327-348.

MARK ANTHONY MILLS.—1820.

A Full Report of the Trial and Honourable Acquittal of
James M'Crone, Esq., upon an Information for Perjury
preferred against him by Robert Cunninghame, Esq.,
Resident Attorney-General of the Isle of Man ; prosecuted
before the Hon. Thomas Gawne, His Majesty's first
Deemster of the said Isle, on Thursday, September the
7th, 1820, and continued by adjournment to the evening
of Saturday the 9th of same month ; containing copies,
taken from the records of the different proceedings had,
and of the evidence given by the respective witnesses in
the course of the trial : As also, Copies of the Correspondences relating to the matter at issue, and of other documents produced thereat ; To which are added, the Arguments of Counsel on both sides—the Judge's Charge—
and other interesting particulars. The whole carefully
arranged and corrected from notes taken at the trial, by
Mark Anthony Mills, Esq., Member of the Hon. Society
of King's Inn, Dublin, and Solicitor and Public Notary of
the Isle of Man.

> " Maxima admiratio est in Judiciis ; quorum ratio duplex est : nam et ex
> accusatione et defensione constat ; quarum essi laudabitur est defensio, tamen etiam accusatio probata persæpe est."—*Cicero de Officiis.*

Isle of Man, 1820. Printed for the Author at the Phœnix

Press, Douglas. Price 2s. 6d. And with a facsimile of the Book referred to in the Proceedings, 3s. *Octavo.* Pp. 79.

1820.

Appendix (No. 1) to the Lex Scripta of the Isle of Man, containing an Act for the better Making and Repairing and Amending of Highways and Bridges. And also an Act to provide for the Commencement and taking Effect of certain Provisions of the above Act of Tynwald. Published by Authority. Douglas : printed and sold by G. Jefferson, Duke Street. 1820. *Octavo.* Pp. 23. Appendix (No. 2), pp. 1 to 8.

1820.

Account of Stock or Dividends belonging to any Hospital, School, etc., in Ireland, Isle of Man, etc. Printed by order of the House of Commons, 4 May 1820. *Folio.*

JOHN SEACOME.—1821.

The History of the House of Stanley, from the Conquest to the Death of the Right Honourable Edward, late Earl of Derby, in 1776. Containing a Genealogical and Historical Account of that illustrious House. To which is added, A Complete History of the Isle of Man, with a comparative view of the past and present state of Society and Manners : containing also Anecdotes of eminent Persons connected with that Island. Manchester : printed and published by J. Gleave, No. 191 Deansgate, and sold by J. Tallis, 16 Warwick Square, London. 1821. *Octavo.*

The House of Stanley, pp. 265.

The title for the Isle of Man portion is, " A Complete History of the Isle of Man ; containing the Situation and

Geographical Description thereof, the ecclesiastical and civil Histories, the whole order of the governments from the earliest accounts, the nature of the Soil, the produce of the Country and the neighbouring Sea, the number of Inhabitants, and description of their Trade ; with a particular Account of its purchase from the Duke of Athol, by the Government, under the reign of George III." Manchester: printed and published by J. Gleave, No. 196 Deansgate. 1821. *Octavo.* Pp. 260.

This is a greatly enlarged edition of Seacome's history. That of 1793 ends at p. 96. Much new matter is here introduced, to which is added a copious appendix. A portrait, with several plates and coats of arms.

MARK ANTHONY MILLS.—1821.

The Ancient Ordinances and Statute Laws of the Isle of Man ; carefully copied from, and compared with, the Authentic Records. Together with copious extracts from the several British Statutes which have reference thereto. Published under the patronage of the Right Hon. Lord Sidmouth, one of His Majesty's Principal Secretaries of State ; His Grace John, Duke of Atholl, Governor-in-Chief ; the Hon. Cornelius Smelt, Lieut.-Governor of the Isle of Man ; the members of the Manx Council, His Majesty's two Deemsters, the House of Keys, and Gentlemen of the Manx Bar, etc. etc. By Mark Anthony Mills, Esq., Member of the Honourable the Society of King's Inn. Douglas: printed at the Phœnix Press. 1821. *Royal Octavo.* Pp. 557. Index, etc., pp. xii.

An Index is added. The last Act in this collection was promulgated on the 1st November 1820. Some copies were struck off in folio. This is the Text-book of the Manx Bar, but many of the earlier Acts are very incorrectly copied from the originals in the Rolls Office.

The Manx Legislature have decided to print the whole of the Manx Statutes from the copies in the Rolls Office, the expense to be defrayed out of the insular revenue.

1821.

The Rising Sun, or Mona's Herald.

> Fiat Lux, et lux fuit—et eundo lucemus.
> " Mens conscia recti famæ mendacia ridet."

The first number of this weekly journal, which was published and edited by Captain Colquitt, appeared on April the 24th, 1821.   In December 1824 the title was altered to *The Manx Rising Sun*, and in April 1826 the present title, *The Manx Sun*, was adopted.   Published on a Saturday.

1821.

The Douglas Reflector, and Isle of Man Magazine.   Douglas: printed by G. Jefferson, Duke Street.   Published by Lane and Son, at the Wellington News Room, Pier ; to whom orders for the work and communications for the Editor are required to be sent, post paid. Sold also by Mrs. Joyner, Post Office, Castletown ; Miss Louisa Cannell, Kirk Michael ; and Mr. John Townsend, Ramsey, by whom orders are received. (Price 5d. British.) *Octavo.*

The first number was published in February ; the publication was only continued for six numbers.

1821.

A Correct Report of the Speech of His Grace, John, Duke of Atholl, Captain-General, Governor-in-Chief, etc. etc. etc., of the Isle of Man, to the Court of Tynwald, assembled at Castletown on the 26th of November 1821. Douglas, Isle of Man : printed by T. Davies, at the Phœnix Press, for the Proprietor. 1821. *Octavo.*

Rev. Hugh Stowell.—1821.

Memoirs of the Rev. Joseph Stowell.

> ——" I had a brother once :
> Peace to the memory of a man of worth !
> A man of letters, and of manners too ;
> Of manners sweet as virtue ever wears,
> When gay good humour dresses her in smiles."
>
> *Cowper.*

By the Rev. Hugh Stowell, Rector of Ballaugh, Isle of Mann. Wellington, Salop : printed by and for F. Houlston and Son ; and sold by Scatchard and Letterman, Ave Maria Lane, London. 1821. 12*mo.* Dedication " To the Pupils of the late Rev. Joseph Stowell," pp. v. to vii. Preface, pp. ix. to xi. Memoirs, pp. 1 to 124. A Sermon by the Rev. Joseph Stowell, pp. 125 to 141.

The Rev. Joseph Stowell was Master of the Free Grammar School at Peel, and also of the Mathematical School, under whose care they became united in 1799. Born 22d December 1772. He died 15th June 1801.

The Rev. Hugh Stowell was also the author of several tracts published in Houlston's Series ; as

No. 17. The Pious Manx Peasant, or the History of William Curphey. He was a pupil of the Rev. Hugh Stowell, canon of Chester.

No. 18. The Pious Manx Schoolmistress (Jane Teare), a living character. Both the above were of Kirk Lonan.

Also the Life of Pat, the Irish Chimney Sweeper.

Also, published by the Religious Tract Society, No. 513, The Happy Man, or the Life of William Kelly, a Tailor in the Isle of Man, who turned Fisherman, and lived for many years of his life on less than two shillings a week. A True History.

SAMUEL HAINING.—1822.

A Historical Sketch and Descriptive View of the Isle of Man :
   designed as a Companion to those who visit and make the
   tour of it.   By Samuel Haining.   Douglas : printed and
   sold by G. Jefferson, for the Author ; sold also by Lane
   and Son, Wellington News Room, Pier ; and J. Townsend,
   Ramsey.   1822.   *Small Octavo.*   Pp. 192.   Map and two
   Views, Castle Rushen and Peel Castle.   ·

The Rev. Samuel Haining was the Minister of the Independent Chapel in Atholl Street, Douglas.   This was the first
Guide Book designed for Tourists in the Isle of Man.

The second edition was published in 1824, " greatly improved."

Mr. Haining made some remarks on the Manx Methodists, which called forth some angry discussions in the public
prints.   A Wesleyan preacher, Mr. Humphrey Stevenson,
discovered seven grammatical errors in one page.   Mr. H.
called Stevenson a *Goliah in grammar !*   These remarks were
left out in the next edition.   Mr. Haining published " A
Sermon on Regeneration : shewing that it is essential to Sal-
vation : explaining its Nature ; exhibiting the advantages
arising from it, etc."   Douglas.   1822.   Price 6d.

C. HULBERT.—No date.—[1822.]

Strangers' Friend ; or a Guide to the Isle of Man, Halton
   Runcorn, Hawkstone Park, and Shrewsbury.   To which
   are added Interesting descriptions of various sublimities
   and curiosities of Nature, in different parts of the Globe.
   By C. Hulbert, Author of the Select Museum of Nature
   and Art, Literary Beauties, and Varieties, etc.

" Perhaps I may see these delightful scenes no more ; but oh ! ye objects,
     do you appear as lovely and delightful to my children and to my
     friends, as ye now do to me."—*Dupaty.*

Shrewsbury : printed by the Author : and sold by G. and W. B. Whittaker, London : Clarkes, Thomson, and Roberts, Manchester ; Kaye, Liverpool ; and Jefferson, Douglas. 24*mo.* Pp. 12-92.

" The Isle of Man," pp. 25 to 42. A Woodcut of Bishop Wilson and a Manx Cottage. The Tour was made in May 1820.

1822.

Banglaneyn y Chredjue Creestee, as oardaghyn crauee Agglish Hostyn, er nyn Soiaghey magh liorish ny ardaspickyn as ny aspickyn as ooilley ny saggyrtyn, ayns y chaglym cooidjagh oc, er ny'reayll ayns Lunnin ayns y Vlein 1562, son shaghney streu mychione y chredjue, as son shickyraghey cordail mychione Crauecaght Firrinagh. Lunnin : Prentit liorish Ellerton as Henderson, Johnson's Court, son yn Prayer-Book as Homily Society, 134 Salisbury Square. 1822. 12*mo.* Pp. 16.

The thirty-nine Articles in Manx.

1822.

Extracts from the Reports given in the *Isle of Man Gazette,* and the *Rising Sun,* on the proceedings at the several Tynwald Courts held in the Isle of Man, by his Grace, John, Duke of Atholl, Governor-in-Chief and Captain-General of the Island, and Cornelius Smelt, Esq., Lieutenant-Governor thereof. From the 5th July to the 1st October 1822 inclusive. Douglas : printed by T. Davies at the Phœnix Press. 1822. *Octavo.* Pp. 130.

Giving an account of the dispute with the Duke of Atholl and the Keys respecting the appointment of Commissioners of Highways. At the Tynwald held at St. John's, on the 5th July, in this year, the Duke of Atholl entertained 180 ladies and gentlemen to " an excellent repast, with wines of the best quality," in a large tent erected on the Fair field.

In this account is also an extract from the House of Keys Journal, 30th July 1822, of "Statement of Charities for Promotion of Education in the Isle of Man, and abuses thereof," pp. 107-121.

HENRY ROBERT OSWALD.—1823.

On the Stratification of Alluvial Deposits and the Crystalization of Calcareous Stalactites, in a letter to John Macculloch, Esq., M.D., etc. etc. etc.   By H. R. Oswald. Douglas : printed by G. Jefferson, Duke Street. 1823. *Octavo.*   Pp. 48.

LIEUT. J. C. BLUETT.—1823.

The Address and Reply delivered by Lieut. J. Courtney Bluett, R.N. (with other proceedings), in an Appeal before the Honourable the House of Keys, assembled at Castletown in the Isle of Man, on Wednesday and Thursday, the 26th and 27th February 1823.   Douglas : printed for John Sumner, *True Manxman* Office. *Octavo.* Pp. 96.

This was an appeal from a Common Law Jury, on a breach of promise of marriage, in which Miss Ritchie obtained £500 damages. The House of Keys awarded £50.   For further matter on this subject see Duggan's "Touchstone," 1845, pp. 36 to 47.   The whole of the Evidence produced on the trial in the Common Law Courts, October 9th, 1822, is here printed.

GEORGE THOMPSON.—1823.

The Sentimental Gleaner, from Esk Bank Academy to the Isle of Man, retrograding to Penrith, Cumberland, *via* Whitehaven.   By George Thomson, author of the "Sentimental Tour to London," etc.

> " Omne tulit punctum, qui miscuit utile dulci
> Lectorum delectando, pariterque monendo."
>
> *Horace.*

Penrith: printed for the Author by J. Brown. 1823. 12*mo*. Pp. 228.

Address, etc., pp. iii. to vi.

The author was a humorous Cumberland schoolmaster.

1823.

The Isle of Man Diary and New Almanack, for the year of our Lord 1823: Being the third after Bissextile or Leap Year, and fourth of the Reign of His present Majesty, King George the Fourth; including a correct Tide Table; as also, Equation, Meteorological Bearings, Distances, Interest, and other Tables; with a variety of additional Articles useful to Gentlemen, Merchants, Seamen, Farmers, and the Public in general. Douglas: printed by T. Davies, at the Phœnix Press, Parade, for the Proprietor. *Small octavo.* Pp. 58. A small Map of the Isle.

HENRY ROBERT OSWALD.—1823.

The Geographical and Topographical Guide of the Isle of Man, intended for the use of Travellers and Tourists, and of those who, visiting this fine Island as sea bathing quarters, or as a cheap, pleasant, and convenient marine residence, are desirous of a succinct description of it.

> " Health in the breeze, retirement in the vale ;
> Where moderation dwells, bath'd in the tide
> Of vigorous ocean."

Douglas: printed and sold by G. Jefferson; sold also by E. Willan, Liverpool; Baldwin, Cradock, and Joy, London, 1823. *Small octavo.* Pp. 76. Index, pp. 2. View of Douglas.

DRS. JAMIESON and DILLON.—1823.

Transactions of the Society of the Antiquaries of Scotland,
Vol. ii., Part ii.   Edinburgh : printed by Alex. Smellie,
Printer to the Society of Antiquaries, for W. and C. Tait.
Princes Street; and T. Cadell, Strand, London.   1823.
Quarto.

Pp. 490-501.—" Account of a Stone with a Runic Inscription, presented to the Society by the late Sir Alexander Setoun,
of Preston, and of some other Inscriptions of the same kind
in the Isle of Man.   A plate of the Runic Inscriptions at
Kirk Michael and Kirk Braddan, with the various readings
from Camden's " Britannia," Gibson's and Gough's editions.
Mr. Oswald of Douglas communicated to the Society several
of these Inscriptions in 1817.

HENRY ROBERT OSWALD.—1823.

Transactions of the Society of the Antiquaries of Scotland.
Vol. ii., Part ii.   Edinburgh : 1823.   *Quarto.*

Pp. 502-508.—" Notes of Reference to the Series of Delineations of the Runic and other Ancient Crosses found in the
Isle of Man."

Three Plates, containing 17 figures of Crosses, beautifully
engraved by W. H. Lizars.   Mr. Oswald of Douglas communicated this paper.

1823.

A Return of the Civil Establishment of this Island ; stating
the name and office of each person ; whether he does the
duty in person, or by deputy ; and by what authority the
appointment is made : stating also the amount of salaries
and allowances of every kind, received by each ; and the

amount of contingent expenses, under separate heads, in the year 1822. Ordered by the House of Commons to be printed, 20 June 1823. *Folio.* 1 Sheet.

1823.

Returns of the Produce of Customs and Expenses of its Establishment. Ordered by the House of Commons to be printed, 25 June 1823. *Folio.* A sheet. Pp. 3.

—— MARSDEN.—[1823.]

Historical Notices of Edward and William Christian, two characters in Peveril of the Peak. Printed by B. Bensley, Bolt Court, Fleet Street. *Small octavo.* Pp. 42. No place or date.

" Peveril of the Peak " was first published in 1822, and the " Historical Notices" have been reprinted in the later editions of that work in "Appendix to Introduction," along with the " Lament for William Dhône," and a copy of the Order of the Privy Council, dated " Whitehall, 5th August 1663," also in " Antiquary's Portfolio," 1825.   This edition was privately printed, and very few copies circulated, being afterwards called in by Mr. Marsden when he left the Island. He resided for some years in the neighbourhood of Castletown. His brother, J. A. Marsden, of Liverpool, planted the grounds at Glen Helen and Rhenass in this Island, now much resorted to by strangers. In the first edition of this List it was, in error, attributed to Col. Wilks, author of the " History of Mysur."

1823.

The True Manxman.   The first No. published by J. Sumner. Continued one year.

1824.

Pigot and Co.'s Directory of the Isle of Man.   *Octavo.*

This was the first introduction of the Isle of Man into their Directories.

1824.

Petition to the House of Commons of the House of Keys of the Isle of Man.   Presented May 1824, with observations.   London : printed by A. J. Valpy, Red Lion Court, Fleet Street.   1824.   *Octavo.*   Pp. 43.

See the Blue Book, 1825, for Answers to the Charges contained in this petition.

1824.

Papers relating to the Isle of Mann, ordered by the House of Commons to be printed, 20 February 1824.   *Folio.* Pp. 2.

Instructions to his Grace the Duke of Atholl, " directing him to exclude the Keys from further attendance at Courts of Tynwald, for the purposes of General Gaol Delivery."

SAMUEL HAINING.—1824.

The Isle of Man Guide ; containing an Historical Sketch, and Descriptive Views of the Island.   Illustrated with a Map and Plates.   Liverpool.   1824.   *Small Octavo.*   Pp. 201.

The Second Edition, " carefully corrected and greatly improved."   Editions published with change of date in 1839-1841.

RT. REV. ROBERT KEITH.—1824.—(Rev. M. Russell.)

An Historical Catalogue of the Scottish Bishops down to the year 1688, by the Right Rev. Robert Keith, etc.   Also, an account of all the Religious Houses in Scotland at the

Reformation, corrected and continued to the present time, with Life of the Author, by the Rev. M. Russell, LL.D. Edinbro': 1824. *Octavo.*

Isle of Man.—The See of the Isles, giving an Account of the Bishops of Man, pp. 293-308. An Edition in 4to. was published at Edinburgh, 1755.

JOHN MACTAGGART.—1824.

The Scottish Gallovidian Encyclopedia, or the original, Anti-
quated, and Natural curiosities, of the south of Scotland ;
containing sketches of eccentric characters and curious
places, with explanations of singular words, terms, and
phrases ; interspersed with Poems, Tales, Anecdotes, etc.,
and various other strange matters ; the whole illustrative
of the ways of the Peasantry, and Manners of Caledonia ;
drawn out and alphabetically arranged. By John Mactaggart.

> " May ne'er waur be amang us."
> *Tinkler's Toast.*

London : printed for the Author ; and sold by Morrison, Fenchurch Street, etc., and Edinburgh, Glasgow, Ayr, etc. 1824. *Octavo.* Pp. 504. Introduction, dated Torrs, Feby. 12th, 1823, pp. xii.

Many of the Sayings and Customs of Galloway are also to be found in the Isle of Man, and which are very curiously illustrated in this little known and scarce work of Mactaggart's. The Isle of Man is noticed at pp. 157-308, and 502.

WM. ROPER.—1825.

A Short History of the Transactions, in the Isle of Man, on
which the House of Keys founded their late Petition to
the House of Commons against his Grace the Duke of
Atholl ; together with Answers to the Charges therein

contained. Published from authentic documents. Second edition. Douglas: printed by G. Jefferson, Duke Street. *Octavo.* Pp. 128. Commonly called "The Blue Book."

A curious exposé of matters connected with the administration of justice, and the *integrity* of persons in office.

The first edition appeared the same year.

1825.

Jefferson's Improved Manks Almanack and Tide Table : showing the Rising and Setting of the Sun and Moon ; also times of High Water for the Isle of Man, and at the different Ports and Harbours in the North, and in St. George's and Bristol Channels, with a variety of other new, accurate, and useful Tables, for the year 1825 ; being the first after Bissextile or Leap Year, and the Sixth of the Reign of his Majesty George IV., with an Appendix.

"They continue this day, according to thine ordinances."
Psalm cxix. 91.

Douglas : printed and sold by G. Jefferson, Bookseller, Duke Street. *Small octavo.* Pp. 60.

Gentleman's Magazine.—1825.

Account of the Isle of Man. Dated "Rosegill, Westmoreland, Aug. 12." Signed G. H. *Gentleman's Magazine.* 1825. Part ii. vol. xcv. pp. 99 to 103.

At page 460, an Account of the disturbances on the Tithe on Green Crop.

E. S. CRAVEN.—1825.

A Legend of Mona. A tale in two Cantos. By E. S. Craven. Douglas : printed by J. Penrice, *Manx Rising Sun* Office, and published by L. Lane, at his Circulating Library, North Quay, Douglas ; sold also by the principal

Shopkeepers throughout the Island. 1825. *Small octavo.* Pp. 44.

The first publication of the Authoress. It is reprinted in Mrs. Craven Green's "Sea Weeds and Heath Flowers." Douglas. 1858.

———— MARSDEN.—1825.

The Antiquary's Portfolio, or Cabinet Selection of Historical and Literary Curiosities, etc. By J. S. Forsyth. In two volumes. London : MDCCCXXV. 12mo.

In Vol. ii. pp. 118 to 151, is " Historical Notices of two characters in Peveril of the Peak," by Mr. Marsden. See a notice under date 1823, page 127, *supra*.

TREVOR ASHE.—1825.

The Manks Sketch Book, or Beauties of the Isle of Man. By T. Ashe. Douglas. 1825. *Oblong Octavo.*

Beautiful Prints of the Island Scenery.

Mr. Ashe was the Author of " Belville and Julia," a Manx Novel, which I have not met with.

Olphar Hamst, in " Notes and Queries," fourth series, vol. ii. p. 340, 1868, says that Captain Thomas Ashe was a sort of literary Jack-of-all-Trades, and author of some twenty works on various subjects, and during his residence in the Isle of Man wrote and published there, " The Manks Monastery ; or Memoirs of Belville and Julia." He was of an Irish family, and died in poverty about 183 . He was the author of " The Hermit in York." Hull. 1823. *Square 12mo.* Pp. 123. Only a few copies printed.

ROBERT STEWART.—1825.

Meteorological Observations made in the Isle of Man. 1822-

25.   By Robert Stewart, Esq., in Brewster's *Edinburgh Journal of Science*, vol. v. pp. 231.

BENJAMIN SMYTHE.—1826.

Map of the Isle of Man.

To the Right Hon. George Canning, M.P., His Majesty's Secretary of State for Foreign Affairs, this Map of the Isle of Man is, by Permission, respectfully dedicated by his faithful and obedient servant, John Drinkwater.   From a Trigonometrical Survey by Mr. Benjamin Smythe.   Published as the Act directs by John Drinkwater, Esq., Sept. 1st, 1826.   Sheet, 24 inches by 36 inches.   Engraved by J. and A. Walker, Pool Lane, Liverpool.

REV. ROBERT BROWN.—1826.

Poems : principally on Sacred Subjects.   By the Rev. Robert Brown, Minister of St. Matthew's, Douglas, Isle of Man.

> " If I one soul improve, I have not lived in vain."
>   *Beattie's Minstrel.*

Published by James Nisbet, 21 Berners Street, London. MDCCCXXVI.   12*mo.*   Pp. 155.

The Poems connected with the Island are :—Page 52, Elegy on the Right Rev. Thomas Wilson, D.D., Lord Bishop of Sodor and Man ; page 60, My Native Land ; page 62, Lines on Viewing Peel Castle by Moonlight ; page 93, Lines on Viewing the Nunnery, near Douglas, in the Isle of Man. The author was Vicar of Kirk Braddan, and died in 1846.

SIR WM. HILLARY, Bart.—1826.

The National Importance of a Great Central Harbour for the Irish Sea, accessible at all times to the largest vessels, proposed to be constructed at Douglas, in the Isle of Man.

By Sir William Hillary, Baronet, author of "An Appeal to
the British Nation on the Humanity and Policy of form-
ing a National Institution for the Preservation of Life from
Shipwreck," etc.   Douglas : printed for G. Jefferson,
Duke Street : Baldwin, Cradock, and Joy, London : E.
Willan jun., Liverpool. 1826. *Octavo.* Pp. 21.

A Plan of Douglas Bay and Harbour.

DR. HIBBERT.—1826.

A Memoir of the Discovery of the *Megaceros Hibernicus*, or
Fossil Elk, in the Isle of Man. Published in the fifth
number of the *Edinburgh Journal of Science*, 1826, vol.
iii., pp. 15, 31, and 129.

"Generally known under the term Irish Elk ; it ought to
have been called Manx Elk, or *Megaceros Monensis*, as the
first described specimen was found in the Isle of Man, and
the remains are abundant for the size of the Island."—
Cumming's "Isle of Man," p. 10, note.

Other remains are known to exist in the Island, and only
require a favourable time for exhumation.

H. R. OSWALD.—1826.

Observations relative to the Fossil Elk of the Isle of Man.
By H. R. Oswald, Esq., F.S.A., Surgeon. Published in
the 3d vol. of the *Edinburgh Journal of Science*, 1826, p. 28.

REV. HUGH STOWELL.—1826.

Memoirs of Mr. William Leece, a native of the Isle of Man ;
with copious extracts from his Journal. By the Rev.
Hugh Stowell, Rector of Ballaugh, Isle of Man.

"No species of writing seems more worthy of cultivation than
Biography ; none can more certainly enchain the heart by irresist-
ible interest, or more widely diffuse instruction to every diversity
of condition."—*Johnson.*

Liverpool : printed for D. Marples, and Chalmers and Collins, Glasgow. Sold also by Westley and Davis, J. Nisbet, and J. and C. Evans, London ; Waugh and Innes, Edinburgh ; and R. M. Tims, Dublin. 1826. *Small Octavo.* Pp. 194.

Inscribed to Mrs. Bell, Oak Hill, Isle of Man. Frontispiece, View of Oak Hill.

Mr. Leece died at Clifton, 11th August 1824. Mr. Stowell also wrote A Narrative of the Life of Miss Sophia Leece.

Dr. Watts.—1826.

Divine and Moral Songs. Translated into Manx. By George Killey, Clerk of Kirk Onchan. Douglas. 1826.

1827.

The First Annual Report of the Isle of Man District Association of the Royal National Institution for the Preservation of Life from Shipwreck. Supported by Donations and Voluntary Subscriptions. Established 1826. Douglas : printed by G. Jefferson, Duke Street. 1827. *Octavo.* Pp. 27.

Sir Wm. Hillary, Bart., was the projector of the Society, which had its origin in the Isle of Man. He wrote the "Appeal to the British Nation" on this subject in 1823. Dated, "Douglas, Isle of Man, 28th Feby."

1827.

The Report of the Commissioners connected with the Isle of Man Herring Fishery. 1827. Dated Edinburgh, 30th April. J. Penrice, Printer, *Manx Sun* Office, North Quay, Douglas. *Folio.* P. 1.

This was in reply to the Report of the Committee of

Legislature of 22d Feby. 1827, desiring to fix a time for the commencement of Herring Fishing, as the Act of 29 Geo. II. cap. 23, allows it at all times and seasons, under a penalty of £100 for any one obstructing the same.

1827.

Report of the Committee of Legislature relative to the Herring Fishery on the coasts of the Isle of Man. J. Penrice, Printer, *Manx Sun* Office, Douglas. *Folio.* Pp. 4. Dated 22d Feby. 1827. Signed by M. Wilks, Geo. Quirk, John Moore, W. L. Drinkwater, J. Quirk, J. Quilliam, John Llewellyn, J. M'Hutchin.

REV. HUGH STOWELL.—1827.

Memoirs of Mr. F. D. P. Geneste.

> " Purpureus veluti cum flos succisus aratro
> Languescit moriens."—*Virgil.*

By the Rev. Hugh Stowell, Rector of Ballaugh, Isle of Man. Liverpool: printed and sold by D. Marples. Sold also by Wightman and Cramp, etc. 1827. *Small 12mo.* Pp. 139.

Francis De la Pryme Geneste, Son of Lewis Geneste, Esq., was born in Douglas, Sept. 20, 1804. Died 1826. An edition appeared in 1843.

P. LYNCH.—1828.

The Life of St. Patrick, Apostle of Ireland, etc. By P. Lynch, Secretary to the Gaelic Society. Dublin: printed by Thomas Haydock and Son, 8 Lower Exchange Street, next door to the Chapel. 1828. 12mo. Refers to the Isle of Man at pp. 155, 156, and in the Appendix, pp. 194-201. A portrait of St. Patrick in his robes and pastoral staff.

H. R. OSWALD, F.A.S.—1828.

Some Observations recommendatory of a General Infirmary for the Isle of Man (Luke x. 35). By H. R. Oswald, F.A.S., Surgeon to the Household. Douglas : printed by G. Jefferson. 1828. *Foolscap Octavo.* Pp. 12.

Gentleman's Magazine.—1829.

On the Round Tower in Peel Castle. A letter dated " Dublin, Dec. 22," signed J. S. *Gentleman's Magazine*, 1829, part ii., vol. xcix., p. 14.

The writer considers that such Towers were built at various periods between the sixth and twelfth centuries, for belfries attached to religious buildings.

1829.

Liorish sheshaght ec Bristol, jeh Agglish Hostyn, son skeaylley lioaryn beggey crauee. Cooney dy Gheddyn Aarloo son Baase : ny yn Chreestee er Lhiabbee dy Hingys. Sold at the Depository, 6 Clare Street, Bristol, etc. Printed by J. Chilcott, 30 Wine Street, Bristol. 1829. 12*mo.* Pp. 20.

Many other tracts of this description were printed at Bristol in the Manx language, as, Coontey jeh saggyrt. 12*mo.* By the Rev. W. Tyndall.

1829.

Copies of the Contracts and Agreement between the Lords Commissioners of his Majesty's Treasury and his Grace John Duke of Atholl respecting the Sale and Conveyance of the Isle of Man.

Ordered by the House of Commons to be printed, 18th May 1829. *Folio.* Pp. 15.

REV. THOMAS HOWARD.—1829.

Plain and Practical Sermons. By the Rev. Thomas Howard, Vicar of Braddan, Isle of Man.

> "I will endeavour that you may be able, after my decease, to have these things always in remembrance."—2 *Peter* i. 15.

Third edition, revised. London. James Nisbet, Berners Street. 1829. Pp. 272.

Dedicated to the Inhabitants of Braddan, Isle of Man. Sermon xviii. *The blessedness who die in the Lord.* Preached on the death of Mrs. Stowell, wife of the Rev. Hugh Stowell, Rector of Ballaugh, Isle of Man. Rev. xiv. 13.

WM. BENNET.—1829.

Sketches of the Isle of Man. By Wm. Bennet, of Wester Duddingston, County of Edinburgh. London : 1829.

1830.

The Rules of the Isle of Man Society for the Promotion and Encouragement of Rural Economy and Industry generally. Douglas : printed by J. Quiggin, at North Quay. 1830. 12*mo.* Pp. 8.

SIR WM. HILLARY, Bart.—1830.

A Letter to the Trustees of the Academic Fund, on the Expediency and Importance of establishing a School of Navigation, as a branch of the Projected College, in the Isle of Man. By Sir William Hillary, Baronet. Douglas : printed and published by G. Jefferson, Duke Street. 1830. *Octavo.* Pp. 15.

THOMAS HOWARD.—1830.

Howard's " Vade Mecum " or Tourist's Companion from Manchester (by the Railway) to Liverpool, and thence through to the Isle of Man. Together with a Map of the Island. Dedicated by permission to Sir George Drinkwater, Knt. Price 2s. 6d. Sold by Worrall and Taylor, Clarendon Buildings, and Mr. Clement, artist, Bold Street, Liverpool. On a sheet in a case. Date on the Map 1830. Published by Quiggin, Douglas.

Mr. Howard issued proposals for publishing a work on the Island, and obtained upwards of 500 subscribers to it, but the MS. was by some means lost and the work never appeared. Connected with it the following advertisement was issued :— "15th September 1828. By Particular Desire, and with high and extensive Patronage, will be published in the shape of a small octavo, a Work, by T. Howard, Esquire, to be entitled An 18 Years' Residence on the Isle of Man. The work is intended to convey, in a manner and style as pleasing and agreeable as possible, correct information on those subjects connected with the Island which must be equally useful to Strangers and Native Residents, whether men of business or pleasure. The work will comprise also the most active and eventful period of the Author's Life ; noticing in a particular manner the many advantages and disadvantages resulting from a married life ; also, every vicissitude likely to amuse or instruct will be carefully narrated, without the slightest intention to outrage the feelings of the scrupulous or wound the keen sensibility of the delicate. The author, solicitous only to please, will, without regard to rank or station, insert every biographical incident that may appear worthy of notice. A very few highly finished sketches of the most interesting views and scenery will be included in the work."

The original subscription book, in the autograph of almost every respectable inhabitant of the Island, is in my possession. Mr. Howard was well known under the cognomen of "The Duke of Norfolk." His portrait was published in 1834.

1831.

The Isle of Man Charities. Liverpool : printed by D. Marples, Lord Street. 1831. *Octavo.* Pp. 139.

" The profits of this publication, should there be any, will be applied towards the building of a Vicarage House in the parish of Malew."—*Note on a Slip.*

This account was drawn up by J. M'Hutchin, Esq., Clerk of the Rolls, and George Quirk, Esq., and is brought down to the year 1827. A Committee of the Tynwald Court has been appointed, and are now investigating the charities up to the present time, 1861.

A large additional mass of information connected with the Charities of the Island has been obtained by this Committee, but they have not, up to this time (1876), given in a report of the same.

1831.

Returns of the Expense of the whole Establishments now maintained in the Isle of Man, and paid from public monies ; also, of the Duties of Customs and Excise in the Isle of Man, where the rates are less than in England or Scotland.

Ordered by the House of Commons to be printed, 9th February 1831. *Folio.* Pp. 6.

H. R. OSWALD.—No date.—[1831.]

The Isle of Man Guide ; being a Historical, Geographical, and Topographical Account of its past and present state ; intended for the use of Travellers and Tourists, and of those who, visiting this fine Island as sea bathing quarters, or as a cheap, pleasant, and convenient Marine Residence, are desirous of a succinct description of it. By H. R. Oswald, F.R.S.

> "Health in the breeze, retirement in the vale,
> Where moderation dwells, bath'd in the tide
> Of vigorous ocean."

Third Edition. Embellished with a Frontispiece Map, four Lithographic Views, and numerous Wood Engravings. Douglas: printed and published by G. Jefferson, Duke Street. (No date.) *Small Octavo.*

Introduction, etc., pp. xv. ; Guide, pp. 125.

George Geneste.—1832.

Statute Laws of the Isle of Man, passed since the year 1821. With an Appendix containing the Regulations of the Insolvent Debtors' Court; the Act of Parliament for Regulating the Trade of the Isle of Man ; and an abridgment of such British Statutes as relate to the Isle of Man. Published by the Authority, and under the patronage of the Honourable Cornelius Smelt, Lieutenant-Governor, the Council, Deemsters, and Keys of the Isle of Man. By George Geneste, Esq., Advocate. Liverpool : printed by David Marples, Lord Street. MDCCCXXXII. *Royal Octavo*, pp. 146.

" Contains, with the exception of one or two temporary Acts which have expired, all the Insular Statutes which have been passed since the publication of Mr. Mills's folio edition of ' The Statute Laws of the Isle of Man.' "—*Preface.*

The last Act in this work was promulgated on the 5th July 1832.

Rev. T. Stephens.—1832.

A Poetical Guide to the Isle of Mann, by a Manksman. Liverpool : printed by S. H. Sankey, Vine Place, Lord Street. May be had of all the Booksellers. 1832. Price eighteenpence. *12mo.* Pp. 53.

A Plate of "A View of Peel Bridge." The Author was Vicar of Kirk Patrick, and died in 1841.

1832.

A Catalogue of the Books, Pamphlets, etc. etc., comprising the Isle of Man Library, on the first day of January 1832. To which are prefixed the Laws for regulating the same. Douglas : printed for the Proprietors by G. Jefferson. 1832. 12*mo.* Pp. 40.

The books are contained in Cases (14) marked A to O. The total number of volumes in this catalogue is 1228. This Library was dispersed by auction. This Catalogue was reprinted in May 1842, with additions made since the former publication.

J. CURRAN.—1832.

Observations on the Rev. Mr. Aitken's Sermon, preached in the Methodist Chapel, Douglas, from John ix. 4, on Friday evening, Nov. 9, 1832. By J. Curran. Douglas : printed and published by G. Jefferson. 1832. 12*mo.* Pp. 16.

EDWARD TAGART.—1832.

A Memoir of the late Captain Peter Heywood, R.N., with Extracts from his Diaries and Correspondence. By Edward Tagart. London : published by Effingham Wilson, Royal Exchange. 1832. *Octavo.*

Preface and Contents, pp. viii. ; Memoir, pp. 332.

This is the Memoir of a Native of the Isle of Man, who was born at the Nunnery on the 6th June 1773, his father being a Deemster of the Island. He was an officer on board the Bounty, when a portion of the crew mutinied, on the 28th of April 1789, and for which he was afterwards tried. The letters of this truly honourable young officer are well worthy of perusal; and those of his warmly attached sister, Nessy Heywood, dated from the Isle of Man, breathe the most heroic devotion and affection for her brother, seldom if ever to be met with.   He died on the 10th of February 1831.

Lieut. John Shipp.—1832.

Memoirs of his extraordinary Military Career. Written by himself. 1832. London. *Octavo.* 3 vols., with his Portrait.

Lieut. Shipp was a native of the Isle of Man. This has passed through four editions, 1834-1840 in one vol., and 1842.

1833.

Proceedings in Chancery, 7th March 1833, Isle of Man, on the Petition of James Tertius Thomson, Esq., of Knockan House, Ballaugh Glen, praying to set aside the writ of arrest "Kelly *v.* Thomson," for Rent not due : Also the Trial at Common Law, "Thomson *v.* Kelly," before His Honour Deemster Heywood and a Special Jury, for £500 damages for said arrest, for which the Jury returned a verdict £150 damages, and costs, in favour of the Plaintiff. Tried at Castletown, 9th October 1833, but appealed against by the defendant to the House of Keys. With an Appendix, containing Copies of the Documents, Letters, etc., read, referred to, and exhibited in Court, illustrative of the whole litigation. Liverpool : printed for the Compiler, by Evans, Chegwin, and Hall, Castle Street. 1833. *Octavo.* Pp. 23. Appendix, pp. ix.

John Wood.—1833.

Plan of Douglas, Isle of Man, from Actual Survey. By John

Wood, 1833, Surveyor, Cannan Grove, Edinbro. Sheet 26 in. by 35 in. This Plan also contains a Plan of Douglas Bay and Harbour, with Sir William Hillary's Breakwater. 1826. Also a Plan of Castletown.

Mona's Herald.—1833.

The first number published August 3, 1833. Douglas : printed by William Walls, New Bond Street, and Robert Farghar, Atholl Street, and published at the *Herald* Office and General Printing Establishment, New Bond Street Lane.

Anne Tallant.—1834.

Octavia Elphinstone, a Manx Story ; and Lois, a Drama, founded on a Legend in the Noble Family of ——. By Miss Ann Tallant. In 2 vols. London : J. Hatchard and Son, 187 Piccadilly. 1834. 12*mo.*

A note at the end of vol. ii. says—This tale is founded on an unfortunate accident which occurred to Miss Ann Fell, of Douglas, a young lady of 17 or 18 years of age, whilst walking on Douglas Head on the evening of Tuesday the 20th 18(19), who fell down the steep rocks at "The Pidgeon's Cove," about three miles to the south of Douglas Head, upon a shelving part of the rock, a considerable distance below, and which was nearly surrounded by the sea. She remained on this rock until Friday the 23d, when she was seen by some boatmen, who conveyed her to Douglas in their boat, and restored her to her parents. The only subsistence she had during her stay on the rock was by a small spring of water trickling down, but so small she could scarcely avail herself of it, scooped up with the aid of a flitter shell, which she had found. Miss Fell died in Douglas in 1875.

J. Taggart.—1834.

A Plan of Douglas, Isle of Man. Surveyed by J. Taggart, Architect. 1834. On a Sheet, 20 in. by 14.

1834.

An Act for better Supplying the Town of Douglas with Water Douglas : printed for the Company by J. Quiggin. 1834. Price Sixpence. *Octavo.* Pp. 16.

1834.

Subscriptions for Building a Tower of Refuge from Shipwreck. on St. Mary's Rock, in Douglas Bay, Isle of Man, on the Plan proposed by Sir William Hillary, Bart. Printed by G. Jefferson. 1834. *Octavo.* Pp. 4.

Total cost of the Tower £254 : 12s. Of this sum Sir Wm. Hillary paid £78 : 6s.

Archibald Cregeen.—1835.

A Dictionary of the Manx Language, with the corresponding Words or Explanations in English ; interspersed with many Gaelic Proverbs : the Parts of Speech, the Genders, and the Accents of the Manx Words are carefully marked ; with some etymological observations never before published. By Archibald Cregeen, Arbory, Isle of Man. "Ballyn dy loayragh shiu ooilley lish glaraghyn," etc.— St. Paul ; 1 Cor. xiv. 5. Douglas : printed and published for the Author by J. Quiggin, North Quay : Whittaker, Treacher, and Arnot, London : Evans, Chegwin, and Hall, Liverpool. MDCCCXXXV. *Octavo.* Pp. 188.

The Author died before he could complete the Second Part, the English and Manx. There is a valuable Introduction to the Manx Language, preceding the Dictionary, giving an idea of the construction of the Language, and forming the outlines of a Manks Grammar. The Author observes, " It appears like a piece of exquisite net-work interwoven together in a masterly manner, and framed by the hand of a most skilful workman, equal to the composition of the most learned, and not the production of chance. The depth of meaning that abounds in many of the words must be conspicuous to every person versed in the language." It is dated " Kirk Arbory, 5th June 1834." According to a list at the end, 418 copies were subscribed for. The Author of this Account purchased the sheets left on hand, from which some Copies were afterwards made up ; some little difference is observable, arising from the few sheets reprinted being in a larger type, when some few words were unavoidably omitted. Mr. George Borrow, the Author of " The Bible in Spain " and other Works, and who for some time resided in the Island collecting its Legendary fragments, remarked that " he reverenced the very ground upon which Cregeen had trod, because he was one of the greatest natural Celtic scholars who had ever lived."

Many of Cregeen's Words are incorporated in the Dictionary published by the Manx Society, vol. xiii. 1866.

1835.

The Ninth Annual Report of the Isle of Man District Association of the Royal National Institution for the Preservation of Life from Shipwreck, from the 5th July 1834, to the 5th July 1835. Douglas : G. Jefferson, Bookseller, Duke Street. *Octavo.* Pp. 4.

The Report was presented at the Tynwald Court held at St. John's, 6th July, and authorised to be published by them.

T. Seppings.—1835.

The Sees of England and Wales, Ireland and the Colonies.
By T. Seppings. London : Simpkins and Co. 1835.
Octavo.

Isle of Man, pp. 18-19. With Arms of the See.

Rev. Hugh Stowell.—1835.

A Sermon preached at the opening of the Mariners' Church,
in the Harbour of the Town of Douglas, Isle of Man, May
24th, 1835. By the Rev. Hugh Stowell, Rector of Ballaugh. Published at the request of the Managers of the
Church. The profits, if any, to be applied to the funds
of the said Church. Douglas: printed by G. Jefferson,
Duke Street. *Octavo.* Pp. 21.

1835.

Self Defence. Being a Statement of Facts of the conduct of
Dr. H. P. Hume towards H. N. Carrington, Esq. By a
Friend to Truth. No place, date, or printer. *Octavo.*
Pp. 52.

Dr. Hume was in practice for some time in Manchester.
This Statement is by Mrs. Carrington.

John Welch.—1836.

A Six Days' Tour through the Isle of Man ; or a Passing
View of its present Natural, Social, and Political Aspect.
By a Stranger. 1836.

    "Comes jucundus in via pro vehiculo est."

Douglas : published and sold by William Dillon, Bookseller. Sold also by Marples and Co., and Lacey, Liverpool ; Thompsons, Manchester ; Simpkin, Marshall, and

Co., London ; and Cummins, Dublin. *Small Octavo.* Pp. 183.

Published at three shillings. A small map and six plates.

LORD TEIGNMOUTH.—1836.

Sketches of the Coasts and Islands of Scotland, and of the Isle of Man : Descriptive of the Scenery, and illustrative of the progressive revolution in the economical, moral, and social condition of the Inhabitants of those regions. In two volumes. By Lord Teignmouth. London : John W. Parker, West Strand. MDCCCXXXVI. 2 vols. 12*mo.*

The Description of the Isle of Man, in vol. ii. chapters 19 and 20, pp. 181-281. A map of the Island. In the Appendix are some Reports on the Harbours, Imports, etc., pp. 406-416 The Author spent a few weeks in the Island in the autumn of 1829.

SIR WM. HILLARY, Bart.—1836.

The National Importance of a Great Central Harbour for the Irish Sea, accessible at all times to the Largest Vessels, proposed to be constructed at Douglas, in the Isle of Man. Third Edition. With an Appendix. By Sir Wm. Hillary, Bart. Author of " An Appeal to the British Nation on the Humanity and Policy of Forming a National Institution for the Preservation of Life from Shipwreck, etc." Douglas : printed by Walls and Fargher, *Mona's Herald* Office. 1836. *Octavo.* Pp. 19.

Dated Isle of Man, 26th July 1826. The Appendix, pp. 14 to 19, dated Isle of Man, 1st January 1836.

1836.

The Tenth Annual Report of the Isle of Man District Association of the Royal National Institution for the Preservation of Life from Shipwreck, from the 5th July 1835, to the 5th July 1836. Douglas : G. Jefferson, Bookseller, Duke Street. *Octavo.* Pp. 4.

Ordered to be published by the Court of Tynwald at St. John's, 5th July 1836.

JOHN DUGGAN.—1836.

By Particular Desire. The Proceedings of a Meeting held in the Court House, Douglas, on Monday evening, 11th July 1836 ; in which is contained the speech of Mr. John Duggan, with an Appeal to his Countrymen. Dedicated respectfully to Lieut.-General Goldie, Speaker of the House of Keys. The proceeds (if any) will be given to that excellent Charity, the Ladies' Soup Dispensary. (Price fourpence) Douglas : G. Jefferson, Printer, Duke Street. 12*mo.* Pp. 12.

On the Fiscal Regulations.

1836.

Temperance Guardian. Commenced. Published by R. Fargher. Continued five years, and merged into the Temperance Advocate.

1836.

Manx Liberal. Commenced September 3d. Published by Penrice and Wallace.

REV. WM. PERCEVAL WARD.—1837.

Isle of Mann, and Diocese of Sodor and Mann. Antient and Authentic Records and Documents relating to the Civil and Ecclesiastical History and Constitution of that Island. Collected and arranged by the Rev. Wm. Perceval Ward,

M.A., Domestic Chaplain to the Bishop of Sodor and Mann. London: printed for J. G. and F. Rivington, by John Taylor junr., Colchester. 1837. 12*mo.* Pp. 185.

JOHN M. JEFFCOTT.—1837.

Statute Laws of the Isle of Man, promulgated since the year 1832. To which is added an Appendix, which contains Rules of the Chancery Court and an Analysis of the Law of the Descent of Hereditary Property in the Isle of Man. Compiled with a Digest of the Provisions of the Statutes ; and published under the patronage of His Excellency John Ready, Lieutenant-Governor, the Council, Deemsters, and Keys of the Isle of Man. By John M. Jeffcott. Douglas : printed and sold by J. Quiggin, North Quay. MDCCCXXXVII. *Royal octavo.* Pp. 134.

Dedicated "To the Hon. John M'Hutchin, Clerk of the Rolls of the Isle of Man." Castletown, September 1837.

The Analysis was drawn up by Mr. M'Hutchin. See continuation in 1841.

J. R. M'CULLOCH.—1837.

Statistical Account of the British Empire ; exhibiting its Extent, Physical Capacities, Population, Industry, and Civil and Religious Institutions. By J. R. M'Culloch, Esq., assisted by numerous contributors. In two volumes. London : printed for Charles Knight and Co., 1837. *Octavo.* Isle of Man, vol. ii. pp. 234-236, 276, 277.

SIR WM. HILLARY, Bart.—1837.

Observations on the proposed Changes in the Fiscal and Navigation Laws of the Isle of Man : Addressed to the Delegates from that Island to His Majesty's Government. By Sir Wm. Hillary, Baronet, Chairman of the Meetings.

Douglas : printed by Walls and Fargher, *Mona's Herald* Office. 1837. *Octavo.* Pp. 15. Dated Fort Anne, 17th April 1837.

A second edition was published the same year in *octavo*, pp. 19, containing additional matter.

Sir George Head.—1837.

A Home Tour through various parts of the United Kingdom. Being a continuation of the " Home Tour through the Manufacturing Districts." Also, Memoirs of an Assistant Commissary-General. By Sir George Head. London : John Murray, Albemarle Street. 1837. 12mo.

Isle of Man, Chapters I. to VI., pp. 1 to 91. Small Map of the Island.

An edition, in two volumes, *post octavo*, in 1840.

1838.

Deed of Association of the Isle of Man Steam Packet Company. Passed 31st July 1838. G. Jefferson, Duke Street, Douglas. *Octavo.* Pp. 15.

Value of Shares £12,000.

1838.

Collections relative to Claims at the Coronations of several of the Kings of England, beginning with King Richard II. London : J. B. Nichols and Son, 25 Parliament Street. 1838. *Octavo.* Pp. 96.

The advertisement is dated " July 26, 1820," and states that the Claims are taken from official and authentic sources. The following relate to the Isle of Man :—

Henry IV.

Claimant.—Henry, Earl of Northumberland.

Right of Claim.—In right of the Isle of Man, which had been granted to him and his heirs by the present King, to hold of him and his heirs, by the service "To carry, by himself or a sufficient deputy, on the Coronation days of the Kings of England, and near the King's left shoulder, that sword naket wherewith the present King was girt when he in partibus de Holdernesse applicuit, and which was called Lancaster Sword."

Answer.—Admitted ; and he performed the service in his own proper person.—See Rymer's "Fœdera," tom. viii. pp. 91-95.

CHARLES II.

"To present Two Falcons to the King on his Coronation."

Claimant.—Charles, Earl of Derby, Lord of the Isle of Man and its appertinents.

Right.—As being seized by inheritance of the Isle and Castle of Pelham, and of the serviory and dominion of Man, in his demesne as of fee, all which are held by such service.

Answer.—Allowed ; it appearing that the Isle of Man was held by the service of giving to the King two Falcons on his Coronation day.

JAMES II.

Claimant.—Henry, Earl of Derby, Lord of the Isle of Man and its appertinents.

Right, etc.—As above.

Answer.—Allowed.

WILLIAM AND MARY.

Claimant.—William Richard George Stanley, Earl of Derby, Lord of the Isle of Man and its appertinents.

Right, etc.—As above.

Answer.—Admitted.

GEORGE II.

Claimant.—James Stanley, Earl of Derby, Lord of the Isle of Man, and its appertinents.

Right, etc.—As above.

Answer.—Claim allowed ; and the Earl performed the service at the Coronation.

CHARLES II.

" On the Coronation day to carry on the King's left hand, during the procession, the sword called Lancaster Sword."

Claimant.—Charles, Earl of Derby, Lord of the Isle of Man and its appertinents.

Right.—As being seized by inheritance of the Isle and Castle of Pelham, and of the signiory and dominion of Man, in his demesne as of fee, all which are held by the service above mentioned.

Fees, etc.—All fees, privileges, and dignities appertinent to the said service.

Answer.—It appearing to the Court that the Isle of Man was held by the service of giving to the King two Falcons on the Coronation day, and not by the service of carrying the sword called *Curtana,* nor by the service of carrying the sword called *Lancaster Sword,* the Earl was admitted to do the service of giving the King two Falcons on his Coronation day ; but not to perform either the service of carrying the sword called *Curtana,* or the service of carrying the sword called *Lancaster Sword.*

N.B.—Afterwards, by the King's favour, the said Earl of Derby did carry the *Third Sword* before the King on his Coronation day.

EDWARD FORBES.—1838.

Malacologia Monensis. A Catalogue of the Mollusca inhabiting the Isle of Man and the neighbouring sea. By Edward Forbes, For. Sec. B. S. President of the Royal Physical Society, etc. Edinburgh : John Carfrae and Son ; Longman, Orme, Brown, Green, and Longmans, London. 1838. 12*mo*. Pp. 63. Dedication, Preface, etc., pp. xii. 3 Plates.

Professor Forbes was a native of the Isle of Man, and one whom the Island was justly proud of. In the preface he states that he had been "induced for some time back to collect materials for the Natural History of that Island, both its Fauna and its Flora. These I propose publishing in the form of catalogues, and commence with the Mollusca, that class being first completed." I am not aware that he continued these catalogues. He was interred in the Dean Cemetery, Edinburgh, and on a granite obelisk is the following inscription :—

EDWARD FORBES,
NATURALIST :
BORN FEBRUARY 12, 1815,
DIED NOVEMBER 18, 1854.

Professor Forbes wrote a Cataloge of Manx Shells, containing 196 names, and of Manx Plants 383, with lists of Crustacea, Radiata, etc. Also Notes on the Geology, etc., of the Island, which were never published.

He was the author of the following relating to the Isle of Man :—

"On some Manx Traditions." Published in the *Mirror*, 1831-32.

"On a Pleistocene Tract in the Isle of Man." Published in *Brit. Ass. Rep. Soc.*, p. 104. 1840.

"List of Pleistocene Fossils from the Isle of Man." Published in *Quart. Jour. Geol. Soc.*, ii. p. 346.

"Notes on the Flora of the Isle of Man."   In Cumming's "Isle of Man."   1848.

"On the Natural History of the Isle of Man."   In the later editions of "Quiggin's Guide."   1842, etc.

There were also published, in a small 8vo. volume, London, 1855, with a portrait, his literary papers, selected from *The Literary Gazette*. His published works consist chiefly of scattered memoirs, and in the "Bibliographia" of Agassiz and Strickland, are 89 in number.

C. A. HALSTEAD.—1839.

The Life of Margaret Beaufort, Countess of Richmond and
    Derby, etc.   By Caroline A. Halstead.   London : Smith,
    Elder, and Co., Cornhill. 1839. *Octavo*. With a Portrait.

The Island is casually mentioned at pp. 109, 155, and 219.   Another edition was published in 1845.

ESTHER NELSON.—1839.

Island Minstrelsy; comprising Old King Death, and other
    poems.   By Esther Nelson.

> —— "What is writ, is writ :
> Would it were worthier !   But—"
>   *Byron.*
> "I leave the summer rose,
>   For younger blyther brows ;
>   Tell me of change and death ! "

London : G. B. Whittaker and Co., Ave Maria Lane ; W. Grapel, Liverpool. MDCCCXXXIX. *Small octavo*, pp. 232.

Miss Nelson was the daughter of the Rev. J. Nelson, Rector of Bride. Miscellaneous Poems, several of which illustrate Traditions and Legends of the Isle.

ANNE TALLANT.—1839.

Octavia Elphinstone : A Manx Story.   By Miss Anne Tal-

laut. In two volumes. London : Saunders and Otley,
Conduit Street. 1839. 12*mo.*

JOHN SEACOMBE.—1840.

The History of the Noble House of Stanley from the Conquest
to the present time (with considerable additions), containing a Genealogical and Historical Account of that Illustrious House, to which is added a Description of the Isle
of Man. Manchester : published and sold by Wm. Willis,
at his Wholesale Warehouse, Hanging Ditch and Old
Church Yard. 1840. *Small octavo.* Pp. 320.

J. PAYNE COLLIER.—1840.

The Egerton Papers, a collection of Public and Private Docu-
ments, chiefly illustrative of the times of Elizabeth and
James I., from the original manuscripts, the property of
the Right Hon. Lord Francis Egerton, M.P., President of
the Camden Society. Edited by J. Payne Collier, Esq.,
F.S.A. London; printed for the Camden Society by
John Bowyer, Nichols, and Son, Parliament Street.
MDCCCXL. *Quarto.* Pp. 509.

Pp. 133-34, Lordship of the Isle of Man. Copy of a Par-
don granted by Henry, Earl of Derby, to Robert Mark Neven,
a felon. Dated at Latham, February 1589.

Pp. 281-82. Isle of Man. Letter from Chief-Justice
Popham to Sir Thomas Egerton, Lord Keeper, respecting the
dispute between William, Earl of Derby, and his three nieces,
daughters of Ferdinando, late Earl of Derby.

1840.

Common Prayer, translated into Manks. 12*mo.*

The Prayer for the Lord and Lady and House of Keys is
not in this edition.

1840.

Jefferson's Guide to the Isle of Man, with Directory, Map,
and Plates.

REV. H. J. STEVENSON.—1840.

Total Abstinence from Intoxicating Liquors on Christian principles, an Antidote of Moral Evil, and a means for the
promotion of good. A Sermon addressed to the Congre-
gation of the Mariners' Church, Douglas, on Sunday,
March 1st, 1840. By Rev. H. J. Stevenson, M.A., Chaplain. Douglas: published by R. Fargher and Co. 1840.
Small octavo. Pp. 23.

WILLIAM KINNEBROOK.—1841.

Etchings of the Runic Monuments in the Isle of Man, with
Remarks. By William Kinnebrook.

> " See the lines graven round it, all are Runic,
> Mystic inscriptions, full of wizard power
> To ward off ill."

London : Longman and Co., Paternoster Row. MDCCCXLI.
Octavo. Pp. 14. Contains 26 plates of etchings.

Dedicated " To the President and Members of the Royal
Antiquarian Society." Fifty copies printed. This work has
become very scarce.

JOHN M. JEFFCOTT.—1841.

The Ancient Ordinances and Statute Laws of the Isle of Man ;
carefully copied from and compared with the original
Records from the earliest date to the year 1841 : with a
copious Index. Douglas: printed and published by J.
Quiggin, Custom House Quay. 1841. *Octavo,* pp. 113 to
140, and Index.

This is a continuation of the "Statute Laws" by J. M. Jeffcott, Esq., published in 1837.

REV. H. J. STEVENSON, M.A.—1841.

The Church the Spouse of Christ: A Sermon preached in St. Stephen's Chapel, Sulby, on Sunday June 20; in St. Patrick's Church, on Sunday June 27th; and in the Mariners' Church, Douglas, on Sunday July 4th, 1841: after which Collections were made in aid of the Funds of the Isle of Man Diocesan Association. By the Rev. H. J. Stevenson, M.A., Examining Chaplain to the Lord Bishop of Worcester, to whom (by permission) it is dedicated. London : J. G. F. and J. Rivington ; Hatchard and Son ; Hamilton, Adams, and Co. Isle of Man : printed by R. Fargher ; sold by G. Jefferson, J. Quiggin, W. Dillon, and J. R. Wallace. 1841. *Octavo.* Pp. 23.

LAWRENCE ADAMSON.—1841.

First Letter to Sir Robert Peel, Bart., on the present Code of Manx Law, and the effects of the Administration of it on the Welfare and Happiness of the different Classes of the Community ; containing the result of five years' close personal observation of the Practical Working of the existing Law. By Lawrence Adamson, an Attorney of the Court of Queen's Bench, at Westminster, and a Solicitor and Master Extraordinary in the English High Court of Chancery. London : Longman and Co., Paternoster Row ; Penrice and Wallace, and W. Dillon, Douglas, Isle of Man. MDCCCXLI. *Octavo.* Pp. 16.

Dated Douglas, August 1841.

CAPTAIN WALLACE.—1841.

Eight Views of the New Churches and Chapels in the Isle of

Man, on Zinc, by Edward De la Motte, from Sketches by Captain Wallace. Douglas: published by W. Dillon; sold also by Pitt and Bogue, 86 Fleet Street, London. Price Seven Shillings. India Proofs, Ten Shillings. *Oblong Folio.*

"Published at the Request of the Bishop of Lichfield, lately of Sodor and Man, as a Memorial of the great exertions of the late Bishop Ward, his predecessor in the latter See."

1841.

Freedom! Righteousness!! and Law!!! versus Manx Injustice, Oppression, and Tyranny: in three letters on the Functions and Liberty of the Press; Manx Advocates, Judges, and Juries; and the Liberty of the Subject in the Isle of Man. By an Englishman. Isle of Man. Sold by Robert Fargher. 1841. 12*mo.* Pp. 16.

1841.

Temperance Advocate. Commenced January 1st. Published by Lees and Robinson, 1st of each Month.

Sir William Hillary, Bart.—1842.

A Letter to the Right Honourable Lord John Russell, Her Majesty's Secretary of State for the Home Department, on the Preservation of Life from Shipwreck. By Sir William Hillary, Bart. Author of "An Appeal to the British Nation on the Formation of a National Institution for the Preservation of Life from Shipwreck;" "The Naval Ascendancy of Britain," etc. Douglas: printed by Robert Fargher, *Mona's Herald* Office. 1842. *Octavo.* Pp. 11.

The Letter is dated, Fort Anne, Isle of Man, 1st Nov. 1838.

1842.

Great Central Harbour of Refuge for the Irish Sea, in Douglas Bay, Isle of Man, by means of Floating Breakwaters. Proceedings of a Public Meeting at the Court House, Douglas, January 18th, 1842. Sir William Hillary, Bart., Chairman. Douglas : printed by Robert Fargher, *Mona's Herald* Office. 1842. *Octavo.* Pp. 19.

At the end is a woodcut, " View of a Refuge Harbour protected by Captain Taylor's Floating Breakwaters."

Sir William Hillary, Bart.—1842.

The National Importance of a Great Central Harbour of Refuge for the Irish Sea, proposed to be constructed at Douglas Bay, Isle of Man. By Sir William Hillary, Bart., author of " An Appeal to the British Nation, on the Formation of a National Institution for the Preservation of Life from Shipwreck ;" " The Naval Ascendancy of Britain," etc. Fourth Edition. Douglas : printed by Robert Fargher, *Mona's Herald* Office. 1842. *Octavo.* Pp. 23.

The Introduction to this Edition is dated " 4th March 1842."

This Edition was published at the request of the " Directors of the National Floating Breakwater and Refuge Harbour Institution," on Captain Taylor's Plans.

Lawrence Adamson.—1842.

A Letter to the Lord Bishop of Sodor and Mann, on the present state of the Law of Real and Personal Property in the Isle of Man, as compared with that of England. By Lawrence Adamson, an Attorney of Her Majesty's Court of Queen's Bench at Westminster, and a Solicitor and Master Extraordinary in the English High Court of Chancery, London : Longman and Co. ; Grapel, Liverpool ; Gibson, Whitehaven ; Dillon, Quiggin, Jefferson, and Cannell, Douglas. 1842. *Octavo.* Pp. 56.

1842.

The Book of Common Prayer in Manx. London : 1842.

THOMAS VOWLER SHORT (Bishop).—1842.

Charge delivered to the Convocation held at Bishop's Court, on Thursday, May 19th, 1842. By Thomas Vowler Short, Bishop of Sodor and Man. Douglas, Isle of Man : printed at the *Manx Sun* Office, North Quay. 1842. *Octavo.* Pp. 15. Not printed for sale.

1842.

Quiggin's Illustrated Guide and Visitor's Companion through the Isle of Man ; with a Directory for Douglas. 2d Edition. 5th Thousand. Douglas : printed and published by J. Quiggin, Custom House Quay, 1842. *Small octavo.* Pp. 130. Map of the Island and Thirty-three Engravings.

"This edition is enriched by an Account of the Natural History of the Island, by Edward Forbes junr., Esq., and by many interesting Particulars furnished by the Rev. C. Radcliffe."—*Preface.*

An edition was published in 1840 and 1838.

JAMES BROTHERSTON LAUGHTON.—1842.

A new Historical, Topographical, and Parochial Guide to the Isle of Man. By James Brotherston Laughton, B.A. Douglas : published by William Dillon. London : Messrs. Simpkin, Marshall, and Co., etc. etc. 1842. 18*mo.* Pp. 184.

A Map, View of Douglas, and several Woodcuts. On the title is a long extract from Sir Thomas Malory.
Editions in 1845 and 1847.

1842.

Dr. Hookwell, or the Anglo-Catholic Family. London: Richard Bentley, New Burlington Street. 1842. 3 vols. 12*mo.*

A Novel: portions of the scene of which are laid in the Isle of Man.

Isaac Dale.—(No date.)

The Mona Melodist. A Selection of Psalm and Hymn Tunes suited to all the Variations of Metrical Psalmody, for Congregational or Family Worship, newly harmonised for Four Voices, with an accompaniment for the Organ or Pianoforte: Dedicated, by permission, to the Lord Bishop of Sodor and Man,'by Isaac Dale. Douglas, Isle of Man: printed and published by J. Quiggin, North Quay. *Folio.*

It was published in two parts. One of the tunes, No. 36, is by the Rev. R. Brown, Vicar of Braddan, which is considered most sublime. Another is by Mr. Cretney, son of old James Cretney of Douglas.

1842.

The Manxman. Commenced in January. Published by W. Walls. Continued eleven months.

Thomas Vowler Short.—1843.

Charge delivered to the Convocation held at Bishop's Court on Thursday, June 8th, 1843. By Thomas Vowler Short, Bishop of Sodor and Man. Douglas: printed by Robert

Fargher, *Mona's Herald* Office. 1843. *Octavo.* Pp. 36. Not printed for sale.

An Appendix on the method of preparing Catechumens for Examination.

1843.

Pigot and Slater's Directory and Topography of the Isle of Man. Manchester, 1843. *Royal octavo.* Pp. 26. With a Map of the Island.

Appended to their Directory of Liverpool.

HUGH STRICKLAND, F.G.S.—1843.

On the Pleistocene Formation of the North of the Island. Published in the 4th vol. of the 2d series of the Proceedings of the Geological Society. Read November 2d, 1843.

REV. HUGH STOWELL.—1843.

Memoirs of Mr. F. D. P. Geneste.

> " Purpureus veluti cum flos succisus aratro
> Languescit moriens."— *Virg.*

By the Rev. Hugh Stowell. Douglas, Isle of Man : published and sold by Wm. Cannell, at his cheap book establishment, Duke St. and Parliament St., Ramsey. 1843. 24*mo.* Pp. 139.

1843.

King William's College Magazine ; or Literary Miscellany. A monthly Periodical, price 6d. The first Number on Saturday, 16th September. W. Cannell, publisher, Douglas.

1844.

Douglas House of Industry, opened February 1838. Fifth Annual Report, for the year ending October 5th, 1843, with the Audited Account, List of Inmates and Out-Pensioners, Donors, and Subscribers. Douglas: printed for the Committee by Robert Fargher, *Mona's Herald* Office. *Octavo.* Pp. 12.

The Sixth Report was also published this year, 1844.

THOMAS VOWLER SHORT.—1844.

Charge delivered to the Convocation, held at Bishop's Court, on Thursday, July 11th, 1844. By Thomas Vowler Short, Bishop of Sodor and Man. Douglas: printed by William Dillon, Duke Street. 1844. *Octavo.* Pp. 39. Not printed for sale.

An Appendix on the Management of Sunday Schools. Addressed to the Rev. Thomas Howard.

J. C. BLUETT.—1844.

The Constitution of the House of Keys; and the Inexpediency and Danger of Changing it : in Two Letters. By J. C. Bluett, Advocate. Douglas: printed by P. Curphey & Co., *Manx Sun* Office. 1844. 12*mo.* Two Pamphlets.

Letter first, pp. 35. Letter second, pp. 35. Addressed " To the Inhabitants of the Isle of Mann, whether Native or Otherwise."

S. S. ROGERS.—1844.

The Manks Farmer's Magazine and Monthly Historical Newspaper. Edited by S. S. Rogers, Esq., A.B. No. 1, Douglas, 8th April 1844. Printed by Wm. Dillon, Duke Street,

Douglas, Isle of Man. *Quarto*, 16 pp. each number. (Price Sixpence.)

SIR WM. HILLARY, Bart.—1844.

Observations on the proposed Changes in the Fiscal and Navigation Laws of the Isle of Man : Addressed to the Delegates from that Island to His Majesty's Government, in the year 1837. By Sir William Hillary, Baronet, Chairman of the Meetings. Third Edition. Douglas : printed by Robert Fargher, *Mona's Herald* Office. 1844. *Octavo.* Pp. 20.

Dated "Fort Anne, April 1837." Contains additional matter from pp. 15 to 20, to that of the first Edition.

1844.

Memorial addressed to the Lieutenant-Governor, the Members of the Council and Keys of the Isle of Man. Douglas : printed by Robert Fargher, *Mona's Herald* Office. 1844. *Octavo.* Pp. 7.

Adopted at a Meeting held in Douglas on the 11th April 1844. Sir William Hillary, Bart., Chairman. To revise the Fiscal and Navigation Laws.

1844.

The Fifth Annual Report of the Isle of Mann Diocesan Association. August 1844. Douglas : Robert H. Johnson, printer, 2 Great Nelson Street. 1844. *Octavo.* Pp. 8.

This Association was established July 16th, 1839.
The Subscriptions for the current year are £252 : 19 : 6.

ELIJAH CHRISTIAN.—1844.

A Light to Lighten the Gentiles. Printed at the *Millennial* Office, Ballasalla. 1844. *Small Octavo.* Pp. 8.

Numbers of Pamphlets and Broadsides, under this and other titles, appeared in this and following years from the same press, under the signature of E. C., or Mary Turnbull, an enthusiast.

WILLIAM KENNISH, R.N.—1844.

Mona's Isle and other Poems. By William Kennish, R.N. Author of "A Method for Concentrating the Fire of a Broadside of a Ship of War," etc. etc.

> "Alas! I'm but a nameless wight,
> Trod i' th' mire clean out o' sight."
> *Burns.*

London : J. Bradley, 78 Great Tichfield Street, St. Mary-le-bone ; Simpkin, Marshall, and Co. 1844. 12*mo.* Pp. 166.

Many curious customs connected with this Island are mentioned in these Poems. The Author "is a native of the Isle of Man, where he passed his early years as a plough-boy, and at the age of twenty-two years he entered the British Navy as a common seaman."—*Preface.*

He died 19th March 1862, in New York, aged 63.

ROBERT JAMES KELLY.—1844.

Sketches in the Isle of Man. By Robert James Kelly.

> " Breathes there a man with soul so dead,
> Who never to himself hath said
> This is my own, my native land !"

Douglas : printed by P. Curphey, *Manx Sun* Office ; Simpkin, Marshall, and Co., Stationers' Hall Court, London. 1844. *Octavo.* Pp. 124.

Dedicated to Edward Moore Gawne, Esq., of Kentraugh.

George Ormerod.—1844.

Tracts relating to Military Proceedings in Lancashire during the Great Civil War, commencing with the Removal, by Parliament, of James Lord Strange, afterwards Earl of Derby, from his Lieutenancy of Lancashire, and terminating with his Execution at Bolton. Edited and illustrated from cotemporary documents, by George Ormerod, D.C.L., F.R.S., F.S.A., F.G.S., of Tyldesley and Sedbury, Author of the History of Cheshire. Printed for the Chetham Society. MDCCCXLIV. *Quarto.* Pp. xxxii. and 371.

Chetham Society, vol. ii.

Many interesting matters connected with the Derby Family and the Isle of Man are mentioned in these Tracts.

Chap. xiii. pp. 280-285, Lord Derby's proceedings in Man, 1643-1651.

1844.

British Archæological Association Journal, December 1844.

Mr. Way communicated drawings of several sculptured crosses in the Isle of Man, the shaft of one of these monuments standing in Braddan Churchyard. Engraved in the *Arch. Journal,* p. 75.

1844.

Third Annual Report of the Isle of Man Agricultural Association, formed 13th March 1841. Price to non-subscribers, sixpence. Douglas: printed by William Dillon, Duke Street. 1844. *Octavo.* Pp. 8. With the Rules and Regulations.

1844.

The National Reformer. Commenced November 16th. Published by Jas. B. O'Brien.

1844.

Oddfellows' Chronicle. Commenced October 25th. Published by Company of Oddfellows, 15th of every month.

THOMAS VOWLER SHORT (Bishop).—1845.

Charge delivered to the Convocation, held at Bishop's Court, on Thursday, May 15th, 1845. By Thomas Vowler Short, Bishop of Sodor and Man. Douglas: printed by Peter Curphey, North Quay. 1845. *Octavo.* Pp. 24.

SAMUEL HAINING.—1845.

Strictures on the Charge of the Bishop of Sodor and Mann, delivered to his Clergy at Bishop's Court, July 11th, 1844. By Samuel Haining. Douglas: printed and published by M. A. Quiggin, 52 North Quay; and sold by the Booksellers. MDCCCXLV. *Small octavo.* Pp. 24.

JOHN DUGGAN.—1845.

The Touchstone; or, a Review of J. C. Bluett's Two Letters in defence of The House of Keys; with important extracts from the Reply of Counsel, and Correspondence, *In Re* Miss Ritchie *v.* Bluett, before the House of Keys, on the 26th and 27th Feby. 1823. By John Duggan, Author of "An Appeal to Manxmen," and "The Last Appeal to Manxmen."

> " Thrice is he arm'd that hath his quarrel just,
> And he but naked, though lock'd up in steel,
> Whose conscience with injustice is corrupted."
>> *Second Part of King Henry VI.*

Douglas: printed by Penrice and Wallace, *Liberal* Office. 1845. *Octavo.* Pp. 47.

Dedicated to "Wm. Kelly, Chairman; S. S. Rogers, Secretary; and all the Members of the Reform Association."

The Author should have followed what he so much admires in Mr. Bluett's letters, " the avoidance of all personality and low abuse." The matter of Miss Ritchie has nothing whatever to do with the "Constitution of the House of Keys." The two pages at the end would have been much better left out of his " Touchstone."

LAWRENCE ADAMSON.—1845.

The People's Case. An Answer to the Letters of J. C. Bluett, Advocate, on the Constitution of the House of Keys. By Lawrence Adamson, an Attorney of Her Majesty's Court of Queen's Bench at Westminster, a Solicitor and Master Extraordinary of the English High Court of Chancery, and a Student of Manx Law.

> " Mannagh vow cliaghtey cliaghtey, nee cliaghtey coe."
> *Manx Adage.*

Douglas: printed at the *Mona's Herald* Office, by Robert Fargher. *Octavo.* Pp. 59.

Dated at the end " Douglas, 1845."

1845.

Truth Seeker. Commenced January 15, and published by Lees and Robinson, on the 15th of every month.

JOSEPH TRAIN, F.S.A. Scot.—1845.

An Historical and Statistical Account of the Isle of Man, from the earliest times to the present date ; with a View of its Ancient Laws, Peculiar Customs, and Popular Superstitions. By Joseph Train, F.S.A. Scot. In two volumes. Douglas, Isle of Man : printed and published by Mary A. Quiggin, North Quay. London : Simpkin, Marshall, and Co., Stationers' Hall Court. Liverpool : Chegwin and Hall, and G. Philip. Glasgow : J. Lumsden and Son. MDCCCXLV. *Octavo.* Vol. I. Introduction and Contents, pp. xxii. Memoir of the Author, pp. 29. History, pp. 401. Vol. II. Contents, pp. v. History, pp. 388.

There are two maps, with several engravings and wood-cuts.

Mr. Train was the correspondent of Sir Walter Scott, furnishing him with many anecdotes and hints for his Novels.

His History is a work of great research, abounding with curious and valuable references.

1845.

Standing Orders of the Court of Tynwald with regard to Railway Bills. 1845. Douglas : printed by P. Curphey, *Manx Sun* Office, No. 6 North Quay. 1845. *Quarto.* Pp. 12.

1845.

A Letter to the Members of the Manx Legislature on the subject of the Petitions praying for the enactment of a Law to reduce the number of Public Houses, and to close them on the Sabbath. Douglas : printed for the Committee of the Isle of Man Temperance Association, by Penrice and Wallace, *Liberal* Office, Parade. 1845. *Octavo.* Pp. 17.

1845.

Church Chronicle. Commenced April 24th. Published by Wm. Dillon, every Thursday.

1845.

The Isle of Man : a Satire. Canto I. By ———. Douglas :

printed by Penrice and Wallace, *Liberal* Office.   1845.
Octavo.   Pp. 19.

On the title is a long quotation from Lord Byron.

The *Hero* does not arrive in the island until the end of
the canto, and the author there gives a synopsis of what is to
be in canto ii., and concludes thus—

> " But O ye Public ! buy, and don't forsake me,
>   Or may the devil roast, and boil, and bake ye."

I am not aware that any more was published.

1845.

Proceedings of a Public Meeting held at the Court-House,
   Douglas, March 18th, 1845, for the purpose of petitioning
   Her Majesty's Government to construct a Great Central
   Harbour of Refuge in Douglas Bay, Isle of Man.   Sir
   Wm. Hillary, Bart., in the chair.   Douglas : printed by
   R. Fargher, *Mona's Herald* Office.   1845.   *Octavo.*   Pp. 15.
   Contains a Copy of the Memorial.

Captain Thurot.—1845.

Genuine and Curious Memoirs of the famous Captain Thurot,
   etc.   This is edited from the edition of 1760, by T. Crofton
   Croker, Esq., and printed by the Percy Society in this
   year, as Part I. of his "Popular Songs, illustrative of the
   French Invasions of Ireland."   *Post octavo.*   Pp. 44.

A Memoir of Thurot, with the various Ballads in Manx and
   English, will be found in the Second Series of " Mona Miscellany," Manx Society, vol. xxi.   1873.

S. Lewis.—1845-48.

Topographical Dictionary of England and Wales, the Islands

of Guernsey, Jersey, and Man, with Atlas and Maps. By
S. Lewis. 7 vols. *quarto.* London : 1845-48.

A Compilation from numerous Authors, and many have
just cause to remember the manner in which this work was
forced upon them. The first edition appeared 1831-33, in
4 vols. *quarto.* Published by subscription.

Robert Kelly.—1845.

An Authentic List of Vessels wrecked on the Coast of the
Isle of Man, from the year 1822 to 1845, both inclusive.
By Robert Kelly, Esquire, Advocate and Notary Public.
Prepared by direction of the Commissioners of Harbours.
Douglas : printed by P. Curphey, *Manx Sun* Office, North
Quay, 1845. *Royal octavo.* Pp. 8.

Total supposed loss of vessels and cargoes, £258,365 ;
total number of lives lost 172.

Sir Walter Scott, Bart.—1845.

Peveril of the Peak. By Sir Walter Scott, Bart. With all
his Illustrations and Notes. Edinburgh : Robert Cadell,
St. Andrew Square. 1845. *Royal octavo.*

This is one of the numerous editions of this novel, the
chief incidents of which are connected with the Isle of Man,
particularly those matters relative to the now venerable ruins
of Peel Castle and William Christian (*Illiam Dhône*).

The pamphlet attributed to Colonel Wilks, but written by
Mr. Marsden, "Notices of Edward and William Christian," is
printed in the Appendix to the Introduction, as well as a
translation of the Lament over " Fair-haired William."

Joseph Train, author of the " Historical Account of the
Isle of Man," is said to have supplied Sir Walter Scott with
many interesting facts connected with this celebrated novel.

Thomas Vowler Short (Bishop).—1846.

Charge delivered to the Convocation, held at Bishop's Court, on Thursday, June 4th, 1846. By Thomas Vowler Short, Bishop of Sodor and Man. London : printed by J. Davy and Sons, 137 Long Acre. 1846. *Octavo.* Pp. 28.

Thomas Vowler Short (Bishop).—1846.

Family Prayer : being an Address to the Inhabitants of the Isle of Man. By Thomas V. Short, Bishop of Sodor and Man. 1846. *Small Octavo.* Pp. 11.

Dated "Bishop's Court, Dec. 31st, 1845." Printed in London.

Thomas Wilson (Bishop).—1846.

Padjeryn Lught-thie liorish Aspick Wilson. A Form of Family Prayer, from the Works of Thomas Wilson, D.D., late Lord Bishop of Sodor and Man. London : printed for the Society for Promoting Christian Knowledge. Sold at the Depository, Great Queen Street, Lincoln's Inn Fields, No. 4 Royal Exchange ; and by all Booksellers. 1846. *Small octavo.* Pp. 17.

In Manx and English.

Rev. J. L. Petit.—1846.

The Archæological Journal. Published under the direction of the Central Committee of the Archæological Institute of Great Britain and Ireland, for the Encouragement and Prosecution of Researches into the Arts and Monuments of the Early and Middle Ages. London : Longman, etc. etc. 1846. *Octavo.* Vol. iii., pp. 49 to 58.

"Ecclesiastical Antiquities of the Isle of Man." By J.

L. Petit. Contains three etchings of Peel Castle and St. German's Cathedral, with fifteen wood engravings of the same.

An excellent account of the Cathedral of St. German's in Peel Castle.

1846.

Manx Press. Printed thrice a month at Ramsey. Price 1d. Printed for the proprietor, R. Busteed, at his Office in Dale Street, Ramsey. *Small folio.* No. 16, Dec. 10th.

REV. J. G. CUMMING, M.A., 1846.

Account of the Geology of the Isle of Man. By the Rev. J. G. Cumming, M.A., F.G.S. Published in the Proceedings of the Geological Society of London. August 1846.

1846.

Lioar dy Hymnyn as arraneyn spyroydoil chyndait gys Gailct veih lioaryn Wesley, Watts, as Scriwdeyryn Elley, son Ymmyd Creesteenyn. Doolish : printit liorish M. A. Quiggin. 1846. *Small octavo,* pp. 191.

Translated by Messrs. Killey, Cretney, and others. Mr. George Killey was the Parish Clerk of Kirk Onchan.

Various editions of Wesley's Hymns in Manx have been published; one, translated by Daniel Cowley of Kirk Michael, about 1778, and one printed by J. Whitham, Douglas, 1799.

SIR WM. DUGDALE, CAYLEY, ELLIS, and BANDINEL.—1846.

Monasticon Anglicanum ; a History of the Abbeys and other Monasteries, Hospitals, Friaries, Cathedral and Collegiate Churches in England and Wales ; also of all such Scotch, Irish, and French Monasteries as were, in any manner, connected with Religious Houses in England, together with a particular account of their possessions as well Temporal as Spiritual, originally published in Latin. A new Edition, enriched with a large accession of materials, now first printed from Leiger-Books, Chartularies, Rolls, and other documents preserved in the National Archives, Public Libraries, and other Repositories ; the History of each Religious Foundation, in English, being prefixed to its series of Latin Charters, by John Cayley, Esq., F.S.A., etc., Sir Henry Ellis, F.S.A., etc., and by the Rev. Dr. Bandinel. London. 8 vols. *folio.* 1846. With numerous plates.

The former edition, 1817-30, was published in 50 parts, at £2 : 12 : 6 each.

Vol. v., pp. 252 to 257. Notices of Russin Abbey. Num. I., Historical Notices ; Synodal Statutes and Constitutions of the Diocese of Sodor, made by Simon, Bishop of Sodor in A.D. 1229. Num. II., Limits of the Land of Russin. Num. III., Transcript of Roll 33 Hen. VIII., 1541-2, Augmentation Office. Num. IV., Transcript from Ministers' Accts. 33 Hen. VIII., 1541-2, Augmentation Office.   As to the Demesne Lands.

The Statutes of Bishop Simon, with a translation, are printed in "Oliver's Monumenta," vol. iii., pp. 176-182, Manx Society, vol. ix., 1862. A reprint of the Isle of Man portion is in the Manx Society's series, vol. xviii., 1871, "Old Historians," pp. 46-77.

Rev. Thomas Howard.—1847.

A Sermon preached at Kirk Braddan Church, on Sunday, December 13, 1846, on occasion of the Death of the Reverend Robert Brown, Vicar of Braddan, by the Reverend Thomas Howard, Rector of Ballaugh. Douglas : printed and published by Robert H. Johnson, 2 Great Nelson Street. 1847. *Post octavo.* Pp. 22.

Published by request. The profits (if any) will be given for the benefit of the poor.

1847.

A Statistical View of the State of Education in the Isle of
Man, furnished by the Teachers to the Committee of the
Isle of Man Educational Library. 1847. P. Curphey,
Printer, *Manx Sun* Office, 6 North Quay, Douglas. *A
Broadside.*

1847.

An Act to render more effectual the Registering and Record-
ing of all Deeds, Conveyances, Wills, and Instruments,
which shall be made of any Lands, Tenements, or Hereditaments, within the Isle of Man. Douglas : printed by
P. Curphey, *Manx Sun* Office, North Quay. 1847. *Royal
octavo.* Pp. 30.

1847.

Letters from the Isle of Man in 1846.

" Recollecting the difficulty I had to procure any previous intelligence relative to the Isle of Man, and that the little I did obtain was, in a great
measure, erroneous, it occurred to me to arrange such information as by my
personal observation I had obtained. It is not my intention to attempt the
character of an historian."—*Jeffrey's Isle of Man.*

"Mona—long hid from those who roam the main."
Collins.

"'Tis Mona, the lone ! where the silver mist gathers,
Pale shroud whence our wizard Chief watches unseen
O'er the breezy, the bright, the loved home of my fathers,
Oh, Mannin, my graih my Cree ! Mannin veg veen."
Island Minstrelsy.

London : Saunders and Otley, Conduit Street. 1847.
12*mo.* Pp. 147.

Contains Ten Letters, with Manx Ballads, Legends, etc.,
and Appendix.

REV. H. MOSELEY, F.R.S.—1847.

Report of the Parochial Schools of the Isle of Man. By the
Rev. H. Moseley, F.R.S., one of Her Majesty's Inspectors
of Schools. 1847. Addressed to the Committee of Coun-

cil on Education.   Douglas : Robert H. Johnson, Printer
and Stationer, 2 Great Nelson Street.   1847.   *Octavo.*
Pp. 22.

Dated Privy Council Office, Whitehall, 31st Oct. 1847.
With a Letter from the Lord Bishop, dated Bishop's Court,
Nov. 30, 1847.

Rev. J. G. Cumming.—1847.

Geology of the Calf of Man.   A Memoir published in the
Quarterly Journal of the Proceedings of the Geological
Society of London, in May 1847, p. 184.   By the Rev. J.
G. Cumming, Vice-Principal of King William's College,
Castletown.

1847.

The Effects of the Manx Fiscal Act of 1844.   Douglas : R.
Fargher, Printer, *Herald* Office.   1847.   12*mo.*   Pp. 12.

J. C. Bluett.—1847.

The Advocates' Note Book, being Notes and Minutes of
Cases heard and determined before the Judicial Tribunals
of the Isle of Mann.   By J. C. Bluett, Esq., of Gray's
Inn, Barrister-at-Law and Advocate at the Manx Bar.
Douglas : printed and published by Robert Heywood
Johnson, 2 Great Nelson Street.   1847.   *Octavo.*   Intro-
duction, etc., pp. xv.   Note Book, pp. 564.

Dedicated to the Hon. Charles Hope, Lieutenant-Governor
and Chancellor of the Isle of Mann.   The Introduction contains a brief sketch of the state of the Common and Statute
Law of the Country.

1847.

Travellers' Guide to the Isle of Man.   Douglas : James
O'Brien, Printer, 40 Duke Street, 1847.   12*mo.*   Pp. 32.

1847.

Quiggin's Illustrated Guide and Visitor's Companion through
the Isle of Man. Third Edition. Douglas: M. A. Quiggin, 52 North Quay. Liverpool: G. Philip. 1847. *Small
octavo.* Pp. 149. 30 woodcut illustrations.

J. B. LAUGHTON, B.A.—1847.

Johnson's Historical, Topographical, and Parochial Illustrated
Guide and Visitors' Companion through the Isle of Man.
By James Brotherston Laughton, B.A. Douglas: printed
and published by Samuel Johnson, Duke Street. 1847.
Small octavo. Pp. 200. Map and plates. Red border
round the letterpress.

1847.

The Queen's Visit to Mona ; or, The Little Orator : a Rhyme.
Containing several allusions to the defection of certain
Functionaries on the above occasion. Douglas : printed
by G. J. Cudd, 8 Thomas Street. 1847. Dated Douglas,
Oct. 1847. 12*mo.* Pp. 12.

REV. JOSEPH GEORGE CUMMING, M.A.—1848.

The Isle of Man: Its History, Physical, Ecclesiastical, Civil, and
Legendary. By the Rev. Joseph George Cumming, M.A.,
F.G.S., Vice-Principal of King William's College, Castle-
town. London : John Van Voorst, Paternoster Row.
MDCCCXLVIII. *Post octavo.* Dedication (to Dr. Short),
Preface, etc., pp. xxxvi. History, pp. 376. Numerous
Views, Geological Maps and Sections.

This Work is principally devoted to the Geological History of the Island.

SIR JOHN PIERS.—1848.

Appeal to the House of Lords between Sir John B. Piers and
Dame Eliza, his Wife, and Sir Hen. Saml. Piers, who
wished to claim the property of the former, and prove the
illegitimacy of his children. Privately printed. *Folio.*
Pp. 30.

Sir John Piers resided at Lecce Lodge, Isle of Man, where
he alleges he was married to Dame Eliza, by Orpen Stewart,
a Priest in Holy Orders, 1815. The case turns on Marriage
Customs of the Isle of Man, and much curious matter is
given.

JAMES GELL.—1848.

Statute Laws of the Isle of Man, promulgated since the Year
1836 : With an Appendix, containing the By-Laws for
the Regulation and Government of Towns ; and the Rules
of the Court of Chancery, etc. etc. Published under the
Patronage of His Excellency the Honourable Charles
Hope, Lieutenant-Governor, the Council, Deemsters, and
Keys of the Isle of Man. By James Gell, Esq., Advocate.
Douglas : printed and published by Peter Curphey, *Sun*
Office, North Quay. Also published by John Mylrea,
Duke Street. London : Steven and Norton, Law Book-
sellers, Bell Yard, Lincoln's Inns, and 194 Fleet Street.
1848. *Royal octavo.* Pp. 230.

WM. NELSON CLARKE, D.C.L.—1848.

A Collection of Letters addressed by Prelates and Individuals
of High Rank in Scotland, and by two Bishops of Sodor
and Man, to Sancroft, Archbishop of Canterbury, in the
Reigns of King Charles II. and James VII. Edited from

Originals in the Bodleian Library, Oxford. With Explanatory and Biographical Notices. By Wm. Nelson Clarke, D.C.L., of Christ Church, Oxford. Edinburgh : R. Lendrum and Co., etc. 1848. *Octavo.* Pp. 184. Maukish Letters to Archbishop Sancroft, pp. 121-170.

Rev. J. M. Neale.—1848.

Ecclesiological Notes on the Isle of Man, Ross, Sutherland, and the Orkneys : or, a Summer Pilgrimage to S. Maughold and S. Magnus. London : Joseph Masters, Aldersgate Street, and 78 New Bond Street. MDCCCXLVIII. *Small octavo.* Pp. 118.

Preface signed " J. M. N., Sackville College, Aug. 16, 1848." " Isle of Man," pp. 1 to 50. The Author appears to have made a hasty visit to the Island, and his remarks, as might be expected, are made without much consideration. It has most gross and glaring faults.

1848.

Manx Jurisprudence, and " Its blessed privileges." The Deed with the altered Date. John Doe and Richard Roe. To which is added, the Affidavit of Adolphus M‘William, Esq., and a letter from John Crawford, Esq., to the Editor of the *Manx Sun.* (A Quotation from the London *Times.*) Douglas, Isle of Man : printed and published by Carre Cook Tupper, 13 South Quay, and sold by all Booksellers. MDCCCXLVIII. *Royal octavo.* Pp. 8.

John Crawford.—1848.

Deed with the altered Date. The Queen against Dumbell. Observations on the Proceedings in this Case, at the Court of Enquiry, held at Castletown, Isle of Man, on the 23d and 24th of August 1848. By John Crawford. 1848. (A Quotation from the *Times*.) Printed for and published by C. C. Tupper, and sold by the Booksellers in London, Liverpool, and the Isle of Man. (Price Twopence.) *Octavo.* Pp. 8.

ALFRED ORMONDE.—No date.   [1848.]

The Clown. Douglas, Isle of Man : printed and published for the Proprietor, Mr. Alfred Ormonde, Minerva Cottage, Prospect Hill, by George John Cudd, No. 8 Thomas Street. Price One Penny. *Folio.* Pp. 4. At the head is a Woodcut of a Clown cutting open a Pie, out of which comes a Young Clown. There are also Woodcuts of the Arms of Man, Douglas Pier Lighthouse, Glen Maye, and Fossil Elk.

1849.

Report of a Committee of the Tynwald Court, appointed to inquire into a Bill for the Preservation of Spawn and Fry of Fish, April 10, 1847. Printed by order of the Lieutenant-Governor for the use of the Members of the Tynwald Court. Douglas : Peter Curphey, *Manx Sun* Office, North Quay, 1849. *Octavo.* Pp. 12. The Report signed by John Moore, John Kelly, R. Harrison. With Minutes of Evidence.

1849.

Report of a Committee of the Tynwald Court, appointed the 5th July 1849 ; with further Evidence touching the Fisheries, November 1st, 1849. Printed by order of the Lieutenant-Governor for the use of the Members of the Tynwald Court. Douglas : Peter Curphey, Printer, *Manx Sun* Office, North Quay. 1849. *Octavo*, pp. 30. The

Report, signed by J. J. Heywood, T. A. Corlett, R. Harrison, Wm. Callister.   With the Minutes of Evidence.

JAMES ROSSER.—1849.

The History of Wesleyan Methodism in the Isle of Man ; with some Account of the Island, and of the Life and Labours of Bishop Wilson ; in a series of Letters addressed to the Rev. George Marsden.   By James Rosser.

> "It is the work of God."
>
> *Page* 193.
>
> " Who the victory gave,
>   The praise let him have,
>   For the work he hath done,
>   All honour and glory to Jesus alone."
>
> *Wesley.*

Douglas, Isle of Man : printed for the Author by Mary A. Quiggin, North Quay.   London : sold by J. Moxon, 66 Paternoster Row.   MDCCCXLIX.   *Small octavo.*   Plates and Map.   Pp. 207.

RICHARD SHERWOOD.—1849.

Plan of the Town and Neighbourhood of Douglas, Isle of Man. Drawn by Richard Sherwood jun., from the Plan lately forwarded to Sir George Grey.   Published by R. H. Johnson, Great Nelson Street, Douglas.   G. Philip and Son, Lithographers, 51 South Castle Street, Liverpool.   August 1849.   A large Sheet.   Surveyed by J. Paris.

BISHOP SHIRLEY.—1849.   (REV. T. HILL.)

Letters and Memoir of the late Walter Augustus Shirley, D.D., Lord Bishop of Sodor and Man.   Edited by Thomas Hill, B.D., Archdeacon of Derby.   London : J. Hatchard and Son, 187 Piccadilly. 1849. *Octavo.* Pp. 505. *Portrait.*

A Second Edition was published in 1850, in which some very injudicious reflections (printed in the first edition) on the Manx Clergy were suppressed.

THOMAS HENRY.—1849.

The Isle of Man Poetically Illustrated. Douglas : printed by Thomas Henry, rear of 7 Athol Terrace. 1849. 12*mo.* Pp. 16.

Dedicated to the Hon. Charles Hope, Lieut.-Governor. It was intended to extend this to eight parts. I have only met with the present one—Part I.

1849.

Statute Laws of the Isle of Man, promulgated on the 8th of March 1849. Douglas : printed (by authority) by P. Curphey, *Manx Sun* Office, North Quay. 1849. *Royal octavo.* Pp. 70. Contains five Acts.

FRANCIS GROSE, F.S.A.—1849.

The Antiquities of the Isle of Man. By Francis Grose, Esq., F.S.A. Extracted from his general Works on the Antiquities of England and Wales. MDCCXCVII. London : John Gray Bell, Bedford Street, Covent Garden. MDCCCXLIX. *Quarto.* Pp. 197 to 214 of vol. vi. ; pp. 161-162 of vol. viii.

Description of the Island, 2 pp. Map of the Island and Eleven Plates. This is made up of the edition of 1797, with the title added.

Reprinted in the Manx Society's series, vol. xviii. 1871. " Old Historians," pp. 153-170.

Rev. J. G. Cumming.—1850.

Great Industrial Exhibition of 1851. Two Letters, showing some of the Productions of the Isle of Man in connection with the Exhibition. By the Rev. J. G. Cumming, M.A., F.G.S., Vice-Principal of King William's College. Douglas: printed for the Local Committee, by P. Curphey, *Sun* Office, North Quay. 1850. *Small octavo.* Pp. 8.

These Letters enumerate the natural and industrial products of the Island, and strongly urge upon the notice of the inhabitants the necessity of sending specimens of the same to the Great Exhibition, for which purpose a local Committee was formed.

1850.

Eye-Salve for the Wesleyans of Mona : containing the facts connected with recent expulsions, and strictures thereon, etc. Carefully compiled and arranged by an Old Wesleyan. Douglas : printed and published by Robert Fargher, etc. 1850. *Large octavo.* Pp. 14.

Rev. Thomas Howard.—1850.

Plain and Practical Sermons. By the Rev. Thomas Howard, Rector of Ballaugh, Isle of Man. London : James Nisbet and Co., Berners Street. 1850.

Dedicated to the Rev. Hugh Stowell, A.M., Honorary Canon of Chester, and Incumbent of Christ Church, Manchester. Sermon XXI.— Preached at Ballaugh Church on Sunday, Oct. 25, 1835, on the Death of the Rev. Hugh Stowell, Rector of Ballaugh, Isle of Man.

"Let me die the death of the righteous, and let my last end be like his."— *Numbers* xxiii.

M. A. DENHAM.—1850.

Popular Rhymes, Proverbs, Sayings, Prophecies, etc. etc., peculiar to the Isle of Man and the Manks people. *Foolscap octavo.* Pp. 17.

The work is inscribed "To Oberon and Titania, King and Queen of Fairies, and the whole Fairy Court, dwelling in the Greater Mona, I dedicate this little Tract on the Popular Rhymes, Proverbs, Sayings, etc. etc. etc., of their native Ysle." Dated at the end "P.B. n'r. D. in com. Dunelm. Oct. MDCCCL. M. A. D."

This brochure was edited by Mr. M. Aislabie Denham, of Piercebridge, near Darlington, and 50 copies only struck off for private distribution. The matter was chiefly supplied him by the author, with other remarks on the Popular Rhymes and Customs of the Isle of Man, at the time Mr. Denham was printing similar tracts connected with the northern counties of England. These are all now, from the few copies printed, become very scarce. Mr. Denham died on the 10th September 1859.

These Proverbs, etc., are printed in the Manx Society's series, vol. xvi., "Mona Miscellany," 1869.

1850.

A Manks Historical and Geographical Dictionary of the places mentioned in the Bible. Douglas : printed and published for the author by James Brown, King Street. N. D.

12mo. No. 1, published Sept. 1850, price 6d. ABA to BAA.

This is all that was published.

BISHOP WILSON.—1851. (REV. H. B. HONE.)

The Lives of James Usher, D.D., Archbishop of Armagh ;

Henry Hammond, D.D., Rector of Penshurst, Kent ; John Evelyn, Esq., author of "Sylvia," etc. ; and Thomas Wilson, D.D., Bishop of Sodor and Man. By Richard B. Hone, M.A., Archdeacon of Worcester and Vicar of Halesowen. Seventh Edition, revised. London : John W. Parker, West Strand. 1851. *Small octavo.*

Life of Bishop Wilson, pp. 249 to 335. With a portrait. The first edition in 1833.

1851.

Harbours—Isle of Man. Copies of Memorial of Inhabitants of Castletown to the Lords of the Treasury, Report of Admiralty, and Correspondence of the Authorities of the Isle of Man with Treasury and Admiralty, etc. Ordered by the House of Commons to be printed, 5th August 1851. *Folio.* Pp. 36.

Nine plans. Contains correspondence on this subject from the 1st January 1846 to the present date.

ROBERT J. MOORE.—1851.

Peel Schools, Isle of Man. To the Trustees of " Christian's Endowed National School," the Trustees of Bishop Wilson's School, and the Promoters of the proposed Infant School, in aid of which the Ladies' Bazaar was held in Peel Castle in August 1848 ; Proposed Terms of Amalgamation of " Christian's Endowed National School," Peel, and Infant School on Bishop Wilson's Foundation, and Clauses of Management to be inserted in Trust-Deed. Printed by P. Curphey, *Manx Sun* Office, Quay, Douglas. *Folio.* Pp. 6.

Dated " Peel, 11th Jany. 1851," and signed " Robert J. Moore."

COMMANDER GEORGE WILLIAMS, R.N.—1851.

Isle of Man. Surveyed by Commander George Williams, R.N. 1847. The Soundings between Maughold Head and Ayre Point, with the Bahama and King William's Banks, are from the Surveys of Capt. F. W. Beechey, R.N., F.R.S. 1843. London : published according to Act of Parliament at the Hydrographic Office of the Admiralty. Nov. 1st, 1851. Large Sheet, 25 in. by 37 in.

The only correct outline map of the Island. The drawings of the different ports, bays, and headlands were most beautifully executed, and are deposited with the Board of Admiralty.

1851.

The Twelfth Annual Report of the Isle of Mann Diocesan Association. August 1851. Douglas : R. H. Johnson, Printer and Stationer, 2 Great Nelson Street. 1851. 12*mo.* Pp. 8.

Total amount of subscriptions, etc., £286 : 15 : 5.

COL. JOHNSON. No date. [1851.]

A Brief Sketch of the Isle of Man ; showing its advantages as a retreat to Visitors and a place of residence to Strangers. By Col. Johnson. Douglas : printed by P. Curphey, *Manx Sun* Office, and by R. Fargher, *Mona's Herald* Office. 32*mo.* Pp. 31.

Some copies have " A Sketch of," etc.

The second edition appeared in the same year. *Small Octavo.* Pp. 16. To which is appended, " Popular Customs and Superstitions of the Isle of Man." With Woodcuts. Printed by R. Fargher. Douglas.

T. R. H. Thomson.—1851.

Plain Directions what to do in Cases of Accident or Medical
Emergency, intended for the use of the Country Popula-
tion of the Isle of Man. By T. R. H. Thomson, M.D.,
Surgeon, R.N. Douglas: printed by P. Curphey, *Manx
Sun* Office. *Octavo.* Pp. 58.

1852.

The Thirteenth Annual Report of the Isle of Mann Diocesan
Association. August 1852. Douglas: R. H. Johnson,
Printer and Stationer, 2 Great Nelson Street. 1852.
Octavo. Pp. 8.

Amount of subscriptions, £263 : 16 : 7.

J. J. A. Worsaae.—1852.

An Account of the Danes and Norwegians in England, Scotland, and Ireland. By J. J. A. Worsaae, For. F.S.A.
London ; a Royal Commissioner for the Preservation of
the National Monuments of Denmark ; author of " Primæ-
val Antiquities of Denmark," etc. etc. With numerous
Woodcuts. London : John Murray, Albemarle Street.
1852. 12*mo.* Pp. 359.

Section X.—The Sudreyjar, or Southern Isles.—Isle of
Man, etc., pp. 276-296. With Woodcuts of the Runic Stones
at Braddan and Michael. A very interesting account of the
Northmen in the Isle of Man, etc.

Rev. G. A. Page.—1852.

An Appeal to British Christians against the Drinking System
of Great Britain. By Gregory Alexander Page, Wesleyan
Minister. Douglas. 1852.

Rev. G. A. Page.—1853.

A Memorial of the Kitterland Disaster, containing a full and circumstantial Account of the Wreck and Explosion of the Brig "Lilly," with several interesting particulars not previously published: to which is added a short Poem on the subject. By the Rev. Gregory A. Page, Castletown. Price Threepence. Douglas. 1853. M. A. Quiggin, 52 North Quay ; J. Mylrea, Duke Street ; M. P. Backwell, Strand Street. Castletown : M. J. Backwell. Ramsey : F. Leech. Peel : N. Pickles. *Small octavo.* Pp. 36.

Mr. Page was the Wesleyan Minister at Castletown. The gunpowder on board the " Lilly " by some means got ignited, and launched into eternity twenty-nine persons who were assisting to save the cargo.

T. J. Ouseley.—1853.

Mona's Isle, and other Poems. By T. J. Ouseley

> " I see the Deep's untrampled floor,
>   With green and purple sea weeds strown ;
>   I see the waves upon the shore,
>   Like light dissolved in star showers, thrown :
>   I sit upon the sands alone,
>   The lightning of the noon-tide ocean
>   Is flashing round me, and a tone
>   Arises from its measured motion,
> How sweet ! did any heart now share in my emotion."
>
> *Shelley.*

London : Woodfall and Kinder, Angel Court, Skinner Street. Shrewsbury : John Davies, High Street. 1853. *Post octavo.* Pp. 230. Preface, etc., pp. viii. "Mona's Isle," pp. 1 to 90.

James Burman.—1853.

Statute Laws of the Isle of Man, promulgated since the year

1848. With an Appendix, containing the additional Bye-Laws for the Regulation and Government of the Towns; Rules of the Court of Chancery respecting Insolvent Debtors, etc. By James Burman, Esq., Advocate, Secretary to His Excellency the Lieutenant-Governor, Clerk of the Council, etc. Douglas: printed and published by Peter Curphey, *Sun* Office, North Quay; London: Stevens and Norton, Law Booksellers, Bell Yard, Lincoln's Inn. 1853. *Royal octavo.* Contents, etc, pp. vi.; Statute Laws, pp. 278.

The Advertisement states this completes the Published Statute Book of the Isle of Man, contained in the series of volumes published respectively by Messrs. Mills, Geneste, Jeffcott, and Gell.

1853.

Customs Reform, Isle of Man. Copies of Treasury Minutes, and of correspondence between the Treasury and the Authorities or other Public Bodies of the Isle of Man, in relation to the recent Customs Reform in that Island. Ordered by the House of Commons to be printed, 19th August 1853. *Folio.*

List of Papers, pp. ii. to iv. Forty-seven Papers. Correspondence, etc., pp. 65.

1853.

Report by the Commissioners for the British Fisheries of their proceedings in the year ended 31st December 1852. Being Fishing 1852. *Folio.* Pp. 33.

Dated Board of Fisheries, Edinburgh, 1st June 1853. In the Appendix will be found many Statistics relative to the Isle of Man Fisheries.

G. H. WOOD.—1853.

Poems. To which are added Critiques on Metaphysical Subjects. By G. H. Wood.

> " But is amusement all ? Studious of song,
>   And yet ambitious not to sing in vain,
>   I would not trifle merely, though the world
>   Were loudest in their praise, who do no more."
>
> *Cowper's Task*, book ii.

Douglas : printed by M. A. Quiggin, 52 North Quay ; published by J. Mylrea, Duke Street. London : Simpkin, Marshall, and Co. Liverpool: G. Philip and Son., MDCCCLIII. *Fcap. octavo.* Introduction, etc., pp. xii. Poems, etc., pp. 263. A long list of Subscribers, pp. 267-277.

Stanzas on Peel Castle, with several others relating to the island and friends.

Mr. Wood was a native of the Isle of Man ; was stationed with his regiment, H.M. 20th Foot, at St. Helena, during the latter years of the captivity of Napoleon, and was present at his burial in 1821.

JOHN CUBBON.—1853.

A Brief Statement of the Charities of St. Matthew's Chapel, Douglas, Isle of Man. By John Cubbon, one of the Wardens. Easter, 1853. R. Fargher, Printer, Wellington Buildings, Duke Street, Douglas. *Folio.* Pp. 3.

1853.

The Fourteenth Annual Report of the Isle of Mann Diocesan Association. August 1853. Douglas: Robert H. Johnson, Printer, etc., 2 Great Nelson Street. 1853. 12*mo.* Pp. 8.

Total amount of subscriptions, etc., £256 : 4 : 6½. Fifteenth Report in 1854, subscriptions, £368 : 6 : 1.

BISHOP WILSON.—No date.   [1855.]

A Form of Prayer to be used at such times as the Fishermen in the Diocese of Mann can be gathered together for Divine Service during the Herring Fishing.   Compiled by Bishop Wilson.   Douglas : M. P. Backwell, Atholl Street. *Small quarto.*   Pp. 16.

The present Bishop Powys caused this Form to be reprinted, and attempted to revive these gatherings, but met with little success.

1855.

Greenhalgh or Greenhugh of Brandlesome, in the County of Lancaster.   1805.   Printed for Thomas Garrett junior, by R. Fargher, *Mona's Herald* Office, Douglas.   A Broadside, with border round, and facsimile of John Greenhalgh's Signature.   A Pedigree.

1856.

The Seventeenth Annual Report of the Isle of Mann Diocesan Association.   1856.   Douglas : Robert H. Johnson, Printer, 2 Great Nelson Street.   1856.   12*mo.*   Pp. 8.

Total amount of subscriptions, £321 : 16s.

JAMES WALKER.—1856.

Isle of Man Harbours.   Report of James Walker, LL.D., F.R.S.L. and E., Civil Engineer, London.   Dated 26th Jan. 1856.   Westminster : Vacher and Sons, 29 Parliament Street.   1856.   *Octavo.*   Pp. 42.   Map and 7 Plans.

Report addressed to Richard Quirk, Esq., Receiver-General of the Isle of Man.

ROBERT J. MOORE.—1856.

Abstract of the existing Bye-Laws for the Regulation and

Government of the several Towns in the Isle of Man.
1856. Printed by P. Curphey, *Sun* Office, King Street,
Douglas. *Octavo.* Pp. 4. Dated " Peel, 16th June 1856.
Robt. J. Moore, H.B."

This Abstract was prepared by Mr. Moore for distribution
in the Town of Peel.

M. SUMMERS.—1857.   (THOMAS CRENNELL.)

Experimental and Practical Christianity exemplified ; or, A
  Brief Memoir of Thomas Crennell of Ramsey, Isle of
  Man.

" Whose faith follow."

St. Paul.

By M. Summers. 1857. Douglas : printed by R. Fargher,
  9 Mona Terrace. 12*mo.* Pp. 35.

REV. W. J. KENNEDY, M.A.—1857.

Tabulated Reports on Schools Inspected in Lancashire by the
  Rev. W. J. Kennedy, M.A., Inspector, and the Rev. W.
  Birley, M.A., Assistant-Inspector. 1855-6. London :
  Eyre and Spottiswoode. 1857. *Octavo.* Pp. 76.

At pp. 41 to 45 are the Isle of Man Schools, inspected by
the Rev. Mr. Kennedy, Her Majesty's Inspector of Schools.
These Reports are annually made and published.

BISHOP POWYS.—1857.

Charge delivered to the Convocation held at Bishop's Court,
  Thursday, June 4th, 1857, by the Bishop of Sodor and
  Mann. Douglas : M. P. Backwell, Printer, Atholl Street.
  Octavo. Pp. 31.

1857.

Ellan Vannin : A Journal of a Tour in the Isle of Mann in the Olden Time. By a School Boy.

> "Buy it. That doth commend a booke, the Stationer saies. Judge your six-pen-orth, your shilling's worth, or higher, and welcome. But, whatever you do, Buy."—*Shakspeare*, *Fol. Ed.*

Liverpool: printed for the Douglas Bazaar, by Egerton Smith and Co. 1857. *Small octavo.* Pp. 12.

This Journal commences Oct. 6, 1805, and ends 28th October. Dated from "Wolstenholme Square, Liverpool, 29th Oct. 1805."

Rev. J. G. Cumming, M.A.—1857.

The Story of Rushen Castle and Rushen Abbey, in the Isle of Man. By the Rev. J. G. Cumming, M.A., F.G.S., Head Master of the Grammar School of King Edward VI., Lichfield. London : Bell and Daldy, Fleet Street. 1857. *Octavo.* Dedication and Introductory Notice, pp. viii. ; Work, pp. 64 ; Appendix, pp. 24 ; 8 Plates.

Rev. J. G. Cumming, M.A.—1857.

The Runic and other Monumental Remains of the Isle of Man. By the Rev. J. G. Cumming, M.A., F.G.S., Head Master of the Grammar School, Lichfield. London : Bell and Daldy, Fleet Street; Lomax, Lichfield ; Kerruish and Kneale, Douglas. *Quarto.*

Dedication to Horace Powys, D.D., Bishop of Sodor and Man. Dated "1st June, 1857." Prefatory Note, pp. v. to viii. Runic Remains, 44 pp. List of Subscribers, 4 pp. Plates 15. Mr. Daniel Wilson's Archæology of Scotland also treats of the Runic Monuments in the Isle of Man.

J. BURKILL.—1857.

Pictorial Beauties of Mona, from drawings made on the spot. By J. Burkill, Esq., author of "Bolton Abbey Illustrated," "The Abbeys and Monasteries of England," etc. 1857. *Imperial folio.* 6 views, tinted lithography, by Day and Son, London.

The views consist of Laxey Village and Bay; Peel Castle from the South; Peel Castle in a Storm; Castletown and Neighbourhood; Ramsey; and Douglas with its Bay.

JOHN PATTERSON.—1857. (JOSEPH TRAIN.)

Memoir of Joseph Train, F.S.A. Scot., the Antiquarian Correspondent of Sir Walter Scott. By John Patterson, Author of "Shadows of the Past." Glasgow: Thomas Murray and Son; Edinburgh: John Menzies. MDCCCLVII. *Post octavo.* Pp. 194.

Mr. Train wrote the History of the Isle of Man (1845), and in this Memoir there are numerous extracts from that work, with other matters relating thereto. He died 7th December 1852.

REV. JOSEPH STEVENSON, M.A.—1858.

The Church Historians of England. *Octavo.* Seeleys, London. 1858.

In vol. v., part i., pp. 385-405, is "The Chronicle of the Isle of Man," translated from the Latin text in Johnstone's "Celto-Normannicæ," corrected in a few places by the original manuscript in the Cottonian Library.

This Chronicle has been printed in part in Camden's "Britannia," at Perth, in 1784; by Johnstone, in 1786, at Copenhagen; in the first volume of Oliver's "Monumenta,"

Manx Society, vol. iv., 1860; and by Professor Munch at Christiania, 1860, with Historical Notes. This latter edition has been reprinted in the Manx Society's series, vols. xxii. and xxiii. Edited by the Right Rev. Dr. Goss.

GILBERT J. FRENCH.—1858.

An Attempt to explain the Origin and Meaning of the early interlaced ornamentation found on the Ancient Sculptured Stones of Scotland, Ireland, and the Isle of Man. By Gilbert J. French, of Bolton. Printed for presentation only. Manchester: printed by Charles Simms and Co. 1858. *Octavo.* Pp. 24. Eight Plates ; three relating to the Isle of Man.

A Paper read at the Salisbury Congress of the British Archæological Association, 6th August 1858.

ELIZA CRAVEN GREEN.—1858.

Sea Weeds and Heath Flowers, or Memories of Mona. By Eliza Craven Green. Douglas : printed and published by H. Curphey, *Manx Sun* Office, King Street ; London and Liverpool ; G. Philip and Son. *Crown octavo.* Pp. 200.

Insular Poems, pp. 1 to 57, with "The Island Harp" at the end.

"A Legend of Mona" was first published by Miss E. S. Craven in 1825. The first 56 lines at the commencement, and the 12 lines at the end of that edition, are omitted in the present one. Mrs. Green was born at Leeds in 1803, and died there in 1866.

1858.

The Nineteenth Annual Report of the Isle of Mann Diocesan Association. 1858. Douglas : printed by H. R. Johnson,

Weekly Advertising Circular Office, Prospect Hill. 1858. 12*mo.* Pp. 8.

Total amount of subscriptions, £353 : 8 : 2.

1858.

The Bentley Ballads, a Selection of the Choice Ballads, Songs, etc., contributed to "Bentley's Miscellany." Edited by Dr. Doran. *Small octavo.* London. 1858.

Pp. 333-350, "The Manxman and his Visitor." Descriptive of a Manxman who was of a cruel disposition when a boy, cruel when a young man, and cruel to the last.

Elizabeth Cookson.—1858.

Mylecharane : The Popular and most Ancient Manx National Song. Air Plaintive.

> O* Vylechrane ! craad hooar oo dthy stoyr,
>> My lomarcan daag oo mee ;
> Nagh dooar mee sy churragh eh dowin, dowin dy liooar
>> As my lomarcan daag oo mee.

  * In Manx, the letter M when preceded by O is changed into V.

The Isle of Mann : printed by M. A. Quiggin, Douglas. 1858. *Square.* Pp. 12.

Contains also "A Manx Myth," and "Manx Scenery," accompanied with a few notes.

C. Cannell.—1858.

Minutes of Cases decided in the Manx Courts, from February 1857, to March 1858 ; including the Two Privy Council Cases of Williams, Deacon, and Co., *v.* Tupper, and Avison and Boardman *v.* Quayle and Quirk. Minuted by C. Cannell, B.A., Student at Law. Douglas, Isle of Man : printed by Robert Fargher, 9 Mona Terrace. March 1858. *Octavo.* Pp. 158.

FREDERIC W. FARRAR.—1858.

Eric, or Little by Little, a Tale of Roslyn School. By
Frederic W. Farrar, Fellow of Trinity College, Cambridge.

> " Tis one thing to be tempted, Escalus,
>   Another thing to fall."
>
> *Measure for Measure, Act. II. Scene* 1.

Edinburgh: Adam and Charles Black, North Bridge.
MDCCCLVIII. *Octavo.* Pp. 396.

The scene of this novel will be recognised by many as
relating to the Isle of Man. The adventure at the Stack is
one of the most thrilling description. Mr. Farrar was a pupil
at King William's College, and it is only justice to him to
reprint the following letter, which appeared in one of the insular papers soon after the publication of Eric :—

HARROW, *April* 18*th*, 1859.

To THE EDITOR OF THE *Manx Sun.*

SIR—I have heard with surprise and regret that some persons who
entertain unkindly feelings towards King William's College have taken the
opportunity to attribute to that institution a state of things described in a
recent story called " Eric, or Little by Little." Now, Sir, had I for a moment
anticipated such a result, I have no hesitation in saying that I should never
have suffered the book to appear in its present shape. To avoid, as I hoped,
the possibility of a consequence so much to be deprecated, I placed in the
preface an emphatic disclaimer of all intention to identify Roslyn with any
existing school ; and I took the same opportunity to express with all humility
a grateful appreciation of past kindnesses which I have received from the
valued friends who are connected with King William's College. It is true that
the scenery of the tale was taken from my own happy and vivid boyish re-
miniscences of your Island. It was a pleasure to reproduce the undimmed
sensations which your seas and rocks had excited ; but if by this innocent
indulgence of happy memories I have done unwitting injury to a school for
which I have quite recently testified my strong regard, I shall be deeply and
sincerely pained. Will you then allow me, thus publicly, to re-affirm (I hope
finally) that Roslyn " was in no way intended to be a picture of King William's College ;" that the incidents of " Eric," so far as they are real and not
imaginary, are derived from many sources ; and that I asserted the truthful-

ness of the book as a whole, not because I was painting the scene of my own education, but because I have had subsequent opportunities of seeing many of the most famous English schools, and forming an opinion of their temptations and advantages, my impressions of which I was desirous to state in the form of a story, mainly intended for the benefit of boys. In conclusion, let me add that I always look back to King William's College with sincere affection, and that I should have the fullest confidence in recommending it as a place of education for any boy in whom I was interested. It has trained many good and able men, and has no need of any defence from me. Indeed, it would be presumption in me to write about it at all, were it not for the circumstances which I have mentioned, and which seemed to call for some notice from me. Yours, etc.   THE AUTHOR OF "ERIC."

REV. WM. MACKENZIE.—1859.

A Lecture on Reformation in the Isle of Man now and before Luther. Published at the request of the "Douglas Religious and useful Knowledge" and of the "Temperance" Societies. By the Rev. William Mackenzie, Minister of North Leith Free Church, and Hon. Secretary to the Manx Society for Publication of National Documents of the Isle of Man. Price One Penny. Douglas: W. Kneale, Duke Street. 1859. *Octavo.* Pp. 16.

WM. SACHEVERELL.—1859.

An Account of the Isle of Man, its Inhabitants, Language, Soil, Remarkable Curiosities, the Succession of its Kings and Bishops, down to the eighteenth century : by way of Essay. With a Voyage to I-Colomb-Kill. By William Sacheverell, Esq., late Governor of Man. To which is added a Dissertation about the Mona of Cæsar and Tacitus, and an Account of the Ancient Druids, etc. By Mr. Thomas Brown, addressed in a Letter to his learned friend Mr. A. Sellers. Edited, with Introductory Notice and Copious Notes, by the Rev. J. G. Cumming, M.A., F.G.S., Warden and Professor of Classical Literature in Queen's College, Birmingham, late Vice-Principal of King William's

College, Isle of Man. Douglas, Isle of Man : printed for the Manx Society. 1859. *Octavo.* Pp. 204.

This is the First volume of the Publications of the Manx Society, reprinted from the Edition of 1702.

ELIZABETH COOKSON.—1859.

Mylecharane : The Popular and most Ancient Manx National Song, rendered into English verse, adapted to the old Manx Air. By Elizabeth Cookson. With Notes. Second Edition.

> O* Vylecharane ! cre dhooar oo dty stoyr,
>   My lomarcan daag oo mee ?
> Nagh dooar mee sy churragh eh dowin, dowin dy looar,
>   As my lomarcan daag oo mee !

* In Manx, the letter M at the beginning of a word, when preceded by O, is changed into V.

The Isle of Mann : printed by M. A. Quiggin, Douglas. 1859. *Small octavo.* Pp. 38.

This Edition contains the Music to Mylecharane, also the Manx Legends—"The Phynnodderee," " A Manx Myth," "Manx Scenery," "The Fairy Wren of Manxland," "The Lore-lei," etc. The Notes to Mylecharane are curtailed and altered.

ELIZABETH COOKSON.—No date. [1859.]

Legends of Manx Land. Second Series. By Elizabeth Cookson.

> " Manxmen love their native dales,
>   Island song, and island tales."

Contains—Olave Goddardson.
>   A Chronicle of Peel Castle.
>   Cutlar Mac Cullock.
>   Illiam Dhôan.

Douglas : printed by H. Curphey, *Manx Sun* Office.   *Small octavo.* Pp. 48.   A second edition the same year.

BISHOP POWYS.—1859.

A Letter from the Bishop of Sodor and Mann to the Rev. the Vicar of Braddan, in reference to Questions on Church Matters which have recently arisen in the Town of Douglas. Douglas : M. P. Backwell, Bookseller, Atholl Street.   No date. *Octavo.* Pp. 8.   Printed for Private Circulation. Dated "Bishop's Court, May 27, 1859."   Addressed to the Rev. Mr. Drury respecting the appointment of Curates to St. George's Church, etc.

REV. JOHN KELLY.—1859.

A Practical Grammar of the Antient Gaelic or Language of the Isle of Man, usually called Manx.

> ——" Si quid novisti rectius istis,
> Candidus imperti : si non, his utere mecum."

By the Rev. John Kelly, LL.D., Vicar of Ardleigh, and Rector of Copford, in the County of Essex.   Edited, together with an Introduction, Life of Dr. Kelly, and Notes, by the Rev. William Gill, Vicar of Malew.   Douglas, Isle of Man : printed for the Manx Society. 1859. *Octavo.* Introduction, etc., pp. xlviii.   Grammar, pp. 92.

This forms the Second volume of the Publications of the Manx Society.   Reprinted from the Edition of 1804, which is not noticed in the Title of this Edition.

The Editor, in his Introduction to this Grammar, says— " This reprint is an accurate transcript of the original work, with corrections only of errors of the press, and of some obvious inaccuracies of the pen," and has " given the work in its original integrity."

It is much to be regretted the Editor did not make foot-
notes where these errors occurred, for in this edition the
alterations and omissions are so numerous as to entirely alter
the original work, which cannot, by any reasoning, be considered as " given in its original integrity."

Mr. Gill died on the 17th October 1871.

REV. EDWARD FORBES.—1859.

Parting Counsel. A Farewell Sermon, preached in St. George's,
Douglas, on Sunday, January 30th, 1859. Also a Pas-
toral Letter from Rome. By the Rev. Edward Forbes,
M.A. Douglas : John Mylrea. London : Wertheim, Mac-
intosh, and Hunt, 24 Paternoster Row. 1859. *Octavo.*
Pp. 24.

1859.

Isle of Man. Copies of Correspondence between the Secretary of State for the Home Department, the Lieutenant-
Governor of the Isle of Man, the House of Keys, and the
Office of Woods, etc., since the 1st of January 1857, as to
the Forests in the Isle of Mann. (Mr. Laing.) Ordered
by the House of Commons to be printed, 13th August,
1859. *Folio.* Pp. 40.

1859.

Report of the Isle of Mann Association of the Church Mis-
sionary Society, from December 1858 to December 1859.
Printed by R. H. Johnson, Prospect Hill, Douglas. *Octavo.*
Pp. 8.   Amount of income for the year, £365 : 12 : 5.

F. LEECH.—1859.

Leech's New Illustrated Tourist's Guide to the Isle of Man,
its Scenery, History, Popular Customs, etc. Ramsey :

F. Leech, Printer and Publisher ; Douglas : J. Mylrea,
Bookseller, etc. ; George Philip and Son, 32 Fleet Street,
London, and 51 South Castle Street, Liverpool ; and all
Booksellers. No date. *Small octavo.* Pp. 160.

With 11 Plates and a Map of the Island.

E. L. BLANCHARD.—1859.

Adams's Descriptive Guide to the Channel Islands, the Isle of
Wight, and the Isle of Man ; with Introductory Sketches
of Southampton, Weymouth, Gosport, and Portsmouth,
the usual Ports of Embarkation. By E. L. Blanchard.
With Maps of the Channel Islands, the Isle of Wight,
and the Isle of Man. A new and enlarged Edition.
London : W. J. Adams (Bradshaw's Guide Office), 59
Fleet Street ; and all Booksellers. 1859. *Small octavo.*
Isle of Man, pp. 95 to 117.

1859.

Amended Standing Orders of the Court of Tynwald with regard to Railway Bills. 1859. Douglas : printed by H.
Curphey, *Manx Sun* Office, King Street. 1859. *Royal
octavo.* Pp. 14.

1860.

An Act for Disafforesting and Allotting the Uninclosed Portion of "The Forest" in the Isle of Man. Douglas :
printed (by Authority) by H. Curphey, *Manx Sun* Office,
13 King Street. 1860. *Royal octavo.* Pp. 24.

Promulgated the 13th November 1860, at St. John's,
being the first act of the present Lieutenant-Governor, F.
Pigott, Esq.

1860.

The Douglas Middle School Magazine. No. 1, January 1860. Douglas : printed by H. Curphey, *Manx Sun* Office. *Foolscap octavo.* Pp. 40.

Only three numbers (for January, February, and March 1860) of this Magazine were published.

J. S.—1860.

Letters, Descriptive, Reflective, and Humorous, on the Isle of Man. By J. S. Supposed to be addressed to a friend in the South. Douglas : printed by R. Fargher, 9 Mona Terrace. 1860. *Small octavo.* Pp. 32.

J. F. CAMPBELL.—1860-62.

Popular Tales of the West Highlands, orally collected, with a translation. By J. F. Campbell. Edinburgh : Edmonston and Douglas. 1860. *Small octavo.* 4 vols.

In the first volume of these interesting Tales, Mr. Campbell has given in the Introduction, p. xl. and pp. l. to lv., specimens of many Tales picked up during a visit to the Island in April 1860. Also in the fourth volume, p. 299 and p. 386, respecting the Legs of Man.

BISHOP POWYS.—1860.

Charge delivered to the Convocation held at Bishop's Court, Thursday, May 31, 1860. By the Bishop of Sodor and Mann. Liverpool : Adam Holden, 48 Church Street ; London : Rivingtons. 1860. *Octavo.* Pp. 30.

1860.

Observations on the State and Condition of the present

Friendly Societies ; and Proposal for the Formation of a Friendly Society on Improved Principles. Castletown : printed by M. J. Backwell, Malew Street. 12*mo.* Pp. 10.

These "Observations" are signed by Mark H. Quayle, J. Gell, R. T. Quayle, and J. T. Clucas. Dated "Castletown, 1st May 1860.

1860.

An Act to Provide for Paving, Cleansing, and Lighting the Streets of the Town of Douglas, and for making and keeping in repair Public Sewers therein, and otherwise improving the said Town. Douglas : printed (by Authority) by H. Curphey, *Manx Sun* Office, King Street. 1860. *Royal octavo.* Pp. 30.

REV. W. MACKENZIE.—1860.

Legislation by Three of the Thirteen Stanleys, Kings of Man, —Acts of Sir John Stanley, A.D. 1417-1430 ; Legislation of the seventh Earl of Derby, A.D. 1627-1647, and his Letter, as published in Peck's "Desiderata Curiosa ;" Acts referring to the Clergy and Landowners, by the tenth Earl of Derby, 1703. Edited, with Introduction and Notes, by the Rev. Wm. Mackenzie, Member of the Free Presbytery of Edinburgh. Douglas, Isle of Man : printed for the Manx Society. 1860. *Octavo.* Pp. 224.

The Third Volume of the Manx Society's Publications.

DR. OLIVER.—1860-62.

Monumenta de Insula Manniæ, or a Collection of National Documents relating to the Isle of Man. Translated and Edited, with Appendix, by J. R. Oliver, Esq., M.D. Douglas, Isle of Man : printed for the Manx Society. 1860. *Octavo.* Vol. i. pp. 244.

This forms the Fourth Volume of the Manx Society's Publications.

Vol. ii. 1861. Pp. 250. With a Map, entitled "Mona Cæsaris." The Seventh Volume of the Manx Society's Publications.

Vol. iii. 1862. Pp. 272. With a Copious Index to the three volumes. The Ninth Volume of the Manx Society. These volumes contain a vast mine of information for the Historian, consisting of copies of Charters and other important documents, as well as numerous extracts from various authors who make mention of the Isle of Man.

W. KNEALE.—No date.—[1860.]

Kneale's Guide to the Isle of Man, comprising an Account of the Island, Historical, Physical, Archæological, and Topographical, and all the information desirable for Visitors and Tourists ; to which is appended a collection of entertaining Manx legends. Illustrated with numerous engravings. Douglas : W. Kneale, 37 Duke Street. *Small octavo.* Pp. 224. A carefully compiled and excellent Guide to the Isle of Man.

A Second Edition was published in 1866. *Small octavo.* Pp. 222.

P. A. MUNCH.—1860.

Chronica Regum Manniæ et Insularum. The Chronicle of Man and the Sudreys, edited from the Manuscript Codex in the British Museum, with Historical Notes, by P. A. Munch, Professor of History in the Royal University of Christiania ; Hon. F.R.A.S.S. To accompany the "Index Scholarum" of the University for the year 1857. Second Season. Christiania, 1860. Printed by Brogger and Christie. *Octavo.* Preface, pp. iii.-xxxiv., dated Rome,

Oct. 4, 1859. Chronica, pp. 1-31. Notes, pp. 32-151. Appendix, pp. 152-191. A plate of Runic Inscriptions.

The Appendix contains copies of many documents from the Archives in the Vatican, etc. etc.

This has been reprinted, with additional documents, edited by the Right Rev. Dr. Goss. Manx Society series, vols. xxii. and xxiii.

H. R. OSWALD.—1860.

Vestigia Insulæ Manniæ Antiquiora ; or a Dissertation on the Armorial Bearings of the Isle of Man, the Regalities and Prerogatives of its Ancient Kings, and the Original Usages, Customs, Privileges, Laws, and Constitutional Government of the Manx People. By H. R. Oswald, Esq., F.A.S., L:R.C.S.E., Member of the Council of the Manx Society.

" Re tam vetustate deficile dictu est."

Douglas, Isle of Man : printed for the Manx Society. 1860. *Octavo.* Preliminary Observations, etc., pp. ix. ; Armorial Bearings, etc., pp. 218.

This forms the Fifth Volume of the Manx Society's Publications, and is illustrated with numerous seals of arms and other antiquities connected with the Isle of Man, which have been most ably discussed in this work.

1861.

Isle of Man Agricultural Society. Rules of the Society, Minutes of Annual General Meeting, Cash Account, List of Subscribers, etc. etc. Isle of Man : printed by John Hampton, Post-Office, Ramsey. 1861. 12*mo.* Pp. 12.

ROBERT J. MOORE.—1861.

Sketch of the Origin, Progress, and present Position of Christian's Endowed National School, and Bishop Wilson's

Infant School, Peel, Isle of Man. By Robert J. Moore, H. B. of Peel, one of the Trustees of the School premises. Douglas : printed by H. Curphey, *Manx Sun* Office, King Street. 1861. *Octavo.* Pp. 15.

The New Schoolhouse was opened on Friday, 28th June 1861.

JOHN FELTHAM.—1861.

Feltham's Tour through the Isle of Man in 1797 and 1798. Comprising Sketches of its Ancient and Modern History, Constitution, Laws, Commerce, Agriculture, Fishery, etc., including whatever is remarkable in each Parish, its Population, Inscriptions, Registers, etc. Edited with Notes, by the Rev. Robert Airey, Curate of Braddan for St. Luke's, Baldwin, and Cronkbourne. Douglas, Isle of Man : printed for the Manx Society. 1861. *Octavo.* Pp. 272.

This is the Sixth Volume of the Manx Society, and contains the Map and Plates of the original edition of 1798.

REV. J. G. CUMMING, M.A.—1861.

The Isle of Man. A Guide to the Isle of Man, with the means of access thereto, and an introduction to its Scenery. Containing also a general synopsis of its Constitution ; Climate ; Language ; Population ; Manners and Customs ; Topography ; Civil and Ecclesiastical History ; Agriculture ; Fisheries ; Mines ; Minerals ; Manufactures ; Antiquities ; Botany ; Geology and Zoology. By the Rev. Joseph George Cumming, M.A., F.G.S., late Warden of Queen's College, Birmingham, and formerly Vice-Principal of King William's College, Isle of Man. London : Edward Stanford, 6 Charing Cross. 1861. *Post octavo.* Preface, etc., pp. xvi. Guide, pp. 230. A Map.

1861.

An Act to provide an Asylum for Lunatics and Insane Persons. Douglas : printed (by Authority) by H. Curphey, *Manx Sun* Office, 13 King Street. 1861. *Royal octavo.* Pp. 43.

1861.

A New Map of the Isle of Man, shewing the local Divisions, Roads, and Geographical features of the Island. Together with the precise site and entire extent of the Forest Wall or Mountain Hedge, laid down from accurate Surveys. May 1861.   25 + 31 inches.

The Disafforesting Commissioners' Map.

Rev. J. H. Gray.—1861.

A Letter to His Excellency Francis Pigott, Lieut.-Governor of the Isle of Man. And a Defence in reply of Certain Charges made by the Bishop of Sodor and Man. By the Rev. J. H. Gray, M.A., Incumbent of St. Barnabas. Douglas : printed and published by Robert H. Johnson, *Isle of Man Weekly Advertising Circular* Office. 1861. *Octavo.* Pp. 24.

1861.

Isle of Man Disafforesting Commission. Declaration of the Boundaries of the Lands in "The Forest," uninclosed or which ought to be uninclosed, as determined by the Commissioners appointed under an Act of Tynwald passed in the Twenty-fourth year of the Reign of Queen Victoria, and entituled "An Act for Disafforesting and Allotting the uninclosed portion of 'The Forest,' in the Isle of Man." Printed by order of the Commissioners. 1861. London : printed by Jas. Wade, Brydges St., Strand. *Folio.* Pp. 22. Dated Ramsey, 24th August 1861.

Signed by George Wingrove Cooke, N. Wetherell, J. H. Patterson. Witnessed by Hans Busk, Secretary to the Commissioners.

GEORGE WILSON, M.D.—1861.   EDWARD FORBES, F.R.S.

Memoir of Edward Forbes, F.R.S., late Regius Professor of Natural History in the University of Edinburgh. By George Wilson, M.D., F.R.S.E., late Regius Professor of Technology in the University of Edinburgh, and Director of the Industrial Museum of Scotland; and Archibald Geikie, F.R.S.E., F.G.S., of the Geological Survey of Great Britain. MacMillan and Co., Cambridge and London. Edmonston and Douglas, Edinburgh. 1861. *Octavo.* Pp. 589. Portrait.

Professor Forbes was a native of the Isle of Man, and the first chapter gives a short account of him. Dr. Wilson died before the work was finished, and Mr. Geikie completed it.

REV. WM. MACKENZIE.—1861.

Index to all the Statute or Tynwald Laws of the Isle of Man, being a combination of all the separate Indexes to the Volumes edited by Messrs. Burman, Gell, Jeffcott, and Geneste, with a New Index to that of Mr. Mills, by A. W. Adams, Crown Solicitor; together with an Abstract by Mr. Burman, Secretary to the Governor and Council, of all the recent Acts of Tynwald, and a Table of the Dates of all the Statute Laws of the Island. By Rev. William Mackenzie, Annotator on "The Stanley Legislation of Man." Douglas: W. Kneale, Duke Street. 1861. *Royal octavo.* Preface, dated 5th March 1861, pp. vii. Index, etc., pp. 87.

WILLIAM HARRISON.—1861.

Bibliotheca Monensis: A Bibliographical Account of Works

relating to the Isle of Man.   By William Harrison, Esq.,
Member of the House of Keys.   Douglas, Isle of Man :
printed for the Manx Society.   1861.   *Octavo.*   Pp. 208.

The Eighth volume of the Society's publications.

REV. H. A. STOWELL.—1862.

Chit Chat on the Isle of Man, with Notices on the Natural
History, and a list of Entomology in the Island.   By the
Rev. A. H. Stowell, Dhoon Chapel.   In the *Zoologist,*
vol. xx.   Pp. 7848-9.

MARY ANNE EVERETT GREEN.—1862.

Calendar of State Papers, Domestic Series, of the Reign of
Charles II. 1663-1664.   Preserved in Her Majesty's
Public Record Office.   Edited by M. A. E. Green.   London :
Longman, Green, Longman, and Roberts.   1862.   *Royal
octavo.*

Various Petitions of Wm. Christian (Illiam Dhône),
Edward Christian, and George Christian ; also other papers
connected with this case.

REV. JOHN CHATER.—1862.

The Voice of the Pious Dead.   A Funeral Sermon for the
late Mr. James Dalrymple (of the Union Mills), by the
Rev. John Chater.   Douglas.   1862.

The proceeds of the sale of this Sermon will be given to
the House of Industry and the Isle of Man Hospital.

1862.

The Queen *v.* John Edward Corkhill.   From the *Manx Sun*
of March 1st, 1862.   Printed by H. Curphey, *Manx Sun*
Office, Douglas.   *Folio.*   Pp. 3.

COL. JOHNSON.—1862.

A Sketch of the Isle of Man ; an Unrivalled Watering Place, By Col. Johnson. Liverpool : printed by Harris and Co., Drury Lane. 1862. 32*mo*. Pp. 30. A Small Map.

An amended edition to the one which appeared in 1851.

JOHN CORLETT LAMOTHE.—1862.

Statute Laws of the Isle of Man, promulgated from the Year 1853 to the Year 1861 inclusive : with a short Appendix containing the Rules of the Chancery and Exchequer Courts, made during that period, etc. etc. Published under the Patronage of His Excellency Francis Pigott, Esquire, Lieutenant - Governor, the Council, Deemsters, and Keys of the Isle of Man. By John Corlett Lamothe, Student-at-Law. Douglas : printed and published by Harriet Curphey, *Sun* Office, King Street : also published by John Mylrea, Duke Street. 1862. *Royal octavo*. Pp. 403.

1862.

History, Topography, and Directory of the Isle of Man. Sheffield Publishing Co., Sheffield. 1862.

1863.

Form of Prayer to be used by the House of Keys at the commencement of each Session. Isle of Man. 1863. Castletown : M. J. Backwell, Printer, Malew Street. 24*mo*. Pp. 6.

Prayers were for the first time read in the House of Keys on the assembling of the House, on Tuesday, 28th April 1863, by the Rev. E. Ferrier, who was appointed Chaplain.

J. O. HALLIWELL.—1863.

Roundabout Notes chiefly upon the Ancient Circles of Stones in the Isle of Man, from rough pencillings dotted down in the Summer of 1862, by J. O. Halliwell. London : John Russell Smith. 1863. *Small quarto.* Pp. 24. 100 Copies.

He considers Glen Helen, with its waterfall, Rhenass, near St. John's, "as perfect Isle of Man." "And take the Isle of Man altogether, it bears away the bell as an Island of Great Britain."

1863.

Isle of Man Agricultural Society. Rules and Prize List, Rules of the Society, Minutes of Annual General Meeting, Cash Account, List of Subscribers, etc. etc. Exhibition to be held at Ramsey, about the first week of August 1863. Ramsey: printed at the General Printing and Bookbinding Office of J. Hampton, Parliament Street. 1863. 12*mo.* Pp. 18.

WM. F. PEACOCK.—No date.—[1863.]

Instructive, Amusing, and entirely Original. Everybody's New Guide, Companion, and Associate (for both Summer and Winter) to the Isle of Man : With a Sail round the Coast, a visit to the Twelve Chasms, a Walk round the Island, and a circumstantial narrative of the prevalent Superstitions. Also, the History (Civil and Ecclesiastical), Constitution, Climate, Natural Productions, Commerce, Herring Fisheries, Mines, Ascents of Mountains, Antiquities, Customs of the Manx, Notes of Where to go, What to see, Routes, Distances, the Hotels ; with personal Adventures, Anecdotes, and an account of Curious Characters whom I met. By William F. Peacock. Price

Sixpence. Manchester : John Heywood, 143 Deansgate. Liverpool : W. Gilling, J. Vaughan, E. Ravenhall. Douglas : J. Mylrea, Duke Street. Ramsey : J. Hampton, Post Office. Peel : E. R. Allpress. London : Simpkin, Marshall, and Co.; and all Booksellers. *Post octavo.* Pp. 72.

Dedicated to Wm. Milner, Esq., of Liverpool. Introductory Chapter dated " Manchester 1863."

ROBERT PATERSON, M.D.—1863.

Manx Antiquities ; or Remarks on the present condition of the Antiquarian remains of the Isle of Man, especially those situated around its coast line (made during a Photographic Tour of the Isle in 1862). By Robert Paterson, M.D., F.R.C.P.E., F.S.S.A., etc. Cupar-Fife ; printed at the Office of the *St. Andrews University Magazine.* 1863. *Octavo.* Pp. 42.

With 12 Views.

1863.

The Gas Question. Address from the Douglas Town Commissioners to the Ratepayers and Gas Consumers of Douglas, including the report on the Supply and Price of Gas to the Town, as furnished by G. W. Stevenson, Esq., C.E., F.G.S. January 1863. (Douglas : printed by Harriet Curphey, *Manx Sun* Office. 1863.) 12*mo.* Pp. 12.

WM. F. PEACOCK.—No date.—[1863.]

The Beauties of Port Erin, and the South of the Island. By Wm. F. Peacock. Price Sixpence. Manchester : John Heywood, Deansgate, etc. *Post octavo.* Pp. 46. Dated at the end " 14th August 1863."

WM. F. PEACOCK.—No date.—[1863.]

The Manx Table Book and Keepsake : Curious, Interesting,
Amusing, and Instructive Memoranda of the Isle of Man
in times past and present. By Wm. F. Peacock. Price
Sixpence. Manchester : John Heywood, Deansgate, etc.
Post octavo. Pp. 65.

B. STOWELL.—1863.

Manxland : a Tale. With an Introductory Sketch of Manx
home Missions. By B. Stowell. London : James Nisbet
and Co., 21 Berners Street. 1863. *Foolscap octavo.* Pp.
199. 4 Plates.

This work of Miss Stowell's gives an account of the Isle
of Man Diocesan Association, founded in 1839, with a few
rural sketches.

REV. JOHN KEBLE, M.A.—1863. BISHOP WILSON.

The Life of the Right Reverend Father in God, Thomas Wilson, D.D., Lord Bishop of Sodor and Man. Compiled
chiefly from Original Documents. By the Rev. John
Keble, M.A., Vicar of Hursley.

" The care of discipline is Love."

Oxford : John Henry Parker. 1863. *Octavo.* In 2
Parts. Preface, pp. xvii. Life, etc., pp. 985.

An able Review of this work will be found in *The Quarterly Review*, No. 239, July 1866, pp. 171-198.

1864.

Disorder ! Disease !! and Death !!! or Order ! Cleanliness !!
and Health !!! Being a report of the Proceedings of the
Douglas Town Commissioners at their meeting held on

Tuesday, March 15th, 1864. Reprinted (with corrections) from the *Mona's Herald* of March 16th, 1864. Fargher, Printer, *Mona's Herald* Office, Douglas. 24*mo.* Pp. 24. Signed, "A Fellow Townsman."

JAMES CHALONER.—1864.

A Short Treatise of the Isle of Man, digested into Six Chapters. By James Chaloner, one of the Commissioners under Lord Fairfax for settling the affairs in the Isle of Man in 1652; and afterwards Governor of the Island from 1658 to 1660. Originally published in 1656, as an Appendix to "King's Vale Royal of England: or, the County Palatine of Chester, Illustrated." Edited, with an Introductory Notice and Copious Notes, by the Rev. J. G. Cumming, M.A., F.G.S., Rector of Mellis, Suffolk; late Warden and Professor of Classical Literature and of Geology, Queen's College, Birmingham; formerly Vice-Principal of King William's College, Isle of Man. Douglas, Isle of Man: printed for the Manx Society. 1864. *Octavo.* Pp. 138.

This forms the Tenth volume of the Manx Society's publications, and contains copies of the Plates and Map which appeared in the original edition, with an extra portrait of Lord Fairfax. The Notes and Pedigree by the Editor add considerably to the value of this edition.

1864.

An Act for Supplying the Town of Peel with Water. Douglas: printed (by authority) by H. Curphey, *Manx Sun* Office, 13 King Street. 1864. *Octavo.* Pp. 8.

CHARLES CLAY, M.D.—1864.

Proceedings of the Manchester Numismatic Society. Manchester : A. Ireland and Co., Printers, Pall Mall Court. 1864. *Small quarto.*

In Part i. pp. 5 to 17, is a paper, " On the Brass, Copper, and other currency of the Isle of Man. By Charles Clay, M.D., President of the Manchester Numismatic Society."

This is illustrated with a Photographic Plate of Manx Coins, and 9 Woodcuts illustrative of the Paper.

1864.

An Act to enable the Trustees of the Peel Grammar School to make sale and dispose of the Old School-House and Premises in the Town of Peel, and to purchase other ground in lieu thereof, and to build a New School-House and Master's residence thereon. Douglas : printed (by authority) by H. Curphey, *Manx Sun* Office, 13 King Street. 1864. *Octavo.* Pp. 7.

1864.

An Act to further amend the Law relating to Weights and Measures. Douglas : printed (by authority) by H. Curphey, *Manx Sun* Office, King Street. 1864. *Octavo.* Pp. 8.

1864.

An Act for the Punishment of Larceny and Embezzlement in certain Cases. Douglas : printed (by authority) by H. Curphey, *Manx Sun* Office. 1864. *Octavo.* Pp. 8.

1864.

An Act for making Compensation for certain claims in regard to certain Lands affected by the Isle of Man Disafforesting Act, 1860. Douglas : printed (by authority) by H. Curphey, *Manx Sun* Office, King Street. 1864. *Octavo.* Pp. 12.

1864.

An Act to amend an Act to Provide an Asylum for Lunatics and Insane Persons, and to provide a Temporary Lunatic Asylum. Douglas : printed (by authority) by H. Curphey, *Manx Sun* Office, King Street. 1864. *Octavo.* Pp. 8.

1864.

The Petty Sessions Act, 1864 : being an Act to consolidate and amend the Acts regulating the proceedings and the Duties of Justices of the Peace. Douglas : printed (by authority) by H. Curphey, *Manx Sun* Office, King Street. 1864. *Octavo.* Pp. 34.

1864.

An Act to consolidate and amend the Acts relating to certain offences and other matters as to which Justices of the Peace exercise summary Jurisdiction, and to define and extend the Powers of the Justices. Douglas : printed (by authority) by H. Curphey, *Manx Sun* Office, King Street. 1864. *Octavo.* Pp. 36.

1864.

Isle of Man. Papers relating to the Isle of Man (Mr. Wm. Ewart). Ordered by the House of Commons to be printed, 28th July 1864. *Folio.* Pp. 70.

Nine Papers. Petitions on Harbours, Breakwater, Commons, etc.

1864.

An Act to further amend an Act to provide for the better Paving, Cleansing, and Lighting the Streets of the Town of Douglas, and for making and keeping in repair public sewers therein, and otherwise improving the said Town.

Douglas : printed (by authority) by II. Curphey, *Manx Sun* Office, King Street. 1864. *Octavo.* Pp. 34.

1865.

An Act to provide for the better Paving, Cleansing, and Lighting the Streets of the Town of Ramsey, and for making and keeping in repair Public Sewers therein, and otherwise improving the said Town. 1865. Douglas : printed (by authority) by H. Curphey, *Manx Sun* Office, King Street. 1865. *Octavo.* Pp. 25.

1865.

An Act for Shortening the Language used in Acts of Tynwald. 1865. Douglas : printed (by authority) by II. Curphey, *Manx Sun* Office, King Street. 1865. *Octavo.* Pp. 4.

1865.

The District Drainage Act. 1865. Douglas : printed (by authority) by II. Curphey, *Manx Sun* Office, King Street. 1865. *Octavo.* Pp. 15.

1865.

Session 1865. Isle of Man Railway. (No name of printer.) *Octavo.* Pp. 109.

1865.

Isle of Man Disafforesting Commission. First award of the Commissioners appointed under an Act of Tynwald, passed in the 24th year of the Reign of Queen Victoria, and intituled, "An Act for Disafforesting and allotting the uninclosed portion of the Forest in the Isle of Man." Printed by order of the Commissioners. 1865. *Folio.* Pp. 59. 3 Maps. Printed in London by J. Wade.

SUETONIUS M. TOD.—No date.—[1865.]

Trout Fishing in the Isle of Man ; where to go, and what baits to use, with a few practical hints on Trout Fishing in general. By Suetonius M. Tod, Esq. Illustrated with Photographs by Lewis, Douglas. Douglas : Matthew Glover, 52 North Quay ; London : Simpkin, Marshall, and Co. ; Liverpool : G. Philip and Son. *Small octavo.* Pp. 62. Two Photographs.

This is the first printed Guide to Angling in the Streams of the Isle of Man.

GEORGE WALDRON.—1865.

A Description of the Isle of Man : with some useful and entertaining reflections on the Laws, Customs, and Manners of the Inhabitants. By George Waldron, Gent., late of Queen's College, Oxon. Printed for the Widow and Orphans. 1731. Edited, with an Introductory Notice and Notes, by William Harrison, Esq., Member of the House of Keys, Author of "Bibliotheca Monensis." Douglas : printed for the Manx Society. 1865. *Octavo.* Introduction, pp. xxiii. Pp. 155. A Plate of Coins.

The Eleventh volume of the Manx Society's publications.

1865.

An Act for the Incorporation, Winding up, and Regulation of Trading Companies and other Associations. 1865. Douglas : printed (by authority) by H. Curphey, *Manx Sun* Office, King Street. 1865. *Octavo.* Pp. 93.

1865.

The Trustees Act. 1865. Douglas : printed (by authority)

by H. Curphey, *Manx Sun* Office, King Street. 1865.
Octavo. Pp. 7.

1865.

Standing Orders of the Court of Tynwald with regard to
Railway Bills, 1859 and 1863. Douglas : printed (by
authority) by H. Curphey, *Manx Sun* Office, King Street.
1865. *Octavo.* Pp. 14.

1865.

Orders, Bye-Laws, Rules, and Regulations, framed and made
by the Douglas Town Commissioners, and confirmed by
the Tynwald Court. Douglas, Isle of Man : printed (by
authority) by James Brown, *Times* Office. 1865. *Octavo.*
Pp. 30.

1865.

The Taverns Amendment Act, 1865. Douglas : printed
(by authority) by H. Curphey, *Manx Sun* Office, King
Street. 1865. *Octavo.* Pp. 15.

1865.

An Act to alter the mode of Promulgating Acts of Tynwald,
1865. Douglas : printed (by authority) by H. Curphey,
Manx Sun Office, King Street. 1865. *Octavo.* Pp. 4.

1865.

An Act to provide additional Burial Ground for the Parish of
Malew. 1865. Douglas : printed (by authority) by H.
Curphey, *Manx Sun* Office, King Street. 1865. *Octavo.*
Pp. 11.

1865.

The Town Bye-Laws and Justices' Jurisdiction Amendment
Act, 1865. Douglas : printed (by authority) by H. Cur-

phey, *Manx Sun* Office, King Street. 1865. *Octavo.*
Pp. 7.

1865.

An Act for the Well-ordering of Common Lodging Houses,
1865. Douglas : printed (by authority) by H. Curphey,
Manx Sun Office, King Street. 1865. *Octavo.* Pp. 12.

EDWIN WAUGH.—No date.—[1866.]

Saint Catharine's Chapel ; or the Pretty Island Bay. By
Edwin Waugh.

> " 'Tis Mona the lone, where the silver mist gathers."

Manchester : John Heywood, 143 Deansgate. *Small duodecimo.* Pp. 32.

This is an account of Port Erin and neighbourhood. Mr.
Waugh is the author of numerous Lancashire songs and
sketches.

1866.

The Twenty-sixth Annual Report of the Isle of Man Diocesan
Association. 1865. Douglas : R. H. Johnson, Printer
and Stationer, Prospect Hill, office of the *Weekly Advertising Circular.* 1866. *Octavo.* Pp. 7.

1866.

The Star of Mona, and Monthly Temperance Advertiser.
The organ of the Manx Union for the Promotion of Tem-
perance. Douglas : Isle of Man, April 12th, 1866. *Folio.*
No. 1, pp. 2 ; No. 2, pp. 4. May 10th. Printed by
Matthew Glover, 52 North Quay, Douglas.

1866.

An Act, entituled the House of Keys Election Act, 1866,

being an Act to render the House of Keys elective ; and for other purposes. Douglas : printed (by authority) by H. Curphey, *Manx Sun* Office, King Street. 1866. *Octavo.* Pp. 159.

1866.

Correspondence with reference to the Fiscal Changes in 1866. Douglas : printed (by authority) by James Brown and Son. *Times* Office. Dated " July 5th, 1866." Folio. Pp. 33.

N. E. S. A. HAMILTON, F.R.S.L.—1866.

The National Gazetteer of Great Britain and Ireland, or Topographical Dictionary of the British Islands, comprising above 30,000 names of towns, villages, parishes, hamlets, castles, seats, and other natural and political divisions ; with a description of their churches, schools, antiquities, manufactures, progress, railways, etc. Compiled from the most recent and trustworthy sources, and corrected by local verification. Edited by N. E. S. A. Hamilton, Esq., F.R.S.L., etc., Assistant in the Department of Manuscripts, British Museum. London : Virtue and Co. 1866.

This work was published in divisions, and was the cause of much annoyance and some litigation to the Manx subscribers. If the information relating to the other portions of Great Britain is drawn from similar *trustworthy sources* as that relating to the Isle of Man, we pity the student who places reliance on the work. It is amusing to find the following as specimens which the work contains respecting insular localities :—

" Balawin, a village in the Isle of Man, 1 mile from Douglas."
" Ballasalla, a village in the parish of Castletown, Sheading of Rushen, in the Isle of Man, 3 miles to the N.E. of Castletown."

" The Site (of the Abbey) now belongs to the Chief Deemster."

" Calf of Man. The island abounds with rabbits and solan geese, the pursuit and capture of which is the occupation of the islanders."

" Kirk Ballaugh, a parish in Michael Sheading, includes the village of Ballamoor, where is a brewery."

" Kirk Braddan, a parish in Middle Sheading, Isle of Man, 2 miles N.W. of Douglas."   " The village, which is considerable, is situated in a pleasant spot."

The information about Castletown and Douglas is much after the same style of fact!

KELLY, GILL, AND CLARKE.—1866.

The Manx Dictionary, in Two Parts. First, Manx and English ; and the Second, English and Manx. Douglas : printed for the Manx Society. 1866. *Octavo.* Pp. 432.

This is the thirteenth volume issued by the Manx Society. The first part is from Dr. John Kelly's Triglot Dictionary, from the MS. in the College Library, Castletown, edited by the Rev. William Gill of Malew ; the second part by the Rev. William Gill and the Rev. J. T. Clarke, of St. Mark's, Isle of Man.

PROFESSOR BROWN.—1866.

Observations on the Cattle Plague in Ireland, and the Cattle Disease in the Isle of Man. Reprinted from the *Veterinarian.* London : printed by J. E. Adlard, Bartholomew Close. 1866. *Octavo.* Pp. 29. Written by Professor Brown, Government Inspector.

That portion relating to the Island is entitled " The disease affecting Cattle in the Isle of Man." Pp. 21-29.

1866.

The Building News. August 17th, 1866.

At p. 546, Engravings, and a short description of St. Olave's Chapel, Ramsey, Isle of Man.

Rev. J. G. Cumming, M.A.—1867.

The Great Stanley, or James VIIth Earl of Derby, and his Noble Countess, Charlotte de la Tremouille, in their Land of Man. A Narrative of the XVIIth Century. Interspersed with Notices of Manx Manners, Customs, Laws, Legends, and Fairy Tales. Copiously illustrated from Manx Scenery and Antiquities. By Alfred D. Lemon and J. T. Blight. By the Rev. J. G. Cumming, M.A., F.G.S., Incumbent of St. John's, Bethnal Green, London, late Warden of Queen's College, Birmingham, and formerly Vice-Principal of King William's College, Isle of Man. London : William Mackintosh, 24 Paternoster Row, E.C. 1867. *Foolscap octavo.* Preface, pp. viii. Pp. 279.

Deemster Parr. (James Gell.)—1867.

An Abstract of the Laws, Customs, and Ordinances of the Isle of Man. Compiled by John Parr, Esq., formerly one of the Deemsters of the Island. Edited, with Notes, by James Gell, Esq., Attorney-General of the Isle of Man. Douglas : printed for the Manx Society. 1867. *Octavo.* Vol. I. Introduction, etc., pp. xvi. Abstract and Notes, pp. 241.

The Manx Society's Twelfth volume.

No date.—[1867.]

The Fishers of Derby Haven. By the author of "The Children of Colverley," "Ferns Hollow," etc. London : The Religious Tract Society. Instituted 1799. Depositories, 56 Paternoster Row, 65 St. Paul's Churchyard, and 164

Piccadilly, and sold by the Booksellers. N.D. *Small octavo.* Pp. 238. 4 plates.

SIR J. Y. SIMPSON, M.D.—1867.

Archaic Sculpturings of Cups, Circles, etc., upon Stones and Rocks in Scotland, England, and other Countries. By Sir J. Y. Simpson, Bart., M.D., D.C.L. Edinburgh : Edmonston and Douglas, Publishers to the Society of Antiquaries. 1867. *Small quarto.* Pp. 200. Numerous plates.

The Isle of Man is alluded to in various instances :—

Page 21. Circle at Oatlands—Cup markings on one of the Stones. Plate viii., fig. 1.

Page 131. Cist at Ballakelly, with a Cup Stone.

Page 56. Cup Stones in the Wood near the Churchyard at Braddan. Plate xxvi., fig. 4.

Page 56. Note. Stones, etc., at Kirk Maughold.

Page 69. At Ballaglonnay, etc., several Cup-marked Stones ; as also near the parish church of Santon.

Page 150. Note on the Great Stone in Santon Churchyard.

The question as to the meaning of these Cups and Circles is left unanswered. They were first noticed on the Cambrian Archæological Association's visit to the Island in the autumn of 1865.

1867.

The Manx Punch. Printed and published by the Proprietor, Thomas John Ouseley, of No. 6 Mona Terrace, Douglas, at his offices, No. 38 Prospect Hill, Douglas, Isle of Man. *Quarto.* Pp. 8. No. 1, July. Price One Penny. Published every Saturday. Woodcut Title.

After a few numbers it merged into an advertising circular.

F. R. RAINES, M.A.—1867.

The Stanley Papers. Part iii. Printed for the Chetham Society, 1867. 3 vols. *Small quarto.*

These volumes contain a Memoir of James, seventh Earl of Derby, with his Private Devotions. In the third volume, separately paged, 1 to 49, is "The History and Antiquities of the Isle of Man," as printed in Peck's "Desiderata Curiosa," 1732, with a Portrait of Bishop Rutter. Many curious particulars are to be found in these volumes relating to the Isle of Man, from MSS. in the Knowsley Library.

1867.

Standing Orders of the House of Keys under the House of Keys Election Act, 1866. Adopted and Confirmed by the House on the 29th October 1867. Printed for the Use of the Members. Isle of Man : printed (by authority) by H. Curphey, *Manx Sun* Office, Douglas. 1867. *Royal octavo.* Pp. 24. With an Index of the Rules and Orders.

By the 55th Rule it is stated, "The Standing Orders to be printed, and a copy furnished to each of the present Members, and to every New Member upon his taking his seat." The Members of the Old House were never allowed to have a Copy of the Standing Orders.

1867.

Methodists' Facts. The Rev. Theophilus Talbot's Appointment to the Douglas Circuit. The doings of the Conference Stationing Committee, and other matters which should be known to all Wesleyans.

"Have I become your enemy because I tell you the truth ?"

Douglas : James Brown, printer, *Times* Office, Wellington Street. *Royal octavo.* Pp. 8.

JAMES WOODS.—No date.—[1867.]

A New Atlas and Gazetteer of the Isle of Man, consisting of seventeen highly finished Maps, compiled from original and authentic sources, describing the Civil and Ecclesiastical Boundaries of each Parish, and the boundaries of the several Baronies, Freeholds, and Quarterlands, as well as the boundaries of the several farms as they are now held in possession. Appended is an elaborate and comprehensive reference table, showing the name of every proprietor of Land in the Island, with the manorial description and extent of Land held by him ; together with an Appendix of useful and interesting information. By James Woods, Surveyor. London : Day and Son (Limited), 6 Gate Street. Isle of Man, Douglas : James Brown ; John Mylrea. Ramsey : John Hampton. Castletown : M. J. Backwell. Peel : Thomas Carran.

Atlas, *folio.* Maps coloured. Pp. 51.

JOHN CHRISTIAN CURWEN. DR. LONSDALE.—1867.

The Worthies of Cumberland. John Christian Curwen. William Blamire. By Henry Lonsdale, M.D., author of " The Life of Watson." London : George Routledge and Sons, The Broadway, Ludgate. 1867. *Post octavo.* Pp. 317.

Portrait of Mr. Curwen. Life of Curwen, pp. 1 to 204.

John Christian of Ewanrigg, Cumberland, and Milntown, Isle of Man, was born on the 12th July 1756, at Ewanrigg, and married his first wife, Margaret, daughter of John Taubman, Esq., of Castletown, at Kirk Maughold Church, in the Isle of Man, on the 10th September 1776, who died February 1778 at Peel, leaving issue one son, John Christian, who became Deemster of the Island, and father of the Rev. William

Bell Christian of Milntown and Ewanrigg. Mr. Christian married for his second wife his cousin, Isabella Curwen, only child of Henry Curwen, Esq., of Workington Hall, at Edinburgh, on the 5th October 1782, and took the name of Curwen. He died on the 10th December 1828, having been a M.P. as well as a Member of the House of Keys.

1868.

Report of the Committee appointed by the Tynwald Court to consider the question of maintaining Telegraphic Communication between the Isle of Man and England. February 1868. Douglas : printed (by authority) by Harriet Curphey, King Street. 1868. *Octavo.*

1868.

Isle of Man ; its Antiquities, etc., with Excursions from Douglas to Peel, Ramsey, Castletown, Laxey, etc., and a paper by Suetonius M. Tod, Esq., on Sea Fishing. Price One Penny. Manchester : Abel Heywood and Son, 56 and 58 Oldham Street. London : Heywood and Co., 335 Strand. Simpkin, Marshall, and Co., Stationers' Hall Court. *Foolscap octavo.* Pp. 22.

JOHN FELTHAM.—1868.—[WM. HARRISON.]

Memorials of "God's Acre," being Monumental Inscriptions in the Isle of Man, taken in the Summer of 1797. By John Feltham and Edward Wright. Edited, with an Introductory Notice, by William Harrison, Esq., Author of "Bibliotheca Monensis." Douglas : printed for the Manx Society. 1868. *Octavo.* Pp. 132.

Introductory Notice, etc., pp. xv. Illustrated with 18 Views of the Old Churches in the time of Bishop Wilson.

ELIZABETH COOKSON.—1868.

Poems from Manxland, with Legends and Translations from the Manx and German.   By Elizabeth Cookson.

" Bannee-Jee-Shiu, Ellan Vannin."

London : Elliot Stock, 62 Paternoster Row.   1868.   *Small octavo.*   Pp. 192.

ARTHUR HELPS.—1868.

Leaves from the Journal of Our Life in the Highlands, from 1848 to 1861, etc.   Edited by Arthur Helps.   Second Edition.   London :   Smith, Elder, and Co.   1868.

Her Majesty did not land on the Isle of Man while her Yacht remained in Ramsey Bay, but the Prince Consort ascended the Hill overlooking the town and bay on the 20th of September 1847, on which spot the Albert Tower was afterwards built to commemorate the royal visit.   The Island is alluded to at pp. 73, 74, and 94.

REV. J. G. CUMMING.—1868.

Antiquitates Manniæ : or a Collection of Memoirs on the Antiquities of the Isle of Man.   Edited for the Manx Society by the Rev. J. G. Cumming, M.A., F.G.S.   London : printed for the Manx Society.   1868.   *Octavo.*   Pp. 140. Plates and Woodcuts.

The Society's Fifteenth volume.   It consists wholly of the Memoirs read at the Douglas Meeting of the Cambrian Archæological Association in 1865, and which were published in their Journal in 1866-7, with some new readings of Runic Inscriptions by Mr. Cumming, and a fuller Account of the Ancient Churches of Man by Dr. Oliver.

Mr. Cumming died in London on the 21st September 1868.

1868.

An Act to prevent the Destruction of Sea Gulls.   Douglas :
printed (by authority) by Harriet Curphey, King Street.
1868. *Royal octavo.* Pp. 16 to 166.

Promulgated 6th July 1868.

1868.

Proceedings of the Society of Antiquaries.   London. *Octavo.*
May 14, 1868.

At pp. 123-124, Description of Two Swords of State be-
longing to the Isle of Man. It is thus noted :—" Henry
Campkin, Esq., F.S.A., exhibited, by permission of J. Latham,
Esq., two Swords of State belonging to the Isle of Man."

These Swords are mentioned in " Records of the Tynwald,"
pp. 20, 21 ; and photographs of the most ancient are given—
Manx Society, vol. xix.   1871.

GEORGE STEPHENS, F.S.A.—1869.

The Old Northern Runic Monuments of Scandinavia and
England, now first collected and deciphered by George
Stephens, F.S.A., Professor of English in the University
of Copenhagen. 1869. *Folio.* Pp. 1112.

Published in Two Parts, with numerous Engravings. A
most complete account, and embracing those of the Isle of
Man.

WILLIAM HARRISON.—1869.

Mona Miscellany.   A Selection of Proverbs, Sayings, Ballads,
Customs, Superstitions, and Legends, peculiar to the Isle
of Man.   Collected and Edited by William Harrison,
Author of " Bibliotheca Monensis."   Douglas : Isle of

Man : printed for the Manx Society. 1869. *Octavo*. Pp. 241. Preface, etc., xviii. pp.

The Sixteenth volume of the Society's publications.

CHARLES CLAY, M.D.—1869.

Currency of the Isle of Man, from its earliest appearance to its assimilation with the British Coinage in 1840 : with the Laws and other circumstances connected with its History. Edited by Charles Clay, M.D., Manchester, etc. etc. etc. The Articles on Paper Currency, Treasure Trove, etc., by J. Frissell Crellin, Esq., M.H.K., Orrysdale, Isle of Man. Douglas : printed for the Manx Society. 1869. *Octavo*. Pp. 215. Illustrated with four Photographic Plates of Manx Coins, and numerous Plates of Card Notes and Coins.

The Seventeenth volume of the Society's publications.

MADAME GUIZOT DE WITT.—1869.

The Lady of Latham ; being the Life and original Letters of Charlotte de la Trémoille, Countess of Derby. By Madame Guizot de Witt. With a Portrait. London : Smith, Elder, and Co., 15 Waterloo Place. 1869. *Octavo*. Preface, v.-vii. Pp. 299.

Portrait of the Countess of Derby, from a painting in the Derby collection at Knowsley, engraved by C. H. Jeens.

Many matters connected with the Isle of Man are mentioned, particularly in the Countess of Derby's letters.

COLONEL SIR HENRY JAMES, R.E.—1869.

Ordnance Survey of the Isle of Man. Colonel Sir Henry James, R.E., F.R.S., etc., Superintendent of the Survey. The Maps of this Survey are on a scale of 25.344 inches to a mile. The length of each Sheet is 1½ mile, and the width 1 mile. The area of each Sheet is therefore 960 acres. To each parish is a Book of Reference, with the title, as :—Ordnance Survey of the Isle of Man ; Book of Reference to the Plan of the Parish of German in Glenfaba Sheading, containing 11,678·560 acres. Colonel Sir Henry James, R.E., F.R.S., M.R.I.A., F.G.S., etc., Superintendent of the Survey. London : printed by George E. Eyre and William Spottiswoode, Printers to the Queen's Most Excellent Majesty, for Her Majesty's Stationery Office. 1869. Price Three Shillings and Six-pence. Pp. 39.

The Maps are published at 2s. 6d. each Sheet. German contains 19 Sheets.

The Survey is also published on a Scale of six inches and one inch to a mile.

DR. M'BURNEY.—No date.—[1870.]

A Lay of Ancient Mona. The Battle of Sky Hill. By Dr. M'Burney, F.S.A.S. Printed by John Christian Fargher, *Mona's Herald* Office, Douglas. *Small octavo.* Pp. 12.

L. JEWITT, F.S.A.—1870.

Grave Mounds and their Contents ; A Manual of Archæ-ology, etc. By Llewellyn Jewitt, F.S.A. London : Groom-bridge and Sons, 5 Paternoster Row. 1870. *Octavo.*

Isle of Man, pp. 76, 78, 274.

NOTES AND QUERIES.—1850-1870.

Notes and Queries : a Medium of Intercommunication for Literary Men, Artists, Antiquaries, Genealogists, etc.

" When found, make a note of."—*Captain Cuttle.*

London : George Bell, 186 Fleet Street. 1850. *Small quarto.*

The first No. commenced, Saturday, November 3d, 1849.

First Series.—1850-1855.

Vol. 3.—Arms of the Isle of Man, pp. 373-510.
    4.—Isabel, Queen of the Isle of Man, p. 423.
    5.—Dial Motto, Kirk Arbory, p. 66.
       Isabel, Queen of the Isle of Man, p. 132.
       Isabel, Queen of Man, and on the title of King, by
          John Gough Nichols, p. 205.
       The Queen of the Isle of Man, p. 234.
       Isle of Man Folk Lore, p. 341.
    6.—Thomas Stanley, Bishop of Man, 1510, p. 130.
       Edmund Chaloner, son of James Chaloner, Gover-
          nor, p. 292.
       Bishop Thomas Wilson's " Sacra Privata," p. 414.
    7.—Inscription on a Penny of George III., p. 65.
       Manx Penny of George III., p. 165.
       Thomas Stanley, Bishop of Man, p. 209.
       Stabit quocunque jeceris, p. 239.
       Edmund Chaloner, son of James Chaloner, p. 334.
       Bishop Hesketh, p. 409.
       James Chaloner, p. 583.
    8.—Bishop Thomas Wilson and his Works, p. 220.
       Cardinal Fleury and Bishop Wilson, p. 245.
       St. Patrick, Maune and Man, p. 291.
       Bishop Ferrar, p. 376.
       Bishop Wilson's " Sacra Privata," p. 470.
       Manx Folk Lore ; Propitiating the Fairies, p. 617.
    9.—Tailless Cats, pp. 10, 111, 209, 479, 480.
       Rumpies, by Edward Forbes, p. 112.
       Tailless Cats, Burmese breed, p. 575.
   10.—The Stanleys in Man, p. 325.

Second Series.—1856-1861.

Vol. 1.—Origin of the name Mona, p. 454.
    2.—Origin of the name of the Isle of Man, p. 20.
       Tailless Cats at Clare Hall, Cambridge, 385.
    3.—Sodor, Origin of the See, p. 129.
       Petition in the Manx Litany, pp. 230, 439.
       Prayers in the Isle of Man for the Earl of Derby,
          p. 268.
    5.—Bishops Richmond and Crigan of Man, p. 172.
       Bishops of Sodor and Man, Arms wanted of, p. 314.
    6.—Arms of the Isle of Man on an Etruscan Vase, pp.
          409-490.
       Bishops of Man. Have they a Seat in the House
          of Lords ? p. 498.
    7.—Bishops of Sodor and Man have no Seats in the
          House of Lords, p. 16.
       Arms of the Isle of Man on Etruscan Vases, p. 31.
       Arms of Man, p. 246.
       Arms of Sicily and the Isle of Man, p. 474.
  11.—Eleanor Cobham confined in Peel Castle, p. 218.

Third Series.—1862-1867.

Vol. 1.—Buck Whalley ; his walk to Jerusalem, p. 452.
    2.—Jerusalem ; or Buck Whalley, pp. 76-149.
              „   „   lived in the Isle of
       Man, p. 314.
    3.—History of the Siege of Lathom House, Bishop
          Rutter the author of, p. 29.
    5.—List of Bishops of the Isles, Sodorensis, etc., p. 412.
    6.—Buck Whalley, p. 297.
       George Waldron, p. 348.
    8.—Isle of Man called Eubonia, p. 454.
  10.—MS. History of the Isle of Man, pp. 330, 440.
  11.—House of Keys, p. 259.

Fourth Series.—1868-1871.

Vol. 2.—Manx Lines on the Manx Fairy Steam Packet, p. 368.

Litany during the Herring Fishery, p. 512.

3.—Ushag beg ruy, pp. 288-493.

Qualtagh Custom, p. 424.

Cade Lamb—Meg, p. 343.

Days of the Week in Manx, p. 552.

Mylecharaine, p. 493 ; Griddle, p. 505.

4.—Thomas Bushel, pp. 159, 244, 368.

The Sudereys, pp. 12, 101, 200.

Hanging or Marrying, pp. 417, 418, 525.

Bishop Robert Farrar, p. 10.

Albert Tower, Ramsey, p. 71.

Earl of Warwick's Place of Banishment, p. 213.

Erse Words denoting the Moon, pp. 229, 303, 458.

5.—Admiral Thurot, p. 47.

Peel Castle Seal, p. 144.

Erse Words denoting the Moon, p. 289.

King William's Bank, p. 382.

First Manx Teetotaller, p. 401.

Manx Song, Mylecharaine, pp. 469, 583.

6.—Manx Song, Mylecharaine, pp. 61, 555.

MS. History of the Isle of Man, pp. 69, 143.

Was James 7th Earl of Derby created a Duke? p. 112.

Mylecharaine, pp. 259, 355, 444.

Arms of the Isle of Man, p. 224.

St. Leonard, p. 371.

Bishop Robert Waldby, p. 459.

Earl of Derby and Calf of Man, 1646 ; Historical Epigram, p. 542.

Ballasalley, p. 475.

7.—Huan Blackleach, *alias* Huan Hesketh, p. 34.

Societas Albertorum, Bishop William Russell, p. 56.

Tynwald Hill, p. 92.

Manx Cats and Fowls, p. 96.

Thomas Stanley, Bishop of Sodor and Man, p. 96.

Burial Places of Manx Bishops, p. 123.

Manx Bishops, pp. 184, 293, 352.

On the title of King or Queen of Man, pp. 249, 332.

Gates, Isle of Man, p. 409.

8.—Gates, Isle of Man, p. 33.

Troparium ; Triforia, p. 88.

Dogs buried at the foot of Bishops, pp. 222, 290, 378, 422, 537.

The Lady of Latham, p. 470.

ACTS OF THE BRITISH PARLIAMENT RELATING TO THE ISLE OF MAN.

The chief Law Officers of England have concurred in declaring the Isle of Man to be an ancient *Kingdom of itself*, and no part of the realm of England. As such they have ever made their own laws; and since the Revestment in 1765, when the Duke and Duchess of Atholl sold the revenues of the Island to the British Crown, the King of England has had the appointment of the Lieutenant-Governor and the chief Officers of State, who, with the 24 Keys (landed proprietors in the Island), continue to make their own laws, subject only to the approval of the Crown of England before being promulgated on the Tynwald Hill, in the same manner as they have been from time immemorial.

The following are the chief of these Acts relating to the Island :—

1536.—An Act for the Dissolution of Monasteries, 27 Henry VIII., Cap. 28. "An Act that all religious houses under the yearly revenue of Two Hundred Pounds shall be dissolved, and given to the King and his Heirs."

It has been stated by some authors that the monastery and priory of Rushen and Douglas, and the Fryers Minors, commonly called the Grey Friars of Bymaken, otherwise Bemaken, in the Island of Man, were dissolved and vested in His Majesty, his heirs, etc., by this Act; but such dissolution and vesting did not take place by virtue of this Act, which has no reference in it to the Isle of Man ; and, according to English jurists, an Act of Parliament does not extend to it, unless it be particularly named therein.—(See the Act of 1729.)

The dissolution was not completed until the reign of Queen Elizabeth, Rushen Abbey being the last monastery dissolved.

1542.—An Act for dissevering the Bishoprick of Chester and the Isle of Man from the jurisdiction of Canterbury to the jurisdiction of York, 33 Henry VIII.

1610.—An Act for assuring and establishing the Isle of Man in the name and blood of William, Earl of Derby, 9th Feby., 8th James I.

This Act is printed in Oliver's "Monumenta," vol. iii. pp. 114-120 ; Manx Society, vol. ix., 1862. Also in Gell's "Abstract of the Laws of the Isle of Man," vol. i. p. 114 ; Manx Society, vol. xii., 1867 ; and in Mill's "Statutes," 1821, pp. 522-526.

1649.—An Act for settling Mannors, Lands, Tenements, and Hereditaments, of the cleare yearly value of £4000, upon Thomas, Lord Fairfax, the Captain-Generall of the forces of the Parliament of England, 29th Septr.

By this Act the Island was conferred on Lord Fairfax, but had no recognition in the Island until February 1652.

1666.—An Act against importing Cattle from Ireland and other parts beyond the Seas, and Fish taken by Foreigners, Anno 18 Charles II. Printed in the Savoy. 1666.

The last clause says, "Provided always that nothing in this Act shall be construed to hinder the importation of Cattle from the Isle of Man in this Kingdom of England, so as the number of the said Cattel do not exceed six hundred head yearly, and that they be not of any other breed than of the breed of the Isle of Man, and that they be landed at the port of Chester, or some of the Members thereof, and not elsewhere."

1676.—Corn, the growth of the Isle of Man, may be imported into Great Britain, 15th Charles II., Cap. 7, Sec. 21.

1692.—An Act dissevering the Bishoprick of Chester and of the Isle of Man from the jurisdiction of Canterbury to the jurisdiction of York, 8th James II., Cap. xxxi.

Printed in Bishop Wilson's Works, 1797, vol. i. pp. 318-321. Also in "The Old Historians of the Isle of Man," Manx Society, vol. xviii., 1871, pp. 107-110.

1721.—Act prohibiting East India Goods being imported into the Isle of Man except through Great Britain, 7th Geo. I., Stat. 1, Cap. 21, Sec. 9.

1726.—An Act for the Improvement of His Majesty's Revenues of Customs, Excise and Inland Duties, enabling the Lords of the Treasury to purchase from James, Earl of Derby, the Isle of Man, 12th George I., Cap. 28.

Sections 25 and 26 are given in Gell's "Abstract of the Laws," etc., vol. i. pp. 94-5; Manx Society, vol. xii., 1867. Sections 22, 23, and 24 also relate to this Act.

1727.—An Act passed, and power given to those entitled to the Island, and to the Trustees of Henrietta Bridgett Ashburnham, an infant, to sell, and for the Treasury to purchase, their Rights and Interests in and over the Isle of Man.

1729.—An Act for the Liability of Seamen to Contribute to Greenwich Hospital was extended to the Isle of Man.

The preamble contains a remarkable declaration and admission by Parliament that to bind the Isle of Man it must be referred to by express name.

1745.—Every Officer or Seaman belonging to the Isle of Man, etc., is required to pay 6d. per month for the use of Greenwich Hospital, 18th George II., Cap. 31.

1764.—An Act respecting Smuggling from the Isle of Man.

1765.—An Act for carrying into Execution a Contract, made pursuant to the Act of Parliament of the 12th of his late Majesty King George 1st, between the Commissioners of his Majesty's Treasury and the Duke and Duchess of Atholl, the proprietors of the Isle of Man, and their Trustees, for the purchase of the said Island and its dependencies, under certain exceptions therein particularly mentioned, 5th Geo. III., Cap. 26.

Called "The Act of Revestment;" received the Royal assent 10th May. £70,000 to be paid into the Bank for the Duke of Atholl on or before 1st June 1765.

A copy of this Act is in Gell's "Abstract of the Laws," etc., vol. i. pp. 107-124; Manx Society, vol. xii., 1867. Abstracts are also given in Mill's "Statutes," 1821, pp. 527-530.

The patronage of the Bishopric and other ecclesiastical benefices, the landed revenue, and other manorial rights, are excepted. Abstracts of many of the Acts of Geo. III. are given in the Commissioners' Report, 1792, Appendix B, No. 44.

1765.—Act to discontinue Bounties on Corn, etc., exported from Great Britain or Ireland to the Isle of Man, 5th Geo. III., Cap. 30, Sec. 11.

1765.—Act respecting infringements on the Revenue of
Spirits, Wines, etc. etc., in the Isle of Man, 5th Geo. III.,
Cap. 39, Sections 1-15.

1765.—An Act for the bettersecuring and further improvement of the Revenues of Customs, Excise, Inland, and
Salt Duties ; and for encouraging the Linen Manufactures
of the Isle of Man, and for allowing the importation of
several goods, the produce and manufacture of the said
Island, under certain restrictions and regulations, 5th
Geo. III., Cap. 43.

Reprinted in 1779.

1765.—Act respecting Bestials, Goods, Wares, and Merchan-
dises, the Produce or Manufacture of the Isle of Man,
may be imported into Great Britain free of Duty, 5th
Geo. III., Cap. 43, Section 11-13.

1765.—An Act for the more effectually preventing the Mis-
chiefs arising to the Revenue and Commerce of Great
Britain and Ireland from the illicit and clandestine Trade
to and from the Isle of Man, 5th Geo. III., Cap. 39.

Received assent 15th May 1765. Was in force two years,
and was repealed 5th July 1825 by Act of 6th Geo. IV., c.
105. From its restrictive clauses was very injurious to the
revenues of the Island. It was called by the Duke, in his
address of 10th April 1805, " The Mischief Act," by which
the Insular revenue sank below £1000 per annum. It was
the first Act of the British Parliament which really affected
the rights and liberties of the people of the Island, and was
no doubt made to compel the Duke to part with his interest
therein.

In 1764 a correspondence commenced between the Lords
of the Treasury and the Duke of Atholl relative to the sale of

the Isle of Man.   The Duke, in his letter of the 20th August
1764, in reply says, "I have been but a few months in possession of the Isle of Man, and never in the least turned my
thoughts towards the sale of it."   *Vide* "His Case," p. 6,
1801.

1766.—An Act for allowing the conveyance from the Ports of
    Southampton and Portsmouth to the Port of Cowes, in
    the Isle of Wight, of goods not liable to Duty on exporta-
    tion, or prohibited to be exported, and of sheep and cattle
    between the said Ports without Cocquets being taken, or
    Bonds entered into for that purpose ; and for extending
    an Act made in the 29th year of the reign of King
    Charles II. for taking affidavits in the country to be made
    use of in the Courts of King's Bench, Common Pleas, and
    Exchequer, to the Isle of Man ; and for appointing Ports
    and places for shipping and landing goods in the said
    Island, 6th Geo. III., Cap. 50, Secs. 2 and 3.

1766.—An Act for Encouraging and Regulating the Trade
    and Manufacture of the Isle of Man ; and for the more
    easy Supply of the Inhabitants there, with a certain quan-
    tity of Wheat, Barley, Oats, Meal, and Flour, authorised by
    an Act made in this Session, to be transported to the said
    Island, 7 Geo. III., Cap. 45, Sections 1 to 8, 10 to 24.

An abstract of this Act, so far as relates to the Isle of
Man, is in the Commissioners' Report, 1805, Appendix B,
No. 44.

To take effect after the 5th July 1767.   The purport of
this Act is to raise a revenue which had fallen in consequence
of the "Mischief Act," the first Act of Parliament after the
Revestment.   By this Act Spirits are prohibited being dis-
tilled in the Island ; forfeiture of £200, with the materials

and utensils. The provisions of this Act are printed in Rolt's "History," 1773, pp. 133-151. Also in Mill's "Statutes," 1821, pp. 532-534.

1767.—An Act to levy New Customs Duties, repealing the Duties existing under local authority, 7 Geo. III., Cap. 45.

An abstract in Gell's "Abstract," vol. i. p. 142; Manx Society, vol. xii.

The Parliament for the first time assumed the power to impose taxes on the people of the Island, and repealing the Duties existing under local authority.

1767.—An Act for amending certain Laws relating to the Revenue of the Post Office, and for granting rates of Postage for the conveyance of letters and packets between Great Britain and the Isle of Man, 7 Geo. III., Cap. 50.

This was the first establishment of a public Post Office in the Isle of Man, by a Packet-boat from Whitehaven, in the county of Cumberland, and the port of Douglas. Given in the Appendix to Rolt's "History," 1773. Abstract in Mill's "Statutes," 1821, p. 534.

1771.—An Act for repairing, amending, and supporting the several Harbours and Sea Ports in the Isle of Man. The produce of the bay fisheries is to be applied for the repair of the harbours, 11 Geo. III., Cap. 52, Secs. 2, 3, 4, 5, 6, 8.

See Act 1814, for the new duties in lieu of these. For the preamble and first section see Gell's "Abstract," vol. i. p. 218; Manx Society, 1867. Also in the Appendix to Rolt's "History," 1773; and in Mill's "Statutes," pp. 534-536.

1772.—An Act for the further encouragement of the Herring Fishery on the Coasts of the Isle of Man; and for obviating a doubt which has arisen with respect to the allowing the bounties upon the British White Herring Fishery in the year 1771, 12th Geo. III., Cap. 58, Secs. 1, 4, 5.

Printed in Rolt's " History," 1773, Appendix.

1775.—Act respecting Bounties to Vessels, etc., and necessaries for Fishing may be exported from the Isle of Man to Newfoundland, 15th Geo. III., Cap. 31, Secs. 1, 3, 5, 6.

1780.—Act respecting Drawback on Salt from Great Britain to the Isle of Man, 20 Geo. III., Cap. 34, Secs. 3-7.

1780.—An Act for granting to His Majesty several additional Duties upon Certain Goods imported into the Isle of Man, and for the better regulating the Trade and securing the Revenues of the said Island, 20 Geo. III., Cap. 42, Secs. 1-11.

The new duties to take effect from the 5th July 1780.

An abstract of this Act is in the Commissioners' Report, 1805, Appendix B, No. 44. Also in Mill's " Statutes," 1821, pp. 537-8.

1781.—An Act for Vesting the Estates of P. John Heywood, Esq., in the Isle of Man, in Trustees, to be sold.

By and under which the estate is now held.

1781.—An Act that Rum imported from Scotland, liable to the same duty as from England, 21st Geo. III., Cap. 28, Sec. 2.

1785.—An Act for reducing the allowances for Waste on Salt and Rock Salt, etc. ; and for regulating the exportation of Herrings from the Isle of Man, etc., 25 Geo. III., Cap. 63, Sec. 9.

1786.—An Act relative to the importation of Herrings into the Isle of Man, 26th Geo. III., Cap. 36, Secs. 1-5.

Upon failure of the Fishery carried on upon the coast, the House of Keys may allow the importation, duty free, of foreign herrings for home consumption not exceeding 1000 barrels per annum.

1786.—An Act for the further Increase and Encouragement of Shipping and Navigation, 26th Geo. III., Cap. 60, Secs. 1-43.

For establishing a registry of ships built in the Isle of Man, or owned by its inhabitants.
An abstract in Mill's "Statutes," 1821, pp. 339, 340.

1786.—An Act respecting the Bounty on Herrings, 26th Geo. III., Cap. 81, Secs. 33-35.

1789.—An Act reducing the quantity of Tobacco to the Isle of Man to 40,000 lbs., 29th Geo. III., Cap. 68, Secs. 40-51.

1790.—A Bill to enquire into the Rights and Property of the Duke of Atholl in the Isle of Man.

1792.—An Act to repeal 5th Geo. III., Cap. 39, and 26th Geo. III., Cap. 41 ; and enacts so much of the 5th Geo. III. as relates to the Isle of Man Bond, be repealed.

1792.—An Act for the Relief of the Coast Trade of Great Britain ; for exempting certain Coast Documents from Stamp Duties ; for abolishing the Bond usually called the Isle of Man Bond ; and for permitting Corn and Grain brought Coastwise to be transshipped into Lighters, for the purpose of being carried through the Canal from the Forth to the Clyde, 32 Geo. III., Cap. 50.

1794.—An Act respecting the Manning of Vessels by British Subjects, etc., 34 Geo. III., Cap. 68, Secs. 1-22.

An Abstract in Mill's "Statutes," 1821, pp. 541, 542.

1798.—An Act for the further encouragement of the Trade and Manufactures of the Isle of Man ; for improving the revenue thereof; and for the more effectual prevention of smuggling to and from the said Island, 38 Geo. III., Cap. 63, Secs. 1-21.   21st June 1798.

With some amendments this Act continued until 5th July 1805.   An Abstract in Mill's "Statutes," 1821, pp. 542-544.

1799.—An Act to entitle Fishers, and Curers of Fish, in the Isle of Man, to the additional Bounty of One Shilling granted by 35th Geo. III., Cap. 56, for every Barrel of Herrings landed in that Isle, 39 and 40 Geo. III., Cap. 85, Sec. 2.

1801.—An Act to continue, until the 5th day of July 1802, an Act passed in the 38th year of the reign of his present Majesty for the further encouragement of the Trade and Manufactures of the Isle of Man, and for improving the revenue thereof; and also to repeal and amend certain of the provisions of the said Act 41 Geo. III., Cap. 54. 20th June 1801.

An Abstract is in Mill's "Statutes," 1821, p. 544.

1801.—An Act for revising and continuing until the 5th April 1802, and amending an Act made in the 39th and 40th years of his present Majesty, for the more effectual encouragement of the British Fisheries, etc. etc., 41 Geo. III., Cap. 97, Sec. 7.

Respecting Bounties for Herrings, etc.

1802.—Act requiring that no goods shall be carried from Ireland to the Isle of Man, etc., but in registered British Vessels, 42 Geo. III., Cap. 61, Sec. 4.

1805.—An Act for granting certain additional rates and duties in Great Britain on the conveyance of letters, 45 Geo. III., Cap. 11.   12th March.

By this Act extra rates on letters to and from the Isle of Man were imposed.

1805.—An Act for regulating and encouraging the Trade, for the Improvement of the Revenue, and prevention of Smuggling to and from the Isle of Man, 45 Geo. III., Cap. 99.   10th July 1805.

From this time the Imperial Parliament commenced to appropriate the Surplus Revenue of the Isle of Man to their own use, and most unjustly as is believed by the Manx people.   For forty years previously it had been kept distinct and apart from all the public revenue.   An Abstract is in Mill's "Statutes," 1821, pp. 545, 546.

1805.—An Act for Settling and Securing a certain Annuity on John, now Duke of Atholl, and the heirs-general of the 7th Earl of Derby, 45 Geo. III., Cap. 113.   12th July 1805.

Printed in Gell's "Abstract," vol. i. pp. 147-8 ; Manx Society's publications, vol. xii.

1805 —Act for Settling and Securing a certain Annuity on John, now Duke of Atholl, and such person or persons as would for ever hereafter, for the time being, have been Lord or Lords of the Isle of Man, if the same had not been revested in His Majesty by an Act passed in the fifth year of his reign, 45 Geo. III., Cap. 123, Secs. 1, 2.

The annuity equal to one-fourth part of the gross annual revenue arising from the duties of Customs.

1808.—An Act for amending an Act of last Session for the prevention of Smuggling, etc., 48 Geo. III., Cap. 84, Sec. 12.

So much of the recited Act as is applicable to Guernsey, etc., shall extend to the Isle of Man. An Abstract is in Mill's "Statutes," 1821, pp. 546, 552.

1810.—An Act for Consolidating the Duties of Customs for the Isle of Man, and for placing the same under the management of the Commissioners of Customs in England, 50 Geo. III., Cap. 42, Secs. 1-14. 2d June.

An Abstract in Mill's "Statutes," 1821, pp. 552-554.

1811.—An Act for explaining and amending an Act passed in the last Session of Parliament for Consolidating the Duties of Customs for the Isle of Man, and for placing the same under the management of the Commissioners of Customs in England, 51 Geo. III., Cap. 52. 31st May.

Empowers the Collector of Customs to retain in his hands the necessary sums of money as may be sufficient to defray the expenses attending the government of the Isle of Man, and other charges incurred in the said Isle.

An Abstract in Mill's "Statutes," 1821, pp. 554, 555.

1811.—An Act to confirm certain Articles of Agreement between the Most Noble John, Duke of Atholl, the Right Honourable Edward, Earl of Derby, the Right Rev. Claudius, Lord Bishop of Sodor and Man, the Honourable Edward Stanley, commonly called Lord Stanley, the Rev. Daniel Mylrea, William Scott, John Cosnahan, and

the Clergy of the Isle of Man, and for other purposes, 51
Geo. III., Cap. 207. 26th June.

Respecting the Ecclesiastical Rights and Impropriate
Tithes in the Isle of Man.

Printed in Gell's "Abstract of the Laws," etc., vol. i. pp.
164-188 ; Manx Society, vol. xii. 1867.

1812.—An Act regulating the export of Wine to the Isle of
Man, 52 Geo. III., Cap. 140.

An Abstract in Mill's "Statutes," 1821, p. 555.

1813.—An Act to Suspend the Exportation of Foreign Spirits
from Great Britain to the Isle of Man under License from
the Commissioners of Customs, and to permit the exportation of a limited quantity of Irish Spirits in lieu thereof,
under License from the Commissioners of Customs and
Port Duties in Ireland, from certain ports in that part of
the kingdom to the said Isle until the 5th day of July
1814, 53 Geo. III., Cap. 110. 10th July.

1814.—An Act to repeal the Duties granted by an Act passed
in the eleventh year of his present Majesty, for repairing,
amending, and supporting the several Harbours and Sea
Ports in the Isle of Man, and for granting new duties in
lieu thereof, and for giving further powers to the Commissioners appointed under the said Act, 54 Geo. III.,
Cap. 143. 27th July.

An Abstract in Mill's " Statutes," 1821, pp. 555, 556.

1815.—An Act for enabling the Commissioners of the Northern Light Houses to erect Light Houses on the Isles
of Man and Calf of Man, 55 Geo. III., Cap. 67. 7th
June.

In 1836, by Act 6 and 7 William IV., Cap. 79, Sec. 40,

13th August, the rates payable to the Commissioners were reduced in amount.

1817.—An Act for the Continuance in Office of persons holding employment under the Crown, on the decease of the King, 57 Geo. III., Cap. 45. 27th June.

This Act included the Isle of Man.

Printed in Gell's "Abstract," vol. i. p. 131 ; Manx Society, 1867.

1820.—An Act to charge additional Duties on the Importation of certain articles into the Isle of Man, and to regulate the Trade of the said Island, 1st Geo. IV., Cap. 61. 15th July.

Printed in Mill's "Statutes," 1821, pp. 507-511.

1821.—An Act regulating the Import of Foreign Corn, etc. 1st and 2d Geo. IV., Cap. 87, Secs. 27, 28.

An Abstract in Mill's "Statutes," 1821, p. 557.

1822.—An Act for granting the Rates of Postage for Conveyance of Letters and Packets between the Port of Liverpool, in the County of Lancaster, and the Isle of Man, 3d Geo. IV., Cap. 105. 5th August.

1824.—An Act empowering the Lords of the Treasury to Purchase all the Manorial Rights of the Duke of Atholl in the Isle of Man, 6th Geo. IV., Cap. 34. 10th June.

1825.—An Act to empower the Commissioners of His Majesty's Treasury to purchase a certain Annuity in respect of Duties and Customs levied in the Isle of Man, and any reserved sovereign rights in the said Island belonging to John Duke of Atholl, 6 Geo. IV. Cap. 34, 10th June.

Printed in Gell's "Abstract of Laws," etc., vol. i. pp. 149, 150. Manx Society, vol. xii. 1867.

1825.—An Act to repeal former Acts relating to Quarantine, etc., 6th Geo. IV., Cap. 78, Secs. 1, 2, 3.

1825.—An Act for the Prevention of Smuggling, 6 Geo. IV., Cap. 108, 109.

The Sections relating to the Isle of Man are printed in Geneste's "Statutes," 1832, pp. 131-133.

1825.—An Act for Regulating the Trade of the Isle of Man, 6 Geo. IV., Cap. 115, July 5th.

By this Act all previous Acts relating to the Customs of the Isle of Man were repealed.

Printed in the Appendix to Geneste's "Statute Laws." 1832.

1826.—Act respecting British plantation Coffee, and the Distillation of Wines and Spirits prohibited.   Penalty £200. 7th Geo. IV., Cap. 48, Secs. 11, 18, 49.   26th May.

1827.—Act to repeal a portion of the 6th George IV. as prohibits Beef and Pork, also Cattle, etc., imported from the Isle of Man, etc., 7th and 8th Geo. IV., Cap. 56, Secs. 3, 13.

1828.—Act respecting Playing Cards for the use of the Isle of Man to have a distinguishing Mark on the Ace of Spades, etc., 9 Geo. IV., Cap. 18, Secs. 3, 8, 9, 20, 30, 32.   9th May.

An abstract given in Geneste's "Statutes," 1832, p. 133.

1828.—Act respecting the importation of Clocks, etc., Spirits, etc., 9 Geo. IV., Cap. 76, Secs. 4, 5, 27, 28.   25th July.

An Abstract in Geneste's "Statutes," 1832, p. 134.

1829.—A Bill for Confirming the Sales and Conveyance made to His Majesty, of the Isle, Castle, Peel, and Lordship of Man, and other Estates in the said Island of Man, lately belonging to John Duke of Atholl.

Ordered to be printed 19th May 1829; but it does not appear to have been proceeded with.

1829.—An Act to Consolidate and amend the Laws relating to the management and improvement of His Majesty's Woods, Forests, Parks, and Chaces; of the Land Revenue of the Crown within the Survey of the Exchequer in England; and of the Land Revenue of the Crown in Ireland; and for extending certain provisions relating to the same to the Isles of Man and Alderney, 10th Geo. IV., Cap. 50. 19th June.

Sections 8 and 113 are printed in Gell's " Abstract," vol. i., pp. 205, 206. Manx Society, 1867. The Revenues were placed under the Management of the Commissioners of Woods and Forests.

1831.—Act to repeal the Duties upon Coals, Culm, or Cinders, imported from the United Kingdom into the Isle of Man, and upon Slate from the Isle of Man, 1st and 2d William IV., Cap. 16, Sec. 1. 23d August.

1831.—An Act to amend and render more effectual an Act passed in the seventh and eighth years of the Reign of his late Majesty, intituled, An Act to amend the Acts for building and promoting the building of additional Churches in populous parishes, 1st and 2d William IV., Cap. 38. 15th October.

An abridgment in Geneste's " Statute Laws," 1832, pp. 134-136.

1832.—An Act prohibiting Tobacco of Irish growth to be imported into the Isle of Man, 2d William IV., Cap. 20, Sec. 5.   24th March.

1832.—An Act for the punishment of Mutiny and Desertion, etc., to extend to the Isle of Man, 2d William IV., Cap. 28, Sec. 32.   9th April.

1832.—An Act respecting Wrecks, etc., 2d William IV., Cap. 84.

An Abstract of the Sections relating to the Isle of Man is given in Geneste's " Statutes," 1832, p. 137.

1833.—An Act for regulating the Trade of the Isle of Man, 3d and 4th William IV., Cap. 60.   28th August.

A fresh consolidation of the Laws relating to the Customs of the Island.

1836.—An Act respecting Lighthouses, 6 and 7 William IV. Cap. 79, Sec. 40.   13th August.

The rates payable to the Commissioners were reduced in amount in the Isle of Man.

1837.—An Act for the Management of the Post-Office, 1st Victoria, Cap. 33.   12th July.

A consolidation of the Post-Office Laws, including the Isle of Man.   And by the Act 1st Vic., Cap. 34, 12th July, was the regulation of the Duties of Postage.   New Postage rates, to and from within the Isle of Man, to commence on the 1st August 1837, were enacted.

1839.—An Act for the further regulation of the Duties of Postage until the 5th day of October 1840, 2d and 3d Victoria, Cap. 52.   17th August.

The uniform rate of 4d. Postage, subsequently reduced to 1d. throughout the United Kingdom, Isle of Man, and the Channel Islands, was established.

1840.—An Act to extend the Powers of the Commissioners appointed for the execution of two Acts for supporting the several Harbours and Sea Ports in the Isle of Man, 3d and 4th Victoria, Cap. 63. 7th August.

1840.—An Act for the regulation of the Duties of Postage, 3d and 4th Victoria, Cap. 96. 10th August.

New Postage rates of the minimum rate of 1d. in the Isle of Man, were continued from the 1st September 1840.

1844.—An Act to amend the Laws relating to the Customs in the Isle of Man, 7th and 8th Victoria, Cap. 43. 19th July.

£2300 per annum was allowed for Harbour purposes.

1845.—An Act for Regulating the Trade of the Isle of Man, 8th and 9th Victoria, Cap. 94. 4th August.

1848.—An Act for rendering certain Newspapers published in the Channel Islands and the Isle of Man liable to Postage, 11th and 12th Victoria, Cap. 117. 4th September.

1853.—The Customs Tariff Act, 16th and 17th Victoria, Cap. 106. 20th August.

New Duties were enacted.

1853.—The Customs Consolidation Act, 16th and 17th Victoria, Cap. 107. 20th August.

Sections 353, 354, refer to the application of the revenue.

The Parliament fully recognised the principle that the Inhabitants of the Island were entitled to the benefit of any additional surplus created by an increase of duties.

Printed in Gell's " Abstract," vol. i. pp. 198, 199.   Manx Society, 1867.

1854.—An Act to alter the mode of providing for certain expenses now charged upon certain branches of the Public Revenue, and upon the Consolidated Fund, 16th and 17th Victoria, Cap. 107.   10th August.

Schedule A.   Charges upon the Customs Revenues of the Isle of Man.

1854.—The Merchant Shipping Act.   10th August.

Section 389 relates to Lighthouses in the Isle and Calf of Man.

Various provisions relating thereto are in Gell's " Abstract," vol. i. p. 226.   Manx Society, 1867.

1860.—An Act to make further provision for improvements in the Harbours of the Isle of Man, 23 and 24 Victoria, Cap. 56.   6th August.

The Commissioners empowered to borrow money on the security of the annual sum of £2300 allowed for Harbours.

1862.—An Act to extend to the Isle of Man the provisions of the Act of Eighteenth and Nineteenth Victoria, Cap. 90. March.

As to payment of Costs to and by the Crown.

1862.—The Merchant Shipping Amendment Act.   29th July.

Includes the Isle of Man, and also relates to Lighthouses.

1863.—The Isle of Man Harbour Act, 26 and 27 Victoria, Cap. 16.   28th July.

This Act authorises taking Harbour Dues at Port-Erin, Isle of Man.

1864.—Isle of Man Harbours Amendment Act, 27 and 28 Victoria, Cap. 62.   25th July.

Relates to the Money advanced for Port-Erin Break-water.

1866.—Isle of Man Customs, Harbours, and Public Purposes Act, 29th Victoria, Cap. 23.   18th May.

This Act was in connection with the Isle of Man Reform Act.   See Gell's " Abstract of Laws," etc., vol. i. pp. 200 and 222 ; Manx Society, vol. xii., 1867, for various Sections relating to the Isle of Man.

AUTHORS WHO MENTION THE ISLE OF MAN,
and not more particularly mentioned in the foregoing account.

Cæsar's Commentaries, B.C. 54.

Printed in Oliver's "Monumenta," vol. i., p. 1.   Manx Society, vol. iv., 1860.

Pliny's Natural History, A.D. 23.

Printed in Oliver's "Monumenta," vol. i., p. 3.

Paulus Orosius, A.D. 416.

Printed in Oliver's "Monumenta," vol. i., p. 6.

Bede's Ecclesiastical History of Great Britain, A.D. 731.

Printed in Oliver's "Monumenta," vol. i., p. 8.

Nennius' History of Britain, A.D. 858.   Great Britain, chap. ii. ;
Ireland, chap. ii.

Printed in Oliver's "Monumenta," vol. i., pp. 11-13.

Annals of Tighernac, *circa* 1084.

Anglo-Saxon Chronicle, 1087.

William the Conqueror.   Printed in Oliver's "Monumenta," vol. i., p. 14.

Jocelinus of Furness, 1112.

Of Man, and the other Islands converted to God, giving an account of St. Patrick's visit to the Island, A.D. 444. Printed in Oliver's "Monumenta," vol. i., p. 15.

Chronicle of Florence of Worcester, 1118.

>Printed in Oliver's " Monumenta," vol. i., p. 18.

William of Malmesbury, 1125.

>Printed in Oliver's " Monumenta," vol. i., p. 23.

Annales Cambriæ, *circa* 1125.

>Printed in Oliver's " Monumenta," vol. i., p. 26.

Ordericus' Ecclesiastical History, 1141.

>Printed in Oliver's " Monumenta," vol. i., p. 28.

The Chronicle of the Princes of Wales, 1150.   " Brut y Tywysogion."

>Printed in Oliver's " Monumenta," vol. i., p. 31.

Henry of Huntingdon's History of England, 1154.

>Lib. i., Lib. ii., Lib. iii.   Printed in Oliver's " Monumenta," vol. i., pp. 32-35.

Annals of Roger de Hoveden, 1192.

>Printed in Oliver's " Monumenta," vol. i., pp. 36-42.

Annals of Innisfallen, 1197.

Ynglinga Saga, 1200.

>Ex Snorro Sturleson, chap. xx.   Printed in Oliver's " Monumenta," vol. i., p. 56.

Matthew Paris, 1236.

>Printed in Oliver's " Monumenta," vol. i., pp. 47-50.

Roger of Wendover's Flowers of History, 1237.

>Printed in Oliver's " Monumenta," vol. i., pp. 51-55.

Haco's Expedition against Scotland, 1248.

From the Flayteyan and Frisian MSS. Printed in Oliver's "Monumenta," vol. i., pp. 58-69.

From the MS. Continuation of the History of William of Newburgh, 1265-75.

Printed in Oliver's "Monumenta," vol. i., pp. 70, 71.

Rotuli Scotiæ, Memb. 5, Nov. Castr., Jan. 5, 1292.

In the Rev. J. G. Cumming's "Sacheverell," pp. 154-5. Manx Society, vol. i., 1859.

Calendar of Patent Rolls, Anno 20 Regis Edwardi Primi, 15th July 1292.

In the Rev. J. G. Cumming's "Sacheverell," p. 154. Manx Society, vol. i., 1859.

Chronicle of Richard of Cirencester, 1348.

Printed in Oliver's "Monumenta," vol. i., p. 72.

Capgrave, Chronicles of England, 1377.

Printed in Oliver's "Monumenta," vol. i., p. 73.

Matthew of Westminster's Flowers of History, 1400.

Printed in Oliver's "Monumenta," vol. i., pp. 74-76.

Hardyng's Chronicle, 1460.

King Arthur. Printed in Oliver's "Monumenta," vol. i., p. 77.

Polydore Virgil, 1470.

Primacy of Scotland and of the Isles of Britain. Printed in Oliver's "Monumenta," vol. i., pp. 78, 79.

Annals of Ulster, *circa* 1496.

Fabyan's Chronicles, 1510.

King Edwyn.   Printed in Oliver's "Monumenta," vol. i., p. 80.

Report of Kelway, Surveyor of the Court of Wards in the 14th of Henry VIII., 1523.

Ann, widow of Thomas, second Earl of Derby, claimed dower in the Isle of Man.

John Leland, 1550.

Printed in Oliver's "Monumenta," vol. i., pp. 81-83.

Grafton's Chronicle, 1568 and 1809.

Manaman Mack Clere, Insula de Man ; Lansd. MSS., 1573.

Printed in Oliver's "Monumenta," vol. i., p. 84.

Buchanan, History of Scotland, 1577.

Printed in Oliver's "Monumenta," vol. i., p. 86.

Letter of John Merick, Bishop of Sodor, on the Antiquities of the Isle of Man ; Cott. MSS., 1577.

Printed in Oliver's "Monumenta," vol. i., pp. 87-99.

Hollinshead's Chronicles of England and Scotland, 1584.

Printed in Oliver's "Monumenta," vol. i., p. 232, Addenda.

Speed's Chronicles, 1618.

Stow's Chronicle.

Olaus Magnus' History of the Goths, Swedes, and Vandals, 1658.

Spelman's Glossary, 1664.

Prynne's Abridgment of the Records in the Tower, 1668.
Printed in Oliver's "Monumenta," vol. i., p. 111.

Ductor Historicus, vol. ii., p. 327.

Formulare Anglicanum, Formula 211.

Wood's Athenæ Oxoniensis, a History of all the Writers and
Bishops who have been educated at Oxford. *Folio.* 1691.

Madox's History and Antiquities of the Exchequer of the
Kings of England, 1711.

Torfæus' Historiæ Rerum Orcadensium, Libri iii. *Folio.*
Havniæ, 1715 and 1697.
Printed in Oliver's "Monumenta," vol. i., pp. 113-116 ;
and vol. iii., pp. 210-217, and 218.

Ryley's Placita Parliamentaria.
Petition of the daughter and heir of King Reginald to
King Edward I. for the Crown of Man, against John Baliol,
King of Scots.

Arms of the Isle of Man, 1735 ; Add. MSS. ; Opinion of
Clarencieux, King of Arms.
Printed in Oliver's "Monumenta," vol. i., pp. 117-122.

Anderson's Royal Genealogies, London, 1736.
Table for the Isle of Man.

Vesyey's Reports, vol. ii., p. 337.
Bishop of Man *v.* Com. Derby, and Com. Derby *v.* D. of

Atholl.   In Canc., 1751, July.   Printed in Gell's "Abstract,"
vol. i., pp. 67-74.   Manx Society, vol. xii.

Mallet's Northern Antiquities, 1770.
   Printed in Oliver's "Monumenta," vol. i., p. 123.

Ridpath's Border History of England and Scotland, p. 382.
   Quarto.   London, 1776.

Wood's Institute of the Laws of England, etc., 1772.
   Printed in Gell's "Abstract of the Laws," etc., vol. i., p.
158.   Manx Society, vol. xii. 1867.

Hutchinson's History of Cumberland ; Account of the Family
   of Edward Christian, vol. iii., p. 146, 1794.

Lord Hailes' Annals of Scotland, Common Law ; 3 vols.,
   Octavo.   Edinburgh, 1797.

Usher, Bishop of Armagh ; List of the Bishops of Man.

Postlethwaite's Commercial Dictionary, Article " Man."

Henry's History of England, B. 1, c. 2, c. 3.

Robertson's History, vol. i., chap. 5.

Robertson's America.

Dalrymple's Essays and Annals of Scotland, 1797.

Debrett's Parliamentary Register.
   On the Duke of Atholl's Claims, vol. iv., pp. 350-1 ; vol.
xxvii., pp. 307, 315, 383, 561.

Peere William's Reports, i., 329.

Christian *v.* Corren.   Appeal from a decree in the Isle of
Man.   Printed in Gell's "Abstract," vol. i., p. 93.   Manx
Society, vol. xii.

Jacob's Law Grammar.

Dr. Ree's Cyclopædia, 1819, vol. xxii.

An Article on the Isle of Man, taken chiefly from Feltham,
Townley, and Woods.

Symson's Description of Galloway, 1684; republished in
Edinburgh, 1823.

Repp's Ancient Forensic Institutions of Scandinavia and Ice-
land.   Edinburgh, 1832.

MANUSCRIPTS.

Harl. 43, A. 70. Charter of Magnus, King of Man, to the Prior of Cunigesheved (Co. Lanc.) 1256.

Respecting privileges. Printed in Oliver's "Monumenta," vol. ii., p. 87 ; Manx Society, vol. vii., 1861.

Charter of Magnus to the Abbot of Furness, date 1256.

Charter of Harald to the same respecting ships.

Charter of Magnus, constituting the Bishopric a feudal barony.

A translation in the Manx Society's third volume, 1860, "Stanley Legislation of Man," pp. 142-3. Date of confirmation, 1329.

Johēs de Athy hēt custodiâ terre de Mā quādiu, tc. Teste Rege apud Northampton, 6 Julii. Cla. A 33, E. 1, m. 4 in dorso.

Printed in Oliver's "Monumenta," vol. ii. p. 271. A.D. 1318.

Harl. MS. 2223, f. 26 ; Mona Insula ; Finis A° 5, E 2, m. 13, 15.

Harl. MS. entitled Recognatio Olavii Regis Manniæ et Insularum.

Insula de Man Comīssa ; Fin. A° 8, E 2, m. 4.

Henricus de Bello Monte hēt totā terrā de Man ad vitam suâ.
Teste Rege ap^d Berewicū suβ Tuedā, 12 Martii.   Fin. A°
10, E. 2, m. 1.

Printed in Oliver's "Monumenta," vol. ii., p. 141.   A.D.
1308.

Willms de Mōte Acuto Comes Sarūⁱ Dofs Insula Manne
Scotia A° 10, E 2, m. 1.

Printed in Oliver's "Monumenta," vol. ii., p. 182.   A.D.
1334.

Insula de Man.   Fin. A° 7, E. 3, m. 11.

Johnēs Stanley pro dom de Man.   Dors. Clau. A° 39, E 3,
m. 7.

Pro Thoma Comiti Warwic' in Insula de Man.   Dors. Cla.
A° 42, E. 3, m. 9.

Walsingham (Historian), 1393, f. 387 ; 17 R. 2.   On Coro-
nets.

Cott. ch. V. 29.   Bond of Wm. Scrope, Seign. de Man, to
Richard Whittington, for £166, date 17 R. 2.   With seal.

Willms de Monte Cuto hēt custodiā Insulæ de Mā cū perti-
nētiis sibi comissā, usq₁ ad festâ Stⁱ Micheſ pr futuř, et
ab esde festo p unū annū ps sequentē.   Teste Rege apud
Twedemouth, 30 Maii.   Eps. p. A° 21 R. 2, m. 10.

De Thoma Comiti Warwic' in Insula de Man ducendo.   Z.
ps. cl A° 22, R. 2, m. 20.

Willm de Montagu Comt de Salisbury ⁱt Seign^r de Man.
Franc A° 1, H. 5, m. 7.

Harl. 56, A. 22.   Grant from Wm. de Montague Seign de
Man of an annual rent of 63s. 8d. to one John Cauleto.
With seal.

Controversy on the Arms of the Isle of Man, 1475.

Printed in Oliver's "Monumenta," vol. iii., p. 24; Manx
Society, vol. ix., 1862.

Records in the Tower.   Pat. 15 E. 4, p. 2, m. 24.

Madox's Formularia Anglican.   No. DLXXII. [par le Grace
de Dieux].

Selden's Titles of Honour.   L. 1, c. 3.   Dissertation on the
Kingdom of Man.

Printed in Oliver's "Monumenta," vol. i., pp. 107-110;
also in Gell's "Abstract of the Laws," etc., vol. i., p. 156;
Manx Society, vol. xii., 1867.

AT LAMBETH.

Chronicon sed valde insigul de episcopis Manniæ, ad. an.
1374.

Collectiones de Episcopis Manniæ.

Catalogue or History of the Bishops of Sodor.

Letter from Sacheverell, Governor of the Isle of Man, to
Archbp. Cant. on the state of Religion there.   Date Oxon,
1 Sep.

Printed in Oliver's "Monumenta," vol. iii., p. 160.

De Episcopis Sodorensibus.

In the Bodleian Library.

Charter of Aufrice de Connaught, granting the Isle of Man to Simon de Montacute, 1305.

Wm. Earl of Salisbury, Lord of Man, granting certain fees to Wm. Hankeford, 30 Ric. II.   French.

Notes of the Foundations of Abbeys in England and Man, 1112-92.

In the Sloane Collection, Brit. Mus.

Catalogue of the Bishops of Man, by Bishop Hildesley.

Ancient Canons of the Manks Church.   The property of John Selden, who died in 1654.   In the Brit. Museum, Seldonian Collection.   Train, vol. i., p. 380.

Sacheverell mentions a very ancient MS. which was put in his hands by the Rev. Henry Jones (nephew and executor to the Right Rev. Dr. Fell, late Bishop of Oxford), giving an exact succession of Bishops for above 200 years, which in his opinion was extracted from the Roll of the Abbey of Rushen.

Printed in his " Account of the Isle of Man," 1702 ; also in the Manx Society's first volume, pp. 85-92, 1859.

The Chronicle of Man and the Isles, in the Cottonian Collection, numbered Julius A. vii.

Printed by Dr. Oliver in " Monumenta," vol. i., pp. 125-215 ; fourth volume of the Manx Society's publications,

1860 ; also in volumes xxii. and xxiii. of the Manx Society's series.

A MS. Record of the Island, preserved in the Castle of Rushen.

The True Chronicle of the Isle of Man.

This is in the Rolls Office, and is prefixed to the old copies of the Statute Book.   It has been continued by successive Clerks of the Rolls until the Revestment in 1765. Printed in Gell's "Abstract," pp. 6-9, vol. i. ; Manx Society, 1867.

Samuel Stanley's Description of the Isle of Man.

In the hands of Mr. Thoresby, who has also MS. "Prospects in the Isle of Man."   *Vide* Gibson's "Camden," vol. i., 1772.

MS. Chronicle of the Kings of Man.   On vellum, in the Cottonian Library, marked Julius A. vii. 3.   1065 to 1316.

Published in Gough's "Camden," 1789, abridged.

MS. Lord's Book.—1609.

A Breefe Collection of all suche Leases within the Isle of Mann, as have been formerly granted by anie of Erles of Derby to the inhabitants thereof, with theire severall dates, what acres they doe contayne, what rentes are res'ved, what estates are in beinge, and what is the true valuation of every p'ticular, rated by the oathes of an especiall jurie, impannelled onlie for that s'vice, who vewed eich sev'rall demyse, and valued the same.   A.D. 1609.

A Quarto MS. on Vellum.

This MS. is in possession of the present Earl of Derby at Knowsley, and will no doubt form one of the publications of the Manx Society, having been placed in the hands of the Council by his Lordship, with the following letter :—

KNOWSLEY, *January 19th*, 1861.

SIR—In the course of partially re-arranging the libraries here, I have come upon the volume, the title of which I enclose ; and as it occurs to me that its contents may be of interest to the resident members of the Manx Society, and perhaps available for some of their future publications, I shall be happy to lend you the volume, and authorise you to make such use of its contents as you may think fit in the interest of the Society. On receiving your answer, I will send it over in such manner as you may advise. I shall of course look to you for its safe return in due time ; and as it is rather in a dilapidated condition, I must beg that it may be carefully dealt with, and not exposed to any farther injury than it has already sustained.—I am, Sir, your obedient servant,

DERBY.

J. R. Oliver, M.D., Hon. Sec., Manx Society.

MS.—1644.

A Discourse concerning the Government of the Isle of Man, by the Rt. Honb. James, Earle of Derby.   A.D. 1644.

This MS. is in the Knowsley Library, a *Small quarto* volume of 78 pages.

It is printed in Peck's "Desiderata," and vol. iii. of the "Stanley Papers," 1867, Chetham Society ; also in the Manx Society's third volume, 1860.

BISHOP RUTTER.—1648.   (MS.)

A choice Collection of Songs composed by Archdeacon Ryter (afterwards Bishop of Sodor and Mann) for the amusement and diversion of the Right Hon. James, Earl of Derby, during his retreat into his Island of Man in the time of the Oliverian Usurpation.

One of the songs is called "Ubonia's Praise ;" another,

"The Little Quiet Nation," "being a prologue to the play acted in Castle Rushen before the Right Hon. James, Earl of Derby, to divert his pensive spirit and deep concern for the calamity of his country, occasioned by the grand rebellion began Anno 1641 ;" a third is styled " Threnodia, or Elegiac Song on the direful effects of the Grand Rebellion, with a prophetic view of the downfall and catastrophe thereof, composed by the reverend author on Scarlet Rocks, near Castletown."

MS.—16—.

A History of the Isle of Man.

A MS. written in the 17th century, beginning A.D. 1205. In *folio*, in the Knowsley Library.

A copy is in possession of Charles Wickstead, Esq., o Shakenhurst, Bewdley, in the county of Worcester, "Stanley Papers," vol. ii., p. ccclxxiv. Chetham Society, 1867.

This appears to be the same MS. as that called the " Blundell MS." 1648, of which various copies are in existence. Mr. Wickstead's copy is defective of the Title as given in the copy belonging to the Manx Society.

WILLIAM BLUNDELL.—1648.   (MS.)

" It then containeth divers Ordinances, Statutes, and Customs,
    presented, reputed, and used for Laws in the Isle of Man,
    that were ratified, approved, and confirmed as well by the
    Honourable Sir John Stanley, Knight, King and Lord of
    the same land, and divers others, his predecessors, as by
    all barons, deemsters, officers, tenants, and inhabitants of
    the same land."

The above is given as the title of this MS. by Mr. Townley in his "Journal," 1789-90, and which he supposes was written by a Welsh Justice. He has given copious extracts from it in his second volume. The MS. then belonged to

Mr. James Oates of Douglas. Feltham, in 1798, states it to be in the possession of Mr. Moore of Douglas (now in the possession of the Manx Society). The author appears to have sought the shelter of the island during the troubles occasioned by the Civil Wars, when, says he, "wearied with being so often awakened at midnight by the King's and Parliament's troops, both equally feared because equally plundering, I resolved to banish myself for a time to the Island of Man, where divers nobility had been banished by our Kings."

The Manx Society are in possession of an imperfect copy of this MS., which contains only the first two books, wanting chapters 14 to 25, also the third book. The title of the volume as given in this MS. is as follows :—"An exact Chronographical and Historical Discovery of the hitherto unknown Isle of Man, containing a true and perfect description of this Island at large ; the History of their Ancient Kings, late Lords and Bishops of the Island ; the Ceremonies of their Inaugurations and Instalments ; together with the Political Government there practised, and their Courts of Justice, and strange manner of the Citations and Form of Pleadings in the Island. As also discovering all their Laws and Customs, as well Political, Legal, or Ecclesiastical, both ancient and modern ; wherein likewise are laid open and rectified the many abusive, erroneous, and misinformed relations of Hector Boetius, and of all those that have hitherto written of this Island. Never hitherto discovered or published by any."

MS. by MR. BLUNDELL, of Crosby.—During the Civil Wars.

"This gentleman employed his leisure hours in collecting the History and Antiquities of the Isle of Man, and by his MSS., which I have seen, gave posterity the clearest and most correct account of it."—*Seacome*, p. 487, Ed. 1793.

This evidently alludes to the above MS. of 1648.   A copy of this MS. is in the library at Knowsley, as appears by an extract from it in "The Stanley Papers," part iii., vol. ii., p. 374 ; Chetham Society, 1867.

There is little doubt this is the author's original MS., from which various transcripts have been made.

A copy is in the possession of M. H. Quayle, Esq., Clerk of the Rolls, said to be written by an unknown author retired here from the troubles occasioned by the Civil Wars.   The Rev. J. G. Cumming considers this to be Mr. Blundell's original MS., and the one made use of by both Sacheverell and Seacome, but the original is evidently at Knowsley.

The Clerk of the Rolls has given permission for the portion not in the Manx Society's possession to be copied for their use.   It will now form one of their series of publications.

MS.—1422 to 1705.

Containing 108 Acts of the Manx Legislature anterior to the accession of the Atholl family, and which have been kept in Castle Rushen.

This MS. contained much interesting information nowhere else to be found.   *Vide* "Memoirs of Train," p. 133, 1857.

DEEMSTER PARR.—1693-1712.

An Abstract of the Laws, Customs, and Ordinances of the Isle of Mann.

John Parr held the office of Deemster from 1693 to 1712. Various copies of this Abstract, which has never been printed, appear to be in existence.   It contains much valuable information as to the state of the law in his day.

This is now in course of publication by the Manx Society, under the editorship of James Gell, Esq., Her Majesty's

Attorney-General for the Isle of Man. The first volume, being the twelfth of the Society's publications, appeared in 1867.

MS.

The Antient Customary Laws of the Isle of Man.

This is a brief compilation, arranged under thirty-nine heads. By whom they were drawn up is not known, but they were considered as of authority at the time Deemster Parr drew up his Abstract, as he often alludes to them. The MS. is in the Rolls Office.

ALEXANDER ROSS.—1744-53.   (MS.)

Mona ; or the History, Laws, and Constitution, Ecclesiastical and Civil, of the Isle of Man, verified by the Records of the Island, and thence extracted by the application, care, and diligence of Mr. Alexander Ross, of Grey's Inn, Gent.

Mr. Ross died in the year 1753. Copied from the original for the use of E. Umfrevill ; now in the hands of George Tollet, Esq., Betley Hall, Staffordshire. The above is from Townley's "Journal," 1789-90, vol. ii., p. 226, where he states that the MS. then belonged to Mr. Oates of Douglas.

Mr. Tollet, now of Wickstead, Nottinghamshire, in a letter to Paul Bridson, Esq., Hon. Sec. to the Manx Society, in the year 1857, dated "Shakenhurst, Bewdley, Worcestershire, 24th May," declines to allow the Society to publish Mr. Ross's MS. as he purposes publishing it.

Mr. Charles Tollet, who took the name of Wickstead, in his letter to Mr. Bridson, gives some extracts from his MS. which clearly proves it to be the same MS. as Blundell's, 1648, and it appears to have the third book, wanting in the Manx Society's copy.

Mr. Ross's MS. is evidently quite a different work.

MS., in Two Volumes, of a Vocabulary or Dictionary of the Manx Language. By the Rev. John Kelly, LL.D., of St. John's College, Cam., Vicar of Ardleigh in Essex.

In the College Library, Castletown. Printed in the Thirteenth volume of the Manx Society's publications, 1866. Edited by the Rev. W. Gill and the Rev. J. T. Clarke.

MS. Triglot Dictionary, by the Rev. John Kelly, LL.D., containing a Vocabulary of the English, Manx, Irish, and Gaelic Languages.

In the College Library, Castletown.

1000 to 1805.

MS. History of the Isle of Man, written by the late Rev. Wm. Fitzimmons, Episcopal Minister of Carrubber's Close, Edinburgh ; a native of the Island.

Formerly in the possession of the late Richard Quirk, Esq., Receiver-General, who presented it to the Manx Society.

MS. on Manx Antiquities, etc.

In the Library of the Society of the Antiquaries of Scotland, Edinburgh. Communicated by Mr. Oswald, of Douglas, 1823, etc.

1843.

MS. Account of Manx Customs, collected for Train's Historical Account of the Isle of Man. By a Native of the Island (Mr. P. Curphey). 1843.

MS. Book of Statutes of the Isle of Man. By James Christian. *Folio.*

In the Knowsley Library.

THE MANX SOCIETY.

*Established in the Year 1858 for Publication of National Documents
of the Isle of Man.*

In this work, treating of what has been printed relative to the
History and Antiquities of the Isle of Man, it would be in-
complete if special notice was not made of the formation and
progress of a Society which has been the means of bringing
not only the present account, but numerous other documents,
before the public, which would otherwise have never appeared.

Early in the year 1858 a few gentlemen met in Douglas
to consider the best mode of forming a Society for publishing
or reprinting everything tending to illustrate the History of
the Isle of Man, an undertaking which required the assist-
ance of many hands. After several meetings a Committee
was formed, who drew up an address which was freely circulated in the Island, as also in England and Scotland, and its
object met with such hearty support, that upwards of one
hundred and twenty members desired to be enrolled in the
Society. Amongst the number were the Earl of Derby, the
Duke of Argyll, several leading Members of Parliament, with
most of the Members of the Insular Government, and others.
A general meeting was accordingly called, when the Society
was formally instituted, and a code of Rules adopted, his
Excellency the Honourable Charles Hope, Lieutenant-Governor of the Isle of Man, being elected President of the Society.

The following is the Address which was sent out, with a
copy of the Rules :—

THE MANX SOCIETY

The Chief "of the multitude of Isles," satellites to Great Britain and Ireland, has local peculiarities of the most interesting and important nature. It has an unexhausted field to the Antiquary and the Statesman—the man of the past and of the future—of conservatism and of progress. Inhabited by an aboriginal tribe of the great Celtic family, with language, institutions, and laws peculiar to itself—never united to Scotland, Ireland, or England—to this day a separate realm independent of the Imperial Parliament, and under its native and aboriginal Legislature, with a singular relation between its Church and State, having, as Lord Coke says, "such laws the like whereof are not to be found in any other place ;" so that "if the ancient discipline of the Church were lost," said Chancellor King, "it might be found in all its purity in the Isle of Man," surely this Island has peculiar claims to have the light of catholic publicity at length cast upon all its documents and peculiarities. It was not in jest merely that Burke, speaking to Dr. Johnson and Boswell about a visit to this Isle, used the famous line of Pope—

" The proper study of mankind is Man."

The central Isle of the British group, connected with Scotland geographically and geologically, with Ireland ethnologically, with England politically, and with the three kingdoms ecclesiastically, merits more attention from the United Kingdom than it has ever received. As during the past it has been, so for the future it promises to be, a beginner of the great central movements of the British Isles. Said to have been the central fane of Druidism in the aboriginal Celtic period, it was certainly the stronghold of the Norsemen long before they took the supremacy of Great Britain and Ireland. They introduced here Trial by Jury, and modified the old Celtic government by constituting the House of Keys to be a representation of the Island, before the judicial and political systems of jury and representation were known in Britain. The highest order of English chivalry, that of the Garter, began with the King and Queen of Man. The Papacy was subdued in this central Isle a full century before Henry VIII., and thus among the European nations, the Manx, like Wycliffe, was the Morning Star of the Reformation, and for 428 years has been to the most catholic extent anti-papal. The latest reforms of the British fiscal and legal systems under Peel and Brougham are said to have been modelled after Manx examples. The records of such central movements of the geographic and organic heart of Great Britain and Ireland must prove in the highest degree interesting to the antiquary, the historian, and the conservative patriot, and may afford data to the patriotic reformer and liberal for prospects and actings as to future progress. The oldest and first-born dependency of England must be an object of interest to the younger brood of giant nations growing up from the loins of the Anglo-Saxon race. It is a singular spectacle in Europe to see a nation with no debt, with no soldiers of its own, with a heavy claim against the British Treasury, and with the taxing branch of its own legislature dormant. Having single-handed cut itself free from the Papacy in 1430, at the end of "the Great Western Schism," and being the only Reformed nation that has not been excommunicated by Rome, it holds towards Papal and Protestant kingdoms a peculiar position in Christendom. Marching in the front rank of European progress, the miniature kingdom of Man preserves with Asiatic immobility the Tynwald government, older far than that throne of the Cæsars on which the Popes have placed their Chair of St. Peter. The Protestantism of Mona, so much indebted to Wycliffe, and not impeded by the growing obstacles that stop the progress of the Luther and Calvin Reformation, seems to have special preparation for the next era and development of Christianity. A nation whose soil is divided as in France, and whose Sabbath is observed as in Scotland, with a domestic Legislature, and a Bible in every family, is in a normal position for progress, ready to move in the van of Christendom, a pilot engine before the catholic train of mankind.

On these grounds it is deemed that a Society for the publication of all the valuable documents illustrating the past, and promotive of the future of the Manx people, will have claims of no ordinary strength on the patronage of the Nobility, Commons, and Churches of the British Empire and Colonies, and of all who look to the United Kingdom as the leading and model nation of mankind. This Society will direct, for the first time, a combined and powerful influence towards the elucidation of the national records and monuments of Man.

The following extract from the Preface to the latest work of the Rev. J. G. CUMMING, the modern historian of the Isle of Man, may be quoted in connection with the preceding statements :—

"It does indeed seem strange that, with all the facilities which steam navigation affords, the Isle of Man, presenting to us certainly some of the most beautiful scenery in the British Isles, and whose political status is of so singular a character, should continue to be so little known. How very few are aware, as I have found by repeated inquiries, of these facts following, very worthy of note :—That its climate is more equable than that of any country in Europe, and its mean annual temperature higher than that of any spot in the same parallel of latitude ; that it has within itself more antiquities in the shape of cromlechs, stone circles, crosses, ruined churches and castles, than any area of the like extent in the British Isles ; that it has been the possession in turn of the Scotch, Welsh, Danes, Norwegians, and English ; that its kings dictated terms to the Kings of Ireland ; that it played a part in the struggle between Bruce and Baliol ; that the land, the people, and their privileges, have been transferred from one party to another by purchase or by mortgage on five separate occasions; that though in the middle of the British Isles, it is not in point of law a part of them; that though a possession of the British Crown it is not ruled by the British Parliament; that though its people have the rights of British subjects, it is no part of England, is not governed by the laws of England, and belongs not to England by colonisation or by conquest; that in all these various changes of hands through which the Island has passed, it has maintained in its integrity its ancient and singular Constitution, and presents the last solitary remains of the ancient Scandinavian Thing, or Court of Justice, which, for the protection of public liberty, was held in the open air, in the presence of the entire assembled people; that its Bishopric is the most ancient of any in Great Britain or Ireland, and has preserved an unbroken succession of Bishops from the first till now; that it contains no records of the Reformation (of the sixteenth century); that the Bishop in the time of King Henry VIII. was also Bishop in the time of Elizabeth, and died in possession; that its ecclesiastical liberty is not encumbered with an Act of Uniformity, or an Act of Mortmain; that, for the better Government of the Church, and for making such orders and constitutions as shall from time to time be found wanting, it is enjoined by law that there shall be a convocation of the whole clergy of the Diocese, on Thursday in Whitsun Week, every year; that Canons drawn up in these Synodal meetings of the Church have received the sanction of the Legislature, and are actually the statute law of the Isle; that the Bishop can himself draw up public prayers to be used in the churches of his Diocese, and that such prayers have been incorporated into the Liturgy of the Manx Church; that the Offertory has never been discontinued, but is in general practice, once at least, every week, in every parish in the Island."

RULES.

1. That the affairs of the Society shall be conducted by a Council, to meet on the first Tuesday of every month, and to consist of not more than 24 Members, of whom six * shall form a quorum; and that the President, and Vice-Presidents, the Hon. Secretaries and Treasurers, shall be considered *ex officio* Members. The Council may appoint two acting Committees, one for finance and the other for publication.

2. That a subscription of One Pound annually, paid in advance, on or before the day of annual meeting, shall constitute Membership; and that every Member not in arrear of his annual subscription be entitled to a copy of every publication issued by the Society. That no Member incur any pecuniary liability beyond his annual subscription.

* The quorum was reduced to three in 1859.

3. That the Accounts of Receipts and Expenditure be examined annually by two Auditors appointed at the annual meeting on the 1st of May in each year.

4. That six Copies of his Work be allowed to the Editor of the same, in addition to the one he is entitled to as a Member.

5. That no Rule shall be made or altered except at a General Meeting, after due notice of the proposed alteration has been given as the Council shall direct. The Council shall have the power of calling Extraordinary Meetings.

In addition to this Address the following was extensively circulated throughout the Island :—

The Council of this Society particularly request your kind co-operation in furnishing them with information on the various details of your parish or district, and beg to call your attention to the following queries :—

Name of the parish, its length, breadth, acreage, and general geologica character ; Celtic remains, such as rocks or stones, which are objects of popular tradition or superstition ; altar stones, cairns, either simple heaps of stones or surrounded by circles of stones, runic stones, or crosses ?

Have any axes, spears, arrow-heads, vases, coins, rings, or other remains been found ? In whose possession are they ? Are there any ruins or remains of ancient buildings, embracing roads, stations, barrows, Treen chapels or yards, civil, military, or ecclesiastical ?

Incumbents, etc., of the livings from the earliest to the present time, with the dates of their induction, etc. In whose gifts are the various Church preferments ?

What benefactions have been given to the parish, particularly since 1827 ?

Parochial registers : their earliest date ? Particular information is earnestly requested, and as ample extracts from them as can be given. No subject is of more importance to the antiquarian and historian, and in no way can clergymen do greater service to the history of the Island than by rendering accessible the valuable documents in their custody.

The Church, when built, its general plan and dimensions ? Are there any remarkable tombs or monumental inscriptions ? Exact copies of these, with all armorial bearings, are particularly valuable. Earliest date on stones, and remarkable ages ?

Notice any peculiarity in the fonts, of what materials composed ; if any screens or carved work, communion plate or Church relics ; if any arms or inscription ? Extent of parish or clerk's glebe ; number of wardens in the parish, or any peculiar mode of election ?

What schools are there in the parish, and how endowed or supported ?

What chapels of other denominations are there in the parish, when built, and how endowed, etc. ?

Is there any library connected with the church or parish ; by whom given, or how kept up ; the number and description of books ?

Are there any words or phrases peculiar to the people of the district ?

Have they any remarkable legends, ballads, or traditions ?

Are any ancient customs or games kept up, or any peculiar customs observed at funerals, or respecting the dead, or marriages or christenings ?

Are there any mineral or remarkable springs of water or wells ?

Natural History : any information on this subject will be very useful. Appearance of rare birds, insects ; mollusca, shells, etc., thrown on the seashore ; plants, etc., that may be considered rare, etc.

These and many other kindred subjects are all worthy of investigation, and the Council recommend that none of these points be lost sight of by those able and willing to communicate information ; in fact, everything should be collected and arranged which can in any way assist in illustrating the past and present condition of the Island, including topography, family or general history, so that each and all may find their appropriate place in some of the volumes offered by this Society.

In what manner the Society has so far carried out their object will be best seen by a reference to the following works which have been published, and already noted in the text of the present volume :—

PUBLICATIONS OF THE MANX SOCIETY.

For the First Year—1858-59.

VOLUME I.

An Account of the Isle of Man, with a Voyage to I-Columb-Kill. By William Sacheverell, Esq., late Governor of Man. 1703. With a dissertation about the Mona of Cæsar and Tacitus, and an account of the Ancient Druids, by Mr. Thomas Brown. Edited, with introductory notice and copious notes, by the Rev. J. G. Cumming, M.A., F.G.S. 300 copies printed. Pp. xvi. 204. A Pedigree.

Volume II.

A Practical Grammar of the Antient Gaelic or Language of
the Isle of Man, usually called Manx. By the Rev. John
Kelly, LL.D. Edited, with an Introduction, Life of Dr.
Kelly, and Notes, by the Rev. William Gill, Vicar of
Malew. 322 copies printed. Pp. xlviii. 92.

For the Second Year—1859-60.

Volume III.

Legislation by Three of the Thirteen Stanleys, Kings of Man,
including the letter of the Seventh Earl of Derby, as published in Peck's "Desiderata Curiosa." Edited, with
Introduction and Notes, by the Rev. William Mackenzie.
402 copies printed. Pp. xix. 224. Plate.

Volume IV.

Monumenta de Insula Manniæ, or a Collection of National
Documents relating to the Isle of Man. Translated and
edited, with Appendix, by J. R. Oliver, Esq., M.D. Vol. i.
315 copies printed. Pp. xv. 244. Plate.

Volume V.

Vestigia Insulæ Manniæ Antiquiora; or a Dissertation on
the Armorial Bearings of the Isle of Man, the Regalities
and Prerogatives of its Ancient Kings, and the Original
Usages, Customs, Privileges, Laws, and Constitutional
Government of the Manx People. By H. R. Oswald,
Esq., F.A.S., L.R.C.S.E. 310 copies printed. Pp. ix. 218.
Ten plates.

For the Third Year—1860-61.

Volume VI.

A Tour through the Island of Mann in 1797 and 1798;

comprising sketches of its ancient and modern History,
Constitution, Laws, Commerce, Agriculture, Fishery, etc.
By John Feltham.   Edited, with Notes, by the Rev.
Robert Airey.   305 Copies printed.   Pp. xvi. 272.   Map.
Four Plates.   Three Woodcuts.

VOLUME VII.

Monumenta de Insula Manniæ ; or a Collection of National
Documents relating to the Isle of Man.   Translated
and Edited by J. R. Oliver, Esq., M.D.   Vol. ii.   311
Copies printed.   Pp. xxi. 250.   Map.

VOLUME VIII.

Bibliotheca Monensis : a Bibliographical Account of Works
relating to the Isle of Man.   By William Harrison, Esq.,
M.H.K.   308 Copies printed.   Pp. viii. 208.

For the Fourth Year—1861-62.

VOLUME IX.

Monumenta de Insula Manniæ ; or a Collection of National
Documents relating to the Isle of Man.   Translated and
Edited, with Appendix and Indices, by J. R. Oliver, Esq.,
M.D.   Vol. iii.   300 Copies printed.   Pp. 272.

VOLUME X.

A Short Treatise of the Isle of Man.   By James Chaloner,
Governor of the Island from 1658 to 1660.   Published
originally in 1656 in King's " Vale Royal of England, or
the County Palatine of Chester."   Edited, with an Introductory Notice and copious Notes, by the Rev. J. G.
Cumming, M.A., F.G.S.   300 Copies printed.   Pp. vii.
138.   Map.   Four Plates.   Five Pedigrees.

For the Fifth Year—1862-63.

VOLUME XI.

A Description of the Isle of Man : with some useful and
entertaining reflections on the Laws, Customs, and Manners
of the Inhabitants. By George Waldron, Gent., late of
Queen's College, Oxon. 1731. Edited, with an Introductory Notice and Notes, by William Harrison, Esq.,
M.H.K. 300 Copies printed. Pp. xxv. 155. Plate.

VOLUME XII.

An Abstract of the Laws, Customs, and Ordinances of the
Isle of Man : compiled by John Parr, Esq., formerly one
of the Deemsters of the Island. Edited, with Notes, by
James Gell, Esq., Attorney-General of the Isle of Man.
Vol. i. 310 Copies printed. Pp. xvi. 241.

For the Sixth Year—1863-64.

VOLUME XIII.

Fockleyr Manninagh as Baarlagh, Liorish Juan y Kelly
Edited by the Rev. William Gill, Vicar of Malew. Part i.

An English and Manx Dictionary, prepared from Dr. Kelly's
Triglot Dictionary, with alterations and additions from
the Dictionaries of Archibald Cregeen and John Ivan
Mosley. By the Rev. Wm. Gill and the Rev. J. T. Clarke.
Part ii. 500 Copies printed. Pp. 432.

For the Seventh Year—1864-65.

VOLUME XIV.

Memorials of " God's Acre," being Monumental Inscriptions
in the Isle of Man, taken in the Summer of 1797. By
John Feltham and Edward Wright. Edited, with an

Introductory Notice, by William Harrison, Esq. 300 Copies printed. Pp. xv. 132. Six Plates.

VOLUME XV.

Antiquitates Manniæ ; or a Collection of Memoirs on the Antiquities of the Isle of Man. Edited by the Rev. J. G. Cumming, M.A., F.G.S. 300 Copies printed. Pp. viii. 140. Twenty-four Plates. Eleven Woodcuts.

For the Eighth Year—1865-66.

VOLUME XVI.

Mona Miscellany. A Selection of Proverbs and Sayings, Ballads, Customs, Superstitions, and Legends, peculiar to the Isle of Man. Collected and Edited by William Harrison. 261 Copies printed. Pp. xv. 241. Music to three Songs.

VOLUME XVII.

Currency of the Isle of Man, from its earliest appearance to its assimilation with the British Coinage in 1840 ; with the Laws and other circumstances connected with its History. Edited by Charles Clay, M.D., Manchester. With articles on Paper Currency, Treasure Trove, etc., by J. Frissell Crellin, Esq., M.H.K. 250 Copies printed. Pp. xi. 215. Illustrated extensively with Photographs, Lithographs, and Woodcuts.

For the Ninth Year—1866-67.

VOLUME XVIII.

The Old Historians of the Isle of Man—Camden, Speed, Dugdale, Cox, Wilson, Willis, and Grose. Edited by William Harrison. 209 Copies printed. Pp. xiv. 199. Three Maps and thirteen Plates.

For the Tenth Year—1867-68.

VOLUME XIX.

Records of the Tynwald and St. John's Chapels in the Isle of Man. By William Harrison. With an Appendix, containing an Account of the Duke of Atholl taking possession of the Isle of Man in 1736. Also, A Lay of Ancient Mona. 263 Copies printed. Pp. xiv. 148. Fourteen Plates.

For the Eleventh and Twelfth Years—1868-69-70.

(No Works issued for these Years or Subscriptions collected.)

For the Thirteenth Year—1870-71.

VOLUME XX.

Manx Miscellanies. Vol. i. Containing—

1. Selections from "Paradise Lost," a Poem, by John Milton, translated into the Manx Language by the Rev. Thomas Christian, Vicar of Marown, in 1796.

2. The Emerald Vernicle of the Vatican. By C. W. King, M.A., with Notes by "Aspen." With a Portrait of Our Saviour.

3. Ancient Portraitures of Our Lord. After the type of the Emerald Vernicle given by Bajazet II. to Pope Innocent VIII. By Albert Way.

4. The Seal of Thomas, Bishop of the Isle of Man. By E. L. Barnwell, M.A. With an Engraving of the Seal.

5. Poetical Description of the Isle of Man in Manx. By Joseph Bridson, 1760. Rendered into English by Mr. John Quirk of Carn-ny-Greie, Patrick.

6. Diary of James, VIIth Earl of Derby, who was beheaded at Bolton-in-the-Moors, October 15th, 1651,
aged 45 years.   With Notes by Mr. Paul Bridson,
Hon. Sec.   250 Copies printed.

VOLUME XXI.

Mona Miscellany.   A Selection of Proverbs, Sayings, Ballads,
Customs, Superstitions, and Legends, peculiar to the Isle
of Man.   Second Series.   Collected and Edited by William Harrison, Esq., Author of "Bibliotheca Monensis."
Pp. xvi. 285.   Two Plates.   With Music to one Song.
208 Copies printed.

For the Fourteenth Year—1871-72.

VOLUME XXII.

Chronica Regum Manniæ et Insularum.   The Chronicle of
Man and the Sudreys, from the Manuscript Codex in
the British Museum, with Historical Notes.   By P. A.
Munch, Professor of History in the Royal University of
Christiania, Hon. F.R.A.S.S.   Revised, Annotated, and
furnished with additional Documents, and English Translations of the Chronica and of the Latin Documents, by
the Right Rev. Dr. Goss.   Vol. i.   Pp. xxviii. 264.   Two
Plates.   155 Copies printed.

VOLUME XXIII.

The Chronicle of Man and the Sudreys.   Vol. ii.   Containing
Documents referred to.   Pp. 265-436.   155 Copies
printed.

INDEX.

ABSTRACT of the laws, Dr. Parr, J. Gell, 224.
Account of stock, etc., belonging to any school, hospital, etc., 118.
Acts of the British Parliament relating to the Isle of Man, 237.
Acts of Tynwald, criminal code, 112.

      ,,   disafforesting the forest, 202.

      ,,   ,,   compensation, 216.

      ,,   ,,   first award, 218.

      ,,   district drainage, 218.

      ,,   Douglas Town's Act, 204.

      ,,   ,,   Amendment Act, 217.

      ,,   ,,   water supply, 144.

      ,,   four new Acts, 105.

      ,   House of Keys election, 221.

      ,,   Incorporation of Companies, 219.

      ,,   lodging-houses, common, 221.

      ,,   lunatic asylum, 208, 217.

      ,,   Malew burial-ground, 220.

      ,,   Peel grammar-school sale, 216.

      ,,   Peel water-works, 215.

      ,,   petty sessions, 217.

      ,,   prevent the destruction of sea-gulls, 230.

      ,,   promulgated in 1814, 106.

      ,,   promulgating Acts, 220.

      ,,   punishment of larceny, 216.

      ,,   railway Act, 218.

      ,,   Ramsey Town Act, 218.

      ,,   registering deeds, 175.

Acts of Tynwald, shortening the language in, 218.
„   summary jurisdiction, 217.
„   taverns amendment, 220.
„   temporary lunatic asylum, 217.
„   town bye-laws, etc., 220.
„   trustees, 219.
„   weights and measures, 216.
„   MSS., 272, 274.
Adams's Guide to Channel Islands and Isle of Man, etc., 202.
Adamson, Lawrence, letter on Manx law, 157.
„   „   the state of the law of real and personal property, 159.
„   „   the people's case, 168.
Address to the people by order of the House of Keys, 1781, 49.
Advocates' Note Book, Bluett, 176.
Agriculture of the Isle of Man, Basil Quayle's view of, 62.
„   „   Thomas Quayle, 103.
Agricultural Society's Rules, etc., 206, 212.
Almanacs, Manx, 69, 112, 115, 125, 130.
Analysis of the petition of the 24 Keys, 74.
Anecdotes of Olave the Black, 47.
Annexing the Isle of Man to Great Britain, 31.
Antiquary's Portfolio, Wm. and Edward Christian's case, 131.
Antiquarian Repertory, lid of a stone coffin, 97.
Antiquaries' Society, swords of state, 230.
Antiquities of the Isle of Man, 182, 228.
„   „   Grose, 42, 52.
„   „   Paterson, 213.
Antiquitates Celto-Normannicæ, Johnstone, 53.
Antiquitates Manniæ, Cumming, 229.
Archæologia Britannica, Lhuyd, 20.
Archæological Journal, Petit, 172.
Archaic sculpturings of cups, Sir J. Y. Simpson, 225.
Ardglass, or the Ruined Castles, 69.
Armorial bearings of the Isle of Man, H. R. Oswald, 206.
Ashe, Trevor, Manx Sketch-book, 131.

Ashe, Trevor, Belville and Julia, 131.

Atholl, Duke of, Address to the Keys, etc., and on his appointment as Governor, 72.

" Articles of Agreement respecting ecclesiastical rights 102.

" Case claiming the Barony of Strange, 27.

" Case of, in the Privy Council, 68.

" Claim of, 54.

" copies of contracts respecting sale of the Isle of Man, 136.

" Curwen, J. C., speech on, 75.

" Extracts from reports of Tynwald Courts, and report by, 123.

" Further observations on rent charges payable out of revenue in favour of, 74.

" Letter of, to the Lords of the Treasury, 36.

" Minutes of the evidence of House of Keys on petition of, 75.

" Observations on the case of the petition of, 72.

" Papers presented to the House of Commons on the claim of, 73.

" Petition of, on the clandestine trade, 58.

" Pitt's speech on the additional compensation to, 58.

" Report from the committee on the petition of, 75.

" Report of Privy Council on the petition of, 71.

" Revenue, observations on, 71.

" Speech to Tynwald Court, 26th September 1821, 120.

" State of proceedings on the petition of, 36.

" Statement of case of, claiming compensation, 76.

Authors who mention the Isle of Man, 257.

Ayloffe, calendars of ancient charters in the Tower, 43.

Baldwin, John, a new Act of an inferior Parliament, 29.

" British Liberty in Chains, 31.

" Liberty Invaded, 30.

Ballad, Winning of the Isle of Man by the Earl of Salisbury, 101.

Ballads, Evans' Old, 101.

Barrow, J., Mona Melodies, 116.

Battledoor for Teachers, Geo. Fox, 11.

Beatson, R., Political Index, 54.

Beauties of England and Wales, 69.

Bell, Mr. (Jeffrey's), Account of the Isle of Man, 99, 100.

Belville and Julia, T. Ashe, 131.

Bennet, William, Sketches, 137.

Bentley Ballads, " The Manxman and his Visitor," 196.

Berger, Dr., Geological Survey, 106.

Bible, Holy, in Manx, 39, 46, 114.

Bibliotheca Monensis, 209.

Bishop of Man *v.* Com. Derby, on alienation, 76.

Blackstone's Commentaries, 98.

Blanchard, E. L., Guide to the Channel Islands, Isle of Man, 202.

Bleau's Atlas, Isle of Man, 11.

Blome, R., Britannia, 14.

Blue Book, Roper's, 129.

Bluett, J. C., Advocates' Note Book, 176.

    „   Address and Reply to the House of Keys on a breach of promise, 124.

    „   Constitution of the House of Keys, 163.

Blundell, William, MS., 270.

Bodleian Library, MS. relating to the Isle of Man in, 267.

Bog timber, remarks on in Gentleman's Magazine, 52.

Book of Rates of Customs, 1731, 24.

Borowlaski, Count, Memoirs of, 117.

Boswell, Henry, Historical Descriptions, 53.

Bridson and Stowell's Letter to their Colleagues, 74.

    „   Woodhouse's answer to, 77.

Briscoe, Christopher, Statute Laws, 64.

    „ Joseph, Acts of Tynwald, 50.

    „ J., Literary Lovers, 50.

Britannia, Camden's, 2, 40, 55.

    „   Blome's, 14.

British Archæological Journal, stone crosses, 166.

British Liberty in Chains, 31.

British Museum, MSS. relating to the Isle of Man in, 267.

British Tourist, Robertson's Tour, 66.

Brown, Professor, on cattle disease, 223.

    „   Rev. Robert, poems, 132.

    „   „   sermon in St. George's, 111.

    „   „   sermons, 113.

    „   Thomas, Dissertation on the Mona of Cæsar and Tacitus, 20.

Building News, St. Olave's Chapel, 223.

Bullock, H. A., History of the Isle, 110.

Burdy, Rev. Samuel, Ardglass, or the Ruined Castles, 69.

Burkill, J., Pictorial Beauties, 194.

Burman, James, Statute Laws, 188.

Butler, Rev. Weedon, Memoirs of Bishop Hildesley, 67.

Bye-Laws for Towns, abstract of, 191.

CALENDARS of ancient Charters, 39, 43.

Calendar of State Papers, Mrs. Green, 210.

Callister, Robert, poems, 53.

    „   Thomas, Description of the Herring-Fishery, 108.

Camden, William, Britannia, 2, 40, 55.

Campbell, John, Political Survey of Great Britain, 42, 45.

    „   J. F., Popular Tales, 203.

Cannell, C., Minutes of Manx Cases, 196.

Carlisle, Nicholas, Topographical Dictionary of Scotland and the Isle of Man, 106.

Catalogue of the Isle of Man Library, 141.

Catechism for the Fishery in Manx, 38.

Challoner, James, Treatise of the Isle of Man in King's Vale Royal, 8.

    „   „   by Rev. J. G. Cumming, 215.

Chancel, A. D., New Journey over Europe, 21.

Charities, Isle of Man, 139.

Chater's Sermon on James Dalrymple, 210.

Chit-chat on the Isle of Man, Stowell, 210.

Christian, Edward and William, Marsden's Historical Notice of, 127.

Christian, William, Judgment of the King in Council on, 12.
      ,,   ,,   Speech of, 45.
     ,,   Elijah, A Light to Lighten the Gentiles, 164.
     ,,   Rev. Thomas, Paradise Lost, in Manx, 63.
Christian Monitor, 34, 38.
Christian's School, Peel, 206.
Chronica Regum Manniæ et Insularum, P. A. Munch, 205.
Chronicon Manniæ, 52.
Chronicle of Man, Rev. J. Stevenson, 194.
Claims at Coronations, 150.
Clara Lennox, Mrs. Lee, 65.
Clark, Rev. Samuel, Mirrour, 14.
Clarke, J. Courts of the Isle of Man, 112.
Clarke, W. N., Letters of Manx Bishops, 178.
Clay, Dr., Currency of the Isle of Man, 231.
     ,,   Proceedings of the Manchester Numismatic Society, 215.
Clown, The, A. Ormonde, 180.
Cobbett's Debates, Duke of Atholl's Claim, 71.
Coke's Institutes, 13, 65.
Collier, J. P., Egerton Papers, 155.
Collins, Captain G., Map, 22.
Commentaries on the Laws, Blackstone's, 98.
Common Prayer-Book in Manx, 35, 38, 46, 98, 155, 160.
Commissioners' report on Smuggling, 34.
     ,,   report, 1792, 78.
Conaant Noa, 45, 101.
Cookson, Elizabeth, Mylecharane, 196, 199.
     ,,   Legends of Manx Land, 199.
     ,,   Poems from Manx Land, 229.
Cooney dy Gheddyn, 136.
Coontey jeh Saggyrt, 136.
Correspondence on Fiscal Changes, 222.
Courts of the Isle of Man, J. Clarke, 112.
Cowley, Daniel, Explanation of the Church Catechism in Manx, 47.
Cox, Rev. Thomas, Magna Britannia, 22.
Craven, C. S., Legend of Mona, 130.

Crawford, John, Deed with the altered date, 179.

Cregeen, Archibald, Manx Dictionary, 144.

Crellin, Margaret, Herring Fishery, 66.

Crennell, Thomas, Summers' Memoirs of, 192.

Criminal Code, the new, 112.

Crossman's Manx Catechism, 109.

Crown Garland of Golden Roses, 11.

Cruttwell, Rev. C., Works of Bishop Wilson, 48.

    ,,   Life of Bishop Wilson, 64.

    ,,   Tour through Great Britain, 68.

Cubbon, John, Charities of St. Matthew's Chapel, 190.

Cumming, Rev. J. G., Antiquitates Manniæ, 229.

    ,,   Geology of the Calf of Man, 176.

    ,,   Geology of the Isle of Man, 173.

    ,,   Great Industrial Exhibition, letters on, 183.

    ,,   Great Stanley, 224.

    ,,   Guide, 207.

    ,,   History of the Isle of Man, 177.

    ,,   Runic remains, 193.

    ,,   Sacheverell's account of the Isle of Man, 198.

    ,,   Story of Rushen Castle, 193.

Curphey, William, Rev. H. Stowell, 121.

Curran, J., Observations on the Rev. Mr. Aitken's Sermon, 141.

Currency of the Isle of Man, Dr. Clay, 231.

Cursory remarks on the Manor Courts Bill, 51.

Curwen, John Christian, Life by Dr. Lonsdale, 227.

    ,,   Speech on the Duke of Atholl's Case, 75.

Customs Reform—Copies of Treasury Minutes, etc., 189.

Customs and Imports, Statement of, 77.

Dale, Isaac, Mona Melodist, 161.

Dalrymple, James, Funeral Sermon on, 210.

Danes and Norwegians in England, etc., Worsaae, 187.

Declaration of the Earl of Derby to keep the Isle of Man, 6.

    ,,   Sir Marmaduke Langdale and Sir Lewis Dives, 7.

Deed of Association of the Steam-Packet Company, 150.

Deed with the altered date, Crawford, 179.

De Foe and Samuel Richardson, Tour through Great Britain, 47.

Denham, M. A., Popular Rhymes, etc., of the Isle of Man, 184.

Derby, Earl of, Declaration to keep the Isle of Man, 1649, 6.

    ,,   Declaration in vindication of, by Langdale and Dives, 7.

    ,,   v. Duke of Atholl, Decision of Lord Hardwicke, 30.

    ,,   History of the Isle of Man, 25.

    ,,   Message from to Charles II. respecting a surrender of the Island, 6.

Description of the Isle of Man, 31.

Desiderata Curiosa—Earl of Derby's History of the Isle of Man, 25, 204.

Dictionary of the Manx Language, Cregeen, 144.

    ,,   Manx and English—Kelly, Gill, and Clarke, 223.

    ,,   of places mentioned in the Bible, 184.

Directory, Pigot's, 127, 162.

Disafforesting Commission, Declaration of the Boundaries, 208.

    ,,   First Award of Commissioners, 218.

Disorder, Disease, and Death, 214.

Divine and Moral Songs, Watts, 134.

Douglas Bye-laws, 220.

    ,,   Middle School Magazine, 203.

    ,,   Plan of, 144, 181.

    ,,   Rev. James, Nénia Britannica, 62.

    ,,   Reflector and Isle of Man Magazine, 120.

    ,,   Town's Act, 204.

    ,,   Amendment Act, 217.

    ,,   Water Act, 144.

Dr. Hookwell, a Novel, 161.

Drinkwater, John, Map of the Island, 132.

Dugdale, Sir William, Monasticon Anglicanum, 10, 173.

Duggan, John, Speech in Douglas, 148.

    ,,   The Touchstone, 167.

Durand, Rev. J. F., Memoirs of Thurot, 32.

Durham, Thomas, Map of the Island, 3.

Ecclesiastical Antiquities, Petit's, 172.

Ecclesiological Notes, Neale's, 179.

Education, state of, 175.

Edwardine, Mrs. St. George, 109.

Effects of the Fiscal Act, 176.

Egerton Papers, J. P. Collier, 155.

Ellan Vannin, Journal of a Tour in, 193.

Encyclopædia Britannica, Article "Isle of Man," 101.

England's Remarques, 14.

England and Wales, Beauties of, 69.

Epistles and Revelations in Manx, 38.

Eric, or Little by Little, F. W. Farrar, 197.

Evans, Thomas, Old Ballads, 101.

Extracts from Reports in the Isle of Man Gazette and Rising Sun, 123.

Eye Salve for the Wesleyans of Mona, 183.

Fannin, Peter, Map of the Island, 56.

Farrar, F. W., Eric, 197.

Fasti Ecclesia Anglicanæ, Le Neve, 21.

Feltham, John, Memorials of God's Acre, 228.

    ,,   Tour through the Isle of Man, 65.

    ,,   ,,   ,,   by the Rev. Robert Airey, 207.

Fiscal Act, Effects of, 176.

    ,,   Changes, Correspondence on, 222.

Fishers of Derby Haven, 224.

Fishery, Prayer for the, 38.

    ,,   Reports on the, 180.

Fitzsimmons, Rev. William, History of the Isle of Man, MS., 274.

Fœdera, T. Rymer, 18.

Forbes, Edward, Memoirs of, by Dr. Wilson, 209.

    ,,   Malacologia Monensis, 152.

    ,,   Rev. Edward, Sermon, 201.

Forests of Man, Boundaries of, 208.

    ,,   Correspondence on the, 201.

    ,,   Disafforesting Act, 203.

Fossil Elk, Dr. Hibbert on the, 133.

    „   Oswald on the, 133.

Fox, George, Battledoor for Teachers, 11.

Freedom, Righteousness, and Law, 158.

French, Gilbert J., on Ancient Sculptured Stones, 195.

Friendly Societies, Observations on, 204.

GALLOVIDIAN Encyclopedia, Mactaggart, 129.

Garnett, T., Observations on a Tour in the Highlands, 67.

Gas Question of Douglas, 213.

Gazette, London, Address to Charles II., 15.

Gell, James, Parr's Abstract of Laws, 224.

    „   Statute Laws, 178.

Geneste, F. D. P., Memoir of, 135, 162.

Geneste, George, Statute Laws, 140.

Gentleman's Magazine, Account of the Isle of Man, 130.

        „   On Castle Rushen Gaol, 100.

        „   On the Round Tower in Peel Castle, 136.

        „   On annexing the Isle of Man, 31.

        „   Reasons for annexing the Isle of Man, 31.

        „   Remarks on Bog Timber, 52.

        „   Runic Monuments at Kirk Michael, 66.

        „   Thurot's action with Elliot, 32.

Geological Survey, Dr. Berger, 106.

Geology of the Calf of Man, Cumming, 176.

    „   of the Isle of Man, Cumming, 173.

Gill, Rev. William, Kelly's Manx Grammar, 200.

Gloucester, Ballad on the Duchess of, 11.

Gospels and Acts, in Manx, 33.

Gough, John, History of the Quakers, 56.

Grammar, Kelly's Manx, 70, 200.

Grave Mounds, L. Jewitt, 232.

Gray, Rev. J. H., Letter to Governor Pigott, 208.

Green, Eliza Craven, Sea Weeds and Heath Flowers, 195.

Green, M. A. E., Calendar of State Papers, 210.

Greenhalgh Pedigree, 191.

Grose, Francis, Antiquities of England and Wales, 42, 52.

    ,,   Antiquities of the Isle of Man, 182.

Guides to the Isle of Man, 122, 125, 128, 139, 140, 156, 160, 176, 177, 202, 205, 207, 212.

Haining, Samuel, Guide, 122, 128.

    ,,   Strictures on the Bishop's Charge, 167.

Halliwell, J. O., Roundabout Notes, 211.

Halstead, C. A., Countess of Richmond, 154.

Hamilton's National Gazetteer, 222.

Harbours, Copies of Memorials, 185.

    ,,   Walker's Report on, 191.

Harbours of Refuge, National Importance of, 132, 159.

    ,,   Proceedings of a Public Meeting on, 159, 170.

Hargrave, Francis, Juridical Arguments on the Duke of Atholl's Claim, 65, 102.

    ,,   Further opinion on said Claim, 102, 105.

Harris, Walter, Life of St. Patrick, and Account of the Isle of Man, 29.

Harrison, William, Bibliotheca Monensis, 209.

    ,,   Memorials of God's Acre, 228.

    ,,   Mona Miscellany, 230.

    ,,   Waldron's Description, 219.

Head, Sir George, Home Tour, 150.

Helps, Arthur, Leaves from the Queen's Journal, 229.

Henry, Thomas, Isle of Man Poetically Illustrated, 182.

Herring Fishery, Callister's description of, 108.

    ,,   A poem, Crellin's, 66.

    ,,   Report on the, 134, 135.

Heylyn, Dr. Peter, Help to English History, 6, 13.

    ,,   Microcosmus, 5.

Heywood, Peter, Tagart's Memoir of, 141.

Hibbert, Dr., on the discovery of the Fossil Elk in the Isle of Man, 133.

Higden, Ralph, Polycronycon, 1.

Hildesley, Bishop, Butler's Life of, 67.

Hill, Rev. Thomas, Memoir of Bishop Shirley, 181.

Hillary, Sir William, Importance of a Central Harbour of Refuge, 132, 147, 159.

      „   Letter to Lord John Russell on the Preservation of Life from Shipwreck, 158.

      „   Letter to the Trustees of the Academic Fund, 137.

      „   Observations on the Fiscal and Navigation Laws, 149, 164.

History, Topography, and Directory, 211.

Holinshed, Ralph, Chronicles, 2.

Hone, Rev. R. B., Life of Bishop Wilson, 184.

Hookwell, Dr., a Novel, 161.

Hooper's Survey of the Revenue Farm Rents, 3.

House of Keys, Address to the People, 49.

      „   Bluett on the Constitution of the, 163.

      „   Form of Prayer for the, 211.

      „   Minutes of Evidence relating to the, 75.

      „   Petition of the, to the House of Commons, 1824, 128.

Howard, Rev. Thomas, Sermons, 107, 137, 174, 183.

Howard, Thomas, Vade Mecum, 137.

Hulbert, C., Guide, 122.

Independent Whig, 25.

Index to the Statutes, Mackenzie, 209.

Intacks, Mill's Impartial Inquiry, 105.

Introduction to first edition of Bibliotheca Monensis, xi.

Irvine, C., Historiæ Scoticæ, 15.

Island Minstrelsy, E. Nelson, 154.

Isle of Man Diary and Almanack, 112.

Isle of Man, a Satire, 169.

      „   Weekly Gazette and General Advertiser, 105.

      „   „   „   New series, 107.

Itinerant, S. W. Ryley, 97.

J. S., Letters descriptive of the Isle of Man, 203.

James, Col. Sir Henry, Ordnance Survey, 231.

Jamieson and Dillon, Drs., on Runic Monuments, 126.

Jeffcott, John M., Statute Laws, 149.

Jeffcott, John M., Statute Laws, continuation of, 156.

Jefferson's Manx Almanack, 130.

      „   Guide to the Isle of Man, 156.

Jeffrey's, N., Account of the Isle, 99, 100.

Jewitt, L., Grave Mounds, 232.

Johnson, Col., Brief Sketch of the Isle, 186, 211.

      „   J., Jurisprudence, 102.

Johnstone, Rev. James, Anecdotes of Olave the Black, 47.

              „   Antiquitates Celto-Normannicæ, 53.

Journal kept in the Isle of Man, Richard Townley, 59.

Jurisprudence of the Isle, Johnson's, 102.

Keble, Rev. J., Life of Bishop Wilson, 214.

Keith, Catalogue of Scottish Bishops, 128.

Kelly, Rev. John, Dictionary in Manx, MS., 274.

        „   „   Edited by Gill and Clarke, 223.

        „   „   Triglot, MS., 274.

        „   Manx Grammar, 70.

        „   „   Edited by Rev. W. Gill, 200.

Kelly, Robert, List of Vessels Wrecked on the Coast, 171.

Kelly, Robert James, Sketches, 165.

Kelly, William, Life, by Rev. Hugh Stowell, 121.

Kennedy, Rev. W. J., Report on Schools, 192.

Keys of the Isle of Man, Address to the People, 49.

        „   Case on behalf of the, 71.

        „   Mode of Election, etc., 71.

        „   Petition to the House of Commons, 128.

King William's College Magazine, 162.

Kinnebrook, Wm., Etchings of Runic Monuments, 156.

Kinnish, Wm., Mona's Isle, 165.

Kneale, W., Guide, 205.

Lady of Latham, Madame Guizot de Witt, 231.

Lambeth Palace Library, MSS. in, 266.

Lamothe, J. C., Statutes, 211.

Langdale and Dives, Knights, A Declaration of, 7.

Laughton, J. B., Historical Guide, 160, 177.

Lay of Ancient Mona, M'Burney, 232.

Leaves from the Queen's Journal, A. Helps, 229.

Lecture on the Reformation in the Isle of Man, Mackenzie, 198.

Lee, Mrs., Clara Lennox, a Novel, 65.

Leece, Wm., Memoir of, 133.

Leech, F., Illustrated Guide, 202.

Legend of Mona, E. S. Craven, 130.

Legends of Manxland, E. Cookson, 199.

Legislation of the three Stanleys, Mackenzie, 264.

Letter to the Manx Legislature on Public Houses, 169.

Letters descriptive of the Isle of Man, by J. S., 203.

Letters from the Isle of Man in 1846, 175.

Lewis's Catechism, and Prayer for the Fishery, 38.

Lewis's Topographical Dictionary, 170.

Lex Scripta, 115.

     ,,   Appendix to, 118.

Lhuyd, Archæologia Britannica, 20.

Liberty Invaded, J. Baldwin, 30.

Liebnitz, G. G., Act of Surrender to the See of Rome, 15.

Literary Lovers, a Novel, J. Briscoe, 50.

London Gazette, Address to Charles II., 15.

London Magazine, Description of the Isle, 31.

Lonsdale, Dr., Life of John Christian Curwen, 227.

Lord's Book, MS., 268.

Lynch, P., Life of St. Patrick, 135.

Macculloch, Dr. John, Western Isles and Isle of Man, 115.

Mackenzie, Rev. W., Lecture on the Reformation in the Isle of Man, 198.

        ,,   Legislation by three of the Stanleys, 204.

        ,,   Index to the Statutes or Tynwald Laws, 209.

Macky, John, Journey through England, 23.

Macpherson's Dissertation on the Kingdom of Man, 38.

Mactaggart's Scottish Galovidian Encyclopedia, 129.

M'Burney, Lay of Ancient Mona, 232.

M'Crone, James, Trial of, 117.

M'Culloch, J. R., Statistical Account of the British Empire, 149.

Magazine, Douglas Middle School, 203.

    ,,   King William's College, 162.

    ,,   Manx Farmer's, 163.

Malacologia Monensis, Forbes, 152.

Manor Courts, cursory remarks on, 51.

Manuscripts, 264.

Manx Advertiser, 69.

Manx Almanack, 69.

Manx Antiquities, Paterson's, 213.

Manx Jurisprudence, 179.

Manx Land, B. Stowell, 214.

Manx Liberal, 148.

Manxman, The, 161.

Manx Mercury and Briscoe's Douglas Advertiser, 61.

Manx Punch, 225.

Manx Rising Sun, 120.

Manx Society, Established 1858, 275.

    ,,   Address and Rules, 276.

    ,,   Publications of, 280.

Manx Sketch Book, T. Ashe, 131.

Manx Spelling Book, Rev. H. Stowell, 114.

Manx Tracts, 136.

Maps of the Island, 3, 11, 22, 56, 132, 186, 208, 231.

Maps of the Parishes, Wood's, 227.

Maria, Mrs. St. George, 112.

Marsden's, James, Historical Notices of E. and W. Christian, 127, 131.

Martin, M., Description of the Western Islands, 17.

Mavor's British Tourist, 66.

Memorandum, Nos. 1 and 2, respecting Customs, 1711, 78.

Memorial of the Landholders, etc., to the Keys, 73.

Memorial to revise the Fiscal Laws, 164.

Memorials of God's Acre, Feltham, 228.

Mercator's Atlas, 5.

Mercurius Politicus, 8.

Mercurius Pragmaticus, 7.

Meredith, John, duel, 97.

Message from the Earl of Derby to Charles II., 6.

Methodist Facts, 226.

Methodist Hymn Book, Manx, 67.

Microcosmus, P. Heylin, 5.

Mills, M. A., on Intacks, 105.

    ,,   Report on Trial of James M'Crone, Esq., 117.

    ,,   Statute Laws, 119.

    ,,   On Tithes, 113.

Minutes of Cases, Cannell, 196.

Miscellanea Scotica, Monipennie's Description of the Isle, 3.

Misson's Travels, 21.

Moll, Herman, Map, 22.

Mona's Herald, 143.

Mona's Isle, W. Kennish, 165.

Mona's Isle, T. J. Ouseley, 188.

Mona Melodies, J. Barrow, 116.

Mona Melodist, J. Dale, 161.

Mona Miscellany, W. Harrison, 230.

Monasticon Anglicanum, Dugdale's, 10, 173.

Monipennie, John, Summarie of the Scots Chronicles, 3.

Monthly Magazine, State of Manners, 70.

Monro, Donald, Description of the Western Isles, 113.

Monumenta de Insula Manniæ, Dr. Oliver, 204.

Moore, R. I., Abstract of Bye-Laws, 191.

    ,,   Amalgamation of Peel Schools, 185.

    ,,   Sketch of Christian's Schools, 206.

Moseley, Rev. H., Report on Parochial Schools, 175.

Munch, P. A., Chronica Regum Manniæ, 205.

Mylecharane, Cookson, 196, 199.

National Gazeteer, Hamilton's, 222.

Neale, Rev. J. M., Ecclesiological Notes, 179.

Neild, James, on Castle Rushen Gaol, 100.

Nelson, Esther, Island Minstrelsy, 154.

Xenia Britannica, Douglas's, 62.

Neve, John Le, Fasti Ecclesiæ Anglicanæ, 21.

Newspapers, Church Chronicle, 169.

    ,,   Isle of Man Weekly Gazette, 105.

    ,,   Manx Advertiser, 69.

    ,,   Manx Liberal, 148.

    ,,   Manxman, 161.

    ,,   Manx Mercury and Briscoe's Douglas Advertiser, 61.

    ,,   Manx Press, 173.

    ,,   Manx Punch, 225.

    ,,   Manx Rising Sun, 120.

    ,,   Mona's Herald, 143.

    ,,   National Reformer, 166.

    ,,   Oddfellows' Chronicle, 167.

    ,,   Rising Sun, or Mona's Herald, 120.

    ,,   Star of Mona, 221.

    ,,   Temperance Advocate, 158.

    ,,   Temperance Guardian, 148.

    ,,   True Manxman, 127.

    ,,   Truth-Seeker, 168.

    ,,   Weekly Gazette and General Advertiser, 105.

    ,,   ,,   New Series, 107.

Nooth, C., Poems, 109.

Notes and Queries, Notices of the Isle of Man in, 232.

Notitia Monastica, Bishop Tanner, 54.

Observations on Acts of Tynwald since the Investment, 50.

    ,,   on Friendly Societies, 203.

Octavia Elphinstone, a Novel, 143, 154.

Olave the Black, Anecdotes of, 47.

Oliver, Dr., Monumenta de Insula Manniæ, 204.

Ordnance Survey, Sir Henry James, 231.

Ormerod, George, Tracts relating to Military Proceedings, 166.

Ormonde, Alfred, the Clown, 180.

Oswald, H. R., Guide, 125-139.

    ,,   on a General Infirmary, 136.

Oswald, H. R., Observations on the Fossil Elk, 133.
      „   Stratification of Alluvial Deposits, 124.
      „   Transactions of Society of Antiquaries of Scotland on
                 Runic Inscriptions, 126.
      „   Vestigia Insula Manniæ Antiquiora, 206.
Ouseley, T. J., Mona's Isle, 188.

Page, Rev. G. A., Appeal to Christians against Drinking, 187.
      „   Memorial of the Kitterland Disaster, 188.
Papers presented to the House of Commons, 73.
   „   presented to the House of Lords, 76.
   „   printed by order of the House of Commons, 1824, 128.
   „   relating to the Isle of Man, 217.
Paradise Lost, in Manx, 63.
Parr, Deemster, Abstract of the Laws, MS., 272.
      „   „   J. Gell, 224.
Pat, the Irish Chimney-Sweeper, 121.
Paterson, Robert, Manx Antiquities, 213.
Patterson, John, Memoir of Joseph Train, 194.
Peacock's Beauties of Port Erin, 213.
    „   Everybody's Guide, 212.
    „   Manx Table-Book and Keepsake, 214.
Peck, Francis, Desiderata Curiosa, Earl of Derby's History of the
    Isle, 25.
Pedigree, Greenhalgh of Brandlesome, 191.
Peel Castle, Round Tower in, 136.
  „ Schools, R. J. Moore, 185.
Perfect Diurnal, 8.
Petit, Rev. J. L., Archæological Journal, on the Ecclesiastical Antiqui-
    ties of the Isle of Man, 172.
Petition to the House of Commons from The House of Keys, 128.
Peveril of the Peak, Sir W. Scott, Bart., 171.
Pictorial Beauties of Mona, Burkill, 194.
Piers, Sir John, and Wife, Appeal to the House of Lords, 178.
   „   Compilations of Different Statements respecting his Duel with
      Mr. Meredith, 97.

Piers, Sir John, and Mr. Meredith, S. Turner's statement on the duel between, 97.

Pigot and Slater's Directory of the Isle, 127, 162.

Pious Manx Peasant, William Curphey, 121.

„   „   Schoolmistress, Jane Teare, 121.

Pitt, Right Hon. William, Speech on additional compensation to the Duke of Atholl, 58.

Plain Instructions in the principles of the Christian Religion, 33.

Poems by Gentlemen of Devon and Cornwall, 61.

„   from Manxland, E. Cookson, 229.

Poetical Guide, Rev. T. Stephens, 140.

Polycronycon, Higden's, 1.

Popular Rhymes, Proverbs, etc., peculiar to the Isle of Man, Denham's, 184.

„   Tales of the West Highlands, Campbell, 203.

Powys, Bishop, Charge to the Convocation, 192, 203.

„   Letter to the Vicar of Braddan on Church matters, 200.

Prayers, Form of, for House of Keys, 211.

Preservation of Life from Shipwreck, 134.

Proceedings in Chancery, Thomson v. Kelly, 142.

Proclamation for continuing officers (1765), 36.

Prynne, William, Animadversions on the Laws, 12.

Quakers, Gough's History of the, 56.

„   Sufferings of the, 26.

Quayle, Basil, View of Agriculture, 62.

„   Thomas, General View of Agriculture, 103.

Queen v. Corkhill, 210.

Queen's, the, Visit to Mona, or the Little Orator, 177.

Quiggin's Illustrated Guide, 160, 177.

Raines, F. R., Stanley Papers, 226.

Reasons for annexing the Isle of Man, 31.

Report of the Agricultural Association, 166.

„   British Fisheries, 189.

„   Church Missionary Society, 201.

Report of Commissioners on the Herring Fishery, 134.

　　„　of Commissioners of Inquiry, 1792, 78.

　　„　of Committee of the Legislature on the Herring Fishery, 135.

　　„　　　　„　　　　　　„　on the Fisheries, 180.

　　„　　　　„　　　　　　„　on Spawn and Fry of Fish, 180.

　　„　　　　„　　　　　　„　on Telegraphs, 228.

　　„　on Day and Sunday Schools, 104.

　　„　on Parochial Schools, Rev. H. Moseley, 175.

　　„　of Deemster, Clerk of the Rolls, etc., on the purchase of the Isle, 1781, 49.

　　„　of Diocesan Association, 164, 186, 187, 190, 191, 195, 221.

　　„　of House of Industry, 163.

　　„　of Port Petition, Ramsey, 71.

　　„　of Privy Council upon the Duke of Atholl's petition, 71.

　　„　of Schools inspected, 192.

　　„　of Society for Shipwrecks, 134, 145, 147.

Return of Civil Establishments (1822), 126.

　　„　of Customs expenses (1822), 127.

　　„　of expenses of all the establishments in the Island, 139.

　　„　of application of surplus revenues, 71.

Revenue, 1786, 75.

　　„　1799-1804, 75.

　　„　1765, view of, 76.

　　„　and Customs, 1765-1805, 76.

　　„　observations on the Atholl, 71.

Richmond, Countess of, C. A. Halstead, 154.

Rising Sun, or Mona's Herald, 120.

Robertson, David, Tour, 63.

　　„　　„　British Tourist, 66.

Rogers, S. S., Manx Farmer's Magazine, 163.

Rolt's History of the Isle of Man, 41.

Roper, William, History of Transactions, The Blue Book, 129.

Ross, Alexander, MS., 273.

Rosser, James, History of Wesleyan Methodism, 181.

Roundabout Notes, J. O. Halliwell, 212.

Round Tower in Peel Castle, 136.

Rules of the Society for Promoting Rural Economy, 137.

Runic Inscriptions, Jamieson and Dillon, 126.

    ,,   ,,   Oswald's, 126.

    ,,   Monuments at Kirkmichael, 66.

    ,,   ,,   Kinnebrook's Etchings of, 156.

    ,,   ,,   Old Northern, G. Stephens, 230.

    ,,   Remains, Cumming, 193.

Rushen Castle, story of, Cumming, 193.

Russell, Rev. M., Historical Catalogue of Scottish Bishops, 128.

Rutter, Bishop, Collection of Songs, MS., 269.

Ryley, S. W., Itinerant, 97.

Rymer, T., Fœdera, 18.

SACHEVERELL, William, Account of the Isle, 16.

        ,,   ,,   edited by Cumming, 198.

Scots Magazine, Abstract of Act 5 Geo. III. for purchase of the Isle, 35.

    ,,   Account of Thurot's Naval Engagement, 33.

    ,,   Appointment of Collector and Comptroller, and Governor Wood, 35.

    ,,   Case of the Duke of Atholl, 35.

    ,,   Contraband Trade, 34, 37.

    ,,   Letter from the Earl of Derby to Cromwell, 35.

    ,,   Notice of the death of John Bourke, 34.

    ,,   Proceedings in the Island on issuing Proclamation, 35.

    ,,   Proceedings in Parliament respecting sale of the Isle, 35.

    ,,   Proceedings in Parliament, 35.

    ,,   Proceedings in Parliament respecting Illicit Trade, 37.

    ,,   Proclamation for continuing Officers after purchase, 35.

    ,,   Short Account of the Isle, 35.

    ,,   Smuggling Clauses of Act of Parliament, 35.

    ,,   Speech of Governor Wood on taking possession of the Isle, 35.

    ,,   Succession of Lady Charlotte Murray to the Lordship of Man, 34.

    ,,   View of the State of the Isle of Man in 1814, 107.

Scott, Sir Walter, Peveril of the Peak, 171.

Seacome, John, Memoirs of the House of Stanley and Isle of Man, 27, 28, 30, 37, 51, 61, 67, 118, 155.

Sea Gulls, Act to prevent the destruction of, 230.

Sea Weeds, Mrs. Green, 195.

Selden, John, Titles of Honour, 4.

Self-Defence, Dr. Hume and H. N. Carrington, 146.

Sentimental Gleaner, G. Thompson, 124.

Sepping's, T., Arms of the See, 146.

Sermons, Rev. R. Brown, 111, 113.

      „   „   John Chater, 210.

      „   „   E. Forbes, 201.

      „   „   T. Howard, 107, 137, 174, 183.

      „   „   H. J. Stevenson, 156, 157.

      „   „   H. Stowell, 100.

      „   Bishop Wilson's, in Manx, 51.

Sherwood, Richard, Plan of Douglas, 181.

Shipp, Lieut. John, Memoir, 142.

Shirley, Bishop, Letters and Memoir of, Rev. Thomas Hill, 181.

Short, Bishop, Charge to Convocation, 160, 161, 163, 167, 172.

      „   Family Prayer, an Address, 172.

Short View of the Isle in 1767, 37.

Simpson, Sir J. Y., Archaic Sculpturings, 225.

Six Days' Tour through the Isle of Man, J. Welch, 146.

Sketches of the Coasts and Islands of Scotland and Isle of Man, Lord Teignmouth, 147.

Sketches of the Isle of Man, Bennet, 137.

      „   „   Kelly, 165.

Sketch of the State of Manners, Watts, 70.

Small, Charles, Letter to " A Manxman," etc., 58.

      „   „   in Manx, 58.

Smuggling, Commissioners' Report on, 34, 78.

Smythe, Benjamin, Map, 132.

Snelling on the Coins of Isle, 38.

Spawn and Fry of Fish, Report on, 180.

Speed, John, Theatre of Great Britain, 4.

Spencer, N., Complete English Traveller, 39.

St. Catharine's Chapel, E. Waugh, 221.

St. George, Mrs., Edwardine, 109.

    "   Maria, 112.

St. Matthew's Gospel in Manx, 29.

St. Patrick, Life of, by P. Lynch, 135.

Standing Orders of the Court of Tynwald on Railway Bills, 169, 220.

    "   "   amended, 202.

    "   under the Election Act, 1866, 226.

Stanley, the Great, Cumming, 224.

    "   History of the House of, Seacome's, 27, 28, 30, 37, 51, 61, 67, 118, 155.

    "   Papers, F. R. Raines, 226.

Stapleton, Major-Gen., case against Deemster Lace, 98.

Star of Mona and Temperance Advertiser, 221.

Statute Laws, 50, 60, 64, 140, 149, 156, 170, 182, 188, 211.

Steam-Packet Company Deed of Association, 150.

Stephens, Rev. T., Poetical Guide, 140.

    "   George, Old Northern Runic Monuments, 230.

Stevenson, Rev. H. J., Sermon, 156.

    "   Rev. J., Chronicle of Man, 194.

    "   John, of Balladoole, Petition for his brother's Estates, 29.

Stewart, Robert, Meteorological Observations in the Isle, 131.

Stowell, Rev. H., Life of Bishop Wilson, 114.

    "   "   Memoir by, of F. D. P. Geneste, 135, 162.

    "   "   "   William Leece, 133.

    "   "   "   Mrs. Stowell, 111.

    "   "   "   Rev. Joseph Stowell, 121.

    "   "   Sermons, 100, 104, 146.

    "   "   Spelling Book in Manx, 114.

    "   "   Tracts, 121.

    "   B., Manxland, 214.

    "   Rev. H. A., Notices on Natural History, 210.

    ,   John, Literary Quixote, or Beauties of Townley, 60.

    "   On the death of Mrs. Callow, 61.

    "   "   n the death of Miss M. Bacon, 61.

Stowell, John, On the death of Miss Nessy Heywood, 62.

    „   „ Retrospect, 57.

    „   „ Sallad for the Young Ladies and Gentlemen of Douglas, 57.

    „   „ Switch for Tom the Gardener, 57.

    „   „ To the Duchess of Atholl, 64.

    „ Kermotte, Address to the Inhabitants, 109.

    „   „   Letter to the Duke of Atholl, 107.

    „   „   Letter to the Hon. John Moore, 109.

    „   „   On the Ruin of the Methodist Friendly Society, 104.

    „   „   Report on the Committee of the Douglas Library, 103.

    „   „   Seneschal's Creed, 113.

    „ Thomas, Statutes, 60.

Strangers' Friend ; or, Guide to the Isle, C. Hulbert, 122.

Strickland, Hugh, Pleistocene Formation of the North of the Island, 162.

Summers, M., Memoir of Thomas Crennell, 192.

Surplus Revenues, Application of, 71.

Surrender to the See of Rome, 15.

Swords of State, Antiquaries' Society, 230.

Taggart, Edward, Memoir of Peter Heywood, 141.

    „   J., Plan of Douglas, 144.

Tallant, Anne, Octavia Elphinstone, 143, 154.

Tanner's Notitia Monastica, 54.

Teare, Jane, the Pious Schoolmistress, 121.

Teignmouth, Lord, Sketches of the Coasts of Scotland and Man, 147.

Telegraphs, Report of Committee, 228.

Temperance Advocate, 158.

    „   Guardian, 148.

Testament, Manx, 45, 101.

Thirty-nine Articles, in Manx, 123.

Thompson, George, Sentimental Gleaner, 124.

Thomson, James T., Proceedings in Chancery v. Kelly, 142.

    „ Dr. T. R. H., Directions in Cases of Emergency, 187.

Thurot, Captain, Memoirs of, Durand's, 32, 170.

    „   Account of his Engagement in Ramsey Bay, 33.

Tithes, Mill's Observations on, 113.

Titles of Honour, Selden, 4.

Tod, S., Trout-Fishing, 219.

Topographical Dictionary, Lewis, 170.

Touchstone, The, by John Duggan, 167.

Tour through the Isle, Feltham's, 65.

    „   Robertson's, 63.

    „   Highlands, Garnett's, 67.

Tower of Refuge, Subscriptions for building, 144.

Townley, Beauties of, J. Stowell, 60.

    „   Richard, Journal kept in the Isle, 59.

Tracts relating to Military Proceedings during the Civil War, Ormerod, 166.

Train, Joseph, Historical Account of the Isle, 168.

    „   Memoirs of, J. Patterson, 194.

Traveller's Guide, 176.

Treatise of the Isle of Man, Chaloner's, 8, 215.

True Manxman, 127.

Truth Seeker, 168.

Turner, S., Statement respecting the duel between Sir John Piers and Mr. Meredith, 97.

Universal Magazine, Tour in the Isle, 1785, 52.

Vestigia Insulæ Manniæ, Oswald, 206.

Waldron, George, Works in Verse and Prose, and Description of the Isle, 24.

    „   Description of the Isle, 28, 48.

    „   „   Edited by W. Harrison, 219.

Walker, James, Report on Harbours, 191.

Wallace, Captain, Views of Churches, 157.

Ward, Rev. W. P., Civil and Ecclesiastical History, 148.

Watts' Divine Songs, 134.

Watts, W. H., Sketch of Manners, 70.

Waugh, Edwin, St. Catharine's Chapel, 221.

Weekly Gazette and General Advertiser, 105.

             „   „   New Series, 107.

Welch, John, Six Days' Tour, 146.

Wesleyan Hymn-book in Manx, 173.

     „   Methodism in the Isle, Rosser's History of, 181.

Western Isles of Scotland, Martin, 17.

Williams, Commander George, Map, 186.

Willis, Browne, Survey of Cathedrals, 23.

Wilson, Bishop, Church Catechism, 20.

        „   A farther Instruction, etc., 22.

        „   Education of Rich and Poor Children, 23.

        „   Form of Family Prayer, Manx, 172.

        „   Form of Prayer for the Fishermen, 191.

        „   Instructions for the Lord's Supper, 27, 46.

        „   Knowledge of Christianity, 28.

        „   Life, C. Cruttwell, 64.

        „   „ H. B. Hone, 184.

        „   „ Rev. J. Keble, 214.

        „   „ Rev. H. Stowell, 114.

        „   Principles and Duties of Christianity, 15, 33.

        „   Sermons, in Manx, 51.

        „   Works, C. Cruttwell, 48.

Wilson, Dr., Memoirs of Edward Forbes, 209.

Winning of the Isle of Man by the Earl of Salisbury, a Ballad, 101.

Wood, G. H., Poems, 190.

     „   John, Plan of Douglas, 142.

Wood's Institute of the Laws of England, 39.

Woodhouse, John, Letter to Bridson and Stowell, 77.

Woods, George, History of the Isle, 101.

Woods, James, Maps of the Parishes, 227.

Worsaae, J. J. A., The Danes and Northmen, 187.

THE END.

www.ingramcontent.com/pod-product-compliance
Lightning Source LLC
Chambersburg PA
CBHW031018120726
47905CB00007B/1960